Dao Disciple

Bruce Sentar

Contents

Chapter 1

The townspeople burst into full celebration. Their weapons couldn't hit the dirt fast enough as they hurried to get food cooking on the hearth, and more than a few merry men were taking their women to their homes for another kind of celebration.

One of victory and life.

They had just stared down at their enemies and won a harrowing victory. Dar couldn't blame them for trying to feel again any way they knew how.

As the village came to life with their return from the southern forest, Dar strode past the townspeople, pulling his ladies along with him. He had a surprise for them. And given that they were all covered in blood and ash from their fight with the ettercaps in the woods, it seemed like the perfect time to surprise them.

The merchant visiting their town walked toward Dar, clearly intending to speak to him. Dar moved away, not interested in dealing with the man at that moment.

Dane Goodhaul wouldn't be causing trouble with several dozen of the ancient races hanging about. And, if he did cause trouble, he'd regret it.

"Come on, girls. I have a surprise for you." He pulled Sasha's arm, who in turn pulled Cherry. He didn't look down the line to see who all was gathered; he was more interested in getting into the cave and the home he'd built before he got stopped.

Being the leader of the town, Dar often found himself needed for this or that. He had a feeling that many would be interested in congratulating him and hearing all the details of the battle.

After all, they'd just killed one of the Mo, an entity that led the devils in this world and were some of the most powerful of the ancient races. If it hadn't been chained up in a massive enchantment, Dar wasn't sure if they would have been able to take it on like they had. He'd need to be stronger for the next one.

His inner world—a place within his body where he could store items, and where the little dao tree absorbed his enemies, turning them into fruit—it had saved him when the little dao tree had absorbed the massive spider. And now he could feel his inner world changing. When he got a chance to meditate and enter his inner world, he'd try to piece together what was happening.

But for now, he was going to surprise his women.

Dar pulled them into the cave from which they harvested stone and various goods. Blair's enchanted salt crystals hung from the walls, collecting and magnifying light, creating a little trail of beacons that led them deeper into the cave.

When he got to the entrance of the home, he'd used his greater dao of granite to shift and form it. It was almost too dark to see it. The girls still seemed puzzled, standing around trying to figure out what they were looking at.

Dar flicked a switch he'd installed and started up the enchantments on their new home.

Sparks caught, and small flames bloomed around the mansion. Dozens of enchanted stone candles came to life, giving and showing the beautiful women around him what he'd been working on.

The candles provided enough light for more of Blair's enchanted crystals to soak up and magnify, banishing the dark completely.

"It's amazing," Sasha whispered in awe, pressing herself to his back. Despite all the grime still on her, she was comfortably soft.

"Come on. There's more." Dar felt like a little kid showing off their latest birthday present. He couldn't wait to watch their reactions as he showed them what he'd built.

He led them through the entrance of two carefully carved pillars. As they stepped inside, the home opened up into a center area that was divided into several sections: one for leisure, another for entertaining guests, and a separate area for cooking and family gathering. Each was separated by two walkways that crossed the massive entry hall.

"How much time did this take?" Mika asked from further back as he led them through the hall.

Dar turned, smiling at how wide her eyes were as she looked around, taking it all in.

"Getting all the stone out was the hardest part, but I needed to do that anyway to get what we needed for the townspeople's homes. Molding what was left into this wasn't too bad. Though, Sasha, I think much of it could use a touch of softness."

Dar's woman only smiled. "Our home will be as comfortable as I can make it." Her blue eyes shone with light, even under the grime.

She walked around inspecting the place, and Dar knew that she was already making a list of all the projects she wanted to complete. Her eyes fixated on some of the tables and countertops. No doubt they'd become workstations for her.

"Of course, you each have your own spaces, but I thought I'd build something grand for myself, and welcome you all to share it." Dar pulled open the stone doors on the opposite side of the grand hall.

Behind it was a large bedroom, complete with a slab of stone. He hoped that, with the right enchantments, it would be a bed more than capable of holding all of them, and any others that joined them in the future.

The girls were moving around the room, taking it all in, but Dar was already moving again. He had one more big surprise. Turning sharply, he entered the bath, nearly bouncing at the reception he expected the room to receive.

The stone candles and lights clicked on, and sure enough, there were several sharp inhales from the women around him.

Dar had carved out a large basin. But, more impressively, he'd used Mika's dao to create lapping waves of water and his dao to add heat, making it a comfortable oasis.

The hot bath warmed the room, giving off a thin layer of steam into the cold air.

"I thought you may want to clean up in here," he said.

The ladies were already moving forward, but Dar held up a hand to slow them. "Before we get in, though, we should wash off a bit in this. We're pretty grimy."

He turned to a crude shower he'd made. Flipping a switch, it sputtered to life. There was a little less water pressure than he'd like, but it would have to do for the moment. Their desire to reach the bath was clear; he was not going to get time to mess around with it.

"What's this?" Cherry asked, reaching out a hand to grab a retreating Neko.

"A shower." He opened his arms.

Predictably, the jaguar demon leapt into his arms. "Neko. No." She narrowed her eyes at the water and hissed.

"I'm going to clean you, Neko. There's no two ways about this." He used a stern voice.

Neko had only been living in their village for a short while. Before that, she'd been more cat than human, and it was still debatable at times. He'd pulled her kicking and screaming out of the woods, where she'd lived as a feral demon since her transformation.

The spirits and demons in the town had taken to her and helped her acclimate to civilization, as was their way. She was both mature in many ways, yet incredibly inexperienced in others.

"Ladies, could you help with our clothes?" Dar noticed that their two maids, Amber and Marcie, had followed them to the stone home. It had taken Dar a while to get used to them serving him in more ways than just housekeeping, but after earning their trust, it felt more natural.

He'd recently given them both fruit from his inner dao tree, allowing them to become immortals. He'd only shared the fruit with a few people, still trying to decide how to proceed.

A whistle sounded as the two maids began undressing him. Dar eyed Blair, who seemed to have invited herself to join the group as well. As they locked eyes, she bit her lip, eyeing him.

Amber and Marcie worked quickly, their hands deftly liberating him and Neko of their clothes. Fully naked, Dar quickly stepped into the spray of water before Neko could get away, ignoring her protests.

"No." Neko clung to Dar even as they both rinsed in the water. He ignored her, petting her and providing calming noises as he tried to get her clean.

Sasha stepped up next to them, helping scrub and rinse them while Dar held Neko.

Once they were clean enough, Dar moved them both over to the bath. Neko pouted, her nose just above the surface, blowing bubbles as she glared at Dar.

"Come on. It isn't that bad—isn't it nice and warm?"

"Wet," was Neko's quick reply.

"I think she'd be long gone if you weren't here," Cherry commented, joining them in the hot bath with a sigh. "It is like a hot spring."

Dar smiled, leaning back against the edge. Soaking in the pool was a pleasant break. They'd been pushing so hard to prepare the town for the winter and protect it against the threat in the woods. He'd barely slowed down, and it was nice to have the moment in his space with his women. It was exactly why he'd wanted the home in the first place—somewhere for them to gather and be together despite what might come.

He looked around, enjoying the relaxation he saw on the girls' faces. He wanted to stay like this forever with them. The girls deserved a chance to enjoy it for a short while, but they needed to get back out and join the rest of the village soon. They'd be missed in all the festivities.

But Dar's tired muscles were finally relaxing in the hot bath, and he really had no desire to move at that moment, especially with the way that Mika sidled up to his right and pressed her toned body against his.

"You should relax more." Her hands wandered around his chest and turned him away from her, giving her his back. Her hands dug into his shoulders and started massaging them.

Dar let out a shuddered breath, enjoying her attention. "We can't stay here for long." He hated saying it, but he knew they had to leave soon.

Something moved in the water next to him, and Amber took up his right arm, Marcie his left. They wouldn't be outdone as they began to massage his arms.

Dar stirred under the water, quickly growing hard. Although, it seemed difficult not to when surrounded by such beautiful women.

"At least let us reward our dao companion before we go join the village in celebration." Sasha came and sat on his thighs, draping herself on his chest. "We all fought well, and you saved the day against that creature."

Her body, as usual, was unbelievably soft as she pressed herself to him.

"The Mo," he clarified as his cock rose and nestled itself in the crevice of her ass.

She rubbed it with slow rocking motions of her hips, pressing her chest to his, and gave him a different sort of massage.

Dar relaxed into all of their soft touches, deciding it wouldn't hurt to stay in the bath a little while longer.

Their group might have spent more time in the bath than Dar had anticipated. By the time he stepped back out of the cave, the village was in full swing.

The people of Hearthway had scrubbed themselves clean of the soot and grime from their battle with the ettercaps and their spiders.

To the south, a bright orange glow filled the sky as the southern forest still raged with a fire. They had managed to turn the fire away from the village, but the ettercaps had killed the forest for miles, and the miles of dead and dry forest were going to burn throughout the night.

"Dar!" Russ, a hunter and one of the leaders of the village, cheered as he came out of his home.

The villagers picked up his cheer and joined him with hoots and whistles.

"I think you need to give a few words." Sasha nudged him before stepping away, pulling Neko with her.

Dar was already tall, but he stepped up on a stump to get everyone's attention. He didn't love having to give the big, grand speeches, but he was growing used to it from leading the town.

"We fought hard today. We ultimately were victorious, but it did not come without a cost. There are those who are no longer with us, and those who might not be able to do their work over the coming days."

Dar paused, allowing the moment to grieve the fallen before lifting his voice up once more. "But we've worked hard, and we've won! Our town is safe." Dar raised his hand and caught a drifting snowflake. "Winter is here, and it is about time we celebrate all of our hard work preparing for it."

The villagers cheered, clanging together wooden utensils.

"So please join me in a feast tonight. Feel free to eat all of the bison you can, because Russ is going hunting again tomorrow, and we are running out of space to store all of this meat."

That only earned him more cheers, townspeople slapping Russ on the back while Russ grinned, enjoying the praise.

Dar stepped down from the stump and walked through the crowd, men cheering him and patting him, women batting their lashes at him. Dar acknowledged them while continuing to move towards his target.

He reached the circle where the leaders of the village met and used for meetings every night at dinnertime.

As expected, the other leaders were already gathered and ready to discuss the day and debrief. There was a lot to talk about given the battle. They needed to figure out the ramifications of their fight.

Dar took his seat, and Amber was quick to arrive with a bowl of meaty stew and a cup of something strong that smelled like bottom-shelf vodka. One sip was all he needed to know that it was distilled and unflavored. He let out a sharp breath, wondering if it might not go to better use for cleaning.

"Strong stuff." Rex raised a glass, his expression a somber one among the celebrating village.

Dar knocked cups with Rex and took a quick sip, trying not to let it linger on his tongue. "You don't look like you have good news."

The avian demon led the village guard and had been a major part of training the population into some semblance of a fighting force before they had marched on the ettercaps.

Rex's eyes wandered to the villagers, picking out dozens who had bandages wrapped around their limbs, or arms in slings. A few sat off to the side of the celebration, being tended to by a woman working to nurse them back to health.

"We were not without losses," he finally said.

Dar nodded. "We knew there would be some. However, I think we pulled through with minimal losses, all things considered. That is something to celebrate."

Any battle would have injuries and death. It was unreasonable to assume that there would be a clean, one-sided battle. And their forces had not been well trained.

The losses would pain their village, but it could have been far worse if they had let the infestation in their southern woods grow and linger. Dar shuddered to think what would have happened if they had let that massive spider continue to struggle out of its seal for the winter and had to take it on when it was fully mobile.

Come spring, that thing might have not only wrecked their small village but then moved on to take out Kindrake or Bellhaven.

"That's the spirit." Russ clapped Dar on the shoulder and swung down into his own spot, his cup sloshing with his drink. The gnoll took a long drink with his muzzle. "We won today, Rex. Celebrate."

"Celebration is all and well, but we should do something for the families that lost someone," Samantha chimed in. The older lady was the self-proclaimed spokeswoman for the children, and apparently by extension, their families.

"What would be appropriate? We've been working together as a village, so everyone has supplies for the winter. We have no currency and no real luxuries to give them, so I'm not sure what would make sense." Dar offered it up, open to any suggestions.

"Salt," Samantha replied. "That merchant came today. Anyone who wants to can trade for things they might want using salt."

Dar felt stupid for not thinking of that. Salt was a valuable commodity for most of the world. The fact that they had Blair, who was able to fill up massive stores of it in one of the caves, wasn't common.

"Set an amount that's appropriate and give it out before the end of the night," Dar agreed, ready to close out that topic. "About this merchant, what do you all think of him?"

"He's a merchant. Nothing too complex about that." Bart shrugged. "We have a few surpluses that we can trade away."

"It is all village stock, so my question is, what do we need in return?" Dar clarified.

Bison meat had gotten out of hand after Russ had finally crossed the Bell River. He had hunted the massive herd that was lingering on the plains on the other side and come back with ten heads of bison on a single day's hunt.

They'd ended up needing to send Blair and Mika down the river to the ocean to collect salt to keep it all from rotting. Luckily, the salt spirit had then filled the boat to the brim with salt that was now stored in granite vessels in a cave.

And now they had a massive surplus, one that could easily be recovered if they sold to the merchant.

"Do we need cut lumber?" Dar suggested.

"We can still harvest wood from the northern forest. I'd suggest things that we might otherwise struggle with. Cloth, for one. Otherwise, we'll all be wearing furs like savages come winter's end." Bart scratched at his chin. "Since Cherry seems to make anything grow, we could see if they have any foreign fruits that might be good for her to grow."

Dar liked the idea of fruits, not only for the village, but to plant more in his inner world.

"Excuse me." The merchant pushed his way into the group. "I couldn't help but notice that this appears to be the decision makers."

Dane Goodhaul rubbed his hands together as he made himself comfortable in the circle. Dar tried not to bristle, annoyed at the pushy merchant. Dar knew that the man had to have somewhat conditioned himself to push past being uncomfortable in social situations in order to be successful in his trade.

The others seemed to be ready to leave Dar to the merchant, so he spoke up first. "Alright. Everyone, enjoy the evening. Celebrate tonight, and we'll talk and plan more tomorrow."

Dar turned to the merchant, looking past him for a moment to jerk his head, inviting the girls to join them.

Dane watched as the women came over and pampered Dar, while also staying out of his way. "Are you a demon?" he asked, tilting his head as he took in their group.

Dar wasn't. He had once been human and now was an immortal, but that was still largely a secret from the world. So he took the easy opportunity. "Yes. Thankfully, I blend in quite well with humans."

Most demons had some sort of appearance that referenced what they'd originally been. Since he had been human, he had none.

"Ah. Well, I see. That explains your size then." The shorter man was eye level, despite Dar still being seated on the stump. "It seems you have quite the food supply. Food is in great demand in Bellhaven this winter."

"We have a strong source of meat." Dar crossed his arms. "But we aren't interested in helping Bellhaven. If you are heading south, we have no interest in trade."

"Dar," Mika admonished. "Last we saw, they were already rationing before the winter started."

"The prince has taken over the city. No doubt he'll solve it." Dar didn't actually believe that, but he didn't want to air all his issues with the merchant. Maybe the prince would manage to pull it together and lead, but the fact that he'd quickly become Mark's hostage upon arrival in Bellhaven didn't bode well.

And, even if he wanted to, if Dar were to give up Hearthway's food to help Bellhaven, he might have a riot on his hands. The spirits and demons of his village wouldn't want to be party to helping restore a city that had tried to kill them all. They'd barely managed to escape with what they had.

Dane smacked his lips. "I see. Given that you are a village with so many non-humans, and according to the rumors I've heard, I can only guess that you were once residents of Bellhaven?"

Dar smiled, not surprised that the man was well informed. It would serve him well to be as he went around trading. "Very recently. Unfortunately, the city became inhospitable to our kind."

Dane nodded rapidly. "That is unfortunate."

"But back to trade. Some of our people may have quantities of salt for trade in the morning," Dar continued. "I think that might be something worth your time? Otherwise, you'll have to work with individuals for small trinkets. We've largely worked as a community to prepare for the winter, so we are mostly stocked with essentials."

"Of course," Dane backed off. "Salt is always a welcome trade. May I trade for food for my men?"

Dar waved his question away. "No. Feel free to join the village for food tonight. No cost, but it would be great if you could share any news or stories you have from your recent travels."

They had plenty of food for a few extra people. Dar just didn't want to support a city that had tried to kill those that he was now duty bound to protect.

Amber heard what he'd said, shooting to her feet to grab him a bowl of meaty stew. "If you don't mind, we'd love to hear news from the capital."

Dar nodded, wanting to hear that information himself. He turned his attention back to the merchant and stuffed his face with food while the merchant began speaking.

CHAPTER 2

Dane finished one bowl of the stew and sheepishly looked back at Amber.

"Go ahead, get him another bowl." Dar jerked his head.

"You have wonderful servants and family." Dane's eyes appreciated the women, but there was no coveting in them. Either that or he was just smart enough to keep that out of his gaze.

"This is Sasha, Cherry, and Mika. My dao companions. And then you have Neko and Blair, two close friends. Finally, you've met Amber and Marcie, my maids," I introduced them quickly.

Dane received his second helping. He'd already told a number of stories, so Dar decided it was only fair to share some of theirs.

"We all fled from Bellhaven when the city became hostile towards ancient races. The city was dealing with repeated devil attacks, and in their panic, a group of nobles used the public's fear, pointing it towards the demons and spirits."

Dar let out a sigh, annoyed just from reliving it as he told the story. "After a harrowing flight from the city, we stopped here, and we've made it a home. We intend to stay here and build up our own city, one that is welcoming and empowering to the ancient races, and creates a more harmonious relationship with humans."

Dar paused, looking over at the burning woods in the distance. "Unfortunately, as we built up this village, we came under attack by a large colony of ettercaps that had built up a fortress in the woods and destroyed the surrounding area to where they were venturing out for food. We made the first move, not waiting for them to organize and attack, destroying them. What you see now is the celebration of that victory."

"The fire is from all of that?" Dane looked over Dar's shoulder. "I can't say I'm entirely comfortable being so close to it."

"Yes. We created a fire line in the woods and a backfire. There's no fuel for it to cross over this way. If anything, that fire will burn out any ettercaps we missed." Dar gave the woods a hard look. "There were thousands of them. I wish there had been a better way for us to deal with them."

"Thousands." Dane paused in eating to repeat with wide eyes.

It was clear the merchant was skeptical of the number, but Dar moved past it, not caring if the man believed it or not. "Ask around if you'd like to confirm. We did several scouting missions ahead of the ultimate battle. The guard captain and his wife could tell you about the ettercap fortress we found."

"Forgive my hesitation," Dane apologized. "It is hard to believe such a young village could survive a colony of ettercaps that size. Then again, I'm not sure of the last time that I've seen so many spirits and demons working industriously together."

"A unique advantage," Sasha interjected, pulling her stump close enough to Dar to lean on him. "But what of

Kindrake? We are rather separate from the Kingdom's capital here."

Dane's eyes raked over Sasha, trying to determine what sort of demon she was, but Dar knew the man would come up short. It had taken Dar a while to get her to tell him. The only marking to indicate she had once been a type of silkworm were two spinnerets in dimples just above her ass.

Given how much she often wanted to fit in with human royalty, Dar had to wonder if that played a role in how human she appeared.

"The capital is... well... rumors that they are preparing a levy to fund a greater military force have been spreading. It is likely that the reason Prince Gregor was sent down to Bellhaven was to get it under control. The city would have had trouble contributing to the levies in the state it was in. It also reaffirms their control of the area. Increasing levies tends to bring unrest, which can be dangerous in already unstable areas." Dane took another bite of his stew, trying to hide a small smile that crossed his face, but Dar noticed it.

"You are happy that a war is coming?" Dar asked, his brow pinched.

"There is always money in a war," Dane explained. "That there is also loss of life is tragic, but it can be quite lucrative. That is if a merchant can figure out the new logistics and predict what goods will be most needed."

He sounded eager for the challenge it would present.

"That changes what you might be trading for," Dar realized. "We have many talents among our village that you might not expect."

Dar watched the man's eyes twinkle, noting that there was an opportunity to trade their skills for goods they needed, but wanting to know more about what was coming.

"So, the levies are being raised for a military. Who's the target?" Dar asked.

"It's all just rumors so far. We likely won't know until they assemble their forces and begin their march. Sailing out to the Mahaklan islands isn't likely; we don't have the fleet for that. So, that leaves just the two neighboring kingdoms. Sineld and Tormac, but we haven't had aggression with either of them for a generation." The merchant showed me his palms in a plea for understanding. "Right now, word is there's going to be heavy demand for metal work. Nails, swords, that type of thing."

Dar shook his head. They had blacksmiths in their town, but they didn't have enough raw metal to sell to Dane in volume. "We have the men, but not the ore. Our village was more concerned about lumber and crops to prepare for the winter."

Dane rubbed his jaw, looking around and then back at the stew. "If you have this much bison meat, do you not have plenty of leather?" Dane pushed. "And if you've been gathering lumber, your scraps might make decent stone-tipped arrows."

Dar smiled. Leave it to a merchant to find the opportunities.

Dar felt Sasha press into him again. She'd been nearly bursting at his side throughout the discussion.

"Go ahead, Sasha." Dar gave her the floor, nearly laughing as words spilled out of her.

"We will need the wool and hides for winter clothing, but we'd be comfortable trading leather, bones, and horns. As for arrows, we'll have to see if we can secure the fletching we need, but we could also use chickens. Speaking of livestock, we'd happily find a trade for goats."

As Sasha spoke, Dane leaned forward, nodding and starting to add small comments to further the discussion.

They went back and forth, both brimming with excitement over the type of deal they could make.

Realizing he was out of his depth, Dar retreated from the conversation, giving Dane a nod indicating that he'd back Sasha's words. Bones and chicken feathers would not have been items he'd expected to be useful. But once Sasha had said it, it made sense.

They had a few wild pigs, but livestock hadn't entered his thoughts at all since founding the village, and bones weren't exactly something he had seen get much use back on earth.

In fact, he thought they were mostly considered waste. Maybe good for fertilizer, but that was about it. Here, though, they would be used for simple tools, handles, maybe even spoons.

He still had much to get used to in Granterra.

"Milord." Amber caught him as soon as he pulled away from Sasha; Marcie hung to her side like usual.

The two of them had grown close. Dar could see the telltale signs of a relationship blossoming between the two of them. They'd even made a comment earlier that made him think they were experimenting with dominance play. And it was clear who the dominant one was.

"We wanted to thank you for our new home." Amber bowed formally and pulled Marcie up to the side.

Where Amber was petite and drew attention to her curves by showing some skin, Marcie was the complete opposite. She covered herself up, but her ample curves were still clear under the clothing.

"Thank you." Marcie's voice was subdued, but that was usual for her. She was shy to a fault, and it didn't help that she let Amber lead her around by the nose.

Marcie bowed as she spoke, her breasts bouncing with the motion despite what he knew to be Sasha's best efforts to contain them.

"You are both very welcome. I expect you to move in and make yourselves comfortable. It will be a long winter, and I have high hopes for the two of you."

They both beamed in response.

Ever since Dar had given them fruits from the dao tree, they had become quite adept with the use of knives, although they still fought with a reckless abandon that spoke of them training to kill rather than protect.

He knew they trained like that to always be his watchful maids, able to react should something endanger their household. It was only more reason to shower them in what he could find.

"I collected many ettercaps and spiders from the fight. Both of you should prepare yourselves to receive more fruits tomorrow."

"Yes, milord." Amber's eyes sparkled with a fevered determination. She was a dangerous one.

Dar caught Marcie's eyes wandering over to the nearby dancing, but he saw Amber's eyes wandering more towards the rod in his pants. He had a feeling she was planning a different kind of thanks.

"Go on. Enjoy the celebration and move your stuff over before you turn in for the night." Dar shooed the two eager maids away. He had to stay and mingle.

Accepting pleasure from the maids had taken him a bit to adjust to when he'd come to Granterra, but that resistance had since melted after seeing their lack of hesitation and enjoyment. It made them feel more secure and a part of the group, and Dar had to admit that it was a hell of a way to bond.

"Do I get my room as promised?" Blair asked from beside Mika. The white-haired salt spirit practically vibrated with sexuality as she tried to hold herself back.

Blair was Mika's old friend and a touch too forward for Dar's tastes, but after he'd voiced it, she'd toned it down.

And she'd repeatedly shown her commitment to their town and Dar.

"Of course. I promised you a room in return for all those enchanted crystals, and I wouldn't go back on my deal. Your room is on the right side; I think you'll figure out which I intended for you." A small smirk tugged at the corner of his lips.

"You sure I can't get a room closer to yours?" Her eyes were hungry.

"Cut it out." Mika slapped Blair's ass, eliciting an excited moan. Blair wiggled her ass in request for another, making the wave spirit roll her eyes. "You are impossible."

Blair turned to Mika like she was about to cry. "But since you joined the family, I have been so pent up."

Dar sighed. This was his life now. But he couldn't say he minded it, given the beautiful women that came with it.

Kissing Mika on her temple, Dar went to leave the circle, but he found himself face to face with a crouching Neko. She sprang from the ground, but vines rose out of the dirt, trapping her ankles. She fell forward and Mika caught her, pulling the grumpy, but clean, cat girl into her lap.

Cherry came to his side as he stepped away. "Where are we going?"

"Moving the stuff from our hut into the cave mansion." Dar was ready to spend his nights in the cave. He'd already carved enough dao characters of quiet into the walls so that they could be as noisy as they wanted in the bedroom and none would know. The little wood hut they'd been using had not provided the same privacy.

While privacy wasn't something the ancient races worried about, Dar was still partial to it.

Cherry put her hand on his chest, whispering. "I know you can feel the change to the little dao tree."

"Something to check on tonight," he agreed. Absorbing the Mo had done something to his little dao tree, and he was eager to figure out just what that was.

"It feels so good. The tree is so full of power." Cherry's voice grew with excitement. And she knew as well as Dar what it felt like; the dryad was connected to the tree inside of Dar.

Cherry looked drunk as she kept her hand on his chest.

Scooping up the petite dryad, Dar draped her long green hair over his arm as he carried her with him. He could tell she was lost in touching him and feeling the change from the tree. It was easier to just carry her than try to herd her anywhere.

Dryads were spirits of a nature dao and obsessed with their trees. Given that Cherry had made Dar's dao tree hers, she was now obsessed with him. Dar would have described her as a fan girl if she wasn't the oldest among them, and far more deadly than a fan girl image portrayed.

Cherry kissed his chest as he walked through the village, earning them more than a few stares and giggles.

"Cherry, calm down."

Her hot breath washed over his chest. "I need it." Cherry's face was flush as she looked up at him with full red lips and emerald-green eyes.

"First, we need to get all our belongings moved over. But maybe when we get to the cave mansion, you might convince me." Dar smirked down at the randy woman.

In response, a warm hand dove into his pants and wrapped around his shaft while still in full view of the other villagers. She pumped him several times before he pulled her arm off him.

"Not here."

"You're such a prude." She sighed and laid back, letting him carry her as she touched him. Little exhales of bliss left her mouth as he carried her into the hut.

Dar looked around, quickly drew all of their possessions into his inner world to store them for the time being. Content that they had gathered what they needed, Dar left for the cave with long, quick strides, Cherry still in his arms.

Cherry giggled in his arms. "You're in a hurry."

"I know better than to make you wait."

Apparently, Cherry took that as full permission to start the moment they crossed into the cave.

Her hands wandered back into his pants, and their warmth enveloped his cock. She began pumping him once more. "Bedroom."

Grunting, Dar lifted her up and tossed her over his shoulder. "Behave."

But behaving did not seem to be on Cherry's mind. Using her access to his neck, she sucked on the nape of his neck, drawing shapes with her tongue.

Dar nearly took the door off its hinges as he slammed the bedroom door closed and activated the dao characters of quiet.

"Yes!" she screamed, flinging herself off his shoulder and landing with more grace than he expected. "Sit." She pointed to a wooden bench.

Though most of the mansion was made with stone, Dar had been mindful to place a number of wooden pieces as well. Not only did it add a little warmth to the otherwise bland structure, but it gave Cherry something to use her dao on.

Clearly, that was also on her mind, because it wasn't long before cords of vines sprang up from the bench, lashing Dar's legs to it and peeling down his pants enough for his cock to spring out.

"There's so much raw power coming from you." Cherry ran her hands along his chest again, her eyes looking hazy and a little crazed.

"Are you okay?" An edge of concern entered Dar's voice. Cherry would never hurt a fly, but the way she was looking at him was strange.

"Better than ever." She kneaded his chest, massaging and feeling him. "It feels so good."

There was no warning as she rose above him and then thrust herself down, impaling herself on him.

Wrapping her up in a hug, Dar held her still even as she wiggled her hips. She moved more, sinking fully down onto him. Dar tried to slow her down. The dryad was petite enough that he was concerned about her going so fast and heavy.

But his worries were baseless; he could feel just how wet she was. Whatever was happening in his inner world was certainly revving her up.

Trying to slow her down, Dar kissed her, cracking open her pink lips and letting their tongues tangle in her mouth. She practically vibrated in his lap.

Giving a frustrated groan, she wrapped her arms around his neck like two firm vines. Using them to get leverage, she began slapping her hips down onto him.

Breaking the kiss, Dar stared into her eyes. They were so fixated on him it was like she was drowning in his attention and would slurp up every ounce of him if given the chance.

Those were crazy eyes.

"Hard. Please, harder," she cried as she threw her entire body weight into his lap with each thrust.

Grabbing onto her hips, Dar's fingers sank into the edge of her tight bubble butt and pulled her down onto him.

Cherry screamed, her eyes filling with tears as she smiled and lifted herself off him, only to slam herself back down. "More."

He'd never seen Cherry like this, but he certainly wasn't going to complain. The vines wrapping around his legs were a token at best. He could tell she'd made them thin and breakable. He stood up, ripping off the vines and breaking the bench.

He looked down, deciding that could be fixed another time.

Grabbing Cherry by the hips, he pressed her to a stone wall and slammed himself into her.

She screamed and clung to him tightly, trying to press herself into him even harder. "More. I need to feel more." Her head was swaying side to side in apparent need.

"I'm going to crush you if I go harder," Dar noted, growing concerned but also insanely turned on.

She bit down hard on his neck in response, giving him a muffled. "Harder."

Unable to deny her, he obliged. He slammed her hard enough into the wall that he was worried it would crack.

Her hips survived, and she squeezed him like she was trying to get him just a little deeper, trying to scratch an itch that she just couldn't reach, which was saying something given that Dar filled her to the brim.

Dar pounded into her as she clawed his back while begging for more.

Trying to up the sensation for her, Dar decided to add more stimulation.

Pinching a small mass of granite from the wall, Dar controlled it with his dao.

The piece rolled itself into a smooth ball and rolled down his arm and chest, settling at the base of his cock. He had no sensation of the ball, but he knew Cherry well enough to not have any problems.

It vibrated back and forth, rolling over where he knew her clit rested.

Cherry screamed, pushing her head back into the wall as he continued to pound her into it.

"Yes. Another one. I want another one!"

He pinched off another piece of granite and let it join the first. The two of them swirled over her.

She came back to his lips, devouring them with a raw passion that consumed him as he felt himself peak.

Ropes of his seed pumped into her, even as she squeezed herself tighter to him.

Stumbling, he caught himself on the bed before he toppled over and let himself fall backwards, landing on the bed.

Cherry stayed latched to him, bouncing eagerly on him for her own release.

As his post-orgasm haze cleared, Dar focused on the two beads he had been using. They went into overdrive, vibrating as they swirled around her.

Cherry finally came up for air, screaming with her own release as she soaked his thighs in her pleasure.

"Fuck," she said as she went limp and flopped down on his chest.

Dar smiled, wrapping his arms around her as she panted. As they came down from the moment, Dar leaned back to look into her eyes. "Going to tell me what that was about?" he asked.

"Tired." She closed her eyes.

He lifted her head, waiting until she opened her eyes again. "Tell me, please?"

CHAPTER 3

Before Dar could press Cherry further, Amber burst into the room. She took about two steps before freezing, a wide smile overtaking her lips at the scene in front of her.

"Milord. I see..." She cleared her throat, trying to retain a professional veneer even as Dar had a nearly sexed out dryad on his chest. "We have an important visitor to the village."

His brows pressed down hard. He didn't like being interrupted, and he was wary of new visitors. "Who?"

"An emissary from The White." Her tone was solemn, her eyes pleading with him to get up quickly.

"Shit." Dar pulled Cherry off of him in a hurry.

The dryad lazily poured herself into him, entering his inner world.

If the dryad disappearing fazed Amber, she didn't let it show. She simply walked over, picking up his pants and holding them out to help him get dressed.

Dar knew trying to fight her and do it himself was a lost cause, so he grabbed a sheet and wiped himself down quickly before stepping into the pants. "What am I dealing with?"

"A big, white bear demon. He says he's from The White, but he wouldn't say more, even to Glump," Amber quickly informed him.

"Strength?" he asked as she pressed down his clothes quickly, trying to make himself a smidge more presentable.

"Strong, but beyond that, I don't know." She looked down in shame.

Dar grabbed her chin and forced it up. "You have just started your journey to become stronger. Don't feel inferior. You could take on a dozen of the guards back at Bellhaven at this point, and you are progressing quickly. Think of where you were a few weeks ago."

"Yes, milord." A smile returned to her lips and buoyed Dar's spirits. "I do not know how strong he is, but he is stronger than Glump."

Dar clicked his tongue. That meant the visiting demon was likely towards the peak of a greater demon, or might even be a grand demon. Thinking back to him being a spokesman for The White, then it was likely he was a grand demon.

The only practitioner of a grand dao in the village was Cherry, whom he didn't think was going to be much help at present.

Whatever had happened to the tree had clearly affected her, and he didn't want to bring her into a fight if he could help it. At least, he wouldn't bring her into it until he had a better understanding of what had come over her.

"Okay, let's go. Lead me to him." Dar motioned Amber forward, and she darted with a speed that made it clear just how dangerous she could be. Stopping after only a couple steps and holding her back straight, she led him out in a manner suiting someone in charge.

The second Dar stepped foot out of the cave, it became glaringly obvious where the demon was.

A furry white head towered over everyone else in the village. Even Dar would have to look up when he talked to the demon. The visitor stood there, tall and domineering, staring out over the crowd. The villagers kept away from him in their celebration, yet Dar could tell the man's presence was putting a damper on things.

"Hello," Dar called out, waving to the demon and hoping to meet him halfway. At least then it would pull him away from the clearly on-edge villagers.

Thankfully, the demon took the cue, moving to greet him.

Dar took that as a good sign. The man wasn't cocky enough to expect Dar to come to him.

Dar got a better look at the demon as he grew closer. He had retained more of his bestial traits than most, and it was clear he had been a polar bear, or at least the Granterra equivalent. Dar had only seen polar bears in a zoo, but this demon definitely seemed larger than those he'd experienced on Earth.

But most things on Granterra were larger and deadlier than their Earth equivalents.

"Hello, I am Karn, emissary from Frost's Fang," the bearman introduced himself, holding out a heavy hand that seemed just barely human enough to use tools.

Dar clasped him by the wrist. "Darius, but my friends call me Dar, leader of this little village."

Karn stared at him, no doubt sensing his mana and his strength. There was little Dar could do to stop him from sensing them.

Amber had been right; this demon was powerful. If he had to guess, he'd place him a notch above Cherry, meaning he might be a grand demon with two grand dao. This wasn't a matter he could take lightly.

"What can we do for you?" Dar continued.

Karn's pitch black eyes blinked. "I have come at the behest of The White to investigate Bellhaven. Rumors...

reached us. She is concerned about what she is hearing."

Shit, Dar cursed internally.

Dar had eliminated Mark during his small trip to Bellhaven recently, putting an end to the group largely responsible for the oppression of the ancient races in Bellhaven, but he was hesitant to tell Karn any of those details.

Without giving away that he was the Black Knight, he couldn't really provide the information, and he wanted to keep that a secret.

There was a bounty on Dar's head for killing a noble, put out by the prince. Despite saving the prince's life, the bounty remained. Apparently, the prince had to uphold appearances and make an example, although Dar thought he should get some sort of break for saving the man's dignity after the prince had been completely bulldozed by Mark.

"I don't know of the rumors, but I know much of the truth. The people you see here fled Bellhaven a month ago." Dar gestured to the celebrating villagers. "After an unfortunate change in leadership, we were no longer welcome in Bellhaven."

Karn growled, and in a flash, it felt like Dar was about to be surrounded by corpses. Dar braced, readying for a fight, but the big bearman calmed after just a moment, stuffing that violent aggression back down.

Dar noted that pissing the bear off was something he should avoid.

"It is unacceptable for humans to treat us this way. Examples must be made," Karn stated with a grunt.

"Agreed. I know the names of those responsible for the aggression they showed us. And since then, I have seen Prince Gregor traveling down to Bellhaven. He may have fixed the problem." Dar tried to give enough that Karn wouldn't storm in and turn the city into a graveyard without learning more.

"No matter," Karn said dismissively. "I will handle this. Bring your people, and we will take back what was yours."

Around them, Villagers were singing and cheering while they drank the terrible liquor and ate meaty stew, oblivious to the talk of yet another battle.

Dar didn't believe more bloodshed was the answer.

Before, the ancient races in Bellhaven had barely survived in the slums. The city had been on the edge of falling apart. Overpopulation continued to make living conditions tougher, caused by the waves of nearby villages seeking refuge from waves of devil attacks within its borders.

"I'm sorry, but I don't think we'll be going back. We want to create something new that isn't hampered by the prejudices in that city."

Karn eyed him, but seemed to accept it for the moment. "What is this celebration for?"

Dar explained, "There have been increased devil attacks in the area. Bellhaven has struggled with it as well. We recently encountered a massive colony of ettercaps that was spreading out and threatening our village. There were nearly a thousand of them, but we fought them and were able to win." He left out mention of the Mo.

Karn frowned. "So many?"

His eyes wandered the village, trying to do the mental math of how the group had been able to eliminate them. But when his eyes took in the fire raging deep into the southern forest, he seemed to be appeased. "Ah."

"Yes. Unfortunately, after our first battle with them, it was clear we needed a more... efficient tactic," Dar said.

"Cowardly." Karn's beady, black eyes fixed on Dar. "They were just ettercaps."

"Any foe is dangerous enough in large numbers. I have no regrets. It was justified by the number of villager's lives I saved in making the decision to burn their webbed fortress, and them with the forest." Dar wasn't backing down.

But Karn wasn't paying attention. Instead, he was looking up at the sky, reading the stars and then looking around, finding landmarks. The big demon frowned.

"I will go investigate this ettercap site," he said in a grave tone. "Then I will go to Bellhaven."

"You are welcome to stay the night here." Dar thought about his freshly cleaned out hut. "We happen to have an empty hut. It is simple, but it's a shelter."

"Show me," Karn demanded.

Dar's face twitched, not used to being commanded since he'd come to Granterra. He wanted to tell the demon off for that tone, but he wasn't an idiot. This demon was powerful enough to wipe their little village off the map, maybe even take Bellhaven with it. For now, he would have to be careful.

The speed with which Karn had become aggressive at the mention of the ancients being abused showed that he was quick to anger. The last thing Dar needed was to wake up in the morning to a village covered in blood because he'd failed to be cautious and diplomatic.

The villagers parted for the two of them as Dar brought Karn to the recently vacated hut. "Here. On your travels to and from Bellhaven, you are free to use it."

"Satisfactory. I will be going now. This ettercap problem concerns me." The big demon lumbered away straight for the raging forest fire. Apparently, fire didn't bother him either. With his dao of heat, Dar could also have walked straight through the fire without harm.

Karn must have had some dao to protect him.

"Is everything alright?" Glump croaked from beside Dar, getting his attention.

"For now." Dar realized more than a few people were waiting in the wings, wanting to know why their new visitor had come.

Dar beckoned over his women and the leadership for the village. "That was Karn. He comes on behest of The White, and he's possibly even stronger than Cherry. He is definitely far more militant.

"Stay out of his way. Hopefully, he'll pass through like a bad storm and we can continue on. He was interested in the ettercaps, so he is scoping the forest out now. And then I believe he'll head for Bellhaven tomorrow."

Bart sucked in a tight breath. "What's he going to Bellhaven for?"

"Investigating rumors around how they were treating spirits and demons," Dar summarized what he had learned from Karn.

More than a few of those present had pained looks on their face as they went through the mental exercise Dar had as well. Bellhaven was in trouble.

It invoked mixed reactions from the group. Glump and Rex looked away as if it wasn't their problem. Let the city pay for what it did to them.

Russ almost looked eager for them to pay their pittance, for driving them out. Bart was no doubt thinking about secondary ramifications as he scratched his chin. Sam was, well, the most caring of their group and thinking of the children that would be caught in the crossfire.

"I think it is about time for me to turn in for the night," Dar told the group, seeing the mix of emotions play across their faces. They all needed time to make up their minds. "I want to be my best for him tomorrow. If he comes back, I offered him our old hut. We are moving out to the cave today and settling in."

That statement earned him a clap of congratulations from Bart, who glanced at his daughter to confirm Dar had made a place for her in his new home. When he saw her smile, it reflected on the old blacksmith's face. "Good.

Enjoy your home. Nothing like living in a place you built yourself."

"Thank you." Dar gave the man's shoulder a squeeze. Bart had become one of Dar's closest allies in the village. The blacksmith and his wife had already made the transition to becoming immortals like Dar's maids. They were among the few he trusted the most.

The group broke up as Dar turned to grab his women and head to the cave, but Glump stopped Dar and pulled him aside to speak for a moment.

"I would be careful with a demon like Karn around." Glump's eyes wandered over Dar's dao companions and then to Blair and Neko. "Demons like him often take what they want, especially if those women are unattached."

Ah, Dar pat Glump on the back, appreciating the heads up.

"Thank you for the advice." Dar would have to keep it in mind. There wasn't much he could do if Karn went after ladies in the village. Technically, Dar hadn't laid claim to Blair or Neko, but he felt a wave of possessiveness at the thought of Karn sweeping them off their feet.

"You should stop being so resistant and bring them into your family. They are good girls, and you are a strong man." Glump clearly didn't understand Dar's hesitation, but how could he? He'd been raised in a world where harems were normal for those powerful enough.

"Will do, old friend. Now, if you'll excuse me, I think my ladies are eager to rest."

Sasha took her cue and grabbed Dar's arm, pulling him away from the conversation. Mika came over on the other side, the two of them hemming him in.

"What are you going to do?" Sasha asked as they walked along with Blair, Neko, and the maids.

"Let's wait until we are inside." Dar pointed with his chin and pulled the ladies along through the cave to the mansion deep within. It wasn't until the door closed behind them that Dar pulled them over to sit down on the stone couches.

Some of Sasha's enchanted cloth was now draped over them, pinned in place with how he molded the stone. It didn't quite mimic a cushion, but Dar never liked overly soft furniture, anyway. They were nice.

Reaching inside himself, he pushed and pulled until a dirty Cherry came out of his inner world.

He raised his brow at her.

"Burying corpses for the little dao tree," she said by way of explanation before hopping on his lap and dirtying his clothes.

"I'm the one who has to get that out of his clothes," Sasha grumbled. "But thank you for joining us. You missed the excitement of one of The White's people coming to visit."

Cherry's brow furrowed, and she turned to Dar, waiting for more.

"His name is Karn," Dar supplied. By the way Cherry's eyes opened wide, she knew the name.

"He is an enforcer. The White sends him out to kill. He's strong and there are many stories of his... swift justice." Cherry's voice was small. "What is he doing here?"

Dar didn't like the sound of 'enforcer', but it wasn't far from what he'd expected after meeting the demon.

"He came to check on rumors of ancient races being mistreated in Bellhaven. But now he's added going to check on the ettercap stronghold. But he didn't seem too interested in it until he looked to the sky and figured out his current location."

Cherry nodded. "Yeah. The White would know of the sealed Mo that was within her territory."

"Do we have a problem?" Dar asked. "If Karn checks it out and finds the Mo gone, what is he going to do?"

The dryad in his lap nibbled on her lip as she pondered it out loud. "If he goes out there and finds it missing, he will eventually report it back to The White. But I think he will assume it is loose rather than that we killed it. That will seem unlikely to him."

"Makes sense. Why would he think that a small village would have been able to kill it?" Mika followed her logic. "Will he try to track it?"

"Maybe?" Cherry hesitated. "Given what kind of creature it was and the dao it possessed, he might not consider it possible for him to track it. But that's all just a guess."

There was a smirk on Neko's lips. "Bear doesn't know that Dar is the best."

"Would there be any consequence if Karn knew I defeated it?"

Cherry shook out her long green hair. "I don't think he'd believe you. If anything, he'd think you were fooled. If that thing had gotten out, it might have been able to do just that, fool us. The Mo that Lilith hunted were immortal and would come back if she didn't seal them."

The spider had seemed tough enough. And when the little dao tree had absorbed the colossal spider, Dar had felt how the creature was connected to its aspect of the dao. Even if they had crushed the thing a million times, it would have continued to come back.

But, with the help of his little dao tree, Dar was sure it was gone for good this time.

"Okay. That settles it. If Karn comes asking questions, we tell the truth. We saw the massive creature, severed its limbs and burnt the web fortress." He looked at the group. "For now, we keep what the little dao tree has done a secret."

The girls nodded in understanding before he continued.

"Considering what you said, and my own impressions of the demon, I think it would be best if I traveled with him to Bellhaven," Dar said seriously.

"Why? They've done nothing for us." Blair crossed her arms and pouted.

Dar knew merchants had continuously cheated the salt spirit in Bellhaven. She had essentially been a walking gold mine as far as those merchants were concerned, given her ability to pull salt from the sea and soil, and salt's use as currency in trade.

Given the chance to exploit her, they had. They'd claimed her salt was monstrous in origin, and therefore lesser. So they'd buy it at a deep discount and then resell it with their stock, pocketing large profits.

"Despite any feelings I might have towards the city, many of the citizens are innocent. It was the nobility that made the power play." Dar let out a heavy sigh. He hated going out of his way to help Bellhaven considering what had happened, but he'd already dealt justice as the Black Knight. It wasn't fair to make them suffer further without additional cause.

Dar saw several options of what could happen when Karn visited Bellhaven, and very few of them were good, and some might affect his village.

Karn could do enough damage that Kindrake would be forced to make a move, or he could do damage on a level that would halt the flow of merchants past their small village. None of those would benefit them. And it could only make the humans more fearful of ancient races.

"I understand." Sasha patted his thigh. "But I can't go with you." She looked apologetic. "The village still needs guidance, and there is much for me to do."

Dar's gaze passed over the rest of the women as he thought about who, if anyone, should come with him.

Blair wouldn't work. Her attitude towards the city wouldn't help Dar's goal to keep Karn from violence.

She'd have to stay behind with Sasha.

Cherry went where he did now that she was tied to his dao tree, so she was a given. And he wouldn't mind having her with him to help navigate his time with Karn. And he had a feeling the maids would insist on coming to make sure he had all he needed.

Noticing Neko listening and based on the look on her face, she'd likely follow him, even if he tried to get her to stay behind.

So the only person that was still a question was Mika.

"What will you do, Mika?"

She had a frown of consternation on her face before giving up with a sigh. "I'm needed here. I need to keep fishing before the river gets too cold, and to help Russ with the boat."

Dar nodded, realizing that, if they wanted to keep the boat up here while they were in Bellhaven, it made more sense for Dar to see if he couldn't hitch a ride with the merchant on his way south.

"Hey. What about me?" Blair shouted, but Mika put a hand on her friend's shoulder and shook her head. She must have had the same opinion Dar did about Blair joining on the trip.

Blair turned to her friend, ready to chew her out, so Dar spoke first. "My goal is to prevent Karn from causing too much damage to Bellhaven, while also looking for more information on this levy that the nation is rallying for in the spring. Can you really say your feelings for the city wouldn't cause conflict with my goals?"

He needed to understand more about any potential oncoming war. Their village was so small—they didn't have resources or people to spare for a levy.

Blair wilted, knowing she couldn't honestly say she would stay out of the way. "No."

"Thank you for being honest with yourself and with me." Dar did his best to reward her for her honesty. "For that, let's talk about spending an afternoon together when I get back."

He'd find some way to spoil her with a date. She deserved to be spoiled after all the help she had given his family recently.

Without a doubt, Blair was strong in many ways and would be a boon to their family, but this wasn't the task for her.

"Of course." She smiled wide, her violet eyes pinched in the corner with her smile. "But just you and me for the afternoon. No one else."

"I wouldn't have it any other way." He smiled. "Now I apologize, but I think I need to get some rest so that Karn doesn't blow through the village tomorrow morning while we're sleeping. I don't want to miss our opportunity."

Dar excused himself, and his dao companions followed him back to the bedroom, while the maids, Neko, and Blair made their way to their own rooms.

While he did need to get sleep, Dar was also excited and anxious. Once he laid down, he'd finally be able to dive into his inner world and see just what had changed from the little dao tree absorbing the Mo.

Chapter 4

Dar settled into bed with his dao companions curled up around him. He paused, enjoying the moment in their new home. Sasha's scent wafted over to him, and he breathed it in, relaxing into the bed she'd softened.

Drifting off, Dar let his mind descend down into his subconscious and his inner world.

Cherry was there already waiting for him, her boundless excitement for the little dao tree always keeping her attached to the space. Sasha had also joined him before in the inner world, but she needed her rest. The fight with the ettercaps had completely worn her out.

"Look at it!" Cherry bounced in front of him the moment he opened his eyes in his inner world. He wondered how she'd even reached him so quickly from wherever she'd been in the inner world.

He looked around slowly, trying to find what she was referencing. Cherry grabbed his face, clearly not willing to let him waste a moment before seeing whatever she was excited about.

She pointed him towards where the little dao tree should have been.

There, in the circle of loose dirt, was still a tree, but he almost didn't recognize it. The little dao tree wasn't very little anymore. It had grown significantly, and now black veins ran through it. They had grafted on part of Cherry's old cherry tree, and it was in full bloom with pink blossoms, while the branches that emanated from the black vein in the tree had pitch black leaves.

Dar moved forward, placing a hand on the rough bark. He closed his eyes, feeling how it connected to him and his dao.

The tree pulsed with life and power. More than ever before. There was some sort of new power that was just out of his reach; the little dao tree had taken on the aspects from the Mo it had absorbed.

"This is… incredible," Dar gasped.

"I know." Cherry beamed up at him with wide, just a tad crazy, eyes. "Can you feel the dao it has aligned with?"

"Yes. It feels like a dao I've already tried to study, but so large." It was faint, like something at the tip of his tongue. He could feel a path to a dao far above those he had studied. "Maybe I should go hunting more Mo."

"Dar, the Mo had a celestial dao, or possibly something beyond even that. It was heavily weakened by the seal. If it hadn't been, we wouldn't have stood a chance," Cherry spoke in a hushed whisper. "We got lucky."

The chill that went down his spine had nothing to do with the weather. "I know. None of us expected something that powerful to be there."

"There's more," Cherry pushed. "What if there are others coming free of their seal? Lilith left this world, and this Mo was only the first we've found that was breaking free from her seal. There are likely others, others that might be weak enough for the little tree to absorb."

"You want me to go after them?" Dar realized. "We could be wrong and not go after one that's weaker. We could easily walk into something way out of our league."

The petite dryad wasn't backing down that easily. "You have people who could scout. You can get support from multiple skilled spirits and demons." Cherry gave him an impatient look.

Dar sighed, running his hand through his hair as he just stared at the newly improved dao tree. He sat down next to it.

Things were just settling down. He'd enjoyed the thought of burrowing in for the winter, working on some small projects. He was planning to exercise his new technique and learn some more dao to get stronger.

But Cherry had a point. He'd be able to progress much faster if he went hunting. He could already feel that his dao was going to take leaps from the changes to the little dao tree.

Cherry came and sat next to him. "Lilith didn't give her life for you to hide, Dar. You are the Black Knight. You are meant to protect this world from the devils. Get out there and find the weakened Mo, kill them."

A punch to the gut. She had to bring up Lilith's sacrifice.

Dar leaned into her, knowing she was right. He'd expanded his path to include building his village and a population of other immortals, but his original path was still there. Devils were attacking the villages in increasing numbers. With Lilith gone, they were either breaking free or just less scared. They would only continue to become bolder and expand, like the ettercaps.

"Okay. So let's say we go after them. How do we locate them?" Dar asked Cherry.

"Well, we found this one by backtracking the ettercaps. Maybe the sudden increase in gremlins and trolls attacking Bellhaven has a similar root cause? We could follow some back to where they are coming from—they are rather stupid," Cherry offered.

It made perfect sense to Dar. "Add it to the list of things to do when we venture to Bellhaven with The

White's emissary. I assume you'll be coming with me to Bellhaven?"

"I sure as shit won't be coming alongside you. In case you forgot, they likely haven't forgotten my face after what happened."

He winced. She was right. After Mark had her tree set on fire, Cherry had lost it and nearly killed the nobility of Bellhaven. "So, you'll ride along in here?"

"Yes. And I'll be bored, so get me all the seeds you can. That way, I can keep busy taking care of trees. Otherwise, I'll just be feeding the little dao tree." She gestured to the side, where a massive mound of ettercap and spider corpses were lying, still needing to be processed.

"That'll be a lot of fruit." Dar sized them up. "I think that might even be enough to help the whole village along in a transformation into immortals."

The pile was like a treasure trove. He stared at it and then looked back at his dao tree. "Guess I can't call it the little dao tree anymore, can I?"

"You still can." Cherry walked around it and pulled down one of the dark limbs. "But you need to see this."

Dar walked around to join her. In her hand hung a cluster of small fruits so dark red that they were nearly black. It wasn't hard to guess what those were; they were from the Mo it had absorbed. Each small fruit rippled with unknown power.

"Any clue what dao those are?" he asked.

"Not a clue, but there are a few new types of fruits started growing on it. I'm unsure if they are all from the Mo or if the tree's evolution has changed the variety we are getting. Although, it could also be that there are just so many of these ettercaps that we are getting some new ones."

Dar plucked one of the new fruits off the branch, rolling it in his hands. "One way to find out."

Cherry turned to say something, but stopped as Dar grabbed and bit into the juicy fruit. Immediately, he could feel the new dao seeping into him. He ate the fruit in a few bites.

Dar waited, wondering what would change. But, as he stood there, the shadows cast by the little dao tree drew his attention. Brow furrowing, he realized that he felt connected to the dimness in that space. He smiled, knowing what dao he'd consumed then.

"Dao of dim." He let out a soft whistle. "We won't be giving these to anyone outside the family."

"Why?" Cherry asked, confused.

"Because, if you put quiet and dim together, you start to get to some very interesting things that have a reputation for being quite deadly."

As much as Dar trusted the villagers, he did have to be careful. He'd given them the quiet dao because it could easily help protect them without being too dangerous. Dim led to shadows and darkness which had other connotations.

Although, he was excited to try it out for himself.

"We are just going to leave them there?" Cherry asked.

"You are free to have one. And we'll share them with the others as well. Amber and Marcie will love it. No doubt they'll start trying to train to use it immediately." Dar plucked a few fruits and set them aside for the morning. "What else do we have?"

"More of the fruits with the sticky dao." Cherry pointed them out, and Dar ate one of those as well. He didn't see a use for it now, but maybe one of these days he'd like to scale a vertical wall like a superhero.

Together, they looked through the tree, searching for others, but there were no other fully formed fruits. Dar was curious to see if the ones that were still growing would mature with the rest of the corpses.

He looked at the pile. It was a lot of work to bury all of those. Even though Cherry was going to stay in his inner world for a while, he didn't want to leave her with the literal mound of work.

So instead, the two of them spent the rest of the night dumping the bodies into the soft soil around the little dao tree and letting it absorb them.

Cherry's excitement hadn't lessened, and with it, her sex drive seemed to increase. There were more than a few times that they took breaks in their work to enjoy each other. During one break, when Dar had pressed Cherry's back up against the tree to take her, she'd nearly lost her mind.

***

"Alright, I think it's about time for me to get up." Dar patted Cherry's apple-red ass. She'd wanted it rough.

"Go ahead. I think I'm going to avoid meeting Karn for now." She lay down in the fledgling grove of apple trees they had started the previous week.

Dar realized that her history as a dao companion with one of the oldest demons might make her recognizable. If she didn't want to meet Karn, that was fine by him.

Rolling over and giving her a peck on the cheek, he left his inner world and settled back into reality on his bed.

Sasha was there on her side, watching him sleep. "Morning." Her hand trailed soft touches along his chest.

"Morning," he grumbled, his body protesting his first movements. He was still sore from fighting his way through the army of devils. "Did I miss anything?"

"No. Amber and Marcie took turns keeping an eye on our visitor. He's still asleep in our old hut."

Dar gave a grunt of affirmation and pulled out one of the fruits of dim for her. "New fruit."

"Wonderful." She took it, a gleam in her eyes. When her face turned to him, sincerity shone in it. "I want you to know that I appreciate this. What you are giving me is priceless."

Dar shrugged. He didn't want to make a big deal of it. "You gave yourself to me, and I think that's worth far more." He claimed her lips for a proper morning kiss, pressing her back to the bed as the fruit rolled out of her hand, forgotten. "But I do need to get going."

Even as he said that, her leg rubbed up against his thigh.

He groaned. It was tempting, but he'd have to make it up to her later. "I need to get going."

Sasha let up with an understanding smile. "The girls brought in breakfast too."

Dar got dressed and padded out into the open area. Amber stood in the kitchen, stirring a pot over the enchanted stove he'd designed. It had taken him a few tries, but he'd figured it out.

"This thing is incredible," she gushed; she kept looking down at the stone surface as the air rippled above it.

"Glad you like it. Just be sure to turn it off when you are done." He walked over to her. "Also, here's a gift." He held out another of the fruits.

Amber didn't ask any questions; she just picked it up and stuffed it in her mouth.

"If ood," she tried to talk with her mouth full. And then her eyes lit up as she swallowed, looking around the room. She licked her lips and smiled. "Dim. I wonder if I can ambush you better next time with this."

"I figured you and Marcie would enjoy this one."

"Yes, milord." She bobbed her head. "May I take Marcie's to her?"

"Has she been a good girl?" Dar asked, holding out the second fruit.

Amber gave him a wicked smile. "Yes. Thank you for the advice the other day."

"Just don't let it get out of hand."

Amber took the fruit and gave him a small curtsy. "I'm just training her for you, milord." Amber's voice dropped down to a low whisper.

As long as the two of them were consenting and enjoyed the play, Dar was perfectly okay with whatever story they built around it. It wasn't surprising to him that Marcie was submissive in bed, nor that Amber was dominant in their relationship.

"Go on, give her a reward." Dar shooed Amber away and gave himself a serving of what she'd been preparing on the stove.

"You spoil them both," Sasha said, walking out of the bedroom.

"If they were lazy, I wouldn't dote on them as much. But, every time I do something, they only work harder." Dar took his bowl and sat down at the table.

He frowned. Having not used the table before, he was now realizing how cold and homely a stone table and chair could be.

This was something he should replace with wood. They just didn't have the spare materials lying around for something like that at the moment.

As if his presence at the table summoned them, Neko and Blair wandered out of their rooms. They followed Dar's lead, grabbing food and a place at the table.

Mika wasn't far behind, reentering the cave. "Morning."

"You rose early," Dar commented. He'd missed his lovely wave spirit when he'd opened his eyes.

"Russ wanted to cross the river early in the morning to hunt at the crack of dawn. And you slept in today," she pointed out.

Dar looked around, but realized his sense of time was lost in the cave. There was nothing to reference. He'd have to figure out a way to resolve that in the future.

"Everyone deserves a good rest after yesterday. But I'm glad to hear Russ went out early in the morning. He needs to keep burning off all that excitement he has."

The table chuckled, clearly in agreement.

Dar laid down a fruit in front of each of them. "Dim." He only said the one word, but that was apparently more than they needed. They each grabbed a fruit and eagerly ate it.

Well, everybody except Neko grabbed a fruit. She smacked it back and forth between her hands, like a cat playing with a ball.

"Don't you want more dao?" Dar was surprised the jaguar demon hadn't immediately eaten it.

"I will eat it, eventually." Neko rolled her eyes. "Just fun."

Dar pulled a lump of granite from the floor, shaping it into a hollow ball with a few round pebbles inside to make some noise. "Knock yourself out."

Neko gave it a tentative tap, her face skeptical. But when it made noise as it rolled, she popped the fruit into her mouth distractedly and played with the ball, batting it around.

"You had to give her something that made noise, didn't you?" Blair narrowed her eyes at Dar while Neko made a racket with the new toy.

"I'm not dumb. You try. You'll understand." Neko held the ball out to Blair, who sighed and put it on the table, hitting it back and forth between her own hands for a moment.

"Sorry, not my style. There are other things I'd like to play with to keep my hands busy." She fixed Dar with a lustful stare, only to be smacked in the back of the head by Mika. "Ouch."

"You told me to," Mika responded, shrugging and ignoring Blair's glare.

Blair rubbed the back of her head. "I know, but did you have to hit so hard?"

"Only way you'll learn. And I keep my promises." Mika gave a proud smile.

Dar ignored them, focusing on his food. Although he hadn't realized it, Blair had clearly asked Mika to help her tame down her intense flirtiness. It was sweet that she'd taken to heart their discussion and his request that she not be quite so forward and instead let them build their relationship naturally.

As he thought about Blair, he remembered something he had meant to ask her a while ago.

"Hey, Blair, think you could do me a favor and show me your bright rune?" Dar pulled Sasha's booklet out of his inner world. He'd added his own dao characters to it. And he intended to add the rest of his companion's to it as well.

Blair's eyes bugged out as he flipped through the booklet containing numerous dao characters. "Whose are in there?"

"Sasha's, and then I started putting mine, and Cherry has added hers."

"Mika?" Blair asked with a strange expression.

"Not yet."

Blair snatched it out of his hand and scrambled for a quill and ink. Then she started jotting down all of her dao characters.

Dar looked to Mika for an explanation.

The wave spirit only gave him a wink and a nod that it was okay. Apparently, Blair adding her dao characters to his booklet had significance that he wasn't aware of.

But then he realized that typically only dao companions shared their dao with each other. This in her eyes must have been an affirmation of her place in his family.

And that was fine. She fit in with their family, and he'd already given her a place in their home. Although his emotions for her were still rather shallow, he planned to make an effort to explore them if there was something more.

He'd already promised her a date when he got back, and he was excited about it. It would help him firm up if there was something deeper there.

Blair finished jotting her dao into the book quickly, then flipped the page and continued until she had added every dao she knew. "Here you go."

"Hold up. Help me figure out which is which. I want to label yours." Dar opened the booklet to the first page she had been drawing in so she could label the dao she had added.

"Bright, like you asked." Blair pointed in the book.

Dar marked it and went through the rest of them with her, marking each page and then sucking the booklet back into his inner world. "It's safe there. No one will get your understanding of dao without first taking my life."

"Not sure if that's as reassuring as you meant it to be," Mika said dryly.

Shrugging, Dar focused back on his meal, chowing down and finishing up the grit-like porridge that they favored in the village.

While Mika was right, he'd be pretty hard to kill. The enchantments covering his body allowed him to fight foes far beyond his limitations. While he wasn't about to take on a full-strength Mo any time soon, he was confident that he was well above average strength in the world.

"Anything else we need to discuss?" He looked around the table, enjoying having them all together. It was a different location, but it was their same family huddle in the mornings.

"Nothing I can't handle while you are out." Sasha patted him on the shoulder. "Go, enjoy your trip."

Dar did a round of kisses with everyone, and against his better judgement, he even gave Blair a peck on the cheek. He could tell she wanted more, but she sat still and didn't push.

Neko and the maids trailed after Dar as he left the cave and set out into the village, looking for Dane Goodhaul and Karn.

As they walked, the merchant was easy to spot. His boat workers stood out like sore thumbs; their shoulders were broad and muscular from carrying heavy cargo all day, making them extra stocky. The big men surrounded the portly merchant as he talked.

"Morning, Dane," Dar called out, even as several of the villagers talked with the merchant. They were holding bags of what he knew to be salt, and Dar was glad they'd gotten their reward and were getting to trade.

"Ah. Dar." Dane turned to him. "Can I help you?"

"Finish up with these people first, but I'd like to talk about hitching a ride down to Bellhaven for a few of us." Dar gave the merchant his most charming smile.

The merchant nodded, focusing back on the trades in front of him. He was in full negotiation mode.

It didn't take long for the merchant to finish; the people of Hearthway mostly wanted luxury items that they had abandoned when they had fled their homes in Bellhaven. They'd bought things like brushes, perfumes, and delicate tools that might require a jeweler to craft.

Dar took it as a compliment that they felt secure enough with shelter and food that they could spend their salt on such items.

When the crowd cleared out, Dane turned to Dar. "What was it you wanted? A ride to Bellhaven?"

"Yes. For myself, the people here with me, and one more." Dar gestured to Neko and the maids.

"Not a problem. Who's the last person?" Dane asked, looking around.

Right on time, Karn stepped out of Dar's old hut. His white fur and stature made him obvious at a glance.

"That one." Dar pointed to the large bear demon.

Dane's face drained of blood, and Dar could see he wanted to say no, but the man was too afraid of The White's emissary. And rightly so. Karn could tear Dane and his whole vessel apart.

"Karn," Dar called out. "I got you a ride to Bellhaven. These ladies and I are also going to join you."

The demon tried to reassess Dar, but after a moment, came to the same conclusion as the first time and shrugged. "I look forward to seeing how the city treats your return."

Dar was curious as well. For Bellhaven's sake, he hoped they opened their arms wide and rolled out the red carpet.

"Come sit. Eat. I think Merchant Goodhaul here will be leaving soon. Lucky for us, river boats are really a quite comfortable way to travel," Dar said.

Karn huffed, but he grabbed a bowl of porridge brought to him from the pot at the central hearth. He downed it in one slug and wiped his mouth. "Let's go. I lost too much time yesterday. Hopefully, this boat can make up for some of it."

Dane was sweating bullets as he watched the demon head towards the river and his boat.

"Don't worry. I'll handle him," Dar tried to reassure Dane, nudging the merchant. But Dane just grunted a weak, high-pitched sound.

Laughing, Dar clapped Karn on the shoulder as he caught up to the demon, Dane hurrying to catch up behind.

Chapter 5

Dane paced up and down his boat as it pushed off the banks of the Bell River.

The merchant was clearly nervous, and Dar couldn't blame him. Karn was clearly powerful and more than a little dangerous. But Dar hoped the merchant pulled it together.

Dar walked over next to Karn, standing at the side of the boat. "What did you find when you looked into the ettercaps?" Dar fished for information.

"Nothing," Karn said simply. But Dar had gotten pretty good at reading Russ' face, and he could see the slightest crease of worry between the bear's brows. However, it didn't sound like he was lying.

Dar realized Karn could have also been saying he found nothing when he'd expected to. That the Mo wasn't where it was supposed to be. He wondered if the bear demon didn't like lying.

"Really? That's good. Our little village doesn't need them to reappear in the spring after the thaw." Dar continued to play the part of a concerned village leader, pretending he knew nothing about the Mo. He wanted to know what Karn was going to do about his thoughts on the Mo.

"The world is a dangerous place. Would you rather not be in a city?" Karn hedged.

Dar worked to not smile. Karn was trying to subtly warn him away, so he must have thought that the Mo was on the loose.

"We left Bellhaven for a reason. It was overcrowded. I imagine most cities are with the increased devil attacks. And regardless, we've found happiness out closer to the wild. Maybe it isn't in our nature to be holed up in a city," Dar added the last part as he watched Neko pace the ship, eyeing the water as if it was going to rise up and attack her.

"What is your companion doing?"

"She can't swim," Dar explained. "And she's new. We pulled her out of the forest for the first time this fall."

"Ah. Still learning," Karn grumbled, his little black eyes trailing after Neko.

The way he followed her didn't sit well with Dar. But then again, Neko was a sight. Her pacing had made what little clothing Sasha could get her to wear ride up. She was nearly showing her pert rear.

Dar cleared his throat, and Amber broke off and went to correct Neko's pending wardrobe failure. He was thankful. Amber and Marcie seemed quite adept at understanding what he wanted.

Karn grumbled and averted his eyes, focusing back on the river ahead of them. "She is an attractive companion."

"That she is, and also quite capable. A wonderful addition to my family." Dar continued to reaffirm his relationship with Neko, not wanting Karn to see any leeway.

Just then, the water in front of the boat exploded. Several sinuous forms rose from the Bell River. Dar's surprise was only overshadowed by his confusion. He hadn't heard of monsters in the river before.

But Dane didn't seem to be surprised. He quickly began shouting out orders. "Crossbows!"

As he shouted, many of the workers hurried to load the contraptions. They readied the weapons and fired into the five serpent monsters that were now clearly visible in the river.

Dar ignored the arrows as they flew over his shoulder. Karn remained stoic, standing between the men and the serpents unperturbed, seeming to do nothing. It was like it didn't concern him at all.

Dar cursed. He couldn't just stand there and watch, although Karn seemed plenty happy to do just that.

Running forward, Dar jumped off the front of the boat with enough power to make the boat shift in the water, the bow nearly ducking under the river's surface.

It was only once he was in the air that Dar realized he couldn't use the Black Knight's weaponry. That would be too recognizable. Changing his plan mid-flight, he prepared to attack.

Crossbow bolts punched into the serpents, but to creatures of their size, they weren't enough to take it down.

With the attack, Dar had made himself a target. The serpents turned to him, lunging for him with wide-open jaws. Each of them snapped forward, trying to catch him.

Dar braced himself, catching one serpent's mouth before it closed in around his waist, wrenching its jaw back open before it could harm him. The enchantments on Dar's body burned bright with power as he overpowered the monster's jaw and tore one of its fangs loose.

The serpent bellowed a screeching cry as it flung its head back, trying to shake Dar free after realizing it had made an error by snatching him.

But Dar had no sympathy for the monster; this wasn't a demon or spirit. He sensed no dao from the creature, only raw, abnormal size and strength.

Slamming the fang he'd pried off into the roof of the monster's mouth, the attack sent spurts of blood into the air as Dar leapt off the creature. The creature's body went limp below.

Dar landed on the bank, rolling to his feet. The remaining serpents were splitting their attention between him and the boat. Two of the remaining monsters focused on the boat, and the other two focused on Dar.

Apparently, monster logic said that if one serpent wasn't enough to kill him, two should do it.

The two serpents that went for him became highly aggressive as they tried to snap and bite Dar in two, working together.

Dar tried to decide on his next move. He needed a weapon.

Sensing around him, Dar was grateful that granite was common enough to be in the ground underneath him. He pulled at the material, using his greater dao to move it. Mottled stone rose, coming to his aid and blocking one serpent while Dar focused on the other.

Dar's hand expelled a wave of heat hot enough to cook meat on contact, blasting the serpent in the face and causing it to jerk off course to avoid the blast.

The serpent's deviated strike made a shallow divot in the bank before the creature pulled itself together to come back around for another strike.

But Dar didn't give it the chance. The wall of stone that had blocked the first serpent quickly became a massive axe. Granite was too heavy and too brittle to make a great weapon, but Dar forced it to hold its shape as he swung for the fences, cleaving the serpent in two.

That was all the other serpent needed. It turned and, with speed Dar didn't expect of a creature of its size, dove back into the river. Ripples of water betrayed its fleeing.

He could chase after it, but Dar wanted to help the boat deal with the other two.

Karn still stood at the front of the boat, his arms crossed as men held long spears, trying to avoid Karn and push the serpents back.

Dar assessed the angle and the force he'd need. There was a new trick he wanted to try. Summoning another block of granite from the ground, Dar placed his palm on it to focus. He formed four large javelins in the block and readied an expendable chunk of granite behind each one.

He'd never tried something like this before, but if he had such control of granite, why couldn't he do it?

Drawing on the mana inside of him, he let it loop around several times, building up before he pushed the dao of combustion through the stone to those four expendable hunks.

The block of granite boomed as it cracked. The four javelins shot forward with explosive power. It was like a medieval rocket battery. And quite effective. The javelins punched through the two serpents with enough force to come clear out the other side.

"Holy shit," Dar gasped as they landed with thuds on the other side of the river, blowing four sizeable holes into the ground with the combination of their force and weight.

The river splashed as the serpent corpses fell back into the water. Dar had to jump back to avoid getting wet.

Cheers went up from the sailors, and men came out with long hooks as they fished into the water. When they came up with the serpents, they hauled their bodies back onto the boat.

Dar took a running long jump back over the river and landed on the boat with a thud, returning to his space at the bow.

"Why did you help them?" Karn asked, a neutral expression on his face.

"Because I was here and I didn't want to see them die?" Dar was confused. Was Karn really so heartless?

"But they are weak. The dao would decide if they should live or die."

Dar's expression froze as he blinked a few times to confirm this was real. This demon thought that the law of the jungle should apply everywhere?

Shaking his head, Dar knew he wasn't going to change Karn's mind, so he turned to more productive activities, helping the crew pull the sea serpents up onto the deck.

Dane Goodhaul approached him. "Thank you for your help." His eyes wandered over to Karn with words unsaid. "We very much appreciate your help with the serpents. Without you, I would have lost men."

Dar was pleasantly surprised. He had half-expected the merchant to cry about almost losing merchandise, but instead, he was concerned for his men.

"It was little trouble." Dar gave his best friendly smile.

"May I inquire, are you a wizard?" the merchant asked cautiously.

"No," Dar said quickly. "I'm a demon. Is that a problem?"

Dane waved his hands quickly. "Not at all! We normally have a few on the boat for protection. If it wasn't for the rumors about Bellhaven, they would be here now. I just haven't seen one as human as you before."

Shrugging in response, Dar moved on. "You should know that that demon is a representative of The White. He's on his way to Bellhaven to assess the situation. What Bellhaven did to my people will have consequences, if it hasn't already."

The merchant's head dipped forward. "Should we turn back?"

"No. Hopefully, I can stop him from killing too many people." Dar didn't believe they were getting through this without Karn at least killing one person. "I'm also interested to see how Prince Gregor intends to turn around the situation. Well, multiple situations."

Bellhaven not only had problems with the non-humans, but there was also a veritable onslaught of devils. And now apparently, the kingdom was headed for war.

Dar needed to get ahead of those issues before they affected Hearthway. Though they hadn't seen the trolls or gremlins up their way, he was concerned that the ettercaps had acted as a barrier. Not much would have been able to come up from the south with them in the forest.

Now they were gone, and Hearthway might start to see other problems wander up from the south.

"Anyway, I wanted to ask how I could repay your help with the monsters." Dane pulled himself back together.

"Helping us find a place to stay in Bellhaven would be nice. Otherwise, just continue trading with Hearthway. The village you saw was only formed in a short, few weeks. I'm sure we'll be producing more items that interest you in the coming days."

Dane gave him a dry look. "Salt, meat, and leather always sell. I'll be back, if for nothing else than a steady supply of those. And let me give you a few coinage for a place to stay."

***

The rest of the trip down to Bellhaven was uneventful. As the boat pulled through the delta and out to open sea, it was less than an hour before they docked at Bellhaven.

Karn didn't even thank Dane, striding off the boat the second it touched the docks.

"It's been a pleasure, but it looks like I have to run," Dar thanked the merchant and followed Karn. Neko and the maids were tight on his heels.

They had only been on the docks for a minute before Dar felt a small shift at his side. He turned and grabbed a boy who was trying to pick his pockets. "Bad move. But I have work for you if you'll be honest."

"Of course, mister." The cheeky brat smiled up at Dar as if he hadn't caught him red-handed.

Dar knew people like this were often born more of desperation than malice. And it was just a kid.

"I have this for you." He held out a silver. "If you can do something for me."

The kid's focus was entirely on the coin, his eyes crossing as he stared. "Sure."

"I need you to run to the noble district and shout that a demon from Frost's Fang just came into the city."

"Mister?" The kid looked nervous.

Dar had fallen behind, but he could see Karn's big white head moving through the crowd ahead of them. He held the kid up so he could see him too. "That big white bearman, you see him?"

"Yes," the kid said.

"Good. Well, he'll kill the whole city if the prince doesn't put on a show." Dar put the kid down. The kid tried to grab for the silver coin, but Dar pulled it back. "Repeat it back. What are you going to do?"

"Go run up to the noble district and shout that The White sent a demon to the city." The boy nodded his head rapidly. There was an eagerness to his expression, but no hint of duplicity.

Dar uncurled his fist and let him have the silver. "Go on. Hurry. Karn is going to walk through the city, and we need the nobility in shape before he gets there."

The boy shot off with the silver in hand, and Dar had confidence the boy would do as he asked. The only question was how effective it would be.

"That was more than he needed to go do that," Amber said as they hurried through the crowd to catch up to Karn.

"Oh, well." Dar wasn't concerned about a silver. If that silver saved enough lives, it was worth it. "Stay close. And, Neko, hold my hand."

The jaguar demon looked shell-shocked and completely overwhelmed in the city. She grabbed his hand, and he held her tightly as he pulled their group through the crowded streets.

Dar took in the city as they walked. If anything, Bellhaven seemed overflowing with people. Before, it had certainly been busy, but not this busy.

He caught up to Karn. "Would you like us to show you the way to the nobles?" Dar remembered where the old duke had lived, and though Mark had lived there on his last visit, he suspected that the prince would be there now.

The big demon scowled for a moment before nodding. "That would make things faster. The sooner I can get out of this wretched place, the better."

"It isn't that bad." Dar tried to take the edge off his statement.

"They pack themselves in far tighter than necessary. It makes the place stink." Karn's little black nose on his wide head wiggled in a way that Dar almost found comical. If it weren't on someone he thought was a murder machine, he might have laughed.

Thankfully, people got out of Karn's way. He had a disgruntled look on his face that made people eager to step aside rather than risk their own day getting far worse.

Dar led him through the city, and the girls followed in the wake.

More than once, Karn's eyes found their way to Neko. It made something in Dar stir angrily. He didn't like having his woman ogled by the demon. He also knew that male demons had a reputation for being territorial; the last thing he needed was a dispute in the city with Karn. That would backfire on both of them and his goals.

Either way, he'd have to work through it for now, and maybe have a talk with Neko once they had some privacy.

They walked uphill through the streets. The crowds grew thinner and the buildings cleaner as they entered the nicer areas of the city.

There was a commotion up ahead that drew Dar's attention. The kid he'd paid earlier was being dragged away by two guards. "I swear. Oh, there, that one!" The kid pointed at Dar's group.

One of the guards stepped forward, drawing his sword on Karn. "Halt."

"That's a bad—" Dar didn't have time to finish the statement before a white clawed hand flew forward and ripped the guard's head from his shoulders.

The second guard let go of the boy and ran screaming deeper into the noble quarter.

"Mister." The boy was frozen with wide eyes.

"You did good. Now get out of here."

The boy didn't need to be told twice. He turned and sprinted down towards the docks. Dar cringed that the poor kid had watched a guard's head go flying.

Neko moved in front of Karn, putting her hands on her hips. "Bad."

"Neko, not now."

"No." She fought Dar to stay in front of Karn. "He's bad. Do you know you are a bad man?"

Dar was worried that Karn would take a swipe at her.

"I am not a bad man. For I am not a man. I am a demon, and that was nothing more than squashing a pest that dared try to bite me." Karn leaned down, so he was eye to eye with Neko.

She swiped, her claws cutting into Karn's nose. "Bad is bad. Don't use words to get out of it."

Somehow Dar could imagine Samantha back in the village using such words to chastise her. Worried Karn would attack Neko, Dar stepped between the two of them, ready to protect her.

Karn held his bloodied nose and growled at Neko. "I'll have to teach you better manners."

Neko clung to Dar's back. "No. Dar is the best. Only he can teach Neko all the things."

There was almost a pause in the world as Karn stared at them, deciding if he was going to start a fight. But, after that moment, he put his bloodied claw back at his side and wiped at his nose with the other.

"We will discuss more of this later. It seems the demons around here might be a touch too human." He targeted the last statement towards Dar.

"Uh. Hello?" A nicely dressed young man wearing a tabard that Dar didn't recognize stopped a few yards from their group. The poor man's eyes were riveted to the headless body laying a foot away from him.

Dar tried to pull his attention back to their group. "Great. This is Karn, a representative of The White. I'm a guest from an outlying village guiding him."

"You are the wizard Darius," the young man said. "There used to be posters everywhere with your face on them."

Dar cringed. It looked like he could not put his past visit behind him so easily.

"Then take us to see the prince before someone else loses their head." Dar looked distastefully down at the decapitated guard.

CHAPTER 6

Dar was glad, for their sake, that the nobility of Bellhaven had been able to roll out the red carpet so quickly.

"Welcome," a richly dressed wizard greeted their party as they reached the duke's old mansion, not more than five minutes after heading through the city.

"I see you've returned to the city." The wizard's eyes narrowed on Dar.

Dar could see he wasn't going to get the warmest welcome, which irked him, given that he was doing it to help them. "Karn, if I hadn't come with you, what are the chances you'd have already killed someone?"

The demon looked at him, surprised at Dar's blunt assessment. "Likely several. But I already killed one."

Karn looked puzzled as he studied Dar. "I do not understand how you survived so long when you are so reluctant to kill. There is a way to the world, a chain of power. Humans are weak. They either serve a purpose, or they do not. And those who do not will perish one way or another. I am simply speeding up the process."

"Thanks for clearing that up." Dar smiled, turning to the wizard and enjoying the look of shock on the poor old wizard's face. At least the wizard looked like he got the picture. Maybe he'd stand a chance.

Providing some extra background, Dar addressed the wizard, "Karn passed through the village I've been establishing with the others who escaped your attempt to cleanse the city of non-humans. He stopped for a night with us on his way here to Bellhaven on behalf of The White. It would seem that she is not pleased with recent events, so I'd recommend you reconsider your attitude."

Karn's beady, black eyes were emotionless as he stared icy death at the wizard. "Did he kill any of our kind?"

"Not that I can personally attest to," Dar answered. "Oh, and you should know, I hid here in the city under the guise of a wizard to avoid persecution," he lied.

The look Karn gave Dar was disgusted. It clearly insulted him that Dar would pretend to be human, but the demon moved on quickly. He pushed past the wizard, knocking him into the wall.

As they stepped inside the mansion, it looked entirely different from the last time Dar had been inside. Almost every strip of cloth, including the rugs, table runners, and large wall tapestries, had all changed to the prince's colors.

Dar looked around, shocked at the opulence. It was all he could do not to whistle. That many dyed fabrics were not cheap. That much coin would be enough to feed Hearthway for several years. And Bellhaven itself was short on food.

Suddenly, Dar felt far less sympathetic to the prince for whatever happened with Karn.

The wizard caught back up with Dar after recovering from being pushed aside by Karn. "Darius, stop at once. The two of you cannot barge through the prince's home without guidance."

"I'd like to see you stop him." Dar pointed to Karn and followed the big bearman as he ripped a door off its hinges rather than open it. Dar smiled. Karn was a bit rough around the edges, but he was also effective.

Dar wondered if The White had any more ambassador-type representatives she sent out on other jobs. Karn was definitely lacking in tact and social skills, and while power might be the law of the ancient races, humans relied on rules to keep order. And while Dar had no doubt Karn could take on a mass of humans, Dar wasn't sure Karn could take on all of Bellhaven.

Karn ducked into the room behind the door he'd ripped off, and Dar paused, waiting. The room was clearly a closet, and the demon would realize it quickly.

"Is he going to kill the prince?" the wizard asked.

"Don't know." Dar shrugged. "I'd rather he didn't, but as a representative of The White, he can do whatever he damn well pleases as far as I'm concerned."

The end of Dar's statement was punctuated by shelving collapsing as Karn strode back out of the closet with a satisfied smile.

It could have also been a grimace. It was hard to tell with his bear-like face.

Guards trooped down the hall, their hands on the swords hanging from their belts.

"Stop at once!" one of the guards in front belted out.

"I wouldn't recommend stopping him. It will only mean your death," Dar scolded the guards. They'd either missed the death of their fellow guard, or they were stupid.

One foolish young guard drew his sword anyway and pointed it shakily at Karn.

Dar cringed. The guard was clearly new. He didn't want to watch the poor kid die. He stepped forward, grabbing the demon's forearm before he reached out and removed the kid's head. "How about I lead from now on?"

Karn's body stiffened at the touch, but Dar was pleased to see his arm remained attached to his body. It appeared he'd at least earned a bit of respect from the old demon.

"You nee—" the guard stammered.

"Don't be a fool." Dar's gaze was stony as he looked at the guards. "He would have already killed you if not for me. And, if you keep pointing that at me, I won't be so helpful anymore."

The young guard froze as his two compatriots pulled him back.

"Great. Now point us to the prince."

"Down this hall, last door on the left," one guard was smart enough to answer Dar. "But we can't let you go unattended."

Dar hooked a thumb over his shoulder. "We have this guy—he was just too slow." Without bothering to continue talking, Dar let go of Karn's arm and brushed past the guards.

He could hear movement behind him. He knew that Neko and the maids were following further back, but what he was mostly listening to was indication that Karn wasn't actively killing guards. So far, so good.

"You are strong," Karn spoke as he caught up.

"Not sure I want to test myself too much against you. After all, you are a grand demon?"

"Yes. But physically, you surprised me. Do not do that again," Karn growled in threat.

Before Dar could say anything in response, Neko whirled around and scolded Karn once again.

"No! Bad," Neko scolded Karn. "Dar is helping you, stupid bear."

Karn's face was one to remember. The shock of being scolded by Neko again was priceless. Karn didn't likely have people scold him a second time after a warning.

"Come on, Neko. Let's not antagonize the bear before we meet the prince." Dar pulled Neko along and pushed through the doors the guards had indicated.

On the other side of the doors, the prince stood. He was joined by several wizards and a few men in military uniform. They seemed to be caught mid discussion.

But what caught Dar's attention most was a woman with antlers rising out of her head. She stepped forward, putting a hand on her sword. "Halt."

"Tami," Karn growled. "Good to see your family is still the pet of Kindrake's ruling class."

Dar didn't miss the familiarity between the two. There was clearly a history there, but from what Dar could assess, she was only a greater demon.

"Excuse me, who let you in?" A man in uniform turned.

The look on his face shifted as Karn pulled himself through the doorway.

"I have been sent by The White to investigate rumors of Bellhaven executing all demons and spirits," Karn said.

Every face in the room froze. They were clearly afraid to blink or breathe after he said that. They all knew that they had a problem. The White did not interfere often. When she did, it was serious.

Golum's eyes slid to Dar. "What are you doing here?"

Dar was starting to question that himself. He'd come with the noble intentions of preventing Karn from slaughtering everyone in the city, but each person just made him want to reconsider that.

"Showing Karn around. How's that laboratory of yours, Golum? Still keeping that spirit in a cage?"

The cold sweat that began building on Golum's face was victory enough for Dar. The prince's face fell as Golum's grew red with rage.

"Enough," the wizard screamed.

Karn lumbered forward, towering over Prince Gregor. "I wish to see how your people treat mine. Show me this laboratory."

Tami stepped forward, keeping herself between Prince Gregor and Karn, but that did nothing to protect Golum.

"I assure you that your people are treated well here in Bellhaven," the prince said. "It is true there was a coup in the city. Those who are no longer in power were using the people's fear of the devil's attacks to create distrust for demons to distract from their political maneuvering to seize power. That has been squashed."

The prince stood his ground before Karn, and Dar had to say that he was a bit impressed the man wasn't cowering.

"Prove it." The bearman huffed hard enough to blow back the prince's hair. "Your treatment of those of my kind that are weak is no different from if I went around slaughtering your children or forcing them into hard labor."

More than a few of the men shifted on their feet, clearly not comfortable with the analogy and what it might mean for their families.

"Golum, show this man to your lab," the Prince ordered.

"Sir. Maybe we let him see the town first?" Golum rubbed his hands nervously and looked past Karn to Dar for help.

"No, I think we should see your lab first." While Dar wanted to save most of the town, he had been sickened by what Golum had done in his laboratory. He had been an enabler for the coup.

The air in the room seemed to shift, anticipation coursing through Dar. It was like watching a building demolished—the calm before the storm. If the Prince had not stopped Golum and the wizards in what they were doing to demons, then Dar no longer had a need to protect them so fully.

Golum twitched and took two fast steps to the side; he looked like he was about to bolt.

Dar kicked the ground. The entire building was made of cut granite, allowing his kick to travel through the ground. A small lip rose before Golum's foot, tripping him as he moved and sending him down in a tumble.

Karn was on the man in an instant, picking him up and biting down on his shoulder and tearing him in two in a brutal display of violence. Golum's body strained and stretched against Karn's powerful neck before his flesh tore. Karn dropped the two separate pieces of Golum on the floor.

The room was silent for a moment except for the wet sound of dripping blood.

Dar had to hand it to Karn. That was definitely one way to get everybody's attention and make a lasting first impression.

The leaders of Bellhaven had their hands halfway to the swords on their belt, but nobody moved. They looked like they were dealing with an unhinged man, trying one last attempt to talk him down. But at least they were smart enough to realize he was homicidal, and they wouldn't be able to stop him if he tried to kill them.

Luckily, they seemed to say the right things, because Karn finally moved over and sat down on a nearby chair. Although, it was clear if anybody tried to leave, they wouldn't make it far.

The rest of the group slowly sat down, seeming to position themselves as far away from Karn as they could. Watching the men squash together into a couch on the far side of Karn's seat was amusing. They tried to look casual as they were pressed against each other.

Dar decided to let them chat, more interested in what they were discussing before he'd entered. He moved over to the large table they'd been standing around. On it was drawn a map with markers and papers that seemed to show military planning.

Dar wondered if it had to do with Kindrake's plans for war, or if it would give him more information on the latest demon attacks as he planned his next rampage. He studied it, trying to understand what it was depicting, but he was having trouble even placing Bellhaven.

"What are you doing?" A female voice caught Dar's attention as he tried to orient himself on the map.

"Trying to read a map," he said, as if it was the most obvious thing in the world. "Shouldn't you be protecting the prince?"

A pretty female face shoved its way between him and the map, only to be pulled back by a growling Neko. "Don't disturb Dar."

Dar looked up at Tami, realizing that she reminded him of the demon that had originally come with the prince.

"Do you happen to know another deer demon? A male?" Dar was curious if they ran in the same circles.

"My brother," she said proudly.

"You do know that he was killed here in Bellhaven for being a demon, right? Hung up outside this very building to rot as a gruesome display to the rest of our kind."

"What?!" Karn's fuzzy bear ears apparently weren't just for show. He whirled around in anger. Barely containing his rage, he stated, "Say that again."

The deer demon looked just as stunned; her mouth hung open, and she turned to the prince. "Is that true?"

"He died in defense of my personage," the prince replied, trying to bend the truth to diffuse the situation.

Dar shook his head, disappointed that the prince was hiding what had been done rather than making it clear that it was unacceptable. Dar had been too optimistic about the change the man would bring to the area.

Instead, it seemed the prince had been busy having his home redecorated and planning military affairs. He wasn't dealing with the domestic unrest that was now knocking on his door.

At this point, Dar was ready to let Karn deliver the wake-up call. "Bullshit."

Dar realized that the knowledge he had was based on the Black Knight. He'd need a viable excuse for knowing about Tami's brother. "We had people here monitoring the situation after we left. He was taken into custody and hung for all to see as an example. And during that, you were hiding up in the manor, making yourself comfortable with those who killed the duke."

"Things are not that black and white. Managing a kingdom isn't as simple as snapping your fingers. Politics are a subtle game. It takes time to make a change." The prince looked like he was fed up with the conversation and ready to be done with it.

"My brother was thrown away for politics?" Tami asked, barely contained rage in her voice. When no one answered her, she turned to Karn. "What are you really doing here, Karn?"

The bearman drew himself up to his full height, giving the woman far more respect than he had the prince and his men.

"The White was told of a city that had grown... rotten." Karn growled with the last word. "I've been sent to investigate and, if need be, remove the rot before it spreads. But I should tell you this, Tami. You should know all about this city since your family are the pets of Kindrake's royalty. I'm sure they knew and filled you in."

Karn's contempt at her family being used by Kindrake instead of the other way around was clear.

While they faced off, Dar assessed the strength of Tami the deer demon. She only seemed to have mastered dao slightly ahead of himself. She certainly was not a match for Karn. But the way Karn spoke of her family, Dar wondered if there was a greater power behind her.

"I will report back to my father," Tami said, struggling to keep her voice even. "There is no need for you to poke your nose in here."

"But I will. Because I can." Karn raised an eyebrow, daring her to make a move.

When she remained passive, he turned to the rest of the people in the room. "I want to see the wizard's laboratories." When no one moved, Karn barked. "Now. Or I will assume the entire city is complicit, and we'll see how long it stands."

Dar looked for the maids and Neko, but they had disappeared. It wasn't until he activated his dao of dim that he realized they had stuffed themselves in the corner and, with everything else happening, remained out of mind.

Tricky girls.

The prince and his men rushed ahead to keep Karn from killing half the nobility, leaving Dar forgotten in their rush. He smiled, taking the opportunity to once again study the map.

But hands slapped down over the map next to him. He looked up, annoyed, once again finding Tami there. She stared him down.

"Shouldn't you be going with them?"

"Nah, I'm good here." Dar shrugged. "I accompanied Karn so he wouldn't just squash the city without fully investigating if there was still corruption. But, from what I'm seeing, there is in fact a need to help push further change in the city. So instead, I'm interested in the latest happenings in the area."

He looked Tami over, wondering how much he should tell her.

Deciding to proceed carefully, he eased into the discussion. "I've heard rumor of war for Kindrake." He paused, trying to read her face. "And I know Bellhaven has been having issues with demons. I was curious which this map was about."

Tami took her hand off the map. "I shouldn't be letting you see this."

"Your brother was a good demon. He didn't deserve what he got. But thank you. I know this is just a little revenge against your master." Dar scanned the map before she tried to stop him once more.

"Master?" She choked on the word. "The prince isn't my master. I'm from the Cervus family; we work directly for the King."

"Looks that way. Hey, this is Bellhaven?" He pointed to a spot on the map. The whole thing was filled with details that didn't matter to Dar; the map covered the entire kingdom. It had taken him longer than he would have liked to point out the city. But he was still learning the surrounding areas.

"Yes. That's Bellhaven, and here's the Bell River all the way up to Kindrake."

His eyes didn't follow her finger, instead looking at the tokens they had been using to describe the devils. "Here were the last three attacks. And what's this? Scouting reports?"

Dar poked a cluster of tokens that were further away from the city. They were too far to be anything that was reported by the city itself.

"Hold on." Tami opened and closed several scrolls, scanning the contents before placing one before me. "I don't know why I'm helping you, but—"

Dar cut her off as he too pitched in, looking at the missives on the table. "Because I'm charming, and you don't see the harm in it. Plus, next to Karn, I'm practically a saint."

"Saint?" she asked curiously.

"Ah, a really good person." Dar quickly pivoted away from the question. "Oh, okay, this is from a scout."

His eyes scanned the scroll several times over. The scout had recorded a large gathering of trolls in the hills northeast of Bellhaven. Hundreds, if not thousands, of the large gray devils were there. And another order of magnitude more gremlins.

That sounded promising.

"What are you going to do with this information?" Tami asked.

"I lead a small village, and we just dealt with an ettercap problem. The last thing we need is trolls marching on us this winter."

"You didn't answer my question. What are you going to do with this?" Tami pressed.

He turned and found her face was nearly pressed into his. "Maybe go kill them."

She scoffed. "Ridiculous."

"Appreciate the vote of confidence," he stated dryly, but then turned his tone more genuine. "Thank you for your help."

"Are you going to catch up with the others?"

Dar thought about it. The temptation was there to let Karn go into full on slaughter on Bellhaven, but Dar knew that was just his current frustration. In the end, he would regret it if Karn killed his way through the city, and the backlash would be even more likely to fall on Hearthway.

"I guess. Otherwise, I think Karn might just kill the prince."

"That would be bad." Tami gave him a monotone reply, conflicted.

"Girls, come on," Dar called as he went to leave. He figured he could pretty easily find Karn in the city; he'd just need to follow the noise.

Neko and the two maids faded out of the shadows.

He didn't miss Tami's gaping mouth as she watched the group leave. Her hand had quickly shifted to her blade in her shock. Dar gave her a wink before turning his back.

But he did note that Tami was armed and armored like a human. It seemed odd, given what Dar had seen so far among most demons and spirits. They often fought without conventional weaponry, like Karn. But Tami wore boiled hide as armor and carried a sword. It appeared there was more to the demon.

CHAPTER 7

Dar moved quickly out of the prince's manor, heading back the way they had come in.

"Milord, what are we to do?" Amber asked.

Dar knew them trailing him all day probably wasn't great for them, but they also didn't have a clear enough plan to know at what time they should regroup. And he was worried what trouble Neko might get into wandering the city.

"You can stay at my place," Tami blurted out. When Dar turned to look at her, she added, "There's no inn in the city that will take you, and I'm interested to hear the full story of what you saw about my brother. I'll need to report it back to the family." She added the last bit as if she was scrambling for an excuse.

Dar wanted to argue, but in the end, she'd been friendly, and he didn't see much harm in accepting her hospitality. And she deserved to know what had happened with her brother.

"Fine. Girls, go with Tami. I need to check on Karn."

Neko snapped a playful salute while the two maids bowed. "Yes, milord. We'll have a place ready for you after your day."

Tami raised an eyebrow at their submissive behavior, but Dar ignored it, not caring to explain. He turned and strode through the city, heading towards Golum's place. It wasn't far, within the same block.

The door to his place had already been ripped off as Dar arrived, and shouting could be heard within.

Slipping in and down the stairs, the confrontation was obvious. Several wizards blocked Karn's path.

"You cannot enter here. Not without Golum's permission."

Dar winced. Soon enough, they'd find out that Golum wasn't going to be giving anyone permission anymore. But for some reason, Karn appeared to be holding himself back from outright killing the three wizards.

"Golum is dead," the Prince tried to mediate. "We need to see what he was working on."

"Dead?" one of the wizards asked. "How can he be dead?" They all wilted.

Prince Gregor used their distraction to walk past them and slide open the door. Karn and Dar followed.

The space was bigger than Dar remembered. Golum had expanded. The reason for the expansion became clear the second the door was opened.

Inside the laboratory, two caged trolls dominated the room. The back of the room was dug out to make room for their large bodies. But other aspects of the laboratory remained the same. There was the workbench full of tools for testing, and the other bank of cages still remained.

The trolls were slumped over. Whether drugged or exhausted, Dar wasn't sure. But the bars weren't warped. Given the troll's brutish strength, Dar was surprised Golum had managed to contain them.

The prince was not happy. "What is the meaning of this! Why are those here in the city?" He pointed a shaking finger at the trolls. "You were given permission to work with the gremlins, not trolls. Do you even realize what would happen if those got out? The casualties they could cause?" He continued to chastise the wizards present.

Dar agreed with the prince. If the trolls got out into the streets of Bellhaven, they could kill dozens before they could be brought down and dealt with. If people didn't have weapons readily available, it might even be worse. And all of that could be exacerbated if panic broke out and crowds trampled each other. It would be a mess.

"The trolls were necessary for his work. Golum was on the verge of changing humanity, allowing us to fight devils on the same level," one of his apprentices pleaded, clearly in awe of their master.

Dar wasn't surprised at the motive. The wizards had been trying to find a way onto the dao path, so far unsuccessful. They still had to use enchanted items in order to wield dao, limiting their power.

The apprentice's statement piqued Dar's curiosity. He wondered if they'd really been close or if it was just more of the same insanity that had possessed Golum the last time Dar had met him.

"I have no report of any breakthrough. I've only seen the same inane ramblings of wizards. Move aside and let us remove this danger from the city," the prince demanded.

"Welcome back." Karn noticed Dar. "Was it like this when you were here?"

Dar stepped through, and luckily, the cage that had once held the spirit was empty. "That cage there used to hold a spirit. They had a small bowl of water and another for food, which is like how they treat pets."

"Master's spirit was killed in a trial," one of the wizard's supplied, not understanding why Karn had come to the city and the impact his statement would have.

Before Karn could remove the man's head, Dar lifted the wizard up and tossed him into a nearby cage. "Spirits are just as sapient as humans. Tell me, how do you feel about being in the cage?"

"I'd just let myself out. As a human, I have that capacity. We are free, never meant to be bound to stupid oaths."

The air in the underground laboratory shifted. Dar wasn't sure how to describe the change, but it was like a prickling across his skin. A fight was about to break out.

Rattling metal sounded behind them. A wrought-iron gate closed, trapping Dar, Karn, and the nobles inside the laboratory. One of the other wizards had pulled a lever against the wall.

"What is the meaning of this?" Prince Gregor nearly screamed. But his question was answered as the cages holding the gremlins and trolls clicked open.

The caged occupants took a moment, staring at the doors. A few moved forward, testing the door as they pushed against it. It swung open easily.

Karn looked at the devils for a moment before turning back to the wizards, his intentions clear across his face.

Dar wasn't interested in watching another wizard be brutally torn apart, so instead, he focused on the trolls coming out of their cages.

"Stay back," he warned the noblemen who had drawn their swords.

Dar could go head-to-head with a troll. He'd done that before and won, but he had progressed his dao considerably since then. But he wasn't sure he wanted to show the full range of his abilities to this group either. He certainly couldn't show any of his Black Knight weaponry in front of the prince given the bounty on his head.

As he decided on his next move, Dar settled into a fighting stance.

Stomping on the floor, he created the same stone javelins backed by granite missile batteries he'd used to take out the serpents.

He fired one into the room; the sound blasting louder than before as it echoed through the underground corridor. He released the others right after.

The javelins blew through gremlins and sent chunks of stone flying throughout the laboratory.

The two trolls were slightly smarter and hunkered down, protecting their face. Their skin held a glossy sheen that told Dar they had used the dao of hard. It was common enough for trolls. They were made much tougher than any gremlin or serpent monster.

"They are still alive," the prince commented.

Dar thought that was pretty clear from the still moving trolls in front of him. He sighed, moving on to his next plan. It seemed that he'd have to get his hands dirty after all.

Striding into the room, Dar was confident in his ability to win the fight. While he might have had trouble with trolls once, he was significantly stronger than he was then. Part of him was interested to see just how he now stacked up against two lesser devils.

A troll picked up a table and swung it at Dar.

Dar let mana pool through his system, increasing his weight and making his skin as hard as stone. He smiled as he gave them a taste of their own medicine.

Dar caught the table with one hand, stepping inside the troll's swing and putting a palm to its chest. As he touched it, he activated the dao of combustion.

The troll's chest exploded under Dar's hand, and the troll toppled backwards as the other came forward, swinging desperately.

Ducking under the swing, Dar stomped on the ground. A pillar of granite shot up, catching the devil in the gut. Dar followed that hit up by dodging the troll's next punch and swinging a reckless haymaker into the troll's jaw.

The troll went down with a satisfying crunch. While it might have also had the dao of hard, it wasn't a match for Dar, who had now mastered a greater dao.

"Sword, please." Dar held out his hand to the prince and the men with him. He remembered when he had had that bent bronze blade and had to hack it through a troll's tough hide.

One of the men rushed forward to give Dar his sword. Dar pivoted back, cleaving the trolls' heads from their bodies in one strike.

Finished with his task, he turned back to the broader group. The wizard who had pulled the lever had already been dispatched.

"Now, Prince Gregor. While I understand the utility of your wizards, I have to wonder if they haven't become too dangerous as they are." Dar looked distastefully over at the remaining wizard on the other side of the gate. "After all, they are complicit in all we see here, and they had no problem trying to kill us."

"I do believe that one man isn't representative of an entire group?" another wizard that had been in the Prince's meeting argued.

"You're going to pretend this was all Golum?" Dar wasn't buying it.

The wizard grimaced. "I am not proud of what he was doing, but he had his reasons. And he was powerful. We weren't strong enough to challenge him."

Karn seemed bored by the chit chat and stepped forward, but Dar interceded. While Dar and Karn could kill them, it would be up to the prince to make any lasting changes. He needed to make this call.

"Each man is responsible for his own actions and must bear the resulting consequences," Prince Gregor proclaimed. "Golum dug his own grave, not that of all wizards. These men are to be unharmed."

The wizards relaxed at his statement.

Karn huffed loudly, a brow arched. He stared the prince down, reminding him that he did not follow the man's orders.

"This has been a poor introduction to Bellhaven," the prince continued, trying again. "Allow us to host you for another few days and try to change your mind. And we have news that The White would be interested in."

"Tell me the news," Karn stated, his focus quickly shifted. It seemed mentioning The White had a profound effect on his temper. Dar filed that away to use later as needed.

"We need to discuss in more detail. Only just before you arrived, I received another set of missives."

Karn was not satisfied with that answer. "Fine, we will discuss later. But I have news of my own that will be quick. Frost's Fang rescinds its protection over Kindrake."

"What?!" Prince Gregor lost all composure. "You can't."

"I was given explicit permission to declare this. This is not the first time, and it certainly won't be the last time, that Kindrake feels it can take advantage of our kind. I spoke with those that fled your city not a few weeks ago. Their stories were difficult to believe, but after what I have seen here, I have the confirmation I needed. Our protection is rescinded," Karn laid out his thoughts.

Dar had been told that The White and her home, Frost's Fang, held power that could crush entire cities overnight, leaving no survivors. And he believed it now after meeting only one resident of Frost's Fang. But he wasn't sure what sort of broader protection they offered.

"Please stay a few days. Let us change your mind," the prince tried again.

"I will stay for several days, but only to understand this devil problem that you have. While our protection is rescinded, the devils must be held at bay."

Karn walked over to the metal gate that had blocked their path and touched it. Dar watched as frost spread throughout it. With a single kick, Karn shattered it.

"If any of your people have demons or spirits... please bring them to me. I will lead them from the city when I go. If I find any have been withheld or hidden, there will be consequences."

Prince Gregor looked to Dar, pleading. "You'll help us?"

"You forget that I was run out of this city. You have absolutely no right to ask for my help, nor am I inclined to give it," Dar scoffed. "I came here to protect you from Karn's wrath should the city have improved. So far, I don't see that as the case. Leadership is clearly lacking, and Karn's decision is his own."

"But it will effectively destroy Kindrake," Gregor pleaded with Dar.

"Sounds like a problem for Kindrake and its leadership, not that of a small village leader." Dar pushed the man off of him and stepped around those gathered. "I'd start by rounding up the spirits and demons in the city like he asked."

***

It wasn't too hard to find Tami's place. The home was attached to Prince Gregor's. As he arrived, Karn shadowed him.

"Karn." Tami's face was dour as she took in the extra guest. "What are you doing here?"

"I've been asked to stay in the city for a few days," he answered simply.

"Yes, but why are you here? Specifically, why are you at my home?" Tami was out of her armor, relaxing on a sofa with Neko while Amber and Marcie worked to make dinner.

"Do we need another serving?" they asked Dar.

"A few extra, I imagine. Karn has a big appetite."

The bear shrugged. “I had a snack earlier.” The demon gave a big, toothy grin. A piece of flesh was stuck between his teeth.

Dar froze, realizing he meant Golum. “Do you normally eat humans?”

“Not often, well... not often anymore. Now that they are organized, it is like disturbing a hive. You often get stung, and it can be annoying to deal with that problem.” Karn took a seat on a couch, and the other side lifted off the ground from his bulk.

“This is why my family doesn’t associate with you or the rest of Frost’s Fang. You are animals.” Tami threw her hands up. “Eating humans? They are more than bees.”

Dar had to agree with Tami. That Karn considered humans equivalent to insects was concerning.

Though, Karn’s mindset explained several actions. He’d have to keep in mind that Karn and the others at Frost’s Fang may consider the human cities to be more like cattle pens or hives.

“Better than being a pet,” Karn grumbled, but it held little bite considering the tone Tami had used with him. Despite their differences, they seemed far more at home among each other.

Dar interrupted their banter with a question of his own. “Karn, what exactly does Frost’s Fang offer protection from?”

Tami quickly jumped in, answering the question. “From the other celestial demons. She doesn’t rule Kindrake, but her presence inside of it keeps The Deep and Crimson from stepping into the nation.”

Tami paused. “Why are you asking?” Her eyes, full of worry, flitted to Karn.

“The White, having heard the rumors, authorized Karn to retract her protection should he not be satisfied with what he found here. He just did that.”

Tami reacted just about as poorly as the prince had. "You can't."

"She can and has. The White explicitly commanded me to come here and assess if it was needed. After Toldove, second chances cannot be given. We must deal with the problem before it gets to that point again," Karn explained.

Tami buried her face in her hands as her thumbs worked the edge of her jaw. "You realize that might as well destroy this city. The Deep One will learn of this and stretch its tentacles up into Bellhaven."

"Now, if only the city had the support of demons and spirits to beat it back to the watery depths. Unfortunately, they killed or drove away all of those who could or would." Karn's face was hard. "You cannot be this blind."

Tami threw her head back in frustration, her antlers scratching the back of her seat. "You cannot be stupid enough to think that The Deep One won't cause trouble for The White if she lets him encroach upon her territory."

"Excuse me," Dar cut in. "Can somebody explain who The Deep One is for me?"

Both demons paused in their fighting, stunned as they slowly turned to look at Dar. Clearly, The Deep One must be well known.

Dar quickly explained, "I'm young for a demon. I haven't been out of Kindrake."

Both demons studied him a bit longer before Tami spoke, "South of here lies an archipelago of human tribes."

"Mahaklan," Dar supplied the name from Mika's stories.

"Precisely. It is ruled by demons, though most of the citizenry is human. But under the sea, around the archipelago, there is a massive swarm of demons. And they are led by a celestial demon that hides on the floor of the sea. The Deep One."

Seeming to have little faith in Dar's knowledge, Tami added, "Crimson is another celestial demon that claims the territory that borders the North of Kindrake, on the other side of the mountain range that Frost's Fang resides in."

Turning back to Karn, Tami resumed their argument. "So, what is The White going to do when they begin to feel ambitious as they succeed in claiming what was once her territory?"

Karn shrugged. "They are no longer a concern for The White."

"No longer a—she has a second celestial dao?!" Tami nearly leapt off her seat. "How?"

Karn shrugged. "I have yet to see it, but she was visited by Lilith recently. Since then, she's had a breakthrough."

"Lilith is in Kindrake as well?"

Karn nodded. "She was at Frost's Fang only several months ago. I do not know if she is still here."

"The Black Knight was in Bellhaven just a week ago," Tami added. "Which would mean she's likely still here. The two were often seen together."

Karn's eyes pinned Dar to his seat, but said nothing.

She paused, working through the new information. "Maybe she continued on to talk to The Deep One and help them with their next celestial dao, too. You know she rarely chose sides, willing to help any who would fight the devils," Tami tried to throw doubt into Karn's decision, but the bear wasn't buying it.

"Unlikely. They do not have that kind of relationship. The Black Knight though... I do wish for a rematch."

Dar tried to keep his face passive, staying out of their discussion. He didn't jump in to supply that Lilith was, in fact, dead, because it would force him to explain more of how he knew the woman so closely. But he was interested in how he'd defeated Karn previously. He must have been stronger back then.

He needed to continue to collect dao and return to that strength if he had any chance of leading Hearthway to a better future. He didn't foresee anything getting easier or less messy in the near term. And he wouldn't get stronger without killing more devils to create fruits and maybe even find another Mo for his little dao tree to absorb.

Wanting to change topics, Dar spoke on what he'd learned. "Karn. I looked at the map before I left. The devil problem they have here is primarily gremlins and trolls. Their scouting reports say that they are coming from the hills northeast of here."

The bear looked down at his hands. "Northeast?" He sighed, commenting to himself, "So the seal there has broken as well."

Tami sat up. "What do you mean as well?"

Karn looked at Dar for a moment, seeming to decide how much to say, before turning back to the woman. "I came through Dar's village. They had set their forest on fire to deal with an enormous ettercap hive." Karn couldn't meet Dar's gaze. "The White knows where all the Mo are sealed in her area. There are two. One was where that ettercap hive had been, the other is in the hills we are discussing now."

"Mo? There are Mo in Kindrake now? How can Frost's Fang pull out now?" Tami was beside herself. "Do you realize the destruction they will reap if they get loose?"

Neko, who had been quiet throughout the entire discussion, puffed herself up. "Don't worry, Dar killed the big spider. He can kill another." Neko stood proudly. Amber was on her in a flash, putting a hand over her mouth.

"Don't listen to her," the maid told the group.

"You might have injured the creature, but the Mo cannot die. That is why Lilith went around sealing all of them." Karn shook his head, taking Neko's outburst for a misunderstanding.

Dar nodded, happy to let Karn believe the Mo was alive. "Then what do we do?"

"Leave it to Lilith," Tami interjected. "If she's here, it is probably to reseal them."

Karn nodded. "That seems highly plausible. She's been at this for longer than either of us have been alive. But she failed to reinforce the seal near Dar's village, so I am not sure we can count on it. And I do not know if she will be there in time to reinforce the Mo leading these trolls before they are able to wreak havoc and become a mess to contain."

Chapter 8

"It sounds like we shouldn't plan on Lilith. What other options do we have?" Dar still wanted to go after the Mo himself. At a minimum, he knew there were a number of devils up in the hills he could use to produce more dao fruits.

"Perhaps we could at least go hunt the devils?" Tami pleaded with Karn, clearly on the same wavelength as Dar, although she had different reasons. "If the Mo were truly loose, we'd already be dead."

Karn grumbled to himself. "Dar, what was the situation when you found the other Mo?"

Given that Karn had already dismissed Neko's blurting out that Dar had killed it as a misunderstanding, Dar didn't hold back. "The ettercaps had formed a massive web fortress in the surrounding woods. The Mo itself looked like a colossal spider. When we found it, it had its head along with two legs outside the seal. It looked like it was slowly breaking free. When we threatened it, the Mo devoured the ettercap and spiders in an effort to speed up the process and escape the seal."

Tami gasped. "Did it escape?"

"We had to beat back the ettercaps and spiders before we were able to reach it and hack away at the Mo. I rode on its head and smashed its eyes repeatedly until the creature collapsed, unmoving." Dar decided to try a bit of a white lie to see if he could help convince them to go after the other Mo in The White's territory. "It disappeared after I defeated it. Perhaps I weakened it enough to draw it back into the seal?"

Karn looked deep in thought before nodding along with that assessment. "That could very well be it. Lilith designed those things to never be found. When I checked the woods next to your village, I found the site of the battle and signs of a creature as large as you described, but no seal. I had thought the worst. But you are right. If it had gotten out, we'd both be no more."

"Then there's hope. We can push back this other tide of devils," Tami pressed.

Dar rubbed his chin in thought. "We don't know if this one has progressed further than the other, but we also have no idea what we are up against. Do you have any more information on what this Mo is, so that we can prepare?"

"It is a giant creature of earth and stone. While you might have been able to smash the previous creature using brute force, this one will be much more resilient."

With that, the group fell quiet. They each had their own motivations for going after the Mo, and their own concerns.

Dar was most curious about which decision Karn would come to. He had no love for the human city, but he did seem to want to keep the Mo within The White's territory contained. Plus, the bearman just seemed inclined to violence.

"Food is ready," Amber said from the kitchen.

"Thank you." Tami stood to get her own.

Dar realized that he needed to have a discussion with his girls, alone. “Is there a room I could use? I would like to discuss this with my dao companions in private.”

“Of course. That room there, on the right.” Tami traded her bowl over to her other hand and pointed at a door.

“You should consider this carefully. It won’t be as easy as the ettercaps, and we are few,” Karn said as he let Amber fill his bowl. “I will take a chance to meditate on this as well.”

“Sure. Just make yourself at home.” Tami rolled her eyes at Karn. “I should be charging you, given the stunt you pulled today.”

“It was necessary. I thought you would be more receptive given that your brother was killed for nothing but having horns.”

Tami focused on Dar. He knew she still wanted the rest of his story, no doubt. “We’ll see.”

“Thank you for your hospitality,” Dar said before ducking into the room with Neko in tow, followed by the maids shortly after.

Closing the door, he let his dao of quiet envelope the group, blocking any potential outside listener.

“How is everyone?” Dar started, taking a seat on the bed.

Neko came to his side with her own food, and the maids sat cross-legged on the ground before him.

“Good. Karn is a vicious animal, but he got things done.”

Neko surprised Dar with her description. She often responded more like an animal than most of them. He realized she must have heard the term used somewhere else.

“Are we really going to go after another Mo from here?” Marcie asked, looking up through her hair that had fallen into her face. “The last one was… dangerous.”

“Agreed,” Dar said, taking the first bite of his food. The girls had made a creamy soup with noodles and sliced vegetables, along with a slice of warm bread covered in hunks of meat that was stuck on with cheese.

Dar smiled, enjoying the luxury of the cheese. It wasn't something they were going to have in Hearthway for some time unless they traded for it. With that thought, he realized he should see if Dane would be able to bring them some goats or milk cows.

"This is great. My compliments to the chef."

"Thank you, milord." Amber somehow managed a sitting curtsy. "I could do a little more with what Tami had here on hand."

Dar let the silence linger, taking the time to enjoy the delicious food. And he needed the chance to think and collect his thoughts.

While it was dangerous to go after the Mo, any delay could end up costing them. They had no idea how much time remained on the seal, and as far as Dar knew, he was the only one who could actually remove the threat.

While Karn believed it possible that the seal recovered and re-trapped the Mo, Dar knew better. He had smashed the previous Mo to pieces with his axe until it had lain flat on the forest floor, yet the seal still hadn't recovered.

Dar took another bite, coming to the clear answer. The only choice was to go after the Mo and remove the threat. The only question was how.

"I need to go," Dar said. "If I don't stop it, one day, it will be a problem we can't handle. While I have faith in us, there's no way we will all ascend to the levels needed to fight an unsealed Mo in the time we likely have before it breaks free. It's not a risk we can afford. So the only remaining question is if you come with me or should head back to Hearthway."

Neko snorted. "Where Dar goes, Neko goes."

"We will serve you as well. I'm only afraid we won't be as much help." Amber looked down at the floor. "You need more than a cook and a servant. You need fighters."

"You two have been training well," Dar tried to encourage them, but he knew their concerns were valid. While they had become immortals with their quiet dao and now had the dao of dim, they were still lesser immortals. At best, they'd be able to handle a single lesser troll each.

In the scheme of the potential battle to come, that was not enough.

Dar wracked his brain, trying to figure out how he could help them improve in only a few days.

He came up short, but he realized part of that was that he hadn't been spending enough time working on his own potential for growth.

Maybe the improvements to the little dao tree opened up new opportunities towards the dao of shadows. Better manipulation of the shadows would go a long way to helping the maids. Trolls weren't exactly the smartest creatures.

Deciding the best course of action was to delay their trip and strengthen, Dar once again spoke up. "Karn has agreed to stay here in the city for several days. I think we should use this opportunity to expand our strength as rapidly as we can."

Neko perked up. "Dao companionship?"

"Yes. But I was thinking I might be able to touch on the greater dao of shadows." His eyes slid to the two maids, who were smiling back at the concept. "Otherwise, how is your dao path, Neko?"

"Sharp, quiet, dim." She gave a feral grin. "I will become a hunter."

They were three lesser dao, but Dar wasn't sure what greater dao they would form. If she could figure it out, it would be great.

Amber licked her lips, meeting Dar's eyes. "Shadow you say?"

"Yes. We have quiet and dim. Now we just need a third," he pondered. "Shadow has a lot of potential."

The maids both nodded with delight in their eyes, following his train of thought.

"Shadow would be perfect," Amber spoke for them. "What about your own dao? Were you not heading towards flame?"

"I still am." Dar had the bright dao from Blair, which would be the perfect complement to the dao that he already had. "But shadow seems far closer. After the little dao tree absorbed the Mo, I think I might have a propensity towards this dao. I could almost feel it calling to me with the dao of dim."

He reached his hand out. It almost felt like he could grasp it. "I'm going to work to develop that dao before we leave and see if I can't help you two along in the process."

His wink made the two maids blush.

"That would be lovely," Marcie said under her breath before speaking up. "Let me take your dishes out."

Once Marcie left the room, Dar raised a brow at Amber in question. She'd left rather quickly at the mention of sharing dao companionship.

"She's just nervous. The play we have been doing lately helps. She does better when... uh... someone else is in control." Amber grinned. "Milord."

Dar rolled his eyes. "I'll trust that you are treating her well. There is no room in my house for mistreating anyone or forcing them to do something against their will."

"I used the colors, like you told me. She's only said red when I asked her to confirm."

"Red?" Neko asked, her cat-like curiosity blooming in her expression.

"We use colors to communicate during sex," Amber explained.

That only made Neko's head tilt in confusion.

"I'll explain another time, Neko. While we have the night, I suggest we work on progressing our dao." Dar didn't exactly want to explain the colors to Neko. The cat girl would probably want a demonstration.

A knock on the door brought Dar out of his thoughts. "Come in." He had a pretty good idea of who was on the other side.

"Hello." Tami walked in with Marcie as she returned from cleaning the dishes.

"How can we help you?" Dar squeezed out a smile.

Tami licked her lips and gave him a pleasant smile. "I was hoping I could talk with you about what you'd seen with my brother."

"Sit." Dar gestured to the unoccupied seat in the room. Once she was sitting, Dar began recounting.

"I first saw your brother when he was coming down the river, standing at the helm of the prince's boat." He debated how to hide the next part, but then decided it didn't matter. "I then was in the city a few days later checking to see if the prince had corrected the treatment of demons. When I entered, I found your brother's body hanging outside the building, his body already starting to rot."

"That would mean he was killed as soon as he got here," Tami surmised. "What of the prince?"

"He was under house arrest. The men he'd come with were active in the city, working for the usurper, though they seemed forced. The prince, nor the rest of his men, were harmed from what I understand. Only your brother was killed," Dar said.

She squeezed her eyes closed. "That's not how they reported it to our family."

"I don't know what they told you, but I've given you the truth. Speaking of your family, how exactly do they work for the kingdom?" Dar was curious about how the arrangement had begun.

Tami nodded, the antlers on her head coming dangerously close to knocking over a candlestick. "My father has lived and worked in service to the royal family of Kindrake since their founding. Hundreds of years. He was fast friends with King Tolmier when he founded Kindrake."

"How would he feel about what's happening here in Bellhaven?"

"I'm not sure you understand just what old demons are like." Tami gave him a rueful smile. "They are a prickly bunch. They sometimes think the cycle of life is completely fair."

"Like Karn?"

"Not quite so brutal, though my father and Karn are of the same era. If anything, my father just wants to be left alone to follow his dao path. Kindrake has become a sort of protection while he tries to chase after The White." She shook her head. "He'll be so distraught to learn that she has acquired her second celestial dao while he is still trying to form his first."

Dar noted that level of strength. That meant that her father had three grand dao if he was working to form them into his first celestial.

Now Dar knew why Karn gave Tami a measure of respect. The bear demon respected strength, and her father clearly had it. If Dar had to guess, Karn only had two grand dao.

"And what will your father do about your brother's death?"

"He won't leave Kindrake, but he may find ways to punish the royal family. If The White pulls back her support though... he'll have tough choices to make. The kingdom is likely to be invaded if news of her withdrawal spreads."

"By whom? You told me of The Deep One. But would he really encroach on The White's territory?"

"The Deep One and his demons are less... human than most. They live in the ocean like apex predators, only coming onto land to satisfy certain needs."

By the way she wrinkled her nose, Dar had a good idea what needs those were.

"But the other two neighboring kingdoms will see an opportunity. And Kindrake has just provoked Tormac as well."

Ah. There was a piece of information that Dar had been looking for. War with Tormac.

"Why? What do we have to gain from the conflict?" he asked.

"Mining rights. The mountains that make up the northern border are incredibly rich with precious metals. Several small skirmishes over a particularly large vein of gold have already occurred in the last few months. It has only calmed down because neither side is going to send an army up into the mountains in the dead of winter."

"But the spring?"

"War will most certainly break out in the spring over the gold, and then the victor will hold not only the gold but the other mineral rich mountains. The real question is how decisive the victory will be. If one side crushes the other, they may push past the mountains into the kingdom proper."

Dar nodded. Once power was gained, those who won often had trouble standing down. "And this may be worsened if The White pulls out?"

Tami nodded. "She will declare that demons and spirits don't join the war effort."

"Ah." Dar understood now. Barring ancient races from a war that was surely going to happen would handicap Kindrake. "You'll lose."

Tami snorted. "We will still have some that are loyal to my father, but it will certainly make the fighting far more precarious than anyone would like. And it will put my father in a tough position with The White."

Dar was pleased with all the information he'd gotten. Finally, the pieces were starting to make sense, and he could figure out what to do with them. "What are you going to do? Now that you know what actually happened to your brother?"

"Send a message to my father and likely step away from this posting to fight the devils. As much as I'd like to outright kill the prince for letting my brother die, politics are a bitch. The best I could do is find an excuse to abandon him."

Dar was disappointed. She was beat down and wouldn't even do anything about her brother's death except flee. He had hoped she was stronger than that.

"Seems we have similar goals. I too would like to fight these devils, maybe even kill the Mo."

She barked a laugh. "You don't think you really killed the Mo, do you?"

Dar paused, giving her a piece. "What if I told you I was one hundred percent positive that I killed the Mo?"

"Dar did," Neko interjected. "We all watched it."

The maids looked away from the conversation, clearly not sure how much to give away.

"Okay, let's say you did. Which is ridiculous. How would you kill this other Mo?" Tami's curiosity got the better of her.

"I need to weaken it first, but once it is down, I can deal the finishing blow." Dar leaned forward, curious to see if he'd just gained an ally in that fight.

Doubt rippled across Tami's face, but eventually she let it all out with a heavy sigh. "A fool's errand. Mo cannot be killed."

Suddenly, Dar was far less interested in the woman. She was too limited in her thinking.

"Well, you may choose to believe what you will. But while I have you here, I was wondering if you'd be interested in trading dao?"

"Trading dao?" she asked, confused.

Dar pulled out his booklet of dao characters of all his dao companions. "I would be willing to trade one for one." Collecting one outside of his dao companions would give him more potential growth.

Tami blushed. "I will not be your dao companion."

"That wasn't the offer," Dar said dryly. He had enough women as it was. "I wanted to simply trade dao characters to broaden my family's strength."

Tami looked at him strangely.

Dar knew it was unorthodox. Without dao companionship to pull each other closer in their dao paths, such a trade would have little value. Almost no value, if Dar hadn't figured out how to study the dao characters and start to ingrain them in his body through meditation.

"Um, sure. Let me get my book."

Tami got up, but before she left, Dar spoke a thought out loud. "Your brother must have had his own book with him. What do you think happened to it?"

She paused and turned woodenly back to him. "That is none of your business."

Dar wondered if the prince had it now and what it might be worth to him. There was a chance Dar could trade protection from the devils to get his hands on it.

As soon as Tami left, Dar turned to Amber. "Go run to the prince's manor. Ask him if Tami's brother kept a book of his dao, and if he would be willing to offer it as a reward or trade."

"Milord, that would be going around her back." Amber smiled mischievously. "Don't you want to woo her? She might be willing to separate from her family."

Dar shrugged. "Not to sound cold, but her value is questionable. She won't even stand up to her brother's death. Is that the kind of person you want in the family?"

Amber shrugged. "I guess not. It is your decision, milord."

Dar would be lying if he said he hadn't considered how her antlers would make wonderful handlebars as he crushed into her, but Dar had two eager maids and a cat girl if he needed a release. Plus, Cherry was still in his inner world, brimming with need.

Tami came back, flipping through her book. "Of course, we must make an equal trade. Lesser for lesser, and such."

"Of course. I'm interested to see if you have any lesser dao that speaks to me," Dar said with a smile.

Tami looked to where Amber had been. "Where's the red-haired one?"

"Off on an errand," he said smoothly.

"Here, I'll trade you." Tami held out the book, gripping it tightly as she held out her other hand, palm open.

Dar wasn't worried about her trying to cheat him or run off with the book. It wasn't in her character from what he'd seen. She seemed reluctant to do anything except stick with the herd, despite any trouble or dangers. And she certainly acted like a prey animal rather than a predator.

He slapped his book in her open palm, and she released her book to his care. Dar didn't waste any time, sitting down and flipping through her book, trying not to focus on any one of her dao characters too long.

Chapter 9

"You've labeled them all?" Tami asked, surprised.

"I share the booklet with my dao companions. All of our dao are labeled so we can share," Dar replied.

Her surprise continued as she flipped through the pages. "How many dao companions do you have?"

Cherry, Sasha and Mika were his dao companions, but he realized that technically he could toss in the two maids.

"Five," he said, hoping to curb her surprise.

"Neko will be six," the cat girl said proudly.

"You will be," Dar promised.

He had no issue bringing her into his harem; it was only a matter of timing. When she'd been hurt by the ettercaps, he had realized just how tightly she fit in with his family. How much she filled a space that they needed. But with everything happening, he hadn't been able to give her the attention she deserved.

Neko gave him a toothy smile, showing off her sharp canines, while she pushed back her shoulders and thrust her chest out.

He rubbed the top of her head and smiled as he gave her back her typical catchphrase. "Neko is the best."

She curled into him, pressing her head against his chest and rubbing her cheeks against him.

Tami sat opposite of them, an eyebrow raised at the display. But Dar didn't care what she thought. He just shrugged it off and flipped through Tami's own book of dao with his free hand while he continued to pet Neko.

He couldn't help but notice as Tami carefully turned the pages of his own book, marveling at the dao characters, using a hand to smooth out each page reverently.

It must have been a bigger deal than he realized to share it with her like this.

Her own book was filled with neat, crisp lines of her own dao characters. They weren't labeled, so Dar was working on instinct, but he wasn't looking for something specific.

Instead, he was searching for a feeling. He was learning to trust his instincts. His dao path seemed to beckon him to grow his dao of dim and quiet into a dao of shadows, and to create that greater dao he needed one more. What that was, he wasn't sure.

But he let the gnawing hunger for the dao of shadows guide him as he flipped through Tami's book. He neared the end of the book, nearly giving up, when he found it.

The dao character leapt off the page, and he felt like it was within his grasp almost immediately.

"This one. What is it?" He turned the book around for her to see.

"Lesser dao of concealment. My family often functions as scouts, given our speed. That dao pushes awareness away from us, sort of like a camouflage, only far more subtle."

"This one then." Dar didn't hesitate. The way his own dao path was drawn to it was enough; he just wanted to know what he was dealing with.

"Sure. Uh. This one." She held up his own book, pointing at the dao of hard.

"Easy enough. If you bring ink, I'll just write it in the back of your book," Dar offered.

Tami bolted out the door in an instant. She was unnaturally quick in her movement, and he could feel the static of mana lingering in the air. She'd said her family was fast, but after seeing it, Dar wanted that one too.

"Here." She thrust a quill and ink pot into his hands.

Dar quickly etched his dao character on the first empty page of her book. "Would you like me to label it?"

"No. It will be the only one I don't know," Tami said quickly, watching him with bated breath before taking the quill and putting her own dao character into his book.

"That speed you just displayed. Any interest in adding that to my book as well? Maybe another has caught your eye?"

She paused. Apparently, that dao was worth far more to her. "Speed is a greater dao. I can offer you acceleration, one of the lesser dao that makes it up? For..." Biting her lip, she flipped through his dao book again. "This one?"

"Dim for acceleration. I accept." He gestured towards the quill still in her hand, and she jotted down another character in his book before handing the quill to him.

Dar could give her one of the many fruits to give her dim, but she had nothing of equal value to trade him. Even if she gave him her entire book, his secret and his fruits were more valuable.

"Anything else catch your fancy?" he asked, hoping to trade more for what would make up speed.

Tami bit her lip as she flipped back through his book. Then she put it down with a sigh. "No. I think those two will give me enough to work on for quite some time." Apparently, she was going to hold that speed dao close to her chest.

But Dar didn't blame her. He remembered fighting the mantis devils. Speed could be quite dangerous, but it was quickly made less valuable the second others also had it. It made sense she'd protect it.

Giving her his best smile, he didn't mention that it wouldn't take him too long to be able to master the two she'd given him.

"Thank you for this. But I think it is best we turn in for the night." Dar wanted time to pore over his own dao.

"Will you be okay with just the one room?"

It had a couch and a bed, though Dar suspected the girls would pile in with him.

"It's fine." He knew for sure that Neko was going to crawl in bed with him, regardless.

Giving a nod, Tami clutched her book to her chest and left.

Neko continued to press into Dar, nuzzling for more scratches. Dar obliged her.

"Amber, Marcie, I am going to work on this dao and try to form the greater dao of shadows. No disturbances, understood?"

"Yes, milord." Amber's face was serious.

"Neko, I need to meditate. You have your own dao to work on, don't you?"

She sighed, pushing her head in one more time before sitting up straight. "Yes. Why can't we cuddle while we meditate?"

"Because..." He didn't have a great excuse. "Another time we'll try. Right now, we both need to focus."

Neko bobbed her head in understanding and crawled onto the foot of his bed, padding around for a moment before curling up in a little ball. Dar watched her for a moment. It seemed far more like sleeping than meditating, but he'd leave her alone.

Taking the book into his inner world, he fell into a trance and found himself next to the little dao tree with the book. Flipping open the book to Tami's dao of concealment, Dar focused on the character and let his channels fill with mana. He slowly inscribed the dao character into himself.

He could feel Cherry's presence hover over him, but she recognized what he was doing and stepped away.

As he cycled his mana for the first time in the shape of the complete dao character, his little dao tree resonated with him.

It was a hair-raising sensation. He felt the vibrations pulsing through him as the mana cycling within him formed the dao character. The vibrations sped up as he increased the speed of the cycles.

It was almost like the dao character was trying to burn itself into him.

Reinforcing himself, Dar grit his teeth, knowing what it would take and ready for the pain. But this time, it never came. Instead, cold certainty trickled through him as he rapidly comprehended the dao character.

It became clear, yet he knew it was concealment. It should have hidden itself more. He couldn't explain why the character blazed to life in his mind and body, and then, with a snapping feeling, settled into place.

His eyes shot open, and he took a deep breath.

"Welcome back." Cherry hung upside down from a tree branch. Pink blossoms lingered on that branch.

That branch was the cutting of her former tree. They'd grafted it onto the little dao tree. Given that one part of it was dark, with nearly black leaves and another part was pink cherry blossoms in full bloom among green leaves, the little dao tree was a strange sight.

"How long was I out?" Dar braced for the news that he'd just missed several days.

"Half an hour?" Cherry tapped her lips, thinking.

His mouth dropped open. "What?"

He'd managed to learn that dao in half an hour? The last two times he'd done the process, it had taken at least a day. Sasha was going to be so jealous. He pondered over what was different. Had his strength made it easier? Was he just better at the process?

He played back through how it had felt and remembered that it had almost felt like the little dao tree had helped him.

"Did you feel anything strange about the tree?"

"It's always pulsing out mana, but I did feel a particularly strong one when you were working on cultivating your dao." She swung down from the tree, a vine supporting her so that she landed effortlessly on her feet.

He couldn't help but let his eyes linger over her petite form. Her green hair was cascading down her back and around her bountiful chest. And she was wearing a diaphanous white dress that was dyed pink along the bottom. Against the backdrop of the tree, she looked even more beautiful.

When he met her eyes and saw the smirk in them, he realized he'd been staring.

"So, I just learned the dao of concealment in that time." He flexed his hands, feeling the dao within him, ready for use. "But that was many times faster than before. I think it is because the dao is related to the power the little dao tree absorbed from the Mo?"

Cherry's eyebrows nearly went up into her hairline. "Do you mean you could rapidly ascend to the full dao that the colossal spider had?"

"No, well, at least not right now." Dar shook his head. "The dao characters didn't come naturally to me. I had to see it first, but then my meditation exercise just now went extremely smoothly."

Cherry still seemed excited. "If that's the case, can you touch upon the greater dao associated with those lesser dao that you have?" She leaned over Dar, her plump, pink lips like cherry blossoms in full bloom.

He cupped the back of her head and kissed her lips, much to Cherry's delight. She squealed and sat in his lap, throwing her arms around his shoulders and pulling him closer.

He'd spent many nights in his inner world making love to Cherry. Her fixation on him as her tree often led to her consuming his time in the most pleasurable of ways.

While she might not claim as much of his waking time as the other women, she had fully lapped all the others when it came to time spent intimate with each other.

She wiggled in his lap, and Dar hated having to hold her still. As much as Dar would happily let himself drown once again in his slightly crazed dryad's attention, he needed to focus on progressing.

It was with great effort that he pulled away from Cherry, who was running her tongue along her pink lips as her eyes bore hungrily into his own.

"I think you were right; the greater dao is within reach," he said.

"Yes, I think the tree has much more to share with us." The cleft of her ass pushed back against Dar's now erect cock. "Maybe we should see what dao you can share?"

"After." Dar pried the dryad off of him. He knew that, if they got started, he'd get nothing further done that night.

Cherry finally caved, bouncing on the soft, loamy soil under the little dao tree before a branch came down and collected the dryad. She disappeared back into the bough of the little dao tree.

Dar shook his head.

Cherry had always had a deep attachment to Dar, begun in a past life when they'd been together. But it had grown far stronger in recent days. He was concerned that he soon wouldn't be able to give her all the attention she was clearly craving.

But for the moment, she seemed happy, so he focused on cultivating his own dao path.

Sinking once again into meditation under the dao tree, he felt himself rooted in place as the three dao circled in his mind. Dim, Quiet and Concealment. The three dao characters floated in his consciousness; he let them spin and circle each other, trying to find the right way that they fit together.

But the little dao tree apparently was impatient. The connection between Dar and the tree blazed to life. He felt it just behind his navel. The tree began burning away the three characters, blurring them and reshaping them into something greater. Dar tried to remain still, not wanting to disturb the tree, which was clearly trying to help him.

Shadow. He felt it settle in, awed at the ease.

As a greater dao, it would be able to do far more than dim. Not only would he be able to make something dim by touching it, but he'd be able to pull and tug on shadows themselves, reshaping them around himself and even others. It would be far easier to protect those he cared about and attack more carefully.

With the dao character clear in his mind, he went to work, carving it into his body. He repeated cycle after cycle of the complex greater dao character in his mind as he had with the lesser dao.

It spun itself to life, etching itself into his very being as it flowed through him. Once again, Dar braced for pain that never came. When he'd forced himself to learn granite or combustion, he'd felt his body nearly ripping apart. But again, the pain never came.

This time, it was a cool, dark sensation that he lost himself in as his mind drifted into the very shadows, pulling him out of himself and along for a merry ride.

In darkness, he found his home. It melded into him as dao characters lit up on his enchanted body, harmonizing with yet another dao and making Dar once again feel as if he was growing in ways he couldn't have imagined.

Power came to him as he became one with the shadows. It was not the same overwhelming might that he'd felt with his dao of granite. This one held a more subtle power. Almost omnipresent, or at least the potential to be present, was always there, but it also felt fleeting.

Dar could already feel the complexity of taming the shadows. They were both fluid and static. Impossible to force. He felt the shadows surrounding his current body. He knew instinctively that they would welcome him, envelop him, and consume him.

Only then did Dar realize the danger he was in.

He couldn't feel his body anymore as he drifted away, sliding through a world of shadows. He flitted from one street of Bellhaven to the next as people moved about. Each of their shadows created strange bridges between one alley and the next.

No one seemed to notice him. He was a part of the shadows, being drawn along them, slipping away through the streets like water through a sieve. Dar tried to slow himself down, but his movements continued. He was swept along the path of shadows, being pulled further and further from his body.

Dar began to worry. He needed to ground himself soon, draw himself back, and not let the shadows take him. He didn't know what would happen if he drifted much further away from his body.

He pulled his attention back to his physical body, trying to re-ground himself and find his physical form.

He slowly pictured the feeling of his rear pressed into the ground, but that faded quickly as he was once again absorbed back into the shadows. So he chose a stronger feeling, focusing on where a piece of the little dao tree's bark dug into his shoulder blade. He managed to lean back, causing a spike of pain in his shoulder and grounding himself in that pain. He was able to pull himself back along the shadows, back towards his body.

Inch by inch, Dar remembered his body and where it was, drawing himself back to the world.

When he felt the crisp air of his inner world once again, he drew a deep breath and his eyes shot open. The light felt brighter than before, but he embraced it, using it to help banish him from the shadows.

"Two hours," Cherry said, sitting down close to him, peering at his face. "You did it."

"Two hours," he repeated, breathless from the exercise. It had felt like only moments. "Shadows are dangerous."

"Yes, they are." Her face was concerned. "I could feel you slipping away. Much like when I travel between trees."

Her ability to flit between trees had always mystified Dar. Now he understood it better. "What is that ability?"

"Something I learned to do with many, many years of practice." Cherry's smile was victorious. "While I might not be the most powerful spirit I've met, I have honed myself on my specialty over a thousand years."

Dar smiled at the not-so-subtle reminder that gaining power was only part of the equation. Learning to use it effectively was another.

"Can you teach me?" Dar asked. "I want to use this, but I don't want to get lost in the shadows."

"Of course, but it is very difficult. I cease to exist for the moment of transfer, turning myself into a plant. Then I let my control of plants carry me through the world and reform myself from a plant leagues away. If you wish to work on it, the first thing you must learn to do is turn some part of you into your greater dao. So instead of turning a fist to mimic granite, you'd become granite. Or have a part of you become a shadow."

Dar was following, but he had to admit, it sounded dangerous.

While it was simple to describe becoming one with dao, the idea of converting himself to an element and reverting back was terrifying. And it would be difficult enough for a single piece of his body. He didn't want to think about the effort to do it for his full body.

Fear flickered through him. What would happen if his brain stopped as it became granite and his consciousness ground to a halt? Would he be able to still function?

His mind began to swirl. What about his blood or his tissue? It would cut off the circulation if even just a hand became something else. How was he supposed to practice and learn it without somehow destroying his body in the process?

Cherry kicked to her feet. "I see you understand the difficulty. But that can wait for a bit. For now, I'll help you take your mind off of it and let you focus on your body."

She crowded over Dar, grabbing his hand and pulling it up to cup her chest, moaning at his touch.

Chapter 10

Dar woke from his time with Cherry to the smell of bacon. He could only think of one arguably better thing to wake up to, smiling up at Amber as she held the plate near his head, wafting the aroma over him.

"Thank you." Dar snatched a piece, making the maid giggle.

Marcie was at the foot of the bed doing the same to Neko, only the demon wasn't waking. Dar watched as Neko's nose rose in the air, sniffing from her spot, curled up at the foot of the bed. Marcie pulled the bacon back, but still asleep, Neko's head just simply followed the bacon right off the edge of the bed.

Marcie kept going, but so did Neko's nose. Marcie took one more step, and Neko tottered on the edge of the bed. She finally woke up, but it was too late. The cat girl fell off the bed, quickly rolling into a crouch to save herself from face planting.

"Morning, Neko." Dar got her attention before she could realize just what happened and jump on top of Marcie, who looked terrified at the same concept. "Looks like you are hungry. Take the bacon from Marcie and say thank you."

Neko sprang up and snatched two pieces of bacon from the maid, shoving them in her mouth and talking around them. "Thank you."

"You are most welcome." Marcie curtsied. "Would you like anything for breakfast?"

"More bacon?" Neko asked hopefully.

"Can you see if they have any milk?" Dar asked, realizing Neko still had a fairly limited palette from only living in Hearthway.

"Milk?" Neko asked curiously, prowling back over to the bed and curling up against Dar's side. "I'm no kitten."

"Specifically, cow's milk or maybe goat's milk. We often drank it where I was from," Dar explained.

"I'll see what I can do." Marcie tucked the plate against her bountiful chest and bowed before she headed out.

Amber handed Dar the rest of his plate of bacon. "Anything you'd like?"

"If we are eating different things, I'd be interested in eggs. How are we paying for all of this?" Dar asked curiously.

The maid gave him a smile. "Sasha sent us here with some coins and a small bag of salt to trade for more coins." She pulled back her dress, revealing her naked hips and a coin purse tied to her thigh.

Dar leaned back in bed and pulled Neko tightly to his side. If he were back at Hearthway at the moment, he'd be meeting with the family and leadership, figuring out tasks for the day. But here, he didn't have those responsibilities. It almost felt like he was on vacation.

He relaxed into the moment, only to have it be broken by the lumbering of Karn outside his door. He groaned as his moment away from responsibilities came to a screeching halt.

Pulling on his clothes, Dar threw Neko hers as well. "Meet me when you're dressed."

Dar slipped outside the room. “Karn, what are you up to today?”

The bear sipped water out of a cup that was comically small compared to his hands and body. “I'll entertain the prince and attend his court for today and tomorrow. I doubt his words or actions will change my mind, but I better see an effort put in.”

Tami stepped out of her room, rubbing tired eyes. “I'm sure he'll have every spirit or demon he can wrangle up serving court in some capacity. You'll see a big change from yesterday. Your threat scared him. I'm sure of it.”

“Wasn't a threat,” Karn grumbled. “You only threaten when you don't follow through.”

The deer woman gave Karn a weak smile in response and grabbed a fist full of leafy greens that had been in a nearby basket, tearing into them, munching like… well… a deer.

“Do you need a bucket to drink from?” Tami asked Karn.

“The cup will do,” Karn ignored the barb.

At that moment, the maids came back into Tami's place with a basket of fresh ingredients and started making themselves at home.

Tami watched them with interest. “You two have dao.”

“Yes.” Marcie nodded as Amber had her back turned.

“Don't bother them,” Dar tried to divert attention from the two girls. They could potentially generate more questions than he wanted to answer. Right now, no one outside Hearthway knew that Dar and several other humans around him had started on the dao path.

The last thing he wanted was that information getting into the hands of the royal family of Kindrake, or the wizards. Immortality and power were far too tempting.

“What about you, Tami? What do you have planned for the day?” Dar asked.

"I was thinking about going and scouting to confirm the report about the trolls in the hills." She gazed over at Karn. "That is, if we were still interested in doing something about it."

"Yes. But first, I will fulfill the commitment I gave your master," Karn said, full well knowing the title would dig under her skin. Dar had no desire to tag along with that.

"What about you Dar?" Tami continued.

"Setting up some trades for my village." He watched Amber work on eggs while Marcie brought milk to Neko, who was padding out of their room. "I'd like to get some basic amenities like milk cows and hens to bring back."

Tami stared at him. "We are talking about the concerns of the kingdom, and you are busy buying milk cows?"

Dar only shrugged. "Not every day can be the life or death of a kingdom. Sometimes you just need to focus on surviving."

Karn gave a deep belly laugh. "I like that. Maybe when we are done here, I will make an effort to just live and survive. Sounds like a happy, simple life."

Dar wasn't sure if the bearman was making fun of him or jealous, but if Karn had a harem back on Frost's Fang, he had reason to want to find a way to settle down a bit.

Neko sat down next to Dar, transfixed on the bowl in front of her. She slowly dangled her tongue down, puzzlement on her face as she took a first tentative lick. Her eyes lit up as she tasted the liquid. Immediately, she was lapping it up, chugging down the contents. Dar knew she'd love it.

Karn put his cup down. "I'll be heading out. Will you stick around to see what can be done about the devils?"

"Of course." Dar wanted to fight them for his own reasons. He could absorb their corpses for the little dao tree.

After experiencing the tree's assistance in developing his shadow dao, Dar knew what his path forward in cultivation would be. He was going to need to kill more Mo and see just how quickly he could advance through his own dao path.

The bear nodded and lumbered out of the space. Tami was still stuffing her face with leaves as fast as she could. It would take a lot of them to keep her body fueled.

"I need to go as well. Don't burn my place down," she said before following Karn out the door.

And in only a moment, Dar realized he was left alone in her home with his women. It was nice to be back in their small group.

"Amber. What did the prince say about trading Tami's brother's book of dao?" Dar asked as soon as he was sure she wasn't going to come right back in.

"He was sending men to find the book after I left. As I was lingering about outside the door, it seems like you gave him the idea to try to offer it to Karn for his support."

Dar scoffed. "Of course he did," he said with an eye roll. "Maybe we should just steal it."

The two maids looked excited at the prospect.

"Don't get your hopes up. If he successfully sells it to Karn, I don't think we will steal it from him." Dar wasn't about to make an enemy of the bear. If he was honest, he liked Karn. The demon was a bit rough around the edges, but he was far more straightforward than most humans Dar had met in Granterra.

Neko raised her cup to Marcie. "More?"

"Sure, kitty," Marcie joked, taking the cup from Neko, who was sporting a milk mustache from her hasty drinking. "If we get goats, you can have this all the time back in Hearthway."

That prompted Neko to turn wide-eyed to Dar, begging.

"Sasha wanted cows or goats. Goats would probably be better. They're hardier than cows," Dar thought aloud.

"Dane Goodhaul should try to find some here in the city, but we'll see what he pulls together as they negotiate."

"I would like to check on the merchant. I can help ensure he is getting Sasha's goats," Neko declared.

Dar and the maids exchanged a glance. One of them should go with Neko, but none of them volunteered. Neko read the silent conversation, crossing her arms.

"I can go by myself."

Dar wanted to tell her no and convince her that she needed someone with her, but he also knew Neko needed to have some more independence. She wasn't a child for all that they often treated her with kid gloves.

"Fine," Dar sighed. "Please check to make sure that you can find your way back to this house. Identify some tall landmarks on your way out. If anyone stops you or gives you trouble, make sure you tell them you are Tami's guest and, by extension, a guest of the prince."

Neko nodded rapidly, excitement bubbling up in her eyes.

"And take your fill of bacon before you leave." Marcie brought over a plate of hot bacon for the cat girl, who happily accepted several strips and downed them with the last of the milk before standing triumphantly.

"Good luck, Neko." Dar waved her out.

The moment the door closed, he let out a heavy sigh. He was fully prepared to have a problem arise from her venturing into the city, but he couldn't keep coddling her.

"She'll be okay." Amber snuck up behind Dar as she whispered in his ear, her hands finding his tired neck and kneading those muscles.

Sinking back into her touch, Dar let go of his worries for the moment. "I know, but I can't help but worry."

"You'll never accept her into your family if you keep thinking of her like a child. She clearly isn't one. I mean, have you seen those tits on her?" Amber pressed her own into Dar's neck for emphasis.

For a moment, he wanted to struggle, but then he realized the maids had him alone, and they were going to take the opportunity.

"Marcie, come here and feed our master."

"Yes, mistress." The mousy maid's tone changed, only confirming Dar's read on the moment.

"Before we get too far, girls, I want to be sure that you both know what you are getting into. Red means stop, yellow means slow down, and if anyone hesitates, you can let them know to keep going with green," Dar explained the rules, wanting to make sure they didn't feel forced.

He had explored this side of his sexuality with more than one ex-girlfriend before he'd been brought to this world. It wasn't something he had prepared for, but he realized he was more than receptive to this sort of bedroom play. He didn't need to be a dominant man in every situation, but done right, it could be so much fun in the bedroom.

"Yes, master." Amber's hands kept working the knots in his shoulders. Marcie came up and handed him his plate of food, but she kept the fork.

Pulling her dress slightly more off her shoulders, slipping it lower on her curves, Marcie leaned forward and speared a hunk of eggs, blowing steam off of them before raising them to his lips with a sort of reverence.

She watched Dar take the bite of food and smiled brightly, licking her lips as she watched him eat.

Dar had no idea being fed could be so stimulating. He chewed the food, feeling Amber press her chest into the back of his head further, while Marcie looked at him hungry for more than food.

"You two." Dar shook his head. "I think I can feed myself. I'd like to see you two in action."

Amber let her fingers trail down Dar's arms, goosebumps rising in the wake of her soft touch.

"Slave, on your knees," she barked at Marcie.

The other woman shot down as if someone had just bolted her knees to the floor, and waited patiently, her eyes wide with anticipation.

Dar crossed his legs and leaned back, watching them with a smug smile on his face. Only half of it was acting. He was definitely turned on.

Amber grabbed Marcie's dress and hiked it up, revealing a silk rope that was no doubt courtesy of Sasha. The rope had been tied around Marcie's body, with a knot lingering just at the cleft of her sex, where the rope dripped with her juices.

The sight of it did something to Dar, and he forgot about the food in his hands, his hunger replaced with other urges.

The more Amber hiked up Marcie's dress, the more he could see of her large chest, which was squeezed tight, bound between a complex knot that rubbed them around the base.

"Say please." Amber pressed into the small of Marcie's back as she finished pulling off her dress, revealing the prize.

"Please, mistress." Marcie's expression shifted. She was already a submissive, mousy woman, but her secret revealed had taken off the quiet mask, showing a lewd woman beneath that panted for her mistress.

Amber was rough, but not uncaring, as she shoved a knee into Marcie's back and pulled her arms back, looping some excess rope over Marcie's shoulder to hold them back and keep her bountiful chest thrust forward. Then Amber proceeded to tie Marcie's arms behind her back.

Dar clicked his tongue. They were playing with bondage, but they were still missing some key points. As their master, he needed to make sure they did it all properly.

"Slap her tits, Amber," he commanded, stepping into his role and trying to keep the excitement from his voice. He was eager, but this type of play required control.

"Yes, master." Amber slapped Marcie's chest hard enough to make them jiggle but not even hard enough to leave a mark.

"Come here," Dar beckoned the pair.

Amber helped Marcie to her feet and brought the bound woman over like she was a platter of food. "Master?"

Dar looked into Marcie's eyes as he let his fingers softly caress her nipples, running around and over them as her skin pebbled with anticipation. He let his fingers savor her soft breasts for just a moment, bringing her pleasure.

Just when her expression shifted, he swiftly slapped each of them, causing her to cry out in surprise. "What do you say to that?"

Marcie hesitated, unsure what he wanted.

He didn't mind; training was half the fun. He grabbed her chin and forced her eyes to focus on him. "You say, Thank you, master."

His other hand slapped her chest again.

"Thank you, master," she breathed.

Her eyes dilated slightly with need as her face flushed. Dar was watching her closely, making sure she was enjoying herself. But she was definitely a total sub.

He wondered about Amber. She dominated Marcie, but was she receptive to being a submissive?

"Amber, lick her chest. Soothe them with your tongue."

The red-headed maid didn't hesitate for a second, diving into the other woman's bosom, her pink tongue flitting out and licking Marcie's nipples while the bound woman cooed and squirmed in her bindings.

Dar's hands wandered over Amber's form, feeling under her dress. He ran his hand along her naked hips until he reached her sex and ran his fingers along it. It certainly wasn't dry; he felt a bead of her want dripping down her thigh.

"Do you have another rope?" Dar asked.

"With our things in the bedroom," Marcie answered excitedly.

"Get it. No hands though." Dar pulled Amber to him, his hand finding her pussy lips and exploring her as she gasped. "You stay with me."

He wanted to get a read on the maid and see if she really was a switch or if he needed to give her enough domination of Marcie. But that was cleared up quickly. The moment Marcie left, Amber melted into him, letting him play with her as she ground herself into his hand.

Dar smiled, not ready to let her climax yet. So instead, he brought his wet fingers out from under her skirt and up to her mouth.

Understanding what he wanted, Amber sucked her own juices off his finger, her tongue eager to please. She worked to get every ounce off before swallowing and opening her mouth for more.

"What do you say?"

"Thank you, master."

"Good girl." Dar petted her cheek and gave her a single tender kiss on the forehead. "Now, I think it is time to check in on our other pet. Do you think she can get the rope without hands?"

"Maybe she needs help." Amber smiled.

"Or punishment for failing a task." Dar stood, hoisting Amber up in his arms, and headed towards the bedroom.

In the room, he found Marcie on her knees, her head buried in a bag and her hips waving in the air as she tried to retrieve their other rope without hands.

"Slave, what's taking you so long?" Dar demanded, making Marcie jump.

"I can't get it," she said, her voice muffled against the bag.

It was everything Dar could do not to settle in behind her plump rear and thrust into her sex as it wiggled in the air. Instead, his hand came down firmly on her ass, leaving a red handprint in its wake.

"Try harder."

After the slap, his hand gently caressed the handprint, cupping the cleft of her rear. He didn't miss the way she wiggled her hips into his hand and thrust herself into the bag, making the rope going through her sex continue to rub her.

"It's a shame you can't get it," Dar sighed. "I was hoping to give you a reward."

Marcie suddenly went into overdrive, pushing things aside in the bag with her face. Sure enough, she came back out, holding another silk rope in between her teeth.

Dar stroked her head. "Good girl." He placed his hand in front of her mouth and she spit out the rope.

Holding her chin, he lifted it up level with the bulge in his pants. "Is this what you want?"

"Yes. Thank you, master," she panted and nuzzled his cock through his pants.

"Amber, lock the door."

"Done, master." Amber was swift in completing the task before presenting herself before him and shrugging her own dress off her shoulders.

He scowled. "Did I tell you to remove your clothes? Bend over the bed."

"I'm sorry, master," Amber pouted but raised her ass high in the air.

Swatting it several times, Dar shook his head. "I'm sorry, Marcie, but she needs to be punished. For now, pull my pants down."

Marcie bit at his pants and tugged them down several inches at a time as Dar pulled on the rope. He felt its strength and flexibility. It would do.

He looped it over Amber's shoulder and down around her breasts, running it behind her back and then finally down to her thighs. Pulling the rope tight, he forced her to open her legs wide. He'd put her into a position that forced her into a spread eagle, yet gave her some control of her arms.

"How does that feel?" Dar asked, worried that he had gone too far.

"Thank you, master. Green." Amber smiled from the bed.

In the time he had worked her over, Marcie had gotten Dar's pants down and his cock sprang free. Both women were looking at it with wide, eager eyes.

"Amber, watch what a good slave deserves." Dar smiled wickedly as he grabbed Marcie's head, pausing for only a brief second. "You need to tap if you want me to stop."

"Yes, master."

"I'm serious." Dar watched her eyes as she nodded before putting his cock to her lips. The moment she opened wide, he shoved it in.

He wasn't gentle, nearly choking her with his cock as she tried to take it, sputtering and drooling over it. Pushing into her warm, wet mouth felt like a release of its own.

He'd held back with them, wanting to progress their relationship and establish trust before they got too intimate. But things had changed since they'd first become his maids. They were now immortals and a part of his family.

Dar let himself go, indulging in the warmth of her mouth and thrusting his cock to the back of her mouth as he forcefully opened her throat. He felt himself rubbing at the back of her throat. Holding it there, Marcie's eyes grew wide as she realized her airway was well and truly blocked by his massive cock.

She moaned and slobbered over him, but then, for a moment, she panicked, flailing, but bound and unable to do anything about it.

Dar could see the moment that fear started to creep into her and he pulled out, bending down and kissing her temple. "Good girl. Do you want it again?"

Adrenaline pumped through her, her concern washed away as Dar ran his hands tenderly over her head. "Yes."

Dar didn't wait for her to open her mouth and accept him this time. He thrusted himself deep into her throat again, though this time she didn't panic quite as quickly. When he saw the flicker of uncertainty in her eyes, he held it just a moment longer before giving her air and comfort.

"I think I'm well and ready."

Marcie looked over at Amber, who was watching from her position spread eagle on the bed. Dar realized she'd gotten a hand wiggled just barely down to her hips and was trying to rub one out.

"It seems your mistress is being rebellious. Let's fix that." Dar hoisted Marcie by her rope, pulling her shoulders even further back and squeezing her breasts.

"Thank you, master," she panted as Dar placed her face in Amber's open crotch, pushing the eager sub's face into Amber.

"I expect her to moan for me."

Marcie started lapping at Amber, eagerly rubbing her face in her mistress' juices. The mousy girl really came out of her shell as a sub. Dar smiled to himself as he lifted her hips and parted the line of rope that had been soaked through by her own eager sex before thrusting himself into her without warning.

She yelped into Amber's sex, but that quickly shifted into a moan as she pushed her hips back into his.

Smacking her ass, Dar let himself enjoy her juicy pussy as he stroked into her and reached around to tweak her nipples. They had been bound tightly for so long he worried that they would be overly sensitive, but she didn't complain. If anything, she relaxed into the pain, enjoying letting someone else control her.

Dar wasn't a sadist, but he would admit he derived some pleasure from the dominance aspect of the act. He enjoyed both the power and watching their pleasure in it. He watched as the buxom maid under him bucked and squirmed as he pinched down harder on her nipples.

"Amber, pet your slave. Tell her how good she's being," he demanded.

Amber's hands ran through Marcie's hair. "You're such a good girl. You are showing our master just how well trained you are."

Grabbing the knot on her back, he pulled hard, using it for leverage as he pounded into Marcie. Soon, she was screaming in the throes of passion as her tits bounced on Amber's thighs. She came undone over Dar, spilling her juices all over his thighs.

"Bad." Dar rolled her over and slapped her chest again. "You finished before me."

"I'm sorry, master. I couldn't help it. You felt so good," Marcie panted, looking both satisfied and repentant at the same time.

"This slave will satisfy you, master." Amber waited on the bed, her legs still spread. "Let me show a lesser slave how it is done."

"No, master. I can redeem myself," Marcie pleaded in a byplay that left him smirking.

"You'll watch," Dar commanded, holding Amber down and cupping her chest. They weren't nearly as large as Marcie's, but they were still a firm handful.

"Let me work you with my mouth, master." Amber opened wide.

Dar flipped her around so that her head hung just off the edge of the bed, and she looked at him upside down. "Open wide."

Dar fucked her open mouth, watching her throat bulge with each thrust and her eyes water as she tried to swallow him whole. She was far more relaxed and managed to not choke on him.

"You'll clean me off, and then we'll see if you can please me," he said.

He smacked her chest, and the moment she winced he knew she wasn't into pain, just submission. He met her eyes, letting her know he saw that and would adjust.

Shifting back into the moment, Dar finished cleaning his cock in Amber's mouth and pushed her back onto the bed. Standing over her, he eased himself inside of her. The maid cooed and encouraged him, thrashing against her bindings as he slowly edged himself deeper and bottomed out.

"Yes, master. Fuck me, master. I need your cock," Amber panted.

Her sex pulsed as she tried to squeeze him inside of her. He let Amber play with him in her sex for a moment while she adjusted to his size. Once it didn't feel quite so constrictive, he pulled out and thrust back in, slowly enjoying the feel of her.

"You feel good. Do you like being on your back for me? I own you."

"I'm yours. Never will I serve another because no other could claim me like you do," she encouraged him, trying to flex her legs and wrap them around his hips, but it only caused the ropes to squeeze her thighs further.

Dar was ready for his release. He pumped himself into her while his finger found her clit and used a knuckle to roll over the swollen pearl.

She tensed under him, trying to keep herself from cumming. Dar enjoyed pushing her to the edge, eventually losing himself and exploding into Amber, pumping ropes of his seed into her ready and waiting sex.

After his release, she relaxed. All it took was one more stroke of her clit to send her into spasms as she keened, finally receiving her release.

"Marcie, now is your chance to make it up. Clean up your master and mistress." Dar pulled out of Amber with a wet squelch and held himself out for Marcie.

She wiggled in her bindings to inch over to him, licking at Dar's once again rock-hard cock. "Yes, master. Thank you, master. I promise not to disappoint you this time."

Dar leaned back, enjoying the feel of her mouth running back and forth around him.

Chapter 11

Dar was sitting calmly on the couch, flipping through one of the books that had been in Tami's home, when the door opened.

Neko strode through proudly. "Goats will go to Hearthway."

"Great." Dar put the book down and checked over Neko, trying to identify anything out of place, but everything seemed fine. "Did you have any trouble?"

Neko's nose flared. She ignored his question, coming over and sniffing his chair. "You had sex with the maids. Where are they?"

"Resting," Dar said with a smirk.

They were currently in his inner world with his family's dao booklet, working on Dar's technique. Having connected with him physically, they were taking the chance to cultivate. And he wondered if the tree would boost them as well, but only time would tell.

Neko made a face of disappointment. "Okay. Oh, and you owe the merchant money."

"No problem. That's to be expected. But you didn't have any issues in town at all?" Dar was skeptical.

She huffed before she spoke carefully, "I am capable. No need to treat me like a kid." Her eyes were filled with more that she wasn't saying.

But he wasn't going to push her. She had come back in one piece.

"Of course you aren't a kid." He pulled Neko into his lap and rubbed her head between her ears.

The cat girl melted into him. Dar realized he needed to give her more independence and treat her like the others. It was easy to coddle her when she could be so naïve and her speech was still developing, but that wasn't fair to her.

"Thank you for checking and making sure we had goats going back to Hearthway. We'll make sure to let Sasha know you could ensure her plans went through."

"Reward." She nuzzled her head into his chest.

Dar continued to rub between her ears while taking his other hand and carefully stroking her ears. They twitched every time he got close to the tips.

"It tickles when you touch the tips. Just rub the base." She grabbed his hand after they twitched again. "But I want a bigger reward, like how you reward Sasha and Cherry after they have a good day."

"Ah." Nerves crept in on Dar; he was fairly certain she meant sex. "I'm not sure that's a reward for them as much as an excuse for both of us to have a little fun."

Neko looked up from where she was in his lap. "Do you not want Neko?"

"No, that's not it at all."

The top of Neko's shirt had pulled down as she rubbed herself against him, and her bounty of creamy skin was on full display, reminding Dar she was very much a woman.

"Then why?" Neko grabbed his hand that had been petting her and pulled it off her head, shoving it on her chest. "These are better than bossy maid's."

His hand squeezed her on instinct, and Neko's face blushed as she bit her lip.

She really was a beautiful woman, and he hadn't been treating her like one. Neko clearly wanted to change that and push them forward, but Dar hadn't really decided if he was ready.

Peals of bells suddenly rang out.

Dar sighed internally; he was relieved that something had broken up the moment so that he didn't have to make an instant decision.

"What's that?" Dar asked, picking Neko up and stepping around the grumpy-looking cat girl. But his brain processed the noise, and he realized he recognized it.

Bellhaven was under attack.

"Come on, Neko. We need to see what's happening." Dar stood up and put Neko down.

"The maids?"

"Cultivating in my inner world," he answered. "Those bells are for an attack on the city."

Outside Tami's house, Dar paused, looking back at her door. Once Neko was out, he put his finger up to the lock and let himself feel the shadows inside of it before using them to fill the void in the lock and twist.

It clicked, locking itself. Dar smiled, satisfied with his new dao.

People were hurrying about on the streets, running home with their belongings and running back out in groups with simple weapons, ready to defend themselves and their home.

Men and women hustled to the eastern side of the city, carrying bows and arrows. It at least seemed that the prince had put together a better system for fighting the devils.

Dar couldn't help but remember his previous experience with the nobility when he'd come to town. They had taken the people out of the slums and shoved them out the front gate with spears in hand. They were entirely used as fodder to help weaken the devils.

As he took a few steps, Karn exited the prince's home, followed by a group of men. Dar slowed, waiting for Karn to catch up.

"Do you know what's going on Karn?"

"A runner interrupted court. There are devils at the eastern wall," Karn grunted.

Dar noticed a spirit and a demon trying to attend to the large bearman, but he ignored both of them. The spirit and demon looked absolutely terrified. Dar wasn't sure if it was because of Karn's overall presence or if it had to do with failing whatever task they'd been given.

Dar eyed them before bringing his focus back to Karn. "Will you help protect the city from the devils?"

"Why would I?" Karn appeared genuinely baffled. "Though I have yet to return to Frost's Fang and formally have The White withdraw her support, I have stated it. I stand by my word. Frost's Fang will not support Bellhaven in this." Karn looked around. "Where's Tami?"

"She left this morning to scout out the devils in the hills to the northeast," Dar reminded him.

Karn frowned. "And she missed this group? I would have thought she'd have seen this coming and given advanced warning."

Dar would have thought so too, but maybe they'd passed each other. The countryside was vast, and even a mass of devils could hide in a forest.

Their group ascended the wall to look out past it and assess the situation. The city's people were stopped short just inside the nearest gate. Guards were arranging those with bows up along the wall while a mass formed. It was what looked like a rather uncoordinated group of tradesmen with spears.

The prince walked up to Karn. "Will you be aiding us?"

"No." Karn said it almost like a declaration.

Dar really wished the prince had taken his advice to heart and made changes in the city. Now innocent people were more at risk because Karn would not engage in the battle. And that was entirely the prince's fault.

The prince scowled, and Neko stepped forward, poking his face on either side of his mouth and tilting it from a frown into an odd grimace. Guards started moving in to intercept her, but Dar gave them a look that slowed them.

Neko ignored the imposing guards. "Turn frown upside down. Dar may help."

Prince Gregor went to yell at her, but then he glanced at Karn. He seemed to remember that he was trying to be more considerate to demons and spirits.

Dar was pleased that he'd made some progress.

"Will you aid us?" Prince Gregor asked Dar.

"Maybe. I'm not particularly interested in fighting for you. But I feel for the people whom you are failing. And I have a new dao that I'm interested in giving some exercise," Dar answered as they got to the top of the wall and saw the mass of devils laid out before them.

It was similar to before. Gremlins were being herded by the much larger trolls into the city walls like fodder.

"New dao?" Karn eyed Dar again. "You are stronger than yesterday."

"I was on the verge of a new greater dao," Dar said by way of explanation. "You know how much fun it is to play with a new dao."

A grunt was all he got in return, but Karn didn't dissuade him from fighting. He had a feeling that was the best he was going to get given he was supporting Bellhaven.

"Can Neko come too?" Neko asked.

"Of course." Dar would be happy to have his ferocious Neko with him. "But let's see how this starts out. I'd hate to jump down there only to turn into a pincushion for the archers."

The prince cleared his throat, seeming to dislike being relegated to an afterthought. "We'll do three volleys once they are in range of the archers. Any more and we end up wasting arrows. Then we'll open the gate with a spear wall to control the funnel. Anything that tries to climb the wall will meet our guards with spears and swords at the top of the wall."

He seemed proud of their defense strategy, and truthfully, it was better than Dar had experienced last time he was in Bellhaven. But they had set the bar quite low.

"I'll wait until after the three volleys." Dar recognized that as the best time to get down there and fight. "What about your wizards?"

"They'll join the volleys and help how they can after. In many ways, they are independent."

"You mean you can't control them," Dar interpreted.

The prince's face twitched, but he didn't respond.

Instead, it was Karn who replied, "Yes, it seems they are working more and more independently these days."

Neko crouched on the edge of the battlement, watching the gremlins rush towards the city. Her tail flicked back and forth like a cat watching a mouse.

"Aim!" the call came, and there was a collective drawing of bows, creating a noise like a great wooden door opening on old hinges. "Fire!"

The twang of a thousand bow strings snapped in the air and the sky whistled with arrows. It looked like some massive swarm of locusts taking to the sky.

The arrows arced high into the sky before they plummeted with much more force, hitting the gremlins like a physical wall. Hundreds were smacked down to the earth, creating barriers those coming after them had to climb over.

"Again."

Another volley was released. But this time, they hit not only gremlins but also the trolls. The arrows did far less to the trolls than the gremlins; the lumbering grey devils shrugged off the arrow fire like pests.

"Again."

This time, one troll fell from what looked like dozens of arrows, but at that point, the devils were close enough to start climbing the walls. The archers replaced their bows with spears.

Dar recognized his chance to join the battle. Taking a running leap, he launched himself off the wall and into the mass of devils below. Letting mana flow through him, he drew upon his dao of heavy and increased his downward momentum, slamming into the ground hard enough to crush the gremlins under him and knocking the nearby ones off their feet.

Landing among the gremlins, he largely ignored them. They were much easier for the city defenders to fight. While the smaller devils were troublesome in numbers, they weren't particularly tough. The trolls were the real problem.

Neko landed on Dar's shoulder in a crouch, then launched herself off of him and over the gremlins, right into a troll. Her claws lashed out and tore swaths in the hairless gorilla like creatures.

Dar was proud of her ferociousness, but he couldn't let her upstage him. Smiling, he charged forward.

As he moved through the gremlins, he activated the dao of hard on his skin and clothes. The little buggers had sharp claws, and their primitive weapons bounced off him as he crushed through them, coming out the other side to the trolls.

As much as he wanted to use brute force and see just how much he'd improved since he'd last fought trolls, it was most important to him to test out his new dao of shadows.

Dar's own shadow sprang up behind him, slashing like a great blade and cleaving through the nearby gremlins. He wielded his shadow like an extra limb as it flowed behind him, materializing in sharp blades and cutting at those who got in range.

Unfortunately, the trolls had thick skin and their dao was related to earth, making them tougher targets. When his shadow hit a troll, it stopped like it had hit a brick wall.

The troll grabbed Dar's shoulders and tried to toss him.

Dar let his dao of heavy weigh him down, locking him onto the ground and stopping the troll from being able to throw him. He grabbed the troll and used his enchanted strength to lift the troll off the ground and slam the devil down on his back.

Deciding to try a closer tactic, Dar held his hand over the troll's face and created shadows under his hand before turning them into sharp blades that tore apart the troll's skin, destroying the devil's head.

Because his dao of shadows was a greater dao, he was largely limited to what he could touch, which meant he was mostly using his own shadow. But he could create his own shadow in many ways.

The blades were a simple but effective use of the dao.

The trolls must have realized the threat that Dar and Neko posed, because they abandoned their work, driving the gremlins forward and coming towards them en masse.

Neko was a sleek and agile fighter as she slipped under the guards of the lumbering trolls, her fingers becoming sharper than steel blades, powered by her dao of sharp.

The trolls found themselves tripping over each other, trying to catch the cat girl, ending up with cuts covering the undersides of their arms and their chests.

Neko spun over one particular troll, latching onto its back before she crossed her arms in a flash and severed the troll's head. As it fell, she jumped off and started fighting another, onto the new troll before the old one even hit the ground.

Dar didn't have much time to appreciate the savage element to Neko's attacks, but he wished he could watch longer.

Focusing on his own fight, Dar continued to use his own skills to fight off the trolls. He stood his ground as trolls came swinging with clubs that were largely small, uprooted trees or massive deadwood branches.

Between the dao of heavy and the dao of hard, Dar stood like a rock, taking the blows without flinching. The trolls tried to hammer him like a stubborn nail, but Dar's body withstood the attack.

Seeing the right moment, Dar grabbed the clubs and wrenched them out of the trolls' hands, swinging them hard enough to shatter them on their previous owners.

Trolls fell before his superior strength, and Dar's shadow stretched out over them, finishing them like a wicked scythe.

It was far easier to take down the trolls than Dar remembered; he had only a few lesser dao the last time he had fought trolls. He'd grown so much in such a short time. He now had two greater dao and, with them, a better understanding of the lesser dao that comprised them.

He and Neko continued to slaughter the surrounding trolls.

Dar was feeling quite confident that they could help eliminate the threat to the city until a massive troll began lumbering towards them, tossing one of the smaller ones aside.

Dar squinted, taking in the troll. It looked like it had huge slabs of stone hanging off its body in some sort of crude armor, and a cudgel made of stone dragged on the ground behind it. Dar recognized its strength; it exuded the power of a greater dao. He licked his lips, ready for a challenge.

The troll swung with enough force to make the air pop as it was displaced. Its stone cudgel hurtled forward in Dar's vision as he braced himself with his dao.

Catching the crude weapon, Dar found himself sliding back, digging furrows in the ground from the force. His arms ached with the effort to hold the weapon from smashing into his face.

"Phew. That is some strength you have there, Big Boy."

The troll bellowed in rage and then it raised its weapon, pausing a moment at the peak before swinging it. Dar watched as it hurtled down towards him like a meteor landing.

As much as Dar wanted to test his strength against Big Boy, he didn't want to exhaust himself in the middle of the enemy lines.

Rolling to the side, the ground exploded with the impact as it hit, sending clods of earth spraying into the air. Dar's feet caught under him, and he shot forward, tackling the creature that was double his size.

As he touched the troll, Dar tried to see if he could use his granite dao to do anything, but it appeared the stone on the troll wasn't granite. It resisted his dao.

So instead, Dar went for another tactic. He let his dao of shadow seep between the stone plates, stabbing into the troll. His victory was short-lived when it didn't work. The blades weren't able to push through the troll's tough skin.

While he might have been able to make a blade out of shadows to cut through gremlins and the weaker trolls, this one had a greater dao and used it to protect itself.

The shadows didn't have the kind of penetrating power Dar needed.

The troll laughed, feeling Dar's failed attempt to harm it and no doubt feeling invincible. The troll pointed and laughed at Dar, opening itself up for attack.

Dar didn't hesitate.

Winding back, he threw a reckless punch right into one of the troll's stone plates before activating his dao of combustion and detonating the surrounding stone.

The explosion rocketed Dar's fist out of the stone. His hand was smoking as he removed it, the troll doubling over.

But Dar wasn't done yet. He continued hitting the troll. Each time his fist touched the troll, his dao of combustion activated and blew another piece of stone apart. Dar kept going until his fists started touching troll flesh. Then he started blowing chunks out of the troll with every explosive punch.

The troll's own control of dao tried to resist each time, but Dar's focused attacks seemed to be enough to break through. The troll stumbled and tried to drag itself off the ground, but Dar didn't relent, changing his target to the troll's head. He clasped it between his palms and rattled its brain with a concussive clap of combustion on each side.

The troll's eyes rolled up into its head as it leaned forward, face planting into the ground.

Dar didn't like to leave things up to chance, so he hauled the massive stone cudgel into the air and slammed it down in an execution of the troll.

The fight would have been easier if he had used one of the Black Knight's weapons lying in his inner world, but he wasn't about to show those off in front of the prince, who still had a bounty out for Dar's alter ego.

Dar looked around for the next target. All around him, trolls lay dead and dying. He and Neko had decimated the stronger devils on their own.

The gremlins were wise enough to stay well away from the duo. Most of the little greedy devils were still pushing into the city, while others on the outskirts had fled without the trolls herding them.

"You hit hard." Neko looked down at the large troll. "And get hit a lot. Sasha is going to be mad that you ruined that shirt."

Dar looked down. Despite extending his dao of hard to his clothes, they'd still been torn apart with the hits from the trolls.

"Let's make sure to buy her some silk before we head back. She'd like that."

Neko giggled and jumped on Dar's back, hitching a ride as he walked back to the city, letting his shadow lash out and clear the way of any gremlins.

Chapter 12

Dar turned, ready to head back to the city after taking on the trolls, but he was intercepted by a giant white form that hurtled itself off the wall and came crashing down before him.

"Neko. Stay back." Dar tried to make sure that Neko didn't get herself killed as he watched a bloodthirsty Karn stride straight for him. He had no idea what Karn was doing.

"Stupid bear." Neko pushed off Dar and landed in a crouch, but she stayed back.

Karn picked up speed like a train pulling out of the station as he charged Dar.

Dar wracked his brain trying to figure out what was going on. But Karn gave him little time to think.

Dar blocked the fuzzy white fist as the demon came swinging. It felt like he'd just gotten hit by a truck. Dar was blown back a dozen feet, even with his dao of heavy.

Karn roared into the air; his black beady eyes of his were filled with the desire to fight.

"Karn, stop. What are you doing?"

But he got no response. It was like the demon was possessed. Karn swung as if to take Dar's head.

At that point, Dar couldn't afford to hold back. So he rolled out of the way and drew upon his dao of granite. Unfortunately, when he pulled, he got no response. It figured he'd be on top of ground with no granite underneath.

Crossing granite off his list of options, he moved on to shadow. He tried to tangle up Karn's feet with his dao of shadows. Karn ignored the dao, ripping his legs out of Dar's attempt to hobble him and stomping down, creating a ripple of ice that rained spikes on Dar.

For all that Dar trusted his dao of hard, he wasn't about to take one of Karn's attacks head on if he could help it.

Blasting the surrounding air with heat, he hoped to stave off more of Karn's ice. But, as they kept coming, it became clear that the demon's grand dao could overpower his lesser heat dao. Dar just had to keep moving.

Every time Karn swung and missed, the air grew several times colder.

Dar wasn't sure what the hell he could pull out to compete against the bear.

"Fight me!" Karn growled, spittle flying from his mouth. "Watching you got my blood pumping. I want to see your strength." He slammed both hands into the ground.

The world around Dar erupted in shards of ice. One managed to touch Dar, burning him with how cold it was and leaving behind a patch of painful red skin.

Dar cursed. Cherry was his best option at that point for help, but he couldn't ask her to come out in full view of the city. Hearing a hiss, he realized Neko was prowling well outside of the fight, glaring angrily at Karn.

He was proud of her for not stepping in and getting tangled up in the fight when it was clear she wanted to.

"Is that all this is about, Karn? You just want to fight?" Dar goaded the bear as he dodged again, making his way towards the forest that the devils had come out of.

There, hidden in the trees, Cherry would be her strongest.

"Don't pretend. I want to see your strength." Karn barreled forward with surprising speed, catching Dar and picking him up in a running tackle before crushing him back down to the earth. "Where is your strength? No need to hide it. If you do, I'll probably end up killing you."

There, staring into Karn's eyes, Dar could see a touch of madness eating away at the demon. He had a lust for battle and blood that had consumed him.

Catching his knees under Karn's bulk, Dar kicked the bear off of him and rolled to his feet. "I don't know what the heck you expect from me Karn."

The bear didn't even seem bothered by being tossed into the air as he rolled to his hands and feet with a crooked chuckle. "Oh, quit playing. I want to see Lilith's little pet fight again."

Dar's gut sank. Somehow, Karn had recognized that he was the Black Knight.

"Don't look like that. Of course I know who you are. Don't you remember when Lilith brought you to Frost's Fang? Your eyes were so lifeless back then." Karn licked his lips. "But the fight was glorious."

Karn charged again on all fours in a running lope that belonged to a bear, not a bipedal creature.

He's crazy, Dar thought. The stupid bear is a maniac.

But there was no time to lament his situation. Dar turned and ran headlong into the forest, using bushes and trees to slow down Karn's charge.

The bear wasn't so easily dissuaded; he crashed through bushes and swatted down small trees.

"Don't run. I want a rematch!" he roared. "You don't have your armor this time. I want to see just what Lilith's little pet is made of."

Dar was backed into a corner, but that was okay. He had gotten Karn into the woods where the view of them was obscured.

"Cherry, stop him." He pushed on his inner world, ejecting the dryad forcefully as he pointed at Karn.

"Wha? Shit!" Cherry slammed her hands on the ground and vines burst out of the ground, grabbing and flinging Karn to the side. "What is going on?"

"I don't know. Karn recognized me as the Black Knight and went crazy," Dar hurried to explain.

"Fucking crazy bear," she cursed before raising her voice. "Karn, calm down."

The demon picked himself back up, panting as those little beady black eyes stared at them unblinkingly. "Ha. I was right. Well met, Cherry."

The dryad rolled her eyes. "Great, introductions are out of the way. Now, can we stop this?"

"If you need this to stop, why doesn't Lilith come out and stop me?" he chuckled, rolling his shoulder.

"Because Lilith is dead," Dar spat.

That pulled Karn up short. "Dead?"

"Dead," Dar repeated. "I saw it myself—a death spirit went with her."

"Impossible. Not to mention, Valdis could bring her back," Karn growled.

Dar was just thankful that Karn seemed to be a little more reasonable for the moment. "I don't know who Valdis is, but Lilith went willingly to her next life. I was there. She pulled me back from another life, and I woke up here about a month ago."

Karn shook his massive head. "The death spirit, Valdis, is one of the oldest and most powerful spirits here. How..." He struggled for words. "Why did Lilith allow herself to die? She had too much to do here."

The way Karn said it, it was almost as if he thought that evading death was entirely within Lilith's realm of control. Just how powerful did everyone think she was, or for that matter, just how powerful had she been?

And here she had sacrificed herself for Dar. Dar had always wondered why, but he realized she'd given the world a chance to have somebody who could destroy, not just contain, the Mo.

Maybe it was time to come clean.

"She did it for me. With what she did to my body when she brought me back, I can kill Mo. Not just weaken them, or put them in a seal. Dead. For good," Dar tried to explain.

Karn leaned against a tree and threw his head back, laughing. "You? Kill a Mo? Laughable." The bear's head snapped down, humor gone. "Wait. Is that what happened back at the ettercaps near your village? Tell me how."

Dar wasn't about to tell him everything, not after what had just happened, but he needed to tell Karn enough. "She put something inside of me. When I was near the weakened Mo, it scoured the creature's body and destroyed it."

Karn licked his lips. "Did it make you stronger?"

"Yes?" Dar wasn't sure why that was important.

"Prove it," Karn growled. "Beat me, and I'll walk away."

"I thought we just got done with fighting."

In response, Karn slammed the ground, and a wall of ice formed around the three of them. "Just hand to hand combat. Since you embarrassed me that day in front of The White, I have awaited the opportunity to fight you again."

Cherry stepped back, looking at Dar for what he wanted to do.

Even with Cherry, Dar wasn't sure they could take Karn if he used his dao. Dar was fairly certain Karn had been holding back so far, and the ice arena he'd created was further indication that was right. Physical combat would also be a challenge, but he at least stood a chance. And hopefully, it would get the battle crazed demon off his back.

"Fine. Rules?"

"Hand to hand only. No weapons, keep your dao to your body. Victory to the last one standing." Karn flexed his massive, clawed hands.

No weapons, Dar scoffed. Those hands were murder mitts.

"Dar," Cherry's voice wavered.

"I got this." He patted the top of her head. "Get out of the arena and watch me do my thing." He turned back to Karn. "I agree with your terms. But after this, we will be good, whatever the result. No further fights."

Dar put his hands up, ready to fight.

There was no starting bell, no countdown. One second, Dar had agreed to the fight, and the next second, a massive white claw was swinging for his head.

Dar just barely reacted in time, ducking under the swing and inside Karn's range. He jabbed forward with several quick strikes as he filled his body with the dao of heavy, hard and strength.

The enchantments on his body glowed with mana as he put everything he had into the fight.

Karn's bestial mouth opened wide, and he lurched forward, biting down at Dar.

Abandoning his assault, Dar braced his forearm to be an object larger than Karn could stuff in his mouth. Unfortunately, it didn't stop the bearman's teeth from scraping along Dar's arm, drawing blood despite the dao of hard.

Karn snapped his mouth closed with jaws that would no doubt crush deer bones like a midday snack. He licked his lips, tasting Dar's blood.

"Going to have to do better than that," Karn said.

Dar slugged the bear in the chest again, but the large demon just shrugged it off. Karn began another running tackle, grabbing Dar and slamming him against the icy wall of the arena.

Putting his arms up to protect his face, Dar weathered Karn's assault as the demon pounded him into the icy wall. He had hoped to tire Karn out, but instead, as the blows rained down, Karn seemed to grow more excited with each punch.

With a scream of rage, Dar pushed Karn off of him. While Karn was unbalanced, Dar slugged the bear in the face hard enough to stagger him.

Dar pressed his advantage with another right hook to the bear's face and an uppercut to his gut; Dar tried to keep Karn off balance. But it wasn't easy. Karn was tough. He only landed a few more blows before Karn blocked a strike, his claws sinking into Dar's arm and twisting his arm.

"Is that all you've got?" Karn squeezed Dar's forearm with enough pressure that only Dar's enchantments were saving him from having his bones crushed.

Jerking forward, Dar head-butted Karn. But he immediately regretted it as he came away seeing stars. He could tell that the hit had affected Karn as well, because his arm came free of the demon's grip. Dar stumbled back, catching himself on the icy wall.

As his vision cleared, Karn's big bear head was tossing itself back and forth, trying to shake his own daze.

Dar noticed that there were specks of blood dotting the bear's white fur. And one look at his knuckles said it wasn't all Dar's blood. Underneath the fur, welts were forming from where Dar had hit him.

The bear demon wasn't impervious, just a hell of a lot tougher than anything Dar had fought before. "Karn, how about we call it quits?"

"Fat chance." Karn wiped at his mouth, streaking his forearm with blood. "I haven't been waiting hundreds of years for this to just stop. This chance will not slip away from me."

Karn put his hands back up, ready to fight once more.

"I'm flattered, but I am not the same person you once fought. I may look the same and have aspects of the same soul, but I have lived a different life. I am a different man." Dar pushed off the icy wall. "That said, if you continue to fight me, you will lose to me as well."

Anger flared in Karn's beady black eyes, and Dar could tell Karn would not back down. Sure enough, he roared as he charged for Dar.

Dar blocked the wild punch, pushing it back across Karn's body as Dar spun, grabbing the bear's extended wrist and locking out the bear's arm. Frozen in that tangled knot, Dar slammed his knee into Karn's hip repeatedly.

Seeing the bear injured during their brief pause had made Dar think about some of his bar fights back on Earth. When opponents had greater strength, he would just hammer the same spot repeatedly until they weakened.

Karn came again and Dar took the hit, driving a left hook back into Karn's hip.

The demon staggered and Dar pushed the demon back, coming in for another round. His fists were a distraction. The real damage was done as Dar used his knee for short, brutal strikes against Karn's hip.

While the demon fought like an angry bear, Dar fought like a human. Duck, dodge, strike the hip. Block, jab, hook to the hip. Again and again Dar took hits as long as he could keep hammering Karn's hip to a bruised pulp.

Eventually, Karn wobbled on his feet. His hips nearly giving out.

"We can call this a tie and walk away," Dar offered once more, feeling at the end of his own strength. His shoulders ached and his head throbbed to the unseen rhythm of his pulse. Even if victory was only a few rounds away, Dar didn't want to take any more of a beating than he had to.

Dar knew that, even after the fight, Bellhaven was only a stone's throw away, and he didn't want the wizards or the prince to see him as a battered and bruised mess.

"No." Karn raised his fists. "I will win."

They stepped back into the fight, both of them sloppy as they teetered on their feet.

But Karn had a surprise for Dar.

The first swing Dar threw wasn't met with hands or arm, it was met with teeth.

Karn's jaw popped open wide at the last second, his inhuman neck muscles bulging under his fur. Karn made one last attempt to bite Dar's arm off.

The world froze for a moment as Dar realized the impending loss of his arm. Karn's jaw was already closing down. Dar knew the teeth could cut right through his dao and flesh.

His arm needed to not be there; it needed to be somewhere else.

Or something else.

Remembering Cherry's words, embracing his dao of shadows, he willed his arm away, to become shadows. There wasn't time to dwell on it.

Dar instead left his right arm up to fate as he focused on winning. Even if he lost it, he wasn't about to lose the fight.

His left fist hammered past Karn's guard as the bear threw everything into removing Dar's arm. Once, twice. Dar's left fist was like a jackhammer into Karn's left hip, using the rebounding force and pushing through it for a third strike.

Something broke under Dar's knuckles, and Karn screamed as he lost his balance and stumbled to the ground, clutching his hip.

Finally.

Dar looked at his right arm; from the elbow to his fingertips was a smokey black form. His lips curled up in victory as that smokey black form faded back to flesh.

"Had enough?" Dar goaded Karn once again.

The bear pushed off the ground trying to stand, but his hip gave out and he fell back down to the ground. Growling, he tried once more to get up, pushing through the pain. But he only made it partway up before he gave up and collapsed.

"You win," Karn conceded.

"Dar!" Cherry jumped onto his shoulders. Her weight would normally have been insignificant to Dar, but this time, it made him stagger to a knee as she peppered him with kisses.

The icy barrier that Karn had erected for their fight shattered and faded. A concerned Neko rushed through the shards of ice, grabbing Dar and shoving her shoulder under his arm to support him.

"Stupid bear. I told you Dar is best."

Rather than be angry, Karn threw his head back and let loose a deep bellied laugh that seemed to go on forever.

When he was done, Karn wiped a tear from his eyes. "Oh. You have good companions, Dar."

Vines rose out of the ground around Karn as Cherry clutched tightly to Dar's back. "I should kill you right now."

"Don't," Dar sighed. "The last thing we need to do is start a fight with The White."

"She won't know for weeks." Cherry argued, her vines poised to finish him.

"And when Karn doesn't come back after investigating Bellhaven for killing demons and spirits? If we kill Karn here, The White is liable to come down here and turn Bellhaven into the next Toldove, or worse. He gets a pass this time. Besides, he wasn't trying to kill me." Dar struggled to his feet, holding his side.

Cherry's vines receded into the ground. "What do you mean he wasn't trying to kill you?"

"He just wanted to beat me to a pulp."

"The stupid bear tried to bite your arm off," Neko blurted out with an angry hiss in Karn's direction.

That Dar did believe. The bear was a loose cannon and too dangerous to stay in the area. He clearly couldn't hold himself back in a fight. "Karn, don't take this the wrong way, but I'd rather you not stay around. After you finish up your tasks at Bellhaven, you need to get the hell back to Frost's Fang. If I see you again, if you pose a threat to my village, I may not be able to let you walk away."

Karn chuckled. "Do you really want to make that threat? Next time, we might not fight with just fists."

Dar would make that bet. He may not be able to defeat Karn at the moment, but he had a feeling that the next time they met he'd be far stronger and maybe even strong enough to kill Karn using his full strength.

"Finish up, Karn, and get out of Bellhaven."

The big demon winced as he gathered his feet under him and lifted his body off the ground, stumbling several steps and using trees to brace himself as he headed back towards Bellhaven.

"Dar, that was dangerous," Cherry admonished him.

"Can you tell me that if I let you kill him here and now that Bellhaven would be here in a month?"

She looked away. "Probably not."

"Besides, until he went psycho, he's been a decent ally. Now help me up; we need to figure out what to do from here."

Neko scooped up his arm and supported his weight as she stood. "I have you."

"Thanks, Neko." He took a few wobbled steps, using Neko as support. But they didn't make it far before something began crashing through the forest.

For a moment, Dar thought it was Karn coming back to settle things, but he realized it was coming from the opposite direction.

Chapter 13

Dar, Neko, and Cherry looked up towards the crashing sound, bracing themselves.

Neko was the first to make out the form. "Tami!" Neko pivoted her head, trying to understand why the deer demon was running through the woods.

But Tami didn't seem to hear Neko as she looked over her shoulder at something that was putting a panicked expression on her face.

"Cherry." Dar pulled her off his shoulder, but she was already catching Tami. Vines sprang from the ground ahead of the demon.

Tami ground to a halt, looking for her way around it, which Cherry had conveniently left open and leading towards their location.

Confusion crossed Tami's face when she saw him. "Dar?"

She looked him up and down, and Dar realized he must have looked a mess after his brawl with Karn.

"I'm fine. What's wrong?"

A high-pitched buzz grew in volume and Cherry wasted no time, snagging Tami with a root and pulling her over to their group. Then she wrapped the four of them in a tight weave of hearty roots from the surrounding trees.

"What—" Tami started, but Dar covered her mouth. "Wait."

Through thin gaps in the roots, Dar could make out mantis type devils. Some even had wings on their back. Dar realized that was the buzzing sound he heard.

They flew through the woods like a swarm of locusts. Dar kept his hand firmly over Tami's mouth, making sure she didn't speak up again and draw the devils' attention.

Neko crouched low, physically displaying that she understood the need for stealth. Cherry watched with eyes narrowed in concern as she pressed herself up to Dar's side.

The mantises zoomed through the woods with incredible speed. Dar was shocked that Tami had stayed ahead of them. Her dao definitely had come in handy.

Dar took the moment to check Tami over. The deer demon had several scratches and bruises, but otherwise, she was unharmed. It was the fear in her eyes that worried Dar the most. She needed to stay calm and, most importantly, quiet in this situation.

As they waited for the mantises to clear out, Dar tried to puzzle through why they were in the woods. If what Karn had said was true, there was a Mo sealed in the hills, but it was connected to earth dao. The trolls and gremlins made sense, but the mantis devils did not.

Dar doubted speed was some derivative of earth. Which meant those devils didn't belong, or at least, didn't fit with what Dar was looking for.

Tami might have the answers to the questions he had once they were in the clear, but for now, they had to wait.

The mantis devils continued searching the woods frantically. So he settled in and gave Tami a look with a raised eyebrow and a finger to his lips.

She nodded. She still looked a touch hysterical, but she'd calmed down. And she definitely seemed to understand the desire to not get caught.

Dar slowly removed his hand from Tami's mouth and pulled Cherry close.

It was going to be awhile before the swarm settled down. Since there wasn't much he could do while they waited, he decided to go into a trance, allowing himself to fall into his inner world.

***

Dar blinked, finding himself once again in the grand space inside of himself.

Cherry had been busy. He hadn't really looked during his last visit, but now he took in the progress she'd made with the few seeds she'd had. They had the start of a small budding orchard.

It was definitely possible there could come a time that having the supply of food would save his life. He was glad they didn't need it for Hearthway during this winter. He had gotten the village to a place where they were comfortable. It would be stable through the harsh season.

He walked over to the little dao tree. It stood there amid the loose loamy soil, his two maids meditating in its shade.

Dar joined the two maids, flipping through his family's book of dao until he found Blair's dao of bright once again. He sat down, drawing on his mana, and meditated slowly on the dao character.

Unlike the ease he had had with the shadow dao, this one came achingly slowly. But he wasn't surprised. He didn't have the tree to help boost this dao.

If Sasha heard him complain, she'd clock him upside the head. He still was able to learn dao at a speed most demons and spirits only dreamt of.

Dar focused on being grateful, pushing aside the distracting thoughts and focusing solely on the bright dao, slowly tracing the pattern in his body. The dao of bright resisted him. He'd get the shape formed, only to have it shoot away, like it refused to be contained within him.

It was a long process of trying and failing to contain mana in the shape of the dao character. But he wasn't discouraged. He'd done this before with other dao and was confident he could figure it out. And he'd made some progress, although quite minimal.

Dar wasn't sure how long he meditated before an external sense brought him out of his session. Slowing his mana until it came to a halt, he gently removed himself from his cultivation.

"Yes?" He cracked an eye open, looking at his two maids now positioned before him.

Both of them were practically vibrating with energy. One look was all it took for Dar to realize that they had not only mastered the concealment dao, but they had also mastered the dao of shadows.

"Incredible, you two!"

They both beamed with his praise. "Thank you, milord. We are honored with all the support you've given us."

Dar waved away their thanks. "You two took the risk of staying with me when I left Bellhaven, and then you took the risk of trying to follow in my footsteps in cultivating dao as an immortal. I can't take the credit for that."

"What has happened since we came here to meditate?" Marcie asked.

Remembering that he was currently hiding in the woods surrounded by hundreds, if not thousands, of devils must have come through on his face, because both girls' expressions turned concerned.

"If..."

"It's fine. Just some trouble. Devils attacked Bellhaven. I went and fought outside the walls, but then... Karn attacked me." He shook his head; that was a tangled mess in itself that required an explanation. "Suffice to say, he had a bone to pick with me from my previous life, and we duked it out in the forest."

"Are you okay?" Amber asked, crouching down to inspect him before realizing it wasn't his physical body.

"Banged up. We parted on rough terms. I was headed back toward Bellhaven, but then Tami was being chased by a swarm of mantis devils. Now we are hiding out buried in tree roots thanks to Cherry's quick thinking." He paused. "I should wake back up and check on things."

"Don't worry about us. We'll stay here until it is safe." Her eyes roamed his inner world, looking for a way she could help when her eyes landed on the massive black stone fortress. "We'll keep ourselves busy."

Dar shook his head. "You can't get in there. Best thing you could do is take those ettercap corpses and toss them down next to the little dao tree. Sprinkle some soil over top, and the tree will absorb them."

"Then we'll do that," Amber said with a finality. "You go take care of what you need to. The last thing your maids should be is a distraction from what needs done."

Winking back at her, Dar took the opportunity. "Unless it is a certain kind of distraction. That is always welcome."

Amber stood back up and straightened her dress. "We take care of your needs. All of them."

The way she lifted her chin and said it with pride still boggled part of Dar's mind, but as he built a relationship with them, it felt more and more natural.

"Thank you, both. I'll be back as soon as I can." Dar kissed Amber and then Marcie before letting himself fade back into the world.

Soft breathing filled his ear, and as he cracked his eyes, he found himself in the dark. Daylight had faded from between the cracks in the roots. But Dar was far from afraid of the dark. His shadow dao kicked in, and the darkness no longer impaired him.

He looked around their small space. Cherry was on his left and Tami on his right, though it looked like she had rolled closer to him in her sleep. The deer girl was actually cute when she was sleeping. She had small freckles that dusted her cheeks that he hadn't noticed before. For once, she looked relaxed.

Neko shifted; she was still awake and alert.

Dar moved, brushing her with his leg. She started silently snapping at him in reflex before relaxing.

She leaned into him, shifting until she was curled against his chest. He took a risk putting his lips inside one of her cat ears, his nose tickled by the fluff that threatened to spill out of them.

"How is it?"

"No movement for several hours," Neko whispered. "I'm tired."

He squeezed Neko to his chest, stroking her back. "Sleep. I'll keep watch." Dar kissed the side of her head.

Neko wiggled into him for a moment before settling down. Soft snores shortly followed.

Releasing his dao of quiet in the surrounding area, he damped down any risk of that noise getting out as the three girls rested. Dar kept his eyes and ears open, but nothing happened. The night was blissfully quiet.

When the first rays of morning started bleeding through the trees, Dar moved himself out of the sleeping pile and pressed his face to the roots, peeking between them.

There were no signs of the mantises, but their passing was clear. Trees all around bore numerous small slashes. Bushes had stray branches sheared off, and nearby, a pile of still wet bones was partially sticking out of the nearby brush.

There was no other way to describe what had come through besides a swarm.

Pushing himself up had made his body ache, a reminder that he was still injured from his fight with Karn. He knew that the enchantments on his body would help him heal rapidly, but it would still take a few more days before he was fully recovered.

"Stupid bear," he grunted under his breath, agreeing with Neko's name for Karn.

"How is it?" Tami asked, apparently awake.

"No mantis that I can see." He made sure his dao of quiet surrounded them before responding, "Looks like you kicked a nasty hive."

Tami shook her head. "I need to go back to Kindrake and report this to my father."

Dar moved so that he could get his back comfortably against the roots and the pressure off his legs. "Yeah? Care to give me the sneak peek?"

"I want to know what happened to you," Tami demanded.

Their conversation had woken Neko. "Stupid bear," she answered simply in response to Tami's statement. Then she wiggled back into Dar and dozed back off.

"What she said. The stupid bear went battle crazy and demanded a fight." Dar rolled his shoulder, poking and prodding himself to see just how bad a shape he was in.

"You fought Karn?" Tami said in disbelief.

"I beat Karn," Dar clarified. "If you think I look bad, you should see him."

"You didn't beat Karn," Tami tried again.

Cherry was the next to wake from the talking. "Oh, but he beat Karn. The two slugged it out like two stupid testosterone fueled demons."

Tami's head snapped to the dryad, assessing her again. "You're Cherry."

It would seem that Cherry was more famous than she had let on. Both Karn, and now Tami, had recognized Cherry on sight. Dar now understood why she wanted to stay hidden when they had first set off.

"Guilty." Dar's dryad shrugged. "And you're Cervus' little brat?"

Tami choked at how Cherry described her father. "You should be careful speaking so casually about my father."

"Nah. He's just a little upstart. I remember when he was this big." Cherry held her hand a couple feet off the ground. "Cute kid though."

Tami pressed a pair of fingers into the ridge of her brow. "What are you doing here?"

"Looking for Mo." Cherry tilted her head with an innocent expression.

"For Lilith?" Tami asked hopefully.

"No, sorry. For the big guy." Cherry pointed at Dar. "You see, he can actually kill a Mo."

Tami looked back at Dar as if she had missed something in her original assessment. "Really?"

"Yes, don't make me repeat myself," Cherry huffed.

"I wouldn't believe it if it wasn't coming from Lilith's dao companion," Tami said, her eyes still roving Dar. "Have you killed a Mo before?"

Dar didn't like Cherry spilling secrets, but at least Tami had no information on how he'd killed the Mo or the benefits it had brought him. People would likely piece it together over time anyway.

"One a few days ago. I came to Bellhaven to see if their devil problem could lead me to another. But that's enough about me. We saved your life last night, and I think telling us what you found that led to that would be a fair repayment."

Tami was a little dazed, clearly still processing everything that had happened. "Yeah. Sure. So, I went up into the hills looking for this sealed Mo that Karn said would be there. But, as soon as I got more than a few miles into the hills, it was absolutely full of devils. Those mantises were... eating gremlins and trolls."

"Eating them?" Dar pushed.

"Yeah. It was almost like there was a war between the two types of devils in the hills. The mantis were clearly winning; they were working in groups and hunting down trolls and gremlins."

Dar thought about the small group of devils that had attacked the city. "Bellhaven was attacked again yesterday. A group of maybe a few hundred gremlins and a dozen trolls. How does that fit in?"

Tami shrugged. "Starving refugees from the fight in the hills, I'd guess." She cringed a bit. "If the devils are eating each other, I doubt there is enough wild game to go around."

Dar nodded. It did explain why the mantises were around and why they'd pursued her so heavily. "That makes some sense. So, we have two groups of devils in the hills. But we do not know what they're fighting over. And meanwhile, Bellhaven is seeing groups of trolls and gremlins flee looking for other sources of food."

Dar couldn't help but be curious about what the devils were fighting over. "Did you go any deeper?"

He felt like she was holding information back. Dar knew she had the dao of speed and concealment. There was little doubt in his mind that she had at least tried to press further into the devil's territory.

Tami hesitated a moment before letting out a sigh. "I guess, if you have Cherry here, I don't have to worry too much about you. There, deep in the hills, was a massive nest. It had a big lumpy bitch that was spitting out eggs. The whole area was locked down tight. Winged mantises patrolled the sky while larger ones guarded what I'm assuming is some sort of queen."

Dar pressed his knuckles into his lips in thought. If the queen devil was producing so many, it needed fuel. While the mantises might be hunting the trolls and gremlins, Dar had a sudden sickening sense.

"Did you get eyes on the Mo that was supposed to be in the hills?" He asked.

"No. I know where Karn said it would be, but I couldn't get that close."

"Was it about where the queen was?" Dar was disgusted at where his thoughts were leading.

"Yes." She looked at him, trying to figure out where he was going.

He grimaced. "The only thing that would make sense is if our Mo problem is someone else's meal ticket. Unless I kill it, they are just going to keep regenerating."

Tami's face was disgusted.

Neko hadn't followed their discussion. "What's happening to the Mo?"

"It is being continually eaten," Cherry filled in for the cat girl. "It might even be allowed to spawn more gremlins and trolls just to feed the hive of mantis devils that have infested the hills."

Dar turned to Cherry, wondering what she thought about all of it. She had the most experience out of all of them. "Cherry, what complications is this going to cause? Obviously we are going to have a very large insect devil problem here eventually, but is this thing continuing to eat the Mo going to keep it contained?"

"It isn't like I have an example of this in the past," Cherry huffed. "But that sort of feeding will make this devil and its spawn stronger over time. The stronger this thing gets, the more powerful devils it is going to produce."

Pressing his head back into the roots, he tried to think of a next step. His first thought was trying to start another giant fire, but past the forest, the growth on the hills was minimal. And some of them could simply fly out of it. He didn't think it would be anywhere near as effective as it had been with the ettercaps.

"What do we know about these mantis devils? Any weakness?" he asked.

"I honestly would have expected them to go to ground by this time of year." Tami tapped her lips. "Like most insects, they don't do well in the cold. But they are still very active."

"Half the reason creatures go inactive in the winter is food scarcity. These guys don't have that. They might be literally eating their way through the winter to keep themselves warm and active," Dar pointed out.

The rest of the group winced.

Another thought started forming in Dar's mind. There was a way they might be able to attack the problem indirectly. But shoring up the plan would have to wait until after he rested, and they could best do that in Bellhaven.

"Cherry, I think it's time we see if we can't get out of here. Neko, stay on high alert. I'm relying on your ears to warn us if anything is coming. Cherry, stay ready to hide us again. Tami... just don't run off." Dar wasn't sure if she'd use her speed to take off towards Bellhaven at the first chance.

"Don't worry. I'll stay with you in case there's more trouble." Tami rolled her eyes as Cherry peeled back the roots and allowed them to exit.

Dar stumbled out; his battered body was sore and stiff with his first few steps.

Neko was there in an instant, supporting him with a smile.

He wanted to argue, but her joyful face at being able to help was too much. He couldn't bring himself to argue with her, and if he was honest with himself, he could use the help. So, arm in arm, they headed towards Bellhaven.

Chapter 14

Thankfully, there had been no trouble getting back to Bellhaven. Despite Dar's misgivings, having Tami with them proved helpful once they got to the gate.

She was known in the city, so the guard didn't bother any of them, although they did receive a number of stares as they walked through the city. Dar wasn't surprised. His outfit was torn and bloody, and he was being helped along by Neko.

Dar had healed, but the walk in had aggravated his injuries even more. Thankfully, Neko never missed a beat and just took more of his weight as they walked.

"Let's get him back to my place before he falls over here in the street and we have to drag him back." Tami turned sharply as they entered the city and started heading uphill towards the nicer area of the city.

Dar was a little out of it as Neko supported him, but he recognized when Cherry slipped away into his inner world.

A block later, Tami paused and looked around. "Where's Cherry?"

"She comes and goes. You get used to it," Dar said with a smile.

Neko snickered and kept moving, prompting Tami to keep going as well.

"Just go lie down and rest. If you walk around the city looking like that, the guards are going to come ask questions." Tami clicked her door open and stepped in.

Dar's eyes narrowed as they scanned the room for Karn, but there was no sign of the demon. Good.

"Neko, make sure he gets some rest. I need to go report to the prince." Tami stepped back out and locked the door, leaving Dar alone.

Dar pushed, and the two maids popped back out of his inner world into Tami's home.

"Dar!" Amber cried upon seeing him. She was so shocked that she dropped the title she always used.

"Not a big deal." He tried to shoo her away as she picked at the remains of his clothes to see just how bad his injuries were.

"Off your feet this instant. Neko, get him on the bed." Amber took charge as Marcie ducked under his other arm and between her and Neko they nearly took all the weight off his legs as they hauled him into Tami's guest room and laid him out on the bed.

Marcie hesitated for a moment before leaning in and whispering something to Amber.

"Yes. Go get them."

The mousy maid bolted from the room, off on some errand.

"Neko, I need help getting him out of his clothes."

The cat girl grinned from ear to ear. "My pleasure." She leaned in and whispered into his ear, her breath tickling him and sending blood south.

"Maybe you should let me do that." Dar grabbed his pants before she tore them.

"No. I can do it." Neko grabbed them and jerked.

The two of them were in a momentary tug of war, which ended up rubbing Dar's manhood. Between that and Neko's chest threatening to spill out, he felt himself rising to attention.

The distraction caused Dar to lose the battle, and his pants were pulled down as his cock sprang up.

Neko looked at it curiously and batted it once, only for it to swing back, sticking up and pointing to the heavens. Her eyes gleamed like a kitten with a new toy, and she batted it again.

"Stop it." Dar tried to grab her hands, but she played with his erection, batting it and watching it stick straight back up. Apparently, his dick was as amusing as cats found a spring doorstop.

Amber was absolutely no help as she doubled over in laughter watching the entire thing. Dar wrestled with the cat girl and tried not to damage her new toy.

"What is—?" Marcie stood in the doorway, frozen for a second by the scene.

Dar paused, fighting Neko as he looked up at the doorway, and Neko took her chance to get in one more smack.

"Enough." Dar grabbed Neko and gently, but firmly, tossed her off of him.

Neko was poised to jump back up, but Amber had enough sense to grab her. "Pussy cat, you are playing with it wrong. Later I'll teach you how to play with it if you are good."

"I know how to use it. I just didn't realize it would be so... fascinating." Neko was still staring at it.

Dar finished shucking his pants and pulled off his shirt before sitting up and closing his legs.

"What's that?" he asked Marcie to change the topic.

"Oh. Just some ointment." She pulled a jar out of the basket. "Let me."

The timid maid undid the lid and sat next to Dar on the bed, liberally applying the ointment before wrapping the worst of his cuts in bandages.

Neko calmed down, and in what felt like an apology, pressed herself to his side, rubbing her face against his shoulder. Her softer side always melted his heart and brought comfort.

But the moment was broken when Cherry popped back out of his inner world.

"Good, we are in private." She looked around. "Dar, you really should take better care of yourself."

He snorted. "I'll remember that next time a big bear demon wants to get in a fight with me."

Cherry was less than amused. "You know what I mean. So, what's next?"

The maids and Neko joined Cherry, pausing and looking to him for the next step.

"If what Tami told us is true, the Mo in those hills is likely in an even weaker state than the one we fought at the ettercaps." Dar tapped the bed in thought. "I might even be able to absorb it in its current state."

Cherry nodded. "From what she said, you'd be putting it out of its misery."

"It's a devil," Neko spat. "Better dead."

Dar knew what Cherry meant, and he agreed. It would almost be a mercy killing to sneak up there and kill the wounded Mo. It was likely being eaten alive, only to regenerate and suffer more.

The thought sent a shiver down Dar's spine. Never in a million years would he wish such a fate on someone, let alone someone who wouldn't die.

"But I need time to heal first." Dar was in no shape to go running through the forest and try to steal a dying Mo's power, especially when that Mo was surrounded by a mass of devils, including one very powerful queen.

"And train," Cherry pushed. "You still have that dao of bright to learn."

Dar wrinkled his nose, annoyed that it had remained out of his grasp for the moment. "I'll continue to train.

Amber, Marcie, and Neko, for this battle, I'm going to ask all of you to sit out."

"But, milord," Amber started to argue.

"No buts. When I go for this Mo, stealth is going to be the highest priority. Bringing multiple people is just going to increase the risk." Dar put a stop to any further conversation on it. "I can't bring any of you."

Neko poked at his chest. "Bring us inside. I will not stay behind while you go."

Amber jumped at Neko's request. "Exactly, milord. Please bring us with you. Even if we cannot share in the journey, we do not wish to leave."

"Exactly, milord." Marcie bowed low.

Dar glanced at Cherry for help.

"Sorry, but I think they have the right to come with you in that capacity, if needed. But all of you should prepare to spend a day in there. That means food, belongings," Cherry coached them.

"Of course." Amber nodded firmly. "We'll have what we need." She turned and beamed back at Dar.

He was wise enough to know that, with all four of them in agreement, he wasn't going to persuade them otherwise. "Fine. We'll be ready to head out tomorrow. I think I'll be healed enough to start the journey."

Dar stood, feeling restless.

"Shouldn't you be resting?" Neko tried to pull him back to the bed.

"No, I'm not feeling tired. I'll walk the city and check in on Dane. I want to see if he's getting things in order to head back to Hearthway soon. Sasha will be getting antsy by now."

Dar picked his pants back up and slipped them on before Neko could get any ideas. They were torn. It made him look a little ragged, but there were more important things than his noble prestige at the moment.

"Snag me a variety of seeds for fruiting plants," Cherry said before she disappeared back into his inner world.

The dryad seemed to be more at home there with every day that passed.

"We have our own shopping to do if we are to prepare for the trip," Amber declared as Marcie stood behind her.

"I stay with Dar," Neko stated as if she were his protector. She hovered by his side, concerned that he was going to topple over.

But Dar felt better; the brief rest in Tami's home had done wonders.

Getting ready, Dar strode out of Tami's place with the girls in tow. The maids split off shortly after, heading to do their own shopping trip. Dar cut for the docks, assuming Dane's boat would be the best place to find him.

"What kind of seeds does Cherry want?" Neko asked, her head on a swivel as they walked through the city streets.

People were going about their days. Farmers walked with tools hanging over their shoulders; they seemed to be coming back from a midday meal and returning to the fields. Women were managing storefronts, working on some form of craft that could be done while they covered a counter.

The men were almost exclusively tucked away in the back room, making whatever was being sold.

While everyone worked, they seemed happy about what they managed. It was a very different experience from what Dar had experienced when he'd toiled through blue-collar jobs back on Earth. There was a lot of pride on their faces in what they built.

People stopped and talked as they worked. There was a sort of casualness about it all, as if they weren't scraping by or working with a manager cracking a whip. There was something simple and enviable about the environment of the city as it buzzed with both productivity and cheer.

Dar realized he had paused, staring at the cheerful laborers around him, lost in thoughts of his previous life. He shook his head, pushing them aside.

He wasn't ever going back. Granterra was his home now. He had people to protect and a little place carved out for his family. One day soon, he might even have the strength to make this world tremble.

Though it had only been a short time, his life back on Earth seemed a distant memory. His life was now in Granterra.

"Dar?" Neko poked him. "Are you okay?"

"Just thinking about things." He ruffled her ears. "So, did you really not get into any trouble when you went into town before?"

"None!" she declared with a finality. "Some men tried to be mean to Neko, but they regretted that."

"Yeah?" Dar asked. She hadn't shown back up at Tami's with the guard in tow, so he could only assume it had been minor. Either that, or she'd taken care of it thoroughly enough that there hadn't been a problem.

Neko's head bobbed, making her cat ears flop. "Neko is the best."

"Yes, you are."

Dar kept his head up as they descended the slope into what he'd call the docks. With the change, the sounds of the city shifted, and the smell of brine filled the air. Buildings shifted from stone to wood, and they had a strange tilt to them as they seemed to lean away from the bay. The side closest to the water swelled with moisture.

"Stay close." He pulled on Neko's hand.

"Not to worry. Neko is tough." She jabbed into the air.

The crowds thinned, yet the street was still crowded as bulky men hauled cargo or pushed carts laden with goods. As they rounded the corner and saw the docks, Dar spotted four large river boats and two ocean faring vessels tied up.

But, as they walked, Dar felt the hairs on the back of his neck stand up. Looking around, he spotted a group of four men slinking out of the alley. A scrappy man in the lead spun a dagger threateningly at Dar.

Blinking, Dar didn't know what to do for a moment. Was he supposed to be scared? A thug with a dagger would be like crushing an ant.

"It seems like you might be in the wrong part of town." Scrappy strode over, as if he was Dar's best friend patting him on the shoulder.

Dar looked past the man to assess the full group. There were two big meat heads and a man with an eyepatch. Fresh claw marks, like he'd gotten into a fight with a tiger recently, spanned eyepatch's right eye, peeking out from under the patch.

His left eye shook with fear, but he wasn't looking at Dar. No, he was looking at Neko pressed to his side.

The cat girl slipped out of Dar's arms and stalked forward. "Bad men get hurt."

"B-b-boss," Eye Patch stammered and tugged at Scrappy.

"Cut it out." Scrappy rolled his shoulder out of his grip and threateningly played with the dagger in his hand. "Where were we? Right, it seems you aren't from around here. Let me introduce you to a few of the rules down here. First, you need to pay the toll."

Dar looked at the man, completely baffled. Did they really think they were going to extort him? He noticed that everybody in the area was averting their eyes from them, clearly not wanting to get involved. Or maybe they were used to these thugs behaving this way. The fear in a few eyes told Dar that the men must have a nasty reputation.

But, for the life of him, Dar couldn't figure out why these men would be a threat. They didn't have any dao that he could tell.

Before Dar even responded, Neko stepped forward, pressing her face into Scrappy's. "Bad men should learn to mind their own business. Plus, Neko has no money for tolls."

The thug tried to lean away from Neko, but she caught him by the hair and hoisted him off his feet. Then she throttled his head into her knee as if he weighed only a few pounds.

His nose crunched into her knee and Scrappy went down, clutching his face.

The two brutes stepped forward, but Neko slipped through their guards. Her fingers became as sharp as claws as she tore into both of their chest. The attacks were deep enough that they both were suddenly far more concerned with stopping the bleeding than trying to grab Neko.

"You bitch." Scrappy got back to his feet, holding his nose.

"Boss. I was trying to tell you. That's HER." Eyepatch grabbed Scrappy and tried to stop him from doing anything else that was stupid.

Dar just watched, amused at the beating Neko delivered.

Neko paused in her attack and stared at Eyepatch. "Did you do what I told you to?"

"Yes. Yes, we did it. Everything is okay. Please leave us alone."

The cat girl turned to Dar as if asking for his opinion.

"Up to you Neko. I'll support whatever you do." Dar thought this would be a good learning experience for her. It seemed like she had successfully intimidated the local gang at the docks, regardless.

She calmed down and spoke carefully, "I will check to see if it is sufficient. If not, I'll find you. But for this, you need to pay me a toll." She held out her hand, very pleased with herself.

Eyepatch didn't hesitate and emptied his pocket of whatever coins he had before sticking his hands into Scrappy's pockets and getting additional coins from him. "That should be enough."

"Good." Neko closed her hands around the coins and shook them in her hand, making a noise. She paused, smiling at the jingling and doing it a few more times before her face returned to being serious as she looked back at them. "Go. You're boring."

They didn't need to be told a second time. The thugs fell over themselves to get away from Neko.

"What exactly did you ask them to do?" Dar asked as they continued their trip to Dane's boat.

"Huh?" Neko was busy shaking the coins in her palm, not paying attention to anything around her.

"Never mind." Dar pulled Neko close, spotting which of the boats was Dane's, although it wasn't what he'd expected.

Dane's boat was covered in small moving forms. As Dar got closer, he realized they were goats.

"Dar!" Dane saw him approach and came down the gangplank to greet him. The merchant's eyes flicked to Neko, who was still amusing herself, shaking the coins in her hand.

Dane eyed Neko warily. It seemed whatever encounter on the docks she'd had earlier had spread, but Dar's attention was on the goats.

"I thought Bellhaven was having a food crisis?" Dar asked.

"They are, but they are also having a land crisis. Livestock doesn't have enough room to graze, so it's butcher or sell them before they lose their value." Dane kept staring at Neko. “But I wasn’t the one that secured all these goats. They came from… some less than reputable men. Started showing up yesterday. I’m going to run out of room here soon.”

Dane’s eyes continued to look at Neko, who didn’t seem aware in the slightest.

It was everything Dar could do not to laugh as he got her attention by placing his hand on hers and stopping her from playing with the coins. He had a pretty solid theory of where those goats came from.

“Neko, did you make the bad men give you goats?”

“Good men give gifts. They were very bad, so they needed to give Neko lots of gifts to become good.” She nodded emphatically. “When we get back to Hearthway, will Neko get more milk with all these goats?”

“Yes, I think this will give us plenty of milk.”

Neko’s smile was too bright for him to even consider chastising her. She hadn’t done anything too terrible, but he hoped they had some townspeople who knew how to care for goats.

“I should thank you too.” Dane smiled. “It seems my time at the docks has become considerably easier as well.”

“Well, at least there’s some good that came out of it.” Dar ran a hand through his hair. “What do we owe you for the goats?”

But Dane shook his head. “They are your goats. I haven’t paid a chit for them. I’ll charge you for shipping them upriver, but that’s it. And it sounds like the lady has your coinage.” He held out his hand for payment.

Neko looked at Dane, aghast that he’d consider taking her toy.

“Pay up, Neko. Otherwise, the goats won’t make it to Hearthway.”

She frowned, her head going back and forth between her hand and the animals before seeming to come to a decision and passing the coins to Dane.

"Here. Take good care of my goats." She unceremoniously dumped her handful of coins in Dane's open palm.

"If you need more, I'm afraid you'll need to work it out with Sasha in either salt or coin," Dar explained as the merchant looked at the pittance of coins in his palm.

"Right, I'll do that." Dane shook his head, clearly trying not to laugh at the situation.

Chapter 15

After the surprise at the docks, Dar wandered around the nearby markets, managing to wrangle seeds for apples, oranges, as well as some plums. The citizens of Bellhaven didn't have a tremendous variety of fruits. He had hoped for some berries, but those were being sold as food and were under strict control, as the nobility worked to ration food.

The shortage hadn't hit yet. People were hungry, but not ravenous.

Dar decided not to push to claim any of their food. He was sure he could find some berry bushes to transfer into his inner world for Cherry. The seeds he had found would have to do for the moment. Looking around to make sure nobody was watching, he secretly sucked them into his inner world.

Neko's eyes were wide as she watched the seeds disappear into his navel. "Cherry will love them. She likes plants."

"Yes, she does," Dar chuckled. The bounce of his abdomen caused him to wince. He'd pushed his body about as far as it was going to go for the day.

"You should have stayed and rested," Neko chastised Dar.

"Sometimes resting is harder than doing things. Besides, we were able to check in on Dane. He wouldn't have been there tomorrow—something about having too many goats to deliver." He fixed Neko with a hard stare. "I'll let it slide because they deserved it, but don't force people to do things for you, Neko."

"Only bad people," Neko agreed.

Dar rubbed a hand into his face, trying to determine how to help her understand. "Neko, bad people won't stop being bad just because you punish them like that."

She paused, looking up at him. "I should have asked for more goats? That seemed like enough."

"No, that's not what I'm saying. Look at what they did after that. They still attacked us," Dar coached.

She put a hand over one of her eyes. "Not Patchy. He was being good when he saw me."

Dar held in his laugh. "Yes, Patchy was terrified of you. But that only made him good to you," he agreed, trying to drive home the lesson. "He hadn't become good to everyone else."

"As long as he is good to Neko and her family, then all is good. I can't be everywhere." Her final statement sounded like Samantha.

"That's a fine way to think, Neko. But, if we ever meet someone that is very bad, I need you to realize that they won't stop being bad. If them being bad would eventually cause problems for the family—"

Neko interrupted him, "Then I kill them. No one threatens my family." She made a terrifying grin that showed off her teeth.

Sometimes, when she was being cute, Dar forgot just how much of a predator Neko actually was. Maybe he didn't have to worry about people taking advantage of her.

He was starting to realize that she was astute at many things, despite her simple language and seemingly simple thought process. Her savageness and perceptiveness did a lot to overcome some of the language and cultural barriers.

He knew that, if something really did threaten the family, the predator in her would come out tenfold.

"There you are." Tami was waiting outside her home as the pair approached. "The prince is looking for you."

"Good or bad?" Dar wanted to know what he was walking into.

"Good. He wants to thank you for helping with the city's defenses today. Then, if you have time later, I think he wants to show you off and try to celebrate demons." Tami hesitated before continuing, "Also, Karn is over there."

"Ah. He's trying to make up to Karn quickly," Dar realized.

"Yeah, though, a fat load that will do him. Karn isn't going to change his mind, not with how beat up he looks. Everyone knows that you did that to him, so that's only made you more terrifying to the prince and his men," Tami continued.

Dar thought about clearing up any misconceptions, but then realized he didn't care. He was okay with them thinking he was terrifying—it might help protect his town.

"Okay, lead on. I'm not sure I want to be paraded around, but I'll go meet the prince." Dar pulled Neko along.

The cat girl frowned. "Dar is tired. Make sure he can sit."

"Of course," Tami agreed, turning heel and leading them in a different direction and into the city's daily court.

Dar had been there once before under the guise of a wizard. He didn't much like the politics of the human city and doubted he was going to appreciate it this time.

But this time, the guards at least looked at him with a measure of respect as they entered.

Rows of wooden pew-like benches dominated the room. The only reason he refused to call them pews is that it would then sound like they were worshiping the prince as he sat up front in a large throne managing the discussion.

Before the prince were a number of high-ranking officials in their own chairs rather than the wooden benches. Everyone seemed to have runners and helpers that flitted about the room, passing papers and jotting down what was said.

The prince looked up from a scroll in his hand. "If it isn't the hero of the day," he celebrated Dar's entrance. "A demon that went out and fought back a dozen trolls on his own."

Despite the prince's encouraging words, the rest of the men present didn't give Dar a warm welcome. Instead, they all seemed to stare at Dar as if they could bore holes in him with looks alone.

He should have known better than to expect them to receive him warmly. They coveted power too much.

"Come, sit. We'd love to hear your thoughts on several things. Karn, unfortunately, is in need of rest."

His words caused a ripple in court. It seemed that Karn's injuries were well known among these men, and now that the prince confirmed it, more of the members of court evaluated Dar with worried eyes.

"I too need some rest," Dar joked, trying to lighten the mood. "But, if you give me a chair, I'll do my best to keep my eyes open and participate."

The room stayed silent, apparently not finding it amusing as they waited to see the prince's reaction.

The prince let out a forced laugh, and the rest of the court joined him. "Come. Someone get this man and his companion a big chair."

A set of servants darted out of the room to do just that, returning in seconds with a heavy wooden chair for Dar. They put it before court, along with the other major nobility. From what Dar could tell, it was a sign of honor.

They had left to go grab a second chair, but Neko had other ideas, curling up in Dar's lap.

Her move caused a few of the men to cough politely, but Neko gave zero shits about them or their decorum. Dar decided she could rest where she wanted to. Stroking her back, he settled into the chair.

"Now that Darius Yigg is here, why don't you go on with the scouting report. We're all eager to hear what you saw today." The prince's tone was bitter as he spoke to Tami. Apparently, her being out of the city prior to an attack was not what the prince had planned.

"I've written out a detailed report for all of your scribes to copy and give you." Tami handed the scroll off to a man that came up to her as she held it out. "But, for brevity befitting the court's constraints, there are two masses of devils in the hills. What we are seeing with the trolls and the gremlins appears to be the losing side fleeing in search of food."

"Will they destroy each other?" a noble asked, a glimmer of hope in his voice.

"Unlikely that both will be wiped out. Both are continuing to produce devils, but it is highly likely that the insect types will win out and use the trolls as a food source to continue growing," Tami answered.

A noble raised his hand to get attention before speaking. "Is it something that the Cervus house can step forward and deal with?"

His question caused a small stir of agreements. They were more than happy to hand this problem off to another to deal with.

"My father is currently unaware of this problem. A boat left yesterday, heading for Kindrake. With it, we sent a missive and will send one on every boat leaving to ensure he gets the message, but that would be weeks away," Tami informed them.

Dar wondered why she didn't use it as an excuse to run up to Kindrake with her speed. But he figured that, no matter how fast she was, sending things via boat would always be much easier in terms of personal effort.

The court mulled over her information.

"Do we think it is likely that danger will come to Bellhaven before your father can get notice?" the prince asked.

"Given what I saw, the battle between the two sides in the hills could be resolved any day. The insects have a clear advantage, as well as more elite devils," Tami reported emotionlessly.

"Could we help the trolls?" a noble asked before he was heckled by his peers.

"Help the trolls?"

"A fucking idiot."

The prince knocked on the side of his throne to settle the court. "Not the worst idea I've heard. We could send a party to harry the insects, helping the trolls indirectly. However, I would not feel comfortable putting people in danger by attempting to give the trolls more direct aid."

The chuckles died down at the prince's suggestion.

"Who do we send?"

"The wizards of course," a noble shouted, slamming his desk. "It is their fault that we don't have spirits or demons to help us. Throw them at the devils and see if we can't kill two birds with one stone."

A wizard stood up, outraged. "We are not marching out there; that would lead to our deaths. And do not downplay your own part in what has occurred. The nobles riled up the rabble to throw out the spirits. Maybe they should be sent to fight."

Dar watched with a cold calculation as the nobles and wizards threw accusations back and forth. The two groups seemed to be competing for attention from the prince. Dar was sure they must have been on edge after Karn's declaration that he was withdrawing The White's protection.

Dar wasn't sure, but he had a feeling that there would be backlash from Kindrake over the withdrawal. Each group was likely trying to position the other to take the blame.

Seeing the discussion for what it was, Dar leaned back in his chair, done with the conversation. They weren't truly trying to solve the issue. They were posturing and trying to position themselves better. It was boring.

He far preferred it when people did something about a problem rather than talk about it.

The prince banged on his throne again, trying to restore order before he turned to Dar. "What do you think, Darius Yigg?"

It rankled Dar that the prince kept using his full name. But he also understood why the prince was doing it.

"I think you all have a very serious problem. The trolls and gremlins are stupid and blunt. To date, you have been defending against small war parties that fled the battle in the hills, and your forces have already become drained. If I had not been out there today, there would have been many more casualties."

He paused, enjoying the way the wizards and noblemen shifted uncomfortably at that fact before he continued. "The insects though? They are far more organized, and there are some that fly among them. I am concerned that they will come in a force large enough to overwhelm Bellhaven should they attack."

The prince kept his face neutral. "But certainly, something can be done."

Dar knew what he was asking. The prince wanted to know if he could fix their problem. The entire court was waiting for Dar to speak.

"As you can see"—he gestured to his bandages—"I'm still a little worse for wear after a scuffle this afternoon. I won't be doing anything today."

The prince gave him a placating smile. "As a citizen of Kindrake, you should take care of yourself, but also rise when the kingdom needs you."

Dar froze. The gall of the man to claim Dar had a duty to do anything for him.

"If my people and I were such honored members of this kingdom, then why were we run out of our homes? Fired upon by the city guard, with one of our most venerated members cut down?" It was everything Dar could do to say those words and not shout them.

He was minimally appeased by the fact that the prince looked uncomfortable at the questions. "Those were the actions of outlaws. You can't hold the kingdom accountable."

"I'd say the ruling nobles of the city damn well represent the kingdom. And I'd love to know what you have done since to punish those that took such actions, showing what is accepted by the kingdom." Dar couldn't help but let some anger seep into his voice.

He knew he couldn't let Bellhaven fall, but he could at least make these men uncomfortable and wring them for all they were worth. "If I went back to my village and asked my people to pick up arms for Bellhaven, they'd laugh their asses off. They would think it was a joke."

Watching the prince's face twitch was priceless. "There are often hard times when we must step up—" the prince started some flowery bullshit again.

Dar really wasn't willing to hear it. "I could kill this entire assembly and walk out of the city unscathed. Yet you dare demand things from me after what happened?"

"It was not a demand," the prince tried to reign in the situation, but he was also keenly aware of the danger Dar posed. His eyes flickered to Tami, looking for her support.

"Dar saved my life earlier. It would be poor form for me to interfere," Tami stated.

Dar smiled. "If I really am your only option, then we should begin negotiations, starting with reparations for what was done to me and my people. Otherwise, I'll not lift a finger," Dar stated his terms plainly.

"Oh. Yes, that can be done." The prince was keeping a calm mask on, but Dar could tell he was seething inside. But Dar had given him a viable option. The prince had things to bargain, and that was what he did all day. "We will discuss later."

Dar knew he would not be able to sit still after that outburst and stood to leave.

"Staff, please get Darius situated in a room, and make sure he's as comfortable as possible while I wrap up court," the prince called out.

Several attendants came to Dar immediately and directed him out of the hall and into another room designed for entertaining nobles. Large plush couches dominated the room with enough table space for food and drink.

"Please, wait here for Prince Gregor. He will not take long wrapping up court."

Dar wanted to tell the servant to get lost, but that was residual anger reserved for the prince. Berating a servant did nothing for him. "Fine. Bring me food and water."

Neko shook her head. "These people are stupid. Maybe Stupid Bear has the right approach."

"What's that?"

"Kill until you get your way. Much easier." Neko nodded.

"That wouldn't go over quite as well as you think," Tami said from behind them as she followed them in.

Dar let his eyes rove the deer demon as she opened one of the cabinets and pulled out a glass and a bottle of liquor. Tami was attractive. The way she sauntered in and made herself at home was far more interesting than how she'd meekly dealt with prior challenges.

"You seemed happy to take a few jabs at the prince."

She sighed as she poured herself a glass. "Small barbs that will amount to little more than me doing my duty poorly. Want one?"

"No thanks," Dar said.

"I'd like one." Neko stepped away from Dar to sniff at the alcohol. Her nose wrinkled, but she was undeterred.

Tami shot him a questioning look. Dar shrugged. Neko was an adult.

Neko returned to his side with a glass in hand, sipping it distastefully, but continuing none the less.

"Tami, are you under an oath here?" The thought had occurred to Dar earlier, when he was trying to figure out her actions and decisions. He'd been surprised she hadn't taken a stronger stance, given the treatment to her brother.

"Yes, well, under oath to my father. That is why I've asked permission to leave this post in my communication to him."

Dar went from thinking poorly of her to being sympathetic. Dao oaths were harsh things; it was no wonder she played within the political rules. She likely had no other choice.

"Shitty of your father to force that on you."

"It's not uncommon for demons and their kids. It is another way for demons to exert control. I assume you have oaths with Neko, for example." She said it calmly, but there was curiosity in her eyes.

"Neko is the best. Dar has never asked for an oath." Neko looked up at him with a brilliant smile.

"No. She isn't going to betray me. Why would I take away her independence?" Dar shrugged at the thought. It seemed abusive to him to put his family under oaths.

"Oh," Tami said, wide-eyed before looking down into her drink. "You really are very different from the other powerful demons I've met."

He shrugged. He was okay with that.

"Dar is the best." Neko took another heavy sip from her drink.

"I'm starting to see why," Tami humored Neko. "Your victory over Karn is already well known in the court. I think the prince will concede to whatever you ask for at this point. He has few options."

Dar leaned forward, looking at Tami. "What do you think I should ask for, then?"

"I don't know... things for your village, noble status?" She struggled to come up with a solid idea.

Dar leaned back, thinking it over. This was a good opportunity to ask for whatever he needed, but he was still trying to piece together what that was. There was so much that Hearthway could use, but was asking for material things really the best option?

They could make or craft many things. It likely wouldn't be long before whatever he asked for would be something they could have had, anyway. There was no doubt in Dar's mind that Hearthway was going to expand rapidly next year.

No, what Dar needed was to ensure the safety and expansion of Hearthway.

Chapter 16

Before Dar could strategize much around what to negotiate for with the prince, the man himself stormed in and plopped himself down on the couch opposite of Dar.

He didn't say a word, simply staring at Dar as servants came in and deposited a number of platters on the table between them.

The servants all shuffled out, and as soon as the door closed, the prince jumped on the food like a starving animal. "You have no idea how hungry I was up there. But it isn't proper to eat during court."

"Looks like pretty fucking hungry," Dar said dryly as he took a block of cheese and scooted a pile of crackers onto a plate for himself before the prince got everything.

Neko watched Dar and mimicked him, shoving what she wanted onto a plate and taking it with her as she leaned back on the couch.

The prince resurfaced from stuffing his face after just a minute. "Can't waste time or food. Too much to do and too little food. So, what do you want in return for clearing out the devils?"

"I don't think you realize how monumental of a task it is to actually clear them out," Dar started. "The chances I go in there and clear them out in one go is impossible."

Tami jumped in. "What he's saying is true. Even my father wouldn't be able to do such a thing."

"Then what are you proposing?" The prince was suddenly far less cordial.

"I'm uniquely qualified to go in and remove the insect devils' ability to continue to amass an army. It will also cut off the increase in trolls and gremlins. My hope is that those two things will create a situation in which the two can fight and dwindle each other down."

"You said the insects were going to win." The prince pointed with a sausage, seeming to give up all semblance of etiquette.

"They will win because they have a queen that is able to breed endlessly," Tami said; Dar noticed that she tried to explain the issue without needing to talk about the Mo. "Darius believes he can stop that, and though I've never heard of what he claims he can do, he has certain credentials that I would be very hesitant to doubt."

The prince leaned forward, interested once again. "So you propose being able to cut off their ability to continue to amass an army?"

"Yes. Once I cut off that ability, the trolls and insects that are still alive will still both need the same scarce resources. They should still fight. The only difference is that their losses won't recover, or at least not anywhere near the extent they are recovering today." Dar put forward his idea. There was no way in hell he was going to fight both armies of devils at the same time.

Although Dar wasn't sure if he'd be able to after he killed the Mo and absorbed its power, he could hope. He could only assume he'd get another nice boost of power and rapidly grow stronger. By the time the devils settled down from their in-fighting, he might be in a position to help further.

"And what do you want for this?" the prince asked. "Would you like what you sent your maid for previously?"

Dar was at least thankful he had the tact to not say that he'd sent for Tami's brother's dao book in front of her. "No. This is worth far more than that. What I want is simple. I want my village, Hearthway, to not be considered part of Kindrake. You have no stake in it, so the kingdom can expect nothing of us beyond trade, as you would a foreign kingdom."

The prince choked on the food he'd been eating. "I could make you Duke of Bellhaven if you wanted. Why would you want to be separate from Kindrake?"

"Why be a duke under the thumb of your people? No, I want Hearthway to be officially separate. In return for me doing this, you'll recognize my family as the rulers of the kingdom." Dar wasn't going to budge. He knew his terms, and he knew the prince was in a difficult position.

"Absolutely not." The prince put down the food and crossed his arms.

Tami looked confused. "Why is it a problem?" she tried to help Dar's cause.

"Because that is a lot of land." The prince shook his head. "Plus, the location... no."

"We will sign and certify that we won't interrupt trade along the Bell River. I know how important a trade route is for Kindrake," Dar tried to reassure him.

That made the prince a little happier, but he still waffled his head back and forth in thought. "No, still can't. I could demand that you and your village deal with this problem."

Dar stood, nearly knocking over the table, and grabbed the prince by his lapel, lifting him up into the air. "You could. And I could kill you. But I don't because that's not what reasonable people do." Dar let that sink in, placing the man back on the floor. "If you demand we serve the kingdom, then we'll rebel. One hundred angry demons and spirits raiding up and down the Bell River, maybe even sacking the farming villages outside Kindrake itself. I'm sure that would go over wonderfully come spring, don't you think?"

Dar knew Kindrake couldn't afford to split their focus or have a weaker harvest come spring.

The prince's face was red with fury. "I'll draft something up acknowledging your… Hearthway as a kingdom outside Kindrake. But you've made enemies today."

"I don't think you can play politics without making enemies. While I may not be your favorite, you now understand me as your equal." Dar smiled, letting go of the prince.

"You must swear oaths to complete the task and to the provisions of not touching trade on the Bell River." The prince fell back to the couch as he talked.

"No." Dar wasn't about to tangle himself up in any of their oaths. "No king would swear such oaths to another. Are you saying that Kindrake is concerned about our little village?"

That rankled the prince. "Then you have to take Tami with you. She'll certify that the job is done. You ask for too much; I at least must have absolute confidence that the job is complete."

Dar looked over at Tami. "Agreed, as long as you clear her of any existing oaths to you before we head out."

The prince's mouth flopped like a fish before he spat out, "Fine."

He knew the prince had secondary plans, maybe even to get them both killed to avoid giving away a chunk of the kingdom. He wasn't about to go into the belly of the beast with someone under oath to him.

Tami gave Dar a concerned look. She likely thought he'd gotten himself into waters deeper than he could handle. But, at this point, it was the clearest way to protect Hearthway. Being separate from Kindrake and untangling themselves from the war that was coming in the spring was the best option.

Dar had thought about becoming something within Kindrake and elevating himself to a noble house, but what did that really do? He would likely waste his time arguing with people who wouldn't change their minds or listen to him, anyway.

Dar felt confident in the path he'd chosen. They'd disentangle themselves from Kindrake while still making sure bigger threats to the area were removed.

"Tami, you are dismissed of any oaths from me," the prince stated. "You'll be back here tomorrow morning to pick up the necessary documents, and I expect them to stay in your possession until he completes the task."

"Understood." Tami nodded.

"As for you." The prince glared at Dar. "You'll leave tomorrow and deal with this problem as soon as possible."

Dar didn't like that the prince was once again trying to issue orders towards him. "I was already planning on heading out tomorrow. This city doesn't exactly give me the warm fuzzies."

The prince grumbled and stood. "I have things to work on. See yourselves out." Without bothering to give Dar any more attention, he stormed out.

"He did not like that," Neko said as soon as they were alone.

"You think?" Tami rolled her eyes. "He was positively livid."

Dar sighed. "That's just his type. They can loan you a piece of anything, but to take something from them... you might as well be taking a pound of flesh."

"Well, it seems you got what you wanted," Tami added.

Dar grinned from ear to ear. "That I did. I also protected my village from being involved in a war next spring."

Surprise turned into a thoughtful smile on Tami's lips. "Was that what you were trying to accomplish with that?"

"No, at least not just that. What I wanted was independence. If it wasn't this war, it would be a famine, or another war. We've been able to live quietly while the devils kept everybody holed up in cities, but when we remove the problem, Bellhaven is going to stretch back out its influence."

Dar grabbed his plate, working to finish his food so that he could get back.

"Was it wise to pick him up? I think you bruised his ego, and possibly his neck." Tami dug into the leafy snack she'd picked out for herself.

"Oh, that was a terrible idea. But it felt good, and I think he'll have his hands too busy to focus on me. If push comes to shove, I can always follow through on my own threat, but I'd just come down to Bellhaven and sack it," Dar laughed. "If Frost's Fang isn't going to protect him, I could easily lead my village down here through the gates and strip the nobles from the city."

Tami's face drained of blood at his statement.

Neko, however, had a feral grin. "Then we'd have ALL the goats!"

"Yes, then we'd have all the goats we could ever want. We could make you a bath out of their milk."

The cat girl's eyes were so wide that they threatened to pop out. "Too bad that would make me a bad Neko."

"Yes, it would." Dar patted her on the shoulder, relieved that she'd come to that conclusion on her own.

Tami shook her head in disbelief at the conversation before her. "I'll be ready tomorrow at dawn. The hills are going to be a whole day's walk for you."

"Then I better go get rested." Dar pushed off the couch, and Neko rose with him, never leaving his side. "I'll see you back at your place, Tami."

He didn't wait for her to finish, heading out on his own. It was clear to him that Tami needed some time to think.

And Dar needed to settle in for the night, rest up while he continued cultivating the bright dao. Unlike the others, he had no dao companionship connection to this dao, nor was the little dao tree connected to it. This one was going to take longer than the others, so he couldn't waste any time.

He went straight back to the room in Tami's home and made himself comfortable, settling down into meditation.

***

"Milord, it is time to get up." Amber shook Dar gently from his sleep.

He had spent a few hours trying to carve the dao of bright into his body, but once again, he had been met with mixed success. Learning a new dao without the benefit of a dao companion or the little dao tree was difficult.

"I'm up," Dar groaned, pushing off the bed and letting his covers fall off of him. Neko was curled up against his side.

Neko stretched out, closing and opening her hands as she yawned. "Too early."

"If you'd like to go to my inner world now, then you can keep sleeping."

Neko cracked an eye and gave him a smile before nuzzling up against him. "Dar is the best."

He chuckled, bringing her into his inner world. He needed to get the maids in there as well. Now that they had brought food with them, they'd be able to survive for several days. And, even if they hadn't, soon some of the trees that Cherry was nurturing might even bear fruit.

He might even have his own little ecosystem soon.

"Food, milord. You need to get going soon." Marcie pushed a plate into his hand.

"Thank you, both. I don't know what I'd do without you two."

They both beamed at his praise. Dar was resistant to having the two girls wait on him, but he had to admit, it was pretty comfortable.

"Milord. We have our supplies." Amber pulled an overstuffed sack from the corner of the room over, and Dar brought it into his inner world.

But then she surprised him, bringing in two more baskets and another more reasonably full sack.

"How long are you guys planning to be in there?" he asked.

"We thought it best to not only prepare for this time, but future times as well."

Dar hoped they wouldn't be cooped up in his inner world that much, but it made sense. "Sounds good. Does that mean you are ready to join Neko?"

"Yes, milord." Amber bowed and held Marcie's hand before he drew them into his inner world.

Right after they entered, there was a knock on his door.

"Come in," he called.

Tami cracked the door and peered inside. "I thought you were talking to someone." She frowned. "Where are the maids?"

"They come and go." He shrugged.

Her eyes wandered to the bedsheet draped over his waist. "Maybe I should come back."

Dar pulled back the sheet, and she averted her eyes before looking back and seeing that he was wearing pants. He smiled, enjoying messing with her.

"Let me eat this meal and then get a shirt on. I'll be ready to go with you here shortly. How was the prince after I left?"

"Irate," Tami sighed, taking a seat. "He made the documents. I have them on the table."

"Did you look them over? Any problems?"

"None. He did as you asked, if minimally. The royal family giving up a piece of their kingdom, no matter how small, is a big move. Are you sure this is what you wanted? You have made an enemy out of the prince. He will look like a fool to his father," she cautioned him.

Dar shrugged. "It doesn't matter. The prince isn't the kind of friend I want. And I was bound to defy an order sooner or later. With this, I'll be able to protect Hearthway."

"You go to great lengths for them." Tami sounded almost a little jealous.

"Of course. I'd go to the ends of the world for my family," Dar said without hesitation.

Focusing back on his food, Dar devoured it with a gusto. He barely even tasted it as he gobbled it down. His shirt was wrinkled, but it wasn't like a nicely pressed shirt saved him from a devil's attack. He didn't much care how he looked while he was in the forest.

"All done. Let's head out." Dar looked around the room, making sure that all of his belongings were safely transported into his inner world.

"Don't you need... things?" Tami looked back over his shoulder into his room with a frown.

"They come and go," he chuckled, enjoying not satisfying her curiosity.

"Sure," Tami said, confused. She grabbed her bag and a cylindrical metal tube that no doubt contained the documents that the prince had prepared.

Dar took it with thanks and stored it in his inner world the first second Tami's back was turned. He knew she was supposed to keep it until the job was done, but he'd rather have it safely tucked away.

It was risky, potentially revealing his inner world, but he was also becoming less cautious as he grew stronger. It would soon be hard for others to tear him down without a fight.

He had two greater dao, and he was closing in on his third. With the third, he'd have the ability to form a grand dao. But he couldn't dwell on that too much. That would take some time, and the next step was to deal with the Mo.

Tami turned back around, noticing that the canister was gone. "Where'd it go?" She looked at his hands.

"Things come and go a lot around me." Dar smiled. "It's safe though."

She frowned but decided not to press for answers. Instead, she belted on her own pack and hung a few filled water skins from her shoulder before thinking better of it.

"Do you think you could make these water skins go and come back when we need them?" She arched an eyebrow.

"Let me see." He took them and held them in his hand for a moment. Tami wasn't turning back around.

Dar decided to wait, slinging them over his shoulder. "Are we going?"

"What about the water skins?"

"I'll carry them for now." He smiled back and as she went to open the door, he made them disappear into his inner world. She whipped back around, her eyes growing wide as they couldn't find the skins.

"How?"

"Dunno," Dar played dumb. "Things just come and go."

Tami snorted. "Fine, keep your secrets. We have a full day's trip ahead of us, and it won't be easy. I hope you are feeling better than yesterday."

He knew she wouldn't believe it, but he was feeling much better. Not quite a hundred percent, but above ninety. With the time it would take them to reach their destination, he had confidence he'd be fully healed.

"Have any more secrets I should know about?" Tami pressed as they walked out of her home and down the street.

"Not sure," Dar said honestly. "But I might still have a few more surprises. Hopefully, we won't need them."

Tami waved to the guards as they approached the wall. Dar always braced when coming and going from the city, expecting trouble, but the guards waved them through without fanfare.

Tami eyed him. "Just don't surprise me too much. Now, are you up for a run?"

Dar looked out of the city gates toward the flat plane. It looked like the forest had been cut back in that area. "Yeah. Might as well speed this up if we can. At least until we get to the forest, I can keep jogging."

Dar knew he had the strength and the power to do many things in this world, but the stamina to run for hours? That just might test his limits. Although, he wouldn't know until he tried.

Chapter 17

Tami stopped running midafternoon when they were well into the forest. "You doing okay?"

Dar leaned against a tree, panting. "Yeah." He held one of the water skins in his hands, already tipping it back and taking a heavy swig. "I'm not exactly the long-distance running type."

"Couldn't tell." Tami smirked. Her sleek form was covered in a healthy sheen of sweat, but she didn't even look tired.

"Let's take a break." He held out her water skin to her before he drank it all.

Tami looked at the waterskin and hefted it several times. "How is this staying full? Does water also come and go around you?"

Dar hadn't even realized it, but the maids must have been refilling the waterskin every time it went back into his inner world. The thought made him grin.

She took a small sip, swishing it around in her mouth before swallowing. "In the woods, we better slow down, anyway. Wouldn't want to risk tripping and ending up with an injured ankle out here."

Dar looked at the leaf-covered ground. She was right. It would be easy to hide a hole or a root and lose their footing. And he wasn't keen on continuing to run, anyway.

It wasn't quite a break, but he could handle walking.

"Alright, let's keep going." Dar pushed off the tree, taking the water skin and pulling it into his inner world the moment Tami wasn't looking.

She didn't even blink when she realized it was gone.

"We'll keep going through these woods for the afternoon. I'm guessing that, a little before night, we'll hit the ravine, but once we cross that, we are officially into the hills. At that point, we will start to see devils regularly," Tami clarified their route.

Dar internalized what she'd said. It also meant that these woods were relatively safe. "So you've explained that your family works for Kindrake, but what do you get out of all of this?"

"What do I get?" she asked, confused.

"Yeah. Do you get paid? Is there some value in dao that your father provides in return?" Dar tried to understand more about his traveling companion.

Tami blinked at his question. It was like she'd never thought about it. "My family has money. I have plenty and am paid. But I… uh…" She struggled to put words to her answer.

Dar couldn't believe it. "You have no idea why you keep doing this, do you? It's just what you've always done. When did you start working for the Kindrake royalty?"

"When I was five," she said, her eyes falling to the ground. "I've worked for my father and for the Kindrake royalty since I was five."

Knowing that she would be far older than she looked, Dar asked the next obvious question. "And how old are you?"

"One hundred and sixteen," Tami said.

He couldn't help himself. He let out a slow whistle. "One hundred and eleven years working the same gig. To me, that sounds like you're a masochist."

"I am not a masochist," she grumbled.

"No, of course not. At least not literally. It just sounds like torture to keep at the same job for that long, though I'm sure the complications of the royal family keep it interesting." Dar couldn't figure out how she wouldn't be bored or wanting something more after a hundred years.

"Well, what have you done with your grand life?" she asked defensively.

Dar shrugged. "Helped those in need. Worked a large number of odd jobs, moved about. Then recently helped a hundred refugees settle in the woods and find their own purpose. You know, build something for ourselves."

"I do plenty for myself."

"Uh huh," Dar made a noncommittal grunt. "I'm sure. When was the last time you just went away on a trip somewhere for fun?"

She stared at him like a deer in headlights. "For fun?"

"You know, go into the woods just to get away from it all, or maybe go find some nice beach and soak in the sun?"

He would have thought he had horns growing out of his head by the way she stared at him. "Never?"

"Damn shame. You aren't living, just working," Dar said. She might be a greater demon with three dao, but she wasn't living. Not as far as Dar was concerned. "Maybe you should do that after we are done here. Just go away, get some time to yourself and think about what makes you happy."

"What makes you happy?" she asked.

"Family," Dar said without a moment's hesitation. "My dao companions, and maybe one day my kids. If I didn't have them, I'd go fishing."

"Fishing? For food?" she asked, trying to understand what Dar meant.

"No, not really for food. I might save one and grill it up, but just to sit there and relax. I'd maybe have a drink by the water, listen to the calming sounds of nature, and just watch the world go by. Let the river and the wind rinse away my thoughts and let the ripples settle." Dar thought back to his past, when he'd take a week off of work and go fishing with a six-pack and a fishing pole that didn't quite work.

But it wasn't actually about catching the fish. There was something about waiting that just made everything else wash away. He'd catch a few fish, but his line would often snag before he reeled it all the way in. He'd have to use it like a king pole to get the fish out.

"You are a very odd demon," Tami said at last. "But I think maybe I'll consider it. I am... tired."

She looked down and sagged. For the first time, it felt like Dar was getting a chance to see the real Tami.

She followed orders. All she did was stay with the herd and do as she was told. And she did that well. But, as a result, she wasn't really her own person when she was around those with authority. Here in the wild, Dar was starting to see inside that shell.

She was vulnerable and confused. Tami needed to figure out who she wanted to be.

"Sorry to hear that, Bambi. I think some time off on your own would do wonders. Just breathe and feel, don't try to think. Let it all come to you," he tried to offer what advice he could, but she'd have to do the heavy mental lifting herself.

"Bambi?" she asked.

"A cute deer from an endearing story where I come from," he explained.

"I am not a deer."

Dar poked the small rack of antlers coming out of her head. "You look like you came from reindeer."

She tossed his hand with a jerk of her head. "I'm a demon, born a demon. My father was once a deer, but not me."

Apparently, it was a sensitive topic.

Dar held up his hands in surrender. "I retract my statement about being a deer. Still, I think Bambi is a great name."

"Well, it isn't my name." She stomped her feet as she walked.

Dar smiled, pleased she was finally showing some more personality.

"Fine. I'm just going to enjoy this walk through the woods." Dar tangled his fingers together and rested them behind his head as he walked. "It is a nice crisp day on the edge of winter. I wonder if it'll snow soon," he chatted idly as they walked.

Tami stopped talking to him; he had a feeling that, after their discussion, she had a few things she wanted to think about.

***

Dar and Tami continued their trek with ease until they crossed the ravine.

"We have already made good time. Do you want to stop here for the night?" Tami asked.

Dar looked at the hills looming ahead, and the sun hanging low in the sky. "I'm fine. Doing this in the dark might actually be best." He knew that his dao of shadows would help him see through the night.

Dar could already see signs of combat past it into the hills. Small trees lay shattered on the ground, and bushes were more often trampled than healthy. It looked like both sides in the war between the two devil species were causing rampant destruction.

"From this point on, let's try to stay hidden." Dar drew on his dao of concealment.

But the second he did, Tami let out a shout and her eyes went wide. "That's my dao."

Dar paused, realizing she'd only given it to him a day ago, but it was too late to hide it. So he let a satisfied smile spread across his face. He could see the question in her eyes, but they didn't have the time to go through it, and Dar still wasn't positive how much information he was comfortable sharing with Tami.

"Not now."

"But..." Tami clearly wanted to talk. Apparently, she could ignore that things seemed to come and go, but that he had learned her dao in a day was just too much.

Dar continued forward, keeping himself in the shadows as best he could.

The gibbering of gremlins sounded in front of them, and he put a finger to his lips as they crept around the devils. The gremlins were all crouched around something, pulling flesh off of it and feasting. Dar wasn't particularly interested in finding out what they were eating.

But, as the sun crept lower, and the shadows extended, Dar realized his shadow was stretching almost all the way to the goblins. With a flick of thought, his shadow scythed through the weak devils, killing them instantly.

"I thought we wanted them to weaken each other," Tami whispered.

"Sure, I won't take all of them down. But I'm not going to miss an opportunity to kill a few if we have it without giving ourselves away," Dar explained, creeping further through the hills. "And be quiet."

The demon rolled her eyes but followed him as they wound their way around the hills rather than crest them. The top of the hills would have given him a full view of the area, but it also exposed him. Dar knew that he was going deeper into devil territory than he ever had. Stealth was much more critical.

It didn't take long before they walked past what looked like an intense battle between the two sides. Fresh corpses of trolls and mantis devils dotted the woods. Not wanting to pass up the opportunity, Dar deposited them into his inner world as they went.

He found it amusing to do it when Tami's back was turned, but she'd clearly figured out he had some way to store everything he took.

"Why are you collecting them?" Tami asked. She didn't seem disgusted, only curious.

"Denying the devils here anymore food," Dar told a half-truth.

Taking these corpses would likely continue to restrict their food supply, but he suspected the devils had plenty of food. And, if they ran short, they would just expand out for more food if needed, like the ettercaps. These devils were voracious, and in most ecosystems, they were the apex predator.

Tami didn't comment on his reasoning, staying low and peering through the darkness while he worked.

Buzzing filled the air, causing Dar to duck low next to Tami as he tried to make out what was coming through the darkness. A troop of flying mantis devils flew through the air above them, like they were on some sort of scouting mission.

Wrapping his dao of concealment tightly around him, Dar waited for them to pass.

"They are more active than last time," Tami commented as they started moving again.

"There wasn't that sort of patrol before?"

"Not that I encountered. And I didn't see graveyards like the battle scene we just passed. It looks like the fight has escalated in just the day since I was last here."

Dar shrugged. It was in their plan for the devils to kill each other. "Fine by me."

As they wrapped around yet another hill, the landscape opened up, and a deep depression nestled itself among the hills.

One look was all it took for Dar to realize that it was their target. Insect type devils moved in and out of a massive hole in the side of the hill; the place was a hive of activity.

"You didn't tell me it was underground," Dar hissed, his initial plan becoming much more complicated.

"I thought that was a given," Tami replied dryly.

Dar shook his head, motioning for them to drop it. There was no use arguing about it at that point. He'd have to figure out what to do.

He called on his dao of granite, wondering if they might get lucky, but it was quiet. There might be some of the stone deep underground, but none was within his reach at the moment, blocking out any shortcuts.

A mantis poked its head out near Dar and Tami, startling the duo.

Tami's sword flashed out, severing its head immediately. Dar then sucked its body into his inner world before it hit the ground and made a noise.

"Okay, so we need to push into there if that is where the queen is?" Dar hoped he was wrong.

"It is, but she isn't too deep underground," Tami replied.

Dar smiled, glad for at least that bit of good news.

Leading the way, Dar wound around the hive until they reached the hill. Then they slipped around the edge of the opening, plunging themselves into near total darkness.

Reaching out with his dao of shadows, Dar could see perfectly in the darkness and probed along the walls, looking ahead. It was all one enormous shadow, and his dao stretched far down here as it was all connected. So he used it to understand the structure of the hive.

The hive seemed to wind in a downward direction, with other passages splitting off as it went. But only one direction was as big as the entrance; Dar assumed that was the queen's path through the hill.

Other weaker devils were working like drones, seeming to be tasked with expanding the hive and cutting it deeper into the earth. They each had a task, some carrying debris to the surface and some digging through the soil with clawed hands.

The mantis devils seemed primarily to be outside the hive, ranging the hills for more prey. Within the hive, Dar spotted large, bulky beetle-type devils roaming the passages, helping the drones move large stones.

Tami tapped his shoulder and urgently pointed down the main passage. He seconded her feelings of urgency. He did not want to get caught down in the hole with all the devils around them.

Stopping his scouting, Dar moved as she'd indicated, wrapping them both in shadowy darkness to avoid the eyes of these devils. As they moved, Dar paused, pushing Tami into the side wall of the tunnel as a group of three beetles pushed out a large boulder that would have given them away.

As the beetles passed by, Dar was able to sense their dao. They were all greater devils.

Grabbing Tami's hand, he pulled her deeper into the tunnels, winding down. With his dao of shadow, he was better equipped to lead them through the dark.

As they reached the center of the colony, they found a massive chamber, one that Dar was wary of probing with his shadows. While the other devils might not detect his use of dao, he had no idea how powerful this queen was and if she would be sensitive enough to feel his dao.

As they creeped closer, Dar spotted a pile that caught his interest.

Corpses were stacked on top of each other, like a food store in the middle of the colony. Several worker devils were next to it, pulling down a body and devouring it.

Dar thought about his options before making a decision. It was likely he would flee when they were done here. If he could do this quietly, he could take these for his dao tree now.

He pivoted to the chamber and unleashed his shadow dao once again, cutting the workers down before drawing them and the mound of corpses into his inner world.

Taking another step, he quickly scanned for any threat as a result of his actions. As he searched using his shadow dao, he realized that the room they were in was not the only one.

"What are you doing?" Tami hissed from her location, crouched at the entrance. Another dead drone was at her feet. "We need to get in and get this done before we are noticed. I didn't sign up to become bug food."

"Calm down." Dar finished and came back over to pick up the drone she'd killed. "They haven't noticed us yet."

"Yet," she emphasized. "They will realize something is wrong."

Dar thought she was giving the devils more credit than they deserved. So far, he hadn't found one that was intelligent enough to rub two brain cells together if it wasn't about killing and eating. He figured the creatures operated largely on instincts.

"Let's keep going." Dar moved towards another of the food stores, but Tami grabbed his arm.

"This way."

Dar was going to object, but then he felt a beetle devil shift towards them.

He pulled her close and clamped his hand over her mouth. She was shocked and about to fight back, but then realization dawned on her, and she froze.

The beetle devil wandered their way. It was a large creature, another head taller than Dar, even when it wasn't standing up straight. Its body was supported by two sets of legs, either for heavy work or for stability given their large, shelled backs.

Dar had no doubt that thing could wrestle a troll, and he wondered if their chitinous back would open up into a pair of wings.

On the back of the devil's head was the start of a large, barbed horn that wrapped around to protrude where its nose should have been. It chittered as it probed the food store entrance.

Dar was close enough to see the sharp chitinous fangs in front of its mouth.

The devil checked the food store, pausing in confusion and looking around. The moment it realized that everything was missing, it screeched.

Acting quickly as it opened its mouth, Dar wrapped the room in shadows and used the dao of quiet to prevent its warning cry from getting out of the chamber.

Dar tried to silence it completely, using his dao of shadow to stab at the devil, but its thick armor made the shadow bounce off its side.

Tami tried to back him up, using her speed to reach the devil quickly. Unfortunately, her sword had the same effect as the shadows. The devil's armor was strong.

Dar had avoided pulling out his weapons in front of Tami, but they didn't have time to be indecisive.

Pulling the Black Knight's axe from his inner world, Dar charged the creature. Swinging in a high, overhand arc, he chopped at the beetle.

Even with the unnaturally sharp blade, Dar's weapon only buried itself a foot into the creature.

The beetle jumped back at Dar's attack, its back exploding in a flurry of wings. The devil shot back forward with a speed that surprised Dar.

Dar barely managed to grab the horn before it gored him, wrestling with the beetle to keep its sharp mouth away from him.

"Tami, use the axe." Dar had dropped it to hold on to the beetle.

The deer demon was there in an instant. She grabbed it and jerked, but it didn't move. "What is this made of?"

The beetle tried to throw him to the side and nearly succeeded.

He didn't have time for this. "You can do it," he encouraged her.

Veins popped out of Tami's arms as she raised the pitch-black axe high into the air before hammering it down on the beetle's back.

The devil squirmed and tried to roll away from Dar to deal with Tami, but Dar held its horn tight, preventing it from moving.

The first few hacks, the beetle grew more and more agitated, but soon it slowed down with each swing. It died slowly as Tami whacked it to death, severing it in half.

"Can we finish this up now?" she huffed, leaning on the axe.

Dar took his axe back from her and sucked it and the beetle into his inner world. "Yeah. Let's get out of here. That thing... was too dangerous."

"That was too fucking close." Tami gave him a small glare, clearly blaming him as she picked her sword up off the ground and sank it into the sheath at her hip. "Let's get this done."

CHAPTER 18

Dar nodded, also wanting to get through the job quickly. As tempting as the other food stores might be, they needed to finish this and get out of the underground hive. And removing other food stores might send up an alert even faster.

Ducking out of the storeroom and following the queen's tunnel to the center of the hive, they passed dozens of devils. As quickly and quietly as they could, they both used the dao of concealment to hide themselves.

The drones completely ignored them, but more than one beetle paused as they passed.

Each time, Dar could feel sweat beading on his face.

When they reached the central cavern, Dar paused, letting a beetle drag in two troll corpses. It was only then that Dar realized what was inside.

The entire wall of the cavern was lined with pulsing sacks of more devils. There were larva-like creatures growing inside.

He shuddered. There were so many. How quickly would a mass of devils like this grow?

The beetle stopped in the center of the room, tossing down the two corpses.

A massive, squishy form shifted, and a delicate female form attached to it picked up the two corpses effortlessly. It started tearing them apart, devouring the two trolls swiftly. The squishy form pulsed behind the queen as it gurgled and spat out another small egg. She carefully picked up and placed it against the wall before regurgitating more gunk to keep it in place.

There, where she had just stuck another soon to be larva, was a giant embedded in the wall. It was covered with gunk and more than a few larval sacks as it slumped forward. Dar realized what he was looking at was the Mo. He could feel its power radiate from it even as it hovered at the edge of death's door.

The queen continued her work on the giant, tearing off much smaller pieces of flesh, seeming to have no issue tearing through the stony exterior. And after the piece was ripped off, its body healed before his eyes.

Dar cringed at the torture. A chill traveled up his spine as he watched, but he didn't dare shiver. He was worried the motion would draw attention.

Tami swallowed loudly beside him, but thankfully he had kept them both wrapped in shadows and could prevent the sound from escaping.

"I didn't come into this room before. We have to destroy this," she said.

"No way. We stop them from using that Mo to feed and get out of here. Can you not feel that devil's strength?" Dar could. The queen was clearly a grand devil, one that was giving off similar levels of strength to Karn.

Dar had been able to beat Karn, but that was when they had limited themselves to only lesser dao. She had an entire army around her; hundreds of those beetle devils would descend upon them if they tried to do anything. Dar was confident, but he wasn't stupid. There was no way he could take on that many.

"Do you think it sleeps? How are we supposed to get to the Mo?" Tami argued.

The heavy fleshy segment of the queen was firmly planted in the dirt, but there was a deep furrow around the outside of the room, indicating she still moved around. The fleshy segment continued to pulse, squirting out yet another larval pod.

Dar realized whatever she was using to fix them to the wall also provided their nutrients. She likely would have to travel around the room, refreshing the other larva at some point.

"For now, we wait. Once she moves away from the Mo, we take our chance." Dar stepped into the room and did his best to stay hidden.

But Tami had other ideas. Her sword lashed along the wall, cutting into the larva and destroying them.

"Stop that."

"You have the dao of quiet and concealment. Keep me hidden. If we let these live, Kindrake is doomed." She slashed again, cutting another handful of larvae.

Dar ground his teeth but did as she asked, keeping them quiet and concealed while the queen had her focus elsewhere. He knew that this wouldn't go unnoticed for long, limiting their time, but he understood why Tami did it. The sheer mass of devils in the space was overwhelming.

He kept watch, nervous the queen would somehow sense what Tami was doing and whirl around to attack. But the devil didn't; it continued to focus on eating and birthing more devils.

"Tami. There are too many." Dar pulled her away as the queen finally moved, taking several steps away from the Mo and revealing more of the giant to them.

It was torn open at the gut, its eyes closed and head bowed.

Dar stepped, moving the opposite direction from the queen, who was circling the chamber. Seeing his opening, Dar rushed to the Mo.

He had killed a Mo once before, but the tree had also come in his moment of desperation. This time, he hoped he'd be able to do it on his own. He remembered the moment the tree had manifested in the world, coming to absorb the Mo. It had been a feeling he'd never forget, and he focused on that feeling.

Tami started to speak, but he motioned for her to stay quiet. He needed to focus.

Focusing back on the feeling when the tree had led, Dar began pulling the little dao tree out of his inner world. It moved slowly at first, but as Dar worked to adjust his process slightly, it flowed more freely. Soon, it popped into being right next to the dying Mo.

The tree barely fit into the chamber floating before the Mo. Cherry swung down from the green canopy to keep an eye on the situation.

The Mo looked up, feeling the presence of the dao tree. Exhaustion spread across its face, and as it took in the dao tree, a flitter of hope shone in its eyes.

It looked at Dar and gave a nod, clearly exhausted from the constant torture. Dar paused for only a moment. It felt different from when he'd taken the other Mo's life. That Mo had been trying to kill him. This one was asking for a mercy kill.

He gave a small nod back before moving quickly. He knew they didn't have much time. Sending a thought to the little dao tree, it plunged its roots into the Mo, the Mo groaning and squirming at the intrusion but not fighting against it. Instead, it sounded like relief.

Unfortunately, the process was far from subtle. The queen spun around, shrieking at Dar and Tami for intruding. The sound increased as she took in what was happening to the Mo.

The queen darted to the edge of her range before Dar could blink, batting him away from the Mo.

He flew across the chamber, crashing into the sticky wall, crushing several larvae behind him.

"Protect the tree," he shouted.

But he hadn't needed to do that. Roots were crashing through the side wall of the chamber, blocking the queen from getting to the tree.

He had a feeling Tami would have lots of questions about the tree later, but for the moment, she stayed on task. She was already moving around the queen, slashing at her even as Cherry shot roots up through the floor, entangling the massive birthing segment behind the queen.

The devil was already hampered by the heavy fleshy appendage that kept spitting out eggs, forgotten on the floor. But with Cherry's added help, the queen's mobility was limited to what little she could stretch.

Even still, the queen and Tami were a blur of motion as Tami hacked and slashed at the queen. Yet, even hampered as the devil was, she kept up with Tami without issue.

Unfortunately, Tami's blade didn't stand up well against the claws of the queen. Dar noticed large gouges torn into her sword following their first exchange.

"How long is it going to take?" Tami cried out, blocking another attack.

Tami could hold the queen off, largely thanks to the queen's more limited mobility, but the queen was still powerful. Dar knew Tami couldn't distract her much longer.

"Just a moment." Dar focused, trying to speed the process, but he was only able to do so much. He watched as the roots pushed their way deep into the earthen Mo.

Its skin was already drying up, cracking and flaking away as the little dao tree absorbed it.

Cherry's roots shot up around the queen, continuing to bind her further while keeping a protective barrier in place between the queen and the little dao tree.

Tami screamed, and Dar realized he needed to get back in the fight. The queen had quickly torn apart her sword and was turning to deal with Cherry's roots.

Needing to do something fast, Dar barreled into the bulky section of the queen, slamming into it with his full force.

It definitely got her attention.

The queen turned, whipping her arms and her sharp claws at him, nearly giving Dar a new haircut as he ducked under and came right back up, hoping to slam into her gut.

As he moved, he was surprised when he didn't collide with flesh when he'd expected to. Instead, he only hit air as the queen sped around the tiny space. Swinging and smacking Tami, who'd tried to ambush her.

This devil was more than they could handle right now. Luckily, Dar and Tami only needed to distract it while Cherry and the little dao tree consumed the Mo.

The back wall crashed to the ground, distracting Dar for a moment.

Looking over, he watched as the Mo crumbled. The little dao tree had done its job. Dar pulled it back, and it returned to his inner world along with Cherry. He breathed a sigh of relief. Having it out of his space was risky.

He did not know what damage to the tree would do to him or its abilities.

Their task was done, but they still had a queen to contend with and an underground filled with enemies to escape. Dar took a deep breath, readying his body for the run.

"Tami, let's go." Dar moved, aiming to get out, but finding himself smacked into the wall yet again by the irate queen.

"Right behind you," Tami shouted, dodging several attacks before darting out of the room.

Looking over his shoulder, Cherry's dao still rooted the queen to the ground. At least one thing had gone their way. But, as he watched, the queen stopped moving, and the breeding section startled to wriggle and shift.

"Fuck," Dar cursed, extracting himself from the wall and not looking back as he charged out of the space. Whatever the queen was going to do, he knew it wouldn't be in his best interest to stick around.

Dar was out of the room quickly and followed Tami as they shot down the tunnel.

Drones were swarming out of every side tunnel, pouring into the larger cavern. Dar put his dao of shadow to work, whipping it around him like a scythe, cleaving through the mass of drones and working to hide them from attacks. His shadow dao worked wonderfully against the mass of weaker devils.

So far, it was working. They charged forward, continuing to slice their way through the tunnel. It wasn't about how many devils they killed, but keeping a path clear as they moved forward.

So far, the devils hadn't been very organized, but as they turned a corner, Dar could see that was about to change. Beetle devils looked like they were forming a wall up ahead, working to seal off their escape with their own bodies.

The beetles then began to advance forward, aiming to stop them and sweep them back towards the queen.

Tami was still sprinting down the tunnel. She jumped high into the air, hoping to clear them, but one unfurled its wings and launched itself upwards, catching Tami and pulling her down into the swarm below.

Dar's heart pounded as he watched the beetle slam Tami into the floor. His Black Knight's axe was in his hand on instinct as he leapt into the crowd of devils.

His weapon bit into the beetle on top of Tami, and he wrenched the devil to the side, toppling over the beetle next to it.

Unfortunately, in those moments, they both stopped moving, giving the devils a chance to swarm them. There were too many to fight head on. Beetles tangled up his axe while drones poured in behind.

His dao of shadow lashed out, but could not penetrate the tough exteriors of the beetle devils. Dar managed to make two more swings of his axe before three of the beetles pinned it down.

Dar pulled his axe back into his inner world and snatched Tami off the ground, diving low. He tried to maneuver under the arms of the devils and break through the blockade, if only for a second.

But more beetle devils stood up ahead. They were surrounded.

"Tami." He shook her, but she didn't respond. Her body was limp. "Fuck. Okay, I'm going to do something and you need to trust me. I don't know what will happen if you resist. Do you understand?"

She moaned in response, and Dar took that as a yes. He pulled her into his inner world, like he had with Cherry and the maids. She flowed into him, successfully tucked away.

Free of the need to protect her, Dar drew another weapon from his inner world. This time, he pulled out a large, curved sword. He wasn't a skilled swordsman, but he wanted something that would work better for what he had in mind.

He swung in wide, nearly spinning arcs. The black blade cut through the beetle's tough hide as they pressed in around him.

A few times, they almost pinned him with their sheer mass of bodies, but he kept them off. Pivoting and sweeping to continue clearing them from his back, pivoting on one foot and sweeping on all sides.

It was a tiring, wild excuse for a fight, and it was slow, but he was making slight progress. Dar managed a single step with each swing, but he wasn't killing anything but drones. They were pressing themselves between the beetles, seemingly willing to take the brunt of the hits.

The larger devils were taking deep cuts, but nothing bad enough to take them out of the fight. If he was going to move further, he needed to take them out as well.

The underground tunnels erupted with a deafening screech that froze all the devils. Dar recognized it as the queen. She had finished whatever she'd been trying to do, and his time was up.

Dar pressed his slight and momentary advantage, slashing into one beetle and killing it while it was frozen. Unfortunately, the moment didn't last long, and more poured back in before he'd even removed his blade from its corpse.

Dar ducked low and picked up a beetle, using it as a battering ram to push his way towards the exit. Unfortunately, it also left Dar's back exposed to the beetles, and something tore into his back.

He might have taken some serious damage from that move, but he made significant progress, breaking free from the other beetles. He slammed down the one he'd been using and bolted for the exit.

Drones tried to block him, but they were fodder for his shadow as he rushed through them. Taking one step out of the exit, Dar was hit from behind. His body lifted off the ground with the impact.

Dar felt the queen's clawed hand tight around his neck as she zipped up into the air with him. She opened her mouth, almost as if it was going to talk, before screeching in his face and then rocketing back down to the ground. She slammed him into the dirt just outside the tunnel.

More buzzing accompanied her as the air filled with flying mantis-type devils, and looking around, Dar saw that the surrounding hills were covered with mantis devils that lacked flight. He wasn't loving his chances.

The queen floated over him, gloating as more beetles poured out of the tunnels and set up a blockade around him.

"I really kicked the hive, didn't I?" Dar joked, but none of the devils laughed. Clearly, a tough crowd.

Dar worked to figure out some semblance of a plan. He was surrounded by multiple layers of devils, and there were more in the air, ready to dive on him. He scanned the ground underneath him, but there wasn't any granite to be found. So his best shot would be his dao of shadows.

The queen landed next to him and snapped out a kick, flinging him into the air. She followed that up by slamming him into the chest of a beetle devil, which then wrapped its arms around him, working to hold him.

Before Dar could even struggle, multiple punches rained down on his face, knocking his head back and forth until he was dizzy. Dar flexed in the beetle's grip, but between its strength and his disorientation, it was useless.

The queen stepped forward, the pair of mandibles on her face clicking open and hungrily seeking his arm.

He wondered why they always went for the arm first. But, as he stared at the appendage he was rather fond of and her descending mandibles, Dar remembered how he'd turned it into a shadow during the fight with Karn.

As quickly as he could, he tried to recreate the feeling.

Her mandibles met nothing but shadows, her jaws closing. Dar felt his arm traveling slightly along the shadows, and he realized he had a risky gamble to make. But he really only saw one option left to him.

Pushing, Dar tried not only to make his arm into shadows, but his whole person. Feeling the way his arm moved along the shadows, he worked to pull the shadows through his body, following it. He pushed everything he was into the greater dao of shadows.

Another hit landed on his head, breaking his focus for a moment, but he ignored the pain as best he could, letting her rain her blows while he worked to shift his body.

Her next blow passed right through him as he faded, although faded might not be the right term. It was like his entire body melted into the darkness, but he was still there.

Evening had descended, filling the area with shadows. Dar was able to slip away, diluted by the massive shadows around him.

Feeling himself fading away, Dar desperately focused to keep his body whole and not allow it to spread throughout the shadows. Dar coached himself, working to think of something to ground himself.

In response, his mind kept slipping back to home. The home he'd built. That cave mansion he'd spent days carefully carving out every last detail.

He could touch and feel each small piece of granite he'd shaped, as if he were right in front of it. So intimate was his knowledge and understanding of the place that it gave him something to grasp in his mind and focus on.

Shadows pulled him along as the world blurred by. He was helpless as every iota of his mind was focused on keeping himself together. He vaguely could feel the devil queen smashing the hills in fury and frustration, trying to find him. But it was useless. She couldn't damage a shadow.

Devils poured out of the hills in search of Dar, but he was long gone.

Spilling through the massive shadow that was night, Dar was traveling at speeds he could only have dreamed of.

He was one with the night, and he only had one destination in mind.

The cave mansion was so locked into his mind, he clung to that single thought to keep himself grounded, even as he threatened to spill out into the great shadow of night and be lost forever.

The countryside rushed by as Dar passed the ravine, the forest, and even Bellhaven, with all its lights trying to break him up and wash him away. He barely stayed in control, but he kept himself centered, flowing up along the Bell River until he settled into a familiar shadow.

He pulled himself back together, reforming his body.

"Dar? Dar!" Sasha screamed in confusion. "Dar, what happened?" A pair of soft hands grabbed his shoulders and tried to shake him.

But he only managed to respond by rolling over and puking blood.

"Dar! Blair, go wake Bart's wife. Tell her we have a patient that needs our help immediately. Make sure she drops whatever she is doing."

Dar groaned and rolled back over, his vision blurry from the strain of tonight.

"Dar, can you focus?"

"Pretty," he said, reaching up and touching Sasha's face. "I hurt."

"I can imagine. You look like a mess, Lug. Let's get you patched up, and then you can tell me all about it." She gently took his hand off her face and kissed his knuckles.

Dar could feel his eyes fluttering shut. They were too heavy for him to keep open. Letting it all go, he relaxed into Sasha's softness. He was safe, at least for that moment. He let himself drift off into sleep.

Chapter 19

Dar slept fitfully; his dreams filled with terrifying swarms of devils devouring the land around him like a plague of locusts.

And the worst part was that he knew it was all his fault. He had started the insect devils on their path of destruction, and he couldn't help but wonder if it might have gone differently should he have chosen another option.

The devils plagued the countryside as Dar watched, holed up in his cliffs. Downstream, the village of Bellhaven hunkered down for the winter and ate what little they could get away with, unsure if they'd be able to find food in the spring.

Dar watched as his dreamworld swirled through the seasons, spring arriving and food growing scarce. Villagers wasting away, too weak to fight back against the horde of insects and instead starving inside the caves.

How had it come to this?

"It's okay, Dar. Dar, wake up." Soft hands roused him from his sleep.

Dar grabbed onto those arms like they were the last life raft in the middle of a sea. "What?"

"You were having a nightmare," Sasha cooed and ran her fingers soothingly through his hair.

Amber was there as well, a wet cloth in her hand. "Milord. You had us worried. You've been out for a little over a day."

He frowned, wasn't she in his inner world?

As if anticipating his question, she answered, "Cherry helped us out once she knew we were safe. Tami is still sleeping, and Neko is pacing outside the room." A smile played on Amber's lips.

"I couldn't let her disturb his rest." Sasha put her hands on her hips. Dar had a feeling getting Neko out of the room hadn't been easy.

But he ignored it all and pulled Sasha off her feet and into his bed. He'd missed her. "I could use some company. Let Neko in."

"Yes, milord." Amber hurried to get his favorite cat girl.

"Dar," Sasha started to complain, but he gave her a squeeze, letting her know that he didn't want to talk. He just needed the comfort of other people.

His nightmare had been so... vivid. Eerily so. It was like the dreams that required checking the entire house before going back to sleep. He couldn't shake the unsettling feeling.

"Is everything fine in the village?" he asked.

"It has been quiet since you left," Sasha responded, not asking any further questions about how he'd appeared in front of her or how he'd gotten injured. Instead, she cuddled into him, letting her soft body mold to his.

Dar heard Neko moving into the room for only a moment before a weight landed on him. She crawled over him, peering into his face before giving him a peck on the cheek. Satisfied that he was well, she cuddled up against his back, pressing her face into his neck to the point he was worried she was going to suffocate herself.

Shifting, he found Neko's head and patted her. "I'm all right. Everything is going to be okay," he comforted the cat girl.

She melted at his words and was swiftly asleep.

"It would seem you aren't the only one having trouble with sleep," Sasha commented, grabbing his arm and wrapping it back around her waist, sandwiching him between the two women. "Please, get some rest. We'll talk in the morning. But I expect to hear everything."

Dar grumbled in agreement and pressed himself against Sasha, burying his nose in her hair and drifting off to a more comfortable sleep. It was the kind of sleep where he could slip into his inner world.

He found himself once again in the extensive field with the black stone keep towering over everything.

As he looked around, he noted that the little dao tree had grown yet again. Now, it towered over the landscape like a hundred-year-old oak. It not only sported a black strip like it had been painted in tar, but a strip of the tree was now smooth, like polished stone. The leaves branching out from that section were a sandy brown that made them look like dead and dried leaves, but they swayed in the wind like any other leaf.

"Amazing, isn't it?" Cherry dropped down from the tree, looking up at it with awe and back at Dar with a thrill on her face.

Dar did a double take as he looked at Cherry. She now had a lock of black and brown in her hair. Dar assumed her connection to the tree was changing her, too.

"I can't believe how big it has gotten." Dar looked up into the leaves, seeing fruits peeking out between the leaves. "It's going to be a bitch to pick those."

"If you need them, I'll pick them." Cherry smiled. "You dropped off many new corpses. I had the maids bury them, and as a result, there are new fruits coming in."

"Anything ripe?" he asked, and the dryad disappeared into the tree before swinging down and dropping off a strange assortment of new fruits.

There were three in total.

Dar picked the first one up. It was heavy and dark, but when he bit in, it was like dark chocolate; it was bitter but delicious. The dao settled into his mind. Brittle. Devouring the others, he felt the dao of sharp and gritty take place.

An odd assortment of dao, he thought. Brittle and gritty were likely coming from the trolls, while sharp had to be from the mantis devils that he had absorbed—both from that battlefield.

Sharp was always welcome, but the other two were odd.

By themselves, they might not have much application, although he did think he could make sanding blocks with the dao of gritty. It would be better than using knives to smooth out wood.

"Nothing spectacular, but I won't say no to more dao," Dar told Cherry. "How are you?" His lovely little dryad was changing along with the tree, and he wanted to make sure she was okay.

"Great," she said excitedly, hopping around Dar. "I feel so... full of life."

"Uh, huh. Can you hold still for a moment?"

Cherry planted herself in front of him, her wide, slightly crazed eyes staring up at him. "Sure!"

He pulled at the different colored locks of hair and lifted them into her view. "Your hair is changing."

"Oh." She held the two locks of hair and gave them a tug to confirm they were indeed part of her hair before she rubbed them as if it was just dirt. But the two locks remained black and brown. "How odd."

"I think you are changing with the tree, Cherry." Dar let some concern creep into his voice. So far, the little dao tree had brought nothing but good to his life, but still, he couldn't help being concerned for her.

She tilted her head. "Of course I am. I'm bound to it. I just wonder what this means? Maybe I should try to learn new dao again."

Dar was surprised at the statement. He hadn't realized she had stopped trying. "Why had you stopped?"

"It just never worked. Outside of my new growth dao, I've struggled to comprehend much." She looked up at the dao tree, specifically the two newly colored segments. "But maybe I'll take a stab at some earth dao."

He had known that spirits were often talented in their related dao at the cost of the broader spectrum, but he didn't realize it was so bad that Cherry had given up.

"The family dao book is yours if you want it." Dar thought that was obvious by now, but he still said it. Picking up the book, he went ahead and wrote down his three new dao.

Flipping through the pages, he passed Blair's dao characters. But what shocked him was that several of them practically leapt off the page. Even though Blair was a fairly flippant person, she was the second strongest among their group, with three greater dao and hoping to form her grand dao.

All of her dao had to do with crystalline minerals. Apparently, that fit well within the earthen Mo abilities Dar had just gained. Dar looked at them all with interest, wondering if he could learn them just as quickly as he had the shadow dao.

The idea kept fluttering in his head, but he tried to set it aside for the moment. First, he needed to finish the dao of bright to build the dao of flame. He needed the firepower the dao provided. Earth and shadow were great for his protection and in a fight, but he knew that this wasn't just a fight.

It was going to become a war, and he needed to be able to do more than wade in as a powerful soldier. Dar needed to bring some real firepower to bear.

Sitting down with little else to do, he returned to Blair's dao of bright.

"I thought for sure you were going to learn her other dao," Cherry said over his shoulder.

"No, I finish what I start." He tapped the dao of bright. "But you are free to flip through the book and learn what you want while I'm meditating."

Dar didn't want to waste any time starting his meditation. Even though he knew it had been a nightmare, it had left him with a sense of urgency he couldn't explain.

Focusing inward, he started once again to cultivate the dao of bright, letting it flow through his channels. He'd practiced it several times already. By now, he had gotten the hang of it and immediately managed to get the dao character swirling through his body.

It sped up faster and faster as he tried to harmonize it with himself, brand it into his very soul and learn the dao. At some point, he had realized it had less to do with his physical body and more with his soul. But the concept of the soul was ephemeral at best.

Dar circled the dao character, filling every inch of him with the knowledge of the dao of bright. The corners of his mind blazed to light, sweeping away the darkness as he embraced bright.

His mind felt so energetic, so full of light as he finally understood the dao of bright. Letting a deep breath out, he slowed down his mana in his channels and let everything settle back down. The dao of bright was complete.

He cracked open an eye to ask Cherry how long he had been out, but she was in her own meditation with the book open before her. Good. Dar hoped it worked for the dryad. She had been stuck at the same level for so long, it almost had to be painful. She had no doubt watched demons like Karn steadily surpass her with some level of jealousy.

Dar left Cherry to cultivate and stood up, needing a break before he even thought about the dao of flame. Bright, combustion, and heat would be the perfect lesser dao to form a greater dao related to fire. His ability to cultivate these lesser dao was much improved, but he knew that the volatile flame dao would be much harder to accomplish. It was something he would have to figure out if he was going to push himself as far as he needed to go.

Karn and the queen were proof that more powerful opponents were out there, and they weren't far away. And, from what he'd heard, even greater opponents might quite literally rise out of the depths of the ocean.

All of it only solidified one of the open questions that had been on Dar's mind. He walked through his inner world until he reached the gate to the black stone keep. The fortress dominated the landscape of his inner world. With every expansion of his inner world, he only unlocked another section of the keep.

At the moment, all he could access was the courtyard, dominated by a training ring and racks of weapons and armor. He wanted to understand what else the keep held, and the only way to find out would be to keep growing his skills.

And he planned to use that growth to help his women. Given the success the maids had had cultivating under his tree, it was about time he brought the rest of his family in here to train at night.

He wasn't alone in his goals. He had his family and, to a greater extent, his village. There were those within the village he knew would fight alongside him in any battle.

Dar stared at the door that stood deeper into the black keep, wondering just what secrets it held. But staring at it wouldn't make it open. Sighing, he accepted that it would have to wait for another time.

Sitting down cross-legged in the practice ring, Dar probed the dao of flame. He wouldn't start it just yet, but at the very least, he could lay the groundwork and start trying to understand it.

***

When Dar woke up, he was lying in bed. His body was sore and wrapped all over in bandages. Shifting, his body sparked reminders that he was still injured, but he enjoyed the soft press of the surrounding bodies. Sasha and Neko had curled themselves around his body while he'd slept, pressing themselves into him.

"Morning." Sasha patted his hand, feeling him awake without even looking.

"Maybe I should go back to sleep." Dar pulled her closer.

She slapped at his hands as they quested for her chest. "Stop that. We should get up. The village knows you got back, and the leaders are eager to hear your tale. I'm eager to hear it as well." She turned and pressed her nose against his. "I don't like my dao companion coming back home beaten to a pulp and carrying an unconscious woman."

"Tami," Dar answered the easy question. "Tami Cervus. Apparently, the Cervus family is a big deal?"

Sasha's eyebrows rose on her beautiful face. "Yes. Her family is a big deal. Maybe I shouldn't have let her sleep with Blair." She bit her thumb.

Dar nearly choked out a laugh. "I don't think Blair would do anything stupid. And Tami was out cold."

Dar pushed himself off the bed, feeling his bones settle. His chest wound strained, threatening to open back up. He let himself back down, grumbling, "Okay, I'm apparently going to need help getting out of bed."

Sasha gave a deep throaty laugh but rolled out of bed. As Sasha shifted aside, a concerned Neko face popped into his field of vision.

Sasha chided the cat girl in exasperation. "You're going to have to get off him if he's getting up, or you could help."

Neko ignored Sasha for a moment, sniffing at Dar before she nodded and sprang to her feet. She grabbed one of Dar's arms to help.

With the help, Dar got upright without freshly tearing open the wound on his chest. He was grumpy. It was going to be a rough morning. But Neko stayed by his side and helped him get dressed before they headed out of the cave to meet with the leaders.

Sasha broke away to go check on Tami after making him promise not to spill too much of the story before she caught up.

Outside, Dar let out a breath of relief. The village was whole, and the sky wasn't dotted with devils. He still couldn't shake off the uneasiness the dream had given him. It had felt eerily real.

"Boss," Glump called as Neko helped him sit down on a stump before scampering away to the central hearth for food. Apparently, she was going to dote on him. "I think you have a story to tell."

"I do. Let's wait for everyone else to join us so that I don't have to tell it too many times. Sasha should be out here soon as well." Dar took his bowl of porridge that was sprinkled with flecks of dried bison meat.

He took a bite, smiling. It wasn't bad at all.

Sasha came striding out with a purpose, and the second she saw him, she reoriented herself towards him.

"I hope you haven't started."

"Nope. Still waiting for Bart and Rex," he said, though Bart was already heading their way.

Sasha nabbed a passing villager. "Can you go see if Rex can join us?"

"Sure," he said.

"Must be big if you are in such a hurry," Glump croaked.

"Do you see how beat up Dar is?" Sasha poked Dar in the chest, making him wince. "Case in point. We have a problem, and I'd like to know what it is."

Bart settled down on his own stump. "Glad to have you back with us."

"Glad to be back," Dar said between mouthfuls. He managed to devour his bowl in short order and sheepishly held it up for more.

Neko didn't hesitate, running off to get him more.

They didn't have to wait much longer for Rex to join them, and Samantha joined as well.

"First, how's the village doing?"

Sasha smacked him over the head. "No, we start with what happened to you."

He sighed. "Fine. We traveled down to Bellhaven with Karn..." He started his story and gave them the details of his trip, going over the time he'd spent with Karn and the nobility of Bellhaven. When he went through the devil attack and the details Tami had shared from her scouting, Sasha's leg started bouncing. He could tell she was barely containing her anxiousness as he closed in on the part about what hurt him.

Finally, he got into their stealth mission through the devil tunnels and destruction of their food source, and at that point, all the leaders were on the edge of their seats.

On his fourth bowl of food after finishing, he quietly ate as everyone just sat, absorbing what he'd said.

"So we aren't part of Kindrake anymore?" Rex asked. "Is there any concern about aggressive action from the kingdom?"

"They have bigger concerns," Dar responded. "Between the devils, the war up north, and The White retracting her aid, I don't see them moving a force to take care of us."

Bart rubbed at his face. "I never thought I wouldn't be part of Kindrake."

"It was necessary to avoid the levies for war this spring. If we were part of Kindrake, they would come and demand that all of our demons and spirits join the war effort."

"Really?" That surprised everyone.

Dar nodded, putting down another finished bowl. "Think about it. If The White pulls her forces, Kindrake is going to scour the countryside for unaffiliated demons and pull them into their forces against the north."

Everyone's faces shifted in understanding. "You are absolutely right," Bart agreed. "I understand why you did it. You just went beyond my expectations."

"There's one more thing we need to talk about." Dar looked around the circle before pulling out a dao fruit of quiet. He still had many of them in his inner world. "Samantha, I'd like you to eat this fruit. Everyone, this fruit is how we can make the humans of our village as strong as lesser demons."

She looked at the fruit and frowned. "It can't be that easy."

"It isn't," Bart spoke up. "Tabby and I have already eaten one. Our daughter helped us with the process."

Samantha looked up from the fruit to the old blacksmith, raising an eyebrow. "I thought you looked better."

"I feel a few decades younger, too." Bart smirked.

"My plan is to help everyone in the village make the transition this winter," Dar explained. "I think as a wonderful teacher to the village, you'd best experience it for yourself so you can help everyone else."

Samantha picked up the fruit and held it close to her chest. "I can do that. Can... can I have another for Jeffry?" She hesitated before asking for a fruit for her husband.

"Of course. I didn't mean to suggest he'd be left out."

"No, I just want him to go first. He's not as healthy as he puts on." Samantha looked at the fruit with hope.

"Sasha, get Amber and tell her she's needed to help someone make the transition to an immortal right away." Dar spoke over his shoulder before turning back to the group. "Anything else?"

Chapter 20

"I hope you realize just how precious this is." Samantha rolled the fruit in her hand as Dar pulled out another.

"For you and for Hearthway, I'll do what we need to survive," Dar offered her the second fruit just as Amber caught up to their circle. "Amber, Sam and her husband are going to need help cultivating their first dao. Think you can do it?"

"Of course, milord." Amber bowed to him before turning to the older lady. "If you are ready, we can start right away."

Samantha shook her head. "We'd better do it before my nerves get the best of me. Jeffry is still in our hut; let's head there."

Dar watched them go with a smile on his face. "Now, is there anything I missed?"

"Russ has been heading out every morning at dawn and bringing back half a dozen bison. We are running out of room. Beyond that, people are taking a well-deserved break from the fields, and many are producing and trading finer wares like brushes and combs. Things they can make in their warm homes," Bart complained with a smile.

"Oh, what a terrible problem to have," Dar chuckled. As far as he was concerned, it sounded like a massive success. "Let's make sure we are getting those hides cleaned up and the bones set aside. When I saw Dane three days ago, his ship looked brimming and ready to set sail." Dar had added in the lost day since he'd returned.

"Oh. Did he manage to find any livestock?" Sasha asked, and Dar felt Neko grow still beside him.

"Plenty." Dar smiled; he was going to enjoy watching her see how many goats arrived. Her wallet may not like the shipping fees, but the cost overall would likely still surprise her.

Sasha narrowed her eyes at Dar, seeing his smirk. She sensed something was amiss, but she didn't push further.

As if their conversation summoned him, Mika came running up into the village, breathing hard. "Trader is coming up from Bellhaven."

"Think that's him?" Sasha asked.

"We haven't seen anyone else on the river lately. It seems the rumors of devils have been keeping others at port." Dar stood with Neko's help. "Come on. Let's go see your merchant friend and your goats."

He paused and looked back at the group. "I think we are going to need a few extra hands, if you can round up some people and ropes."

The cat girl shrank away from Sasha, using Dar as a barrier. "They were cheap."

"How cheap?" Sasha asked, squinting at Neko.

"Free," Dar said, chuckling. "Just shipping costs, we were told."

That brought Sasha up short. "Free? How..."

"Neko is the best." Neko peered around Dar proudly, then darted back behind him.

Dar rolled his eyes at her antics, but filled Sasha in. "Some less than scrupulous types tried to cause Neko trouble. They learned their lesson and made amends using goats."

Sasha blinked several times, unable to respond.

"I know. But they deserved it for attacking Neko," Dar chuckled. He didn't enjoy taking from people, but some had it coming.

"Well, let's see how many goats we have to deal with." Sasha pulled her hair back, ready to work. "I have no idea where we are going to keep them, though. Goats like to climb fencing, and we don't even have the materials to make a solid fence."

"I thought we could just keep them inside the wall once we have it finished." Dar scratched the back of his head.

Sasha sighed. "Like some backwater farming village? I thought Hearthway was better than that." She crossed her arms.

"Just for the winter. We'll figure out something come spring." Dar did his best to give her a charming smile.

She sighed even harder. "It'll have to do."

As they walked the Bell River, Dane's boat came into view as it pulled up along the bank. The men on the boat were in a flurry of activity as an undercurrent of goats ran around the surface of the boat.

Dane looked up from ordering around his men, shocked to see Dar approaching. "Dar! We managed to get most of them up the river. Lost a few, but who could tell with all of these?"

He smiled like a merchant about to get paid, though there was a flicker of confusion at seeing Dar there.

"Dar." Sasha's voice was low and dangerous. "You said a lot, but that's more than a lot."

"Neko's the best!" sounded from Dar's right before Sasha's sharp gaze made the cat girl hide behind Dar again. "Neko's the best?"

Sasha rubbed her temple. "Why did you think we needed so many goats?"

Dar decided to defend the cat girl. "It was my idea. I told her about milk and cheese. And I can't say I wouldn't love some of those to be a staple in everyone's diet."

"Fine." Sasha shook her head, muttering, "Goat milk for everyone."

Dar shrugged. Adding some dairy would be good for everyone.

Dane's men threw down a long, wide board. They didn't even have to try to herd them before the goats started spilling out onto the bank.

Thankfully, Bart and half the village turned up, ready to help unload. A group of them ran along the sides of the mass of goats, shouting and waving their hands, trying to drive them toward the village.

If nothing else, Dar figured the warmth put off by the homes would keep them close. And the southern woods were barren enough to act as a barrier. Assuming they didn't go for a swim in the Bell River, they'd likely stay close enough. And they could afford to lose a few.

Dane came down the gangplank not long after the goats, rubbing his hands and looking at Sasha. "We also have a dozen hens and a rooster, as you asked."

"And silk," Neko piped up, trying to save herself.

"And silk, among other goods you offered to buy," Dane agreed.

Sasha pulled her purse out of the folds of her dress. "Fine. Let's talk coinage. We also have a few dozen bison hides and their bones we can trade." She tapped the side of her purse. "Maybe even a few hundred pounds of salted meat if you could handle it."

"Meat and furs?" Dane gave a grin that only merchants had when they smelled money. "With the coming winter, I'd be very interested in those."

Dar left the two of them to handle the bargaining. Instead, he frowned, looking at the deck of the boat.

Ignoring everything else, he walked up the gangplank to a man with what looked like a freshly injured shoulder.

"Did you encounter trouble on the river?" Dar wanted to know if the river had a monster problem.

"No, sir. This was a devil problem in Bellhaven," the sailor answered, wincing as he tried to stand.

"Ah, you fought the devils at the gate," Dar realized.

But the sailor shook his head. "No, it's from the devils yesterday." He hesitated to say more, looking towards Dane for permission.

"Dar, what are you doing?" The man had caught Dane's attention.

"Asking after this wounded man. He says that there was another devil attack yesterday?" That would have been the day after Dar had absorbed the Mo.

Dane looked nervous as well. "I thought you knew, since you were already back in your village."

"Spit it out." Dar felt his stomach sink.

"Flying devils attacked Bellhaven. They swooped in and started ripping people off the street and carrying them away. After the first attack, we boarded and headed out. I heard that another attack had happened when we met people fleeing on the delta."

"Flying?" Dar wanted clarification. "What did they look like?"

"Big bugs," the wounded sailor answered his question before Dane. "Like massive bugs. They were so fast. One second the thing was landing on the other side of the dock, the next it had its claws in my shoulder and tried to fly away with me."

"It's okay. We killed it," Dane told the man, trying to offer some level of comfort. "Someone got lucky and knocked it out of the sky with a bolo. Everyone picked up something and crushed it there on the docks." Dane shook his head. "I think Bellhaven has become too dangerous even for me."

Dar looked out over the sky, almost expecting to see a swarm like in his nightmare, but there was nothing but blue skies. "I understand. Let's get everything unloaded as quickly as we can so that you can be on your way."

"That would be good. I feel like I can't put enough distance between me and Bellhaven right now." Dane turned back to Sasha. "You have a deal. Just help us get this all unloaded." The reminder of the danger was enough to make the merchant expedite his haggling.

With the deal made, Sasha was more than happy to help. Dar smiled. That meant she had completely fleeced the merchant. Bellhaven must have been terrifying.

Dar grabbed one of the villagers heading back, realizing it was one of Glump's dao companions. "Come back and bring a full pot from the hearth? Let's feed these merchants and help them on their way."

"Yes." She nodded. There was an eagerness in her step as she hurried away.

Dar regretted he couldn't do it himself, but he imagined that if he tried to lift and carry a pot over, Sasha would beat him silly for risking aggravating his injuries.

"What now, Dar?" Neko asked, still supporting him.

"We need to talk as a family, because things just went from bad to worse." The fact that the insect devils were already attacking Bellhaven was wrong. It should have taken them more time to clear out the rest of the trolls and gremlins.

"Back to the cave?" she asked.

He looked around. Everybody had things well in hand unloading Dane's boat. He would just get in the way if he hung around.

"Back to the cave," Dar agreed, bending down to kiss Neko's forehead.

But the girl threw her head back and instead claimed his lips with her own.

He almost pulled back, but by that point, Neko was well and truly one of his women. She had a piece of his heart, and he'd kill any who tried to take her from him. It was stupid that he kept treating her like something else.

"Come on, before we put on too much of a show." Dar stroked Neko's cheek and tugged for her to keep walking.

The cat girl was nearly vibrating with excitement as she pulled him along. "I'm okay with a show."

"Of course you are," Dar chuckled. "But I would rather not put one on. Besides, we need to talk with the family, so try to contain yourself for now."

As they walked, the goats were being herded back to the village, where people were more than happy to accept them, giving them handfuls of grass and attention. Meanwhile, the goats were starting to headbutt each other and establish their own rule.

There were so many goats around that Dar and Neko couldn't walk in a straight line through the village. But the bounce in Neko's step as she walked and her chant of "milk" every time her eyes landed on a goat made it almost worth the ridiculous number of them.

He hoped Neko knew only the females gave milk. And, if they were ever short on meat, they would be set.

Dar spotted Marcie walking by and waved her down.

"Milord?" She hurried up to his side.

"Do me a favor and gather up the family. I think we need to have a talk." Dar replied.

"Right away." She bowed and then darted away, finding Amber almost immediately. The two set off to collect the rest of the family.

Neko pulled on him to head back to the cave, and he let her lead him back into the darkness where his shadow dao stretched out, probing around him. With it and his dao of granite, the cave came alive with details he couldn't normally see. Nearly everything was within his reach, and he'd never felt safer.

But that strange feeling was cut off as soon as they entered his well-lit home, and he didn't have the same reach with his shadow.

"Dar." Tami stood up from the couch and winced, a hand shooting up to her head.

"Tami," he greeted her; Neko pouted before bringing him over to the sitting area and helping him into a large chair. "What do you remember?"

Tami settled back on the couch, holding her head in her hand. "I remember the mother fucking beetle that slammed me into the ground. Memory is fine."

"Yeah, well after that, the devil queen got loose. She dropped that big birthing section of her body and came swinging for us," Dar explained.

Tami looked shocked. "How did you survive?"

"I escaped. How else?" Dar shook his head. "No way I could take that whole hive myself. I took you and ran. But there's more news."

Neko crawled up on Dar's armrest and leaned on him, making small purring noises as she settled down.

"When my family gathers here, I'll discuss it. But Tami, I think Bellhaven is in some serious trouble."

Cherry came skipping in next before perching herself on his other armrest, eliciting an eye roll from Tami.

"Darn. If I had come just a moment earlier, I could have had an arm rest perch. What do you say, Pussy Cat? Want to trade?" Blair sauntered in.

"No." Neko pressed herself harder into Dar's side.

Blair gave a heavy, drawn-out sigh. "Figures."

"I haven't forgotten about my promise," Dar reminded her. "Though if you want to spend time with me like this, you can take it. Otherwise, I'd ask you to let me heal up before we spend some time together."

Blair licked her lips. "I'm not afraid to do all the work."

"We have a guest." Dar pointed at Tami. "But noted." He winked.

The salt spirit's face turned bright red, not at the mention of Tami, but his wink.

"You are playing with fire," Mika said as she walked in. "Don't promise her anything you aren't willing to back up."

"I'm not that bad." Blair tried to bat Mika away as the wave spirit grabbed her friend and pulled her to a spot further away from Dar. "But I'm more than ready."

"You are always ready." Mika rolled her eyes. "Dar, what is this about?"

"News from Bellhaven," he answered. "Sasha and the maids should be here soon."

As if on cue, the well-dressed demon strut in with the two maids in tow behind her. "We are here, love. Go ahead. I heard most of it when you were talking to Dane."

Dar laced his fingers together and made eye contact with everyone in the room. "Devils have started to raid Bellhaven. Insect types with flight have been breaching the walls and raiding the city for... food."

"You mean humans?" Mika asked.

"Yeah..." Dar hated the sound of it. "They are raiding the city, taking people out of the streets. It seems that our plan went to shit, Tami."

The deer demon sat shocked at the news, staring into nothingness. But when he said her name, her eyes moved and locked on his. "We need to go back. Now."

She got up like she was going to pack immediately.

"Can't." Dar shook his head. "Dane just headed north, and I doubt there's going to be another boat headed south anytime soon."

His trip through the shadows had been dangerous. It wasn't something he would attempt again unless his life was in danger. He'd nearly lost himself, and he needed to learn better control before risking it again.

"I can run." She stood again and wobbled on her feet.

Even if they had a way down to Bellhaven, he wasn't sure what good they would do against the queen as they were.

Sasha's silk ribbons shot out of her dress and caught Tami, helping her settle back down. "It doesn't seem like you can stand, much less run. Dane will carry the news to Kindrake. Maybe this is something we let them and your family handle."

"I don't get it. There were signs of the insects fighting the trolls all over the hills. Why are they already attacking Bellhaven?"

Dar could only guess. "What if the queen is that hungry? She's been eating that Mo near constantly for weeks or even months."

"You think it's about food?" Tami looked up, surprised.

"I do. Those insects were feeding themselves through the winter cold, but now the queen is active and needs to replace her food source. If she wants to continue to grow that hive as quickly as she was, that is going to require a vast amount of food."

What Dar didn't want to say was that Bellhaven might as well have been a livestock pen for the powerful devil.

"What are we going to do then?" Tami asked.

Dar looked around the room. Cherry was the only one who could potentially stand a chance against the grand demon, but he couldn't send her in against not only it but the whole hive.

They needed more strength.

Dar's first instinct was to hunker down and grow his own dao, and he'd do that, but there was another opportunity sitting right here. "Blair. I think I have a way to help you finish your grand dao."

Her dao path was on minerals and crystals. It wasn't exactly earth, but given how her lesser and greater dao had reacted after Dar had absorbed the most recent Mo, he realized it was at least under the umbrella of earth.

The salt spirit cocked her eyebrow. "Help how?"

"We can discuss in more detail after. Just know I have a way." His eyes drifted over to Tami. While she'd seen the tree, she didn't know its ability to help everyone along their dao path.

And that was the kind of information that could get Dar in trouble if she relayed it back to her father. He was slowly growing past the need for concern, but he'd rather not tempt fate.

"We need to prepare for when the devils are done with Bellhaven."

"Done with Bellhaven?" Tami nearly shouted. "What does that mean?"

This was the part Dar was going to hate the most. "That means we plan for Bellhaven to fall to the devils."

Tami shook her head in disbelief, and the girls around Dar all looked solemn at the thought. "We need to do something," she shouted accusingly, as if it was his responsibility to save the city.

"There's nothing we can do in our current state. Think about it, Tami, if those beetles came to Bellhaven in force along with a troop of those flying mantises, what could we do? At most, we could isolate and kill some, but what then? Next time, there would be more." Dar's voice was rising as he spoke.

Leaving Bellhaven to its fate didn't sit well with him either. He hated that he couldn't step forward and crush an army under his heel. But that wasn't reality in this situation. He was one man, and while strong, he couldn't take on an army yet. They needed to prepare.

Tami was stunned into silence as she tried to process the information.

Sasha played mediator. "It sounds like we all need time to think, and most importantly, we all need to grow stronger. It sounds like you and Blair need to spend some quality time together."

Neko's claws sank into his shoulder at the mention of that, and he realized she was getting jealous at the thought that Blair might step in before her.

"Yes, Blair. Let's talk. Neko, can you help me to the bedroom?"

The cat girl grabbed him a little too tightly as she helped him to his feet.

Chapter 21

Once in the bedroom, Dar turned to Neko. "You don't have to be jealous."

"Can I stay?" she asked, turning her head to the side in question.

"Sure." Dar patted the bed as he settled down and Blair stepped into the room, carefully closing the door behind her.

"I'm confused," she blurted. "You held off for so long, and suddenly, it's come into the bedroom?"

He shook his head. "Not like that. I still want to have that date with you before we take those steps. I brought you here because I want to take you into my inner world."

She cocked an eyebrow and came over, sitting next to him on the bed. Obviously, she'd heard about it from being around his family, but she hadn't seen it yet.

Thankfully, Neko relaxed.

"You could have just said that."

"Not with Tami out there. She's under a number of oaths to her father, and this is a secret I still want to keep."

"Ah." Blair settled as she understood. "You wanted her to think it was dao companionship type activities. Not cool. Don't tease me like that." Blair tried to touch Dar, but Neko's hand flashed out and knocked it away as she possessively clung to him.

Dar pulled Neko off of him. "Don't do that."

"But..." Neko started to complain, but one stern look from Dar was all it took to make her bite back whatever dispute she was going to have. "Fine."

"Good." He turned back to Blair. "If you want to relax, I can bring you in now. I think showing is better than trying to explain in this instance."

"Bring me inside you; isn't it supposed to be the other way around?" she joked while batting her eyes.

Dar let out a sigh; he had set himself up for that one with the lusty spirit.

"Come on, relax." He started to draw her into his inner world and felt a moment of resistance before she relaxed and was swept inside.

Now he needed to deal with Neko.

Neko looked properly chastised as she kept her head down, not looking at Dar. All the same, she felt his attention. "Neko is next."

"Yes, you are." He ruffled her hair between her cat ears. "Will you behave yourself if I let you in there with Blair?"

She bobbed her head excitedly. "Yes. As long as Neko is next. I can't lose to the salty bitch."

Feeling that she needed some encouragement, he pulled her close and kissed her again. Her soft lips were a contrast to her rough, but not unpleasant, tongue as they kissed.

Soon Neko grew more aggressive, her hands questing over his body.

Dar replied in kind, feeling her soft curves and letting his hands squeeze her thighs and cup her hips as he pulled her closer.

"Neko." He paused before regaining his thoughts. "We need to get back to work."

She nodded with a cute grunt as she head-butted his chest. "Stupid Dar."

"Soon," he promised her, opening up his inner world and swallowing her.

Flopping back on the bed, he stared at the ceiling, wondering how his life had become like this. He was a damn lucky man, but he also needed to make sure he took care of all the women in his life.

It took him a moment to clear his head, but eventually fell into meditation and his inner world.

When he appeared, both girls were slowly meandering around, looking at his inner world.

Neko was the first to notice him and jumped into his arms. "It's so pretty."

"This is really something." Blair was doing a slow circle. "Why don't you just live here?"

"Because, while you all physically can enter, my body remains outside," Dar said. "I would still have to maintain myself and stay safe."

"Shame." Blair walked over to one of the waist-high orange trees. "It seems like you are planning to grow food here."

He nodded, carrying Neko over with him. "Back up plans. Or at least, something that we can subsidize the village's food stores with."

"You are taking great care of Hearthway. I can't believe you've been thinking of all these plans and implementing them to keep everyone safe, sheltered, and fed. Most would help their people with the bare minimum and then tax them for their own gains." Blair let her fingers trail through the small tree.

"Dar is the best." Neko smiled.

"Wasn't I just 'stupid Dar'?" he countered.

The cat girl's smile went flat. "You can be both," she said with full seriousness.

Dar didn't know what to say in reply to Blair. He was just doing what he felt was right. "I take care of my own and those around me. That's just who I am, and it won't stop."

"So what is it that you wanted to show me?" she changed the topic, looking around his inner world.

"The little dao tree." He pointed to the strange tree that dominated the space.

"Little?" Blair looked at the tree and then back at Dar, confused. "I'd hate to see the big dao tree."

He rolled his eyes. "It used to be little. With each of the two Mo I've absorbed, it has grown significantly. But that's also what I wanted to show you."

He stepped over to the tree and pointed at the part that looked more like polished stone. "The Mo I just absorbed had a dao related to earth. The maids tested that shadow part of the tree. Cultivating near it significantly improved their comprehension of that type of dao."

"You do know there is another way to help me with the comprehension of dao?" Blair ran a finger along his arm, leaving a trail of goosebumps.

He cleared his throat. "Yes, but I don't have dao greater than your own. This tree can push you past your current blockade, or at least, that's the hope."

Blair stepped away from him and put her hand on the tree. "Oh," she moaned. "I can feel it."

"Good. I hope it works for you."

She pressed herself to the tree before she threw off her shirt.

Dar averted his eyes, but she just turned and pressed her back to it, sliding down to the dirt with a sigh.

"This will do." She didn't waste any time settling down to work on her dao path.

He was glad to see that she could be serious when she needed to be. Blair was a sexually charged person, but she clearly saw the value in pursuing her dao under this tree.

"I will try too," Neko declared, jumping out of his arms and running over to the dark part of the tree. She followed Blair's example, freeing herself of her top and pressing her back to the tree.

Dar wasn't sure if the shirtless part was necessary, but maybe it helped. He made sure to look away before Cherry popped in and teased him. Instead, he flipped open the family dao book and sat down cross-legged to start his own pursuit of his dao path.

Flame.

He knew it was a dangerous dao to try to force, but it was the best dao for him at that moment with what they faced.

Meditating, Dar began the process. Bright, combustion, and heat circled each other in his mind as Dar tried to find the right combination that would make flame.

Granite had taken him so long to finally piece together, but Dar hoped that his third greater dao would be easier. He knew he didn't have the dao tree to help him on this one, but he pushed those stray worries away.

Everything else faded out until those three dao were the only remaining thoughts in his mind.

Round and round they spun. Dar watched and waited for the three of them to make something greater. To his surprise, it didn't take long until the three clicked and uncontrollable heat burst through Dar's mind as he stared at the greater dao.

The greater dao was made up of his three lesser dao. Even though he knew them individually, it still functioned as a dao character he didn't understand when they combined to form the dao of flame. It was hard to focus and the pathway through his channels was then three times longer than a single lesser dao.

It made inscribing it into his body three times harder to do while maintaining his focus on the dao character for that increased length, making the difficulty increased by an exponential degree.

Sudden dread of what it would be like to inscribe a grand dao into his body flooded him and threatened to break his focus.

Dar closed those thoughts off like he'd just closed a fire door in his mind, containing the burning blaze and making it his sole focus. He chastised himself for the distraction.

The flame dao was rampant by that point. It wanted to consume fuel to keep itself active, and at the moment, his mind was the only source it had access to. Dar slowly started channeling mana into its form, trying to control it through comprehension.

When he completed the first pass, it was like the dao wanted to leap out of his mind and set his body aflame. It didn't seem to care that it could destroy him. Using his dao of heat, Dar did his best to disperse it before he truly caught on fire.

Cycling his mana again, the dao of flame fought to overcome his dao of heat. Dar fell into a rhythm of tug of war with the dao as he worked to feed it within his body, yet keep it from harming him.

It was a delicate balance, like walking a tightrope wire. Dar was only part way done, but he knew what he needed to do at that point.

He kept at it, not caring how much time it took to master the skill he knew they needed—until finally, the dao of flame solidified in his mind. As he finished, mana rushed back into him, and he felt himself grow stronger, the weakness fading from him.

"Phew," he breathed out a breath, half-expecting it to be fire. But it wasn't. Dar reminded himself that he wasn't a dragon.

Flexing his hands, Dar thought of something crazy. Why stop there? He could go straight for the grand dao. It's not like he had time to waste with the insects already attacking Bellhaven.

Focusing inward once, Dar took the dao of shadow, the dao of flame, and the dao of granite. The three were made of three lesser dao, so in the end, it was like trying to match up nine lesser dao. The complexity and permutations had increased an entire fold.

But that just made him want to get started sooner, not knowing when he'd find the right way to combine them. He wanted that grand dao.

When Dar put the dao of granite next to the dao of flame, nothing happened. Noting that, he tried something else. When the dao of flame touched the dao of shadows, the lesser dao of dim and bright pulsed, both racing towards each other.

When those pulses touched, it was like someone had set off a bomb in Dar's chest. Dar was flung out of his meditation and out of his inner world, physically jolting off the bed before puking blood.

"Dar!" Cherry was there in an instant. She must have returned to his inner world while he was cultivating. "Dar, speak to me."

"Hurts," he croaked.

It felt like his chest cavity was burnt so badly that all that was left was cooked charcoal.

"Hold on, I know Sasha bought a few healing potions from the merchant."

Dar was suddenly ever grateful for his wife's forethought.

Cherry came running back with a vial and unceremoniously pushed Dar's head back, sticking the neck of the vial into his mouth. It clanked against his teeth, but cool liquid flowed through his throat and eased his pain.

"Thank you, and remind me to thank Sasha for buying these." His eyelids felt heavy.

"Shh," Cherry shushed him, stroking his cheek. "You'll be alright. What happened?"

"Grand dao," Dar grumbled. "I tried to see what it would be like to cultivate a grand dao."

He could almost hear Cherry roll her eyes with the way she responded, "That was reckless—there's no way a grand dao would be that easy."

"I tried to combine shadow and flame. The dao of bright and dim reacted. They collided and exploded inside of me."

Cherry cursed under her breath. "Dar, there are just some dao that don't go together."

"Could have told me that sooner," he grumbled.

"Normally, it just doesn't work," she huffed. "You're experimenting with this new way to form dao. It hasn't been done before. How was I supposed to know that the resulting issue would be so severe?"

Dar closed his eyes, chiding himself. If things were really so easy, he would have soared to the celestial dao in weeks or months, not years. But he'd had to try. "You're right. I'm just hurt and angry."

"I understand." She kissed his forehead. It was one pleasant sensation among a world of agony. "Sasha is going to be livid. Do you want her to find out now or later?"

"Later?" Dar hesitated. "Where are Neko and Blair?"

"Neko broke through to a greater demon while you were cultivating and has been out for a day. Blair is still holed up next to the tree. I think she might really do it this time." Cherry realized he was missing a piece of information. "You've been out for almost a day."

A day. Without the tree to help him, it had indeed been longer yet again.

"If I can't combine flame and shadow, then I have to learn a different greater dao." Dar sighed, feeling like letting the cold stone floor consume him. "Fuck."

"Don't beat yourself up too hard. Let's find a dao related to earth. What grand dao were you even trying for?"

Dar paused, not having an answer for her.

She must have read his face. "See, that's why you need to slow down. Look through the dao book and see if there aren't some earth related dao that the tree can help you with. Lean into your advantages rather than trying to take the hard road."

Cherry patted his face with that sage advice and stood. "I'm going to go get Sasha so we can get this over with."

"Ugh," he groaned. Now he really wanted the floor to swallow him up.

It was some of the worst dread of his life as he waited there on the cold stone floor and Sasha's footsteps came closer. He heard her enter the room. He laid there in silence for a long while before he opened his eyes to Sasha's silent crying as she leaned against the bed.

He cursed. Her scolding him wouldn't be fun, but seeing her cry was absolutely heartbreaking.

"I'm sorry, Sasha," he whispered.

"Why?" That was all she said before she walked over and put a hand on his chest. "Why do you do this to yourself? First it was the ettercaps, then going to Bellhaven and returning torn up, and now this?"

His heart sank.

He hadn't been thinking about what coming home injured would do to her or any of the other women in his life.

Her eyes were filled with worry, not for herself, but for him. He reminded himself she never cared for battle.

She was softer. While she could run a tight ship in his household, she wasn't used to so many life-or-death moments.

"I'm so sorry, Sasha, but I have to push myself."

"For what? A stupid city that scorned us?" She slapped the side of the bed.

"No, Sasha, for you, for everyone here. When Bellhaven is gone, we'll be next. To wallow in inaction would be to doom our future." Dar opened his arms for her, and she knocked the wind out of him as she collapsed on him.

"I hate it."

Dar shushed her, petting the back of her head. "I know. But I can't stop. It's who I am. Every day, I'm going to push myself. That's the only way that I can ensure you and everyone here is still alive."

Tears flowed down Sasha's face, wetting his chest.

He squeezed her tightly. He knew the path they were on would hurt not only himself but those around him, but it was the right choice. Because it could also save them all. Nothing was easy, at least nothing worth doing.

Chapter 22

The potion had helped with the pain, but it didn't completely solve Dar's problem.

As he thought about it, it made sense that dim and bright wouldn't want to work together, but he hadn't expected the reaction. Based on the way they'd destroyed his body, they were completely incompatible. Dar really wasn't excited at the thought of continuing to tinker with them. He had to find another way to progress his dao path.

That meant he was left with pairing shadow and granite with something else, or fire and granite. Fire and granite made more sense as he thought about it. After all, there was an obvious evolution involving those two.

But, if he went that route, he needed to form a fourth greater dao before he'd be able to go after the grand dao. He rubbed his head in frustration. They didn't have a lot of time.

Pulling the family's dao book from his inner world, he flipped through it on the kitchen table. Once again, Blair's dao drew his attention. They were all related to minerals and part of earth.

Intrigued, his fingers traced the dozen lesser dao she had given his family, a thought forming. Malleable, tough, conductive. Those attributes sounded a whole lot like metal. She had them split up differently, but the more Dar looked at those three lesser dao, the surer he grew that they could form a metal.

"What are you doing?" Sasha came back in with a bowl of food. But her face said she was just as likely to throw it at him as give it to him.

"Just research."

"Put it away. I think we should ban you from looking at that book for the day." She put down the hot bowl of porridge hard enough to slosh it on the kitchen table.

Dar let the book fall back into his inner world and carefully pulled the bowl closer to himself. "You are right. Food sounds much better than dao." He was starving and was far more interested in stuffing himself than studying.

"I should take it back. That was my book once upon a time."

"You should cultivate a new dao. The tree seems more than capable of helping Blair. I bet it could do wonders for you or the rest of the girls."

She sighed and took a seat opposite of him. "Do you really think this is going to come down to some big battle?"

"Positive," Dar said between mouthfuls. "If it isn't the devils, it'll be Kindrake, or even another nation. Sasha, we are surrounded by hornets' nests. And we have already kicked half of them."

"Fine." She held her hand out, and Dar summoned the book again for her to browse. "But, if you are going to make me push for another dao, then you should think about helping Neko, too. And I'm pretty sure she'd rather not cultivate at a tree."

Dar nudged her, understanding her meaning. He'd already been thinking about it. He'd grown closer and more attached to Neko. There was an intimacy in the way she cuddled him and cared for him in her own way that had been progressing, and he was interested in getting even closer to her.

Having seen her in her wilder state, he'd had some trouble seeing her as a woman, but the more time they'd spent together, the harder it was to see her as anything else. And most importantly, the harder it was getting to see her as anything but his.

"I know. Maybe if I'm not all beat up, I should take her to the bedroom."

Sasha nodded. "But remember, it's her first time. Be a gentleman." Sasha got to the back of the dao book, tilting her head in question. "You need to complete it with what you've just learned."

Dar took the book and rather than ask for a pen, he used his dao of combustion and heat to spark a small flame. He used the tip of his finger to burn the dao into the page.

He enjoyed the small gasp he heard from Sasha as he pressed his finger to the pages.

"Dar! You could have burnt the whole thing!" She took the book back and held it to her chest protectively before pulling it back and scanning what he'd added. "Flame sounds interesting."

"Earthen dao, or something along shadow, would be a lot easier with the dao tree."

Sasha shook out her mane of black hair. "Earth doesn't appeal to me, though shadow is interesting. But what would I do with that?"

Dar didn't have an answer, but she should decide that on her own, anyway. "Tami's dao of acceleration is pretty universally helpful." He moved the pages back a few.

There was no argument from Sasha. Speed was always an advantage if it compromised nothing else. "Have you learned it yet? Care to help me along?" Sasha smiled up at him, giving him a wink.

Dar laughed. Apparently, she was loosening back up after his near-death experience. He leaned over, giving her a kiss and pulling her closer.

She tossed the book aside, about to jump in his arms just as Mika walked into the room.

"What are you two doing?" Her eyes landed on Dar. "Did he hurt himself again?"

"He most certainly did," Sasha sighed. "Tried to combine two incompatible dao."

Mika winced. "It is painful enough when we dabble in it. I'm assuming you went full throttle." She gave him a knowing look. "I can only imagine the damage. No pain, no gain, though."

Sasha was less than amused with Mika's disregard. "So, we are looking at all the dao our family has acquired. Dar wants to push us all a step forward before we have a conflict."

"Makes sense." Mika pulled the book closer to her. "Not a lot for me here though."

"Sorry, Mika." Dar felt a little silly that some of their specializations were too different from each other.

"Don't be. There'll be one or two lesser that might interest me, and I can always branch out." She flipped through the book and landed on acceleration. Dar had a feeling all of them would want that one.

Sure enough, she pointed to it. "This seems handy."

Cherry came wandering back in. "Oh good. Sasha didn't kill you."

"Gee. Thanks." Dar rolled his eyes.

"No new bruises, either. Seems like you got off easy. You should have seen her when I first told her you were hurt again." Cherry was peppy as always as she sat up next to Dar. "So, are you going to try it again?"

"No, I'm going to shift focus. I have a new plan."

"Good," Sasha said from the other side of the table. "Now, if we are finished with breakfast, let's get back to working on the village. What do we have?"

Dar leaned back, realizing that he needed to get back to work on the wall. "I'll roll some balls of granite out and see if I can't make progress on the village wall."

"Please don't strain yourself." Sasha sounded worried.

"I'll stick to using my dao for the heavy lifting and just walk alongside it." Dar lifted himself out of his chair. Things hurt, but not so much anymore that he couldn't function. It felt more like he'd had a brutal exercise at the gym the day before and he needed to take it easy. And what Sasha was asking for would use dao instead of his body, anyway.

Wanting to get it done, he headed out of their home. As he stepped outside the cave, Dar pulled on his dao of granite and sectioned off a large round ball of granite that went up to his chest.

Instead of pushing it, he hovered his hand over the surface and pushed it with his dao.

He smiled as the motion was far easier than when he had just formed his greater dao of granite. Now he had three greater dao, and his capacity to manipulate mana had grown with each one.

In its own way, this was an exercise of his power, he realized.

Spurred by that thought, Dar went to work, rolling balls of granite with dao alone. Each time he brought a ball out to the unfinished wall, he would make a new section only two feet tall. For now, he was hoping to keep the goats in more than monsters out.

It would probably take a week of just hauling granite out for him to make a wall tall enough for protection, but for now, he could make the base.

Dar realized as he headed back for another round that he was feeling better than when he had started. It was almost as if each time he drew in mana and poured it out through his dao that it was slowly but subtly healing him.

Dar flexed his arms, feeling less pain. He figured anything was possible with the energy that powered magic.

"Dar," Neko greeted him on one of his trips through the village. The sun was high in the sky, but that did little to warm the chilly day.

Villagers hurried between buildings or clustered near the central hearth. The kilns were also popular. People huddled around them, happy to shovel out and grind up more of the stone that would eventually be used for concrete.

Dar had told Bart it wouldn't set right in the winter, but the old blacksmith hadn't stopped the prep work. They continued to crush and cook what limestone he could find in the caves. Come spring, they would have all the concrete they could want.

"Neko, what have you been up to?"

"Practicing. My new dao is going well."

"What did you form?"

"Claws." Neko demonstrated, a glowing claw ghosting over her hand. In the past, she had done something similar with the dao of sharp, but that had only given off a faint glow at her fingertips. This was far more.

Dar was fascinated by it. Reaching out, he took her hand in his, turning it back and forth to study the claws. Neko was pleased with his touch, purring as he examined her hand.

Reaching out, he pressed his finger to the tip, drawing blood. Neko quickly pulled her hand out of his, frowning at him. "No hurting Dar."

Dar nodded, too lost in his thoughts to reply. Where Dar and everyone else seemed to focus on something elemental, Neko had instead focused on something almost conceptual.

She wasn't actually creating anything physical with the glowing claws over her hand. Instead, it was like the concept of powerful claws wrapped around her hand. In its own way, it was quite unique, almost more of a technique.

Dar wondered if, by putting the villagers on their own dao paths, some of them might learn similar techniques. Or maybe he could even learn it from Neko. The creativity of all the different paths might lead to some amazing new ways to use dao and mana.

"What are you planning for your greater dao?" Dar asked as he rolled the ball of granite into its spot and pushed the material out and into the next section of the wall.

"Predator," Neko answered happily. "Make everyone prey by becoming the ultimate predator."

Dar would have laughed, but she'd proven that she could break the mold with her claws. He wouldn't put it past her to make everybody else prey. "I'm excited to see it one day."

Neko beamed up at him, happy with his approval. "You seem better."

"I'm feeling better. This exercise of my dao is quite good for me." He scooped Neko up, his ribs only protesting slightly.

Momentarily amazed at the change in his body, he almost dropped Neko, but he could feel for a moment all the enchantments on him pulsing and drawing mana along with him. He followed the mana, feeling it focus more than usual on the potent dao character between his legs as it continued to restore his body at an amazing rate.

Neko rubbed herself against him until her lips found his neck. She nibbled and suckled on his neck enough that he knew he was going to have a hickey.

"What's gotten into you?" he asked.

"I got my greater dao. Neko is good enough now," she whispered happily.

Dar was shocked by her statement. "You were always good enough."

But the cat girl shook her head. "You only slept with those with a greater dao."

"The maid's," Dar pointed out.

Neko shook her head again. "Doesn't count. They were yours for other reasons."

Dar hadn't realized how close she had been watching and feeling less than by not being with him. "I want you to know that I wasn't holding off for you to reach your greater dao." Dar felt dirty at the thought.

"Then why?" She kissed his neck again.

"Because you were fresh out of the forest, and you didn't know any better." Dar sighed, trying to think about how to explain it to her without her misunderstanding or feeling worse. "I was concerned you had attached yourself to me not because you wanted to be part of my family, but because we were your shelter, your support system. If you did this because you wanted to cling to that support, I don't know if that would be right. It would feel like I was taking advantage of you."

She stopped kissing his neck for a moment and batted his head until he turned to look at her. She let out a small growl. "I am no helpless kitten. Dar is the best, and Neko deserved the best." She pulled his head down for a kiss on the lips.

More than a few of the villagers watched and giggled. A few nudged each other like they'd won some sort of bet.

"Bed," Neko demanded. "I will put your concerns to rest. Will you accept me as part of your family or push me away again?"

Dar realized he'd delayed too long if she felt so strongly. He didn't want her to ever feel like he'd reject her. "I'd happily go with you, Neko. I'm lucky to have you as part of my family."

"Yes, you are the lucky one, now hurry." She swiped at his neck, and her dao of sharp scratched his neck.

"Feisty," he joked, but she gave him a flat, unamused face.

"Horny," she clarified. Her hands flexed against his shoulder in a signal that she was ready to take another swipe at him if he didn't hurry up.

Dar laughed. Her pushiness was cute, and her reaction had settled his resolve even further. He was eager to explore their connection.

"Dar." Mika caught him at the entrance to their home. But Neko gave her a look that made her immediately step aside, laughing. "I see she finally got tired of waiting."

"Hush." Neko wrinkled her nose. "Or join. But don't stop him."

"Maybe after you've had your first ride." Mika laughed and hurried off.

Dar suspected the rest of his family was about to know not to disturb Neko and him. He already knew that the girls had accepted Neko into their family; it was time he did the same.

Closing the door to his room, he activated the dao of quiet over the door and put Neko on the bed, hovering over her.

"You are amazing, Neko." He forced her head to the side and kissed along her jawline, coming to her chin and working his way up to her lips.

Surprisingly, the tension bled out of her, and she melted like a puddle into the bed. "Tell me I'm the best."

"You're the best cat girl I've ever known."

"The only." She gave him a token pout, but her smile bled through, regardless.

Dar pressed her to the bed as he kissed her, his hands finding her firm toned rear and giving it a good squeeze.

A part of him still couldn't believe this was his life. All of his women loved him, and he could enjoy each without guilt. They were a family.

Neko grabbed the back of his head and crushed their lips together as their tongues twirled in each other's mouth.

Dar savored her soft lips and the wonderful curves of her hips as he felt himself rise to the occasion.

The change didn't go unnoticed by the lovely woman under him. She hooked her ankles behind his hips and rubbed her hips up into his growing erection. Neko gave a lusty growl into his mouth as she continued to press herself against him and rolled on top.

Neko started bouncing herself against him before pushing off him with a growl of frustration. She pulled his clothes off. Her face was flush with lust as she breathed heavily with need.

"Stupid pants," she cursed as she fumbled with Dar's drawstring.

"Let me." Dar lifted his hips off the bed, but his cat girl wasn't patient enough.

Pulling out her claw, she delicately sliced the drawstring and pulled on his pants, his erection coming free and pointing straight up. Neko's eyes shone as she batted it once before sitting down and clenching it in the cleft of her ass.

She was so soft and firm, but what made her unique was the base of her cat tail brushing the head as she bounced on top of him.

Dar reached around and grabbed it, massaging the base.

Neko moaned and started bouncing harder. "Yes," she hissed as she pushed back, causing his erection to poke harder into her rear as she ground on it.

He could feel the wet heat coming from her as her sex pressed against the front of the minimal clothing she wore. She liked to call them pants, but they were barely any fabric.

"Why don't we do something about your clothes?" He tugged at her top.

Neko raised her arms and wiggled as Dar pulled it free, letting her chest flop back down. The perfect, perky mounds topped with a tight little cherry of a nipple were a delectable treat. He forgot about her pants and pulled her down to lick and suck on her tits.

"Ah!" Neko shouted as he enjoyed her chest, his hands coming around to cup and lift them.

She wasn't as big as Sasha, but they were a little more than a handful, and so soft.

He couldn't get enough of Neko as she blushed and squirmed on top of him as he played with her chest.

Neko threw her head back, letting out a shout of frustration as she made claws over her hands and cut away her own pants, ripping them off. "I'm ready. Stop teasing me."

Dar slowed down, kissing her breasts, trading between them evenly as if he was worshiping two twin peaks. Then he lifted Neko off his lap and laid her down on the bed. What Sasha said before stood out in his mind. He wanted to make sure her first time was special.

There, with her hair spilled out behind her, naked with a pink blush on her face, she looked like the visage of innocence.

Dipping his finger into her sex, he pushed her labia aside and felt the wet paradise waiting for him. He drew a thick bead of her juices and circled her clit, feeling it swell under his touch as Neko calmed down. Her breath became steady as she stared at him. The only thing about her that moved was her cute little cat tail as it flailed underneath her.

"More?" he asked, seeing how transfixed she was.

"Yes," she said, quiet as a whisper.

He continued to circle her clit slowly, rewetting his finger every time it became dry. Once he tried to speed up, but she silently grabbed his hand and slowed him back down, soft purrs coming from her.

After a few minutes, Neko shook underneath him, building up to something. It was a quiet, breathy release as she sighed and melted back into the bed. But she looked anything other than finished as she opened her legs wider, looking up at him hungrily.

Dar slid up over her in the bed and kissed her softly on the lips. Her hands weren't the hungry grabbing of before. Now she gave soft touches that trailed over his shoulder and down his arms.

"You like it slow, and loving." It hadn't taken long for him to pick up on her style. He had to admit that he was surprised. She was ferocious outside of bed, but his cat girl was sensitive. She wanted to be loved thoroughly.

Dar gently pushed himself against her sex, letting her coat his tip before working himself past her lower lips.

Neko let out a sigh of relief as he pushed in.

She was tight, but not unbearably so. Dar had to wiggle his hips to make progress until he found himself buried to the hilt.

"Slow," she breathed, closing her eyes and letting her arms hang around his neck.

"My lovely Neko, who knew you were such a lover."

"Shhh." She pressed her head back into the bed and savored the moment, her fingers dancing on the back of his neck as he slowly pressed himself in and out of her.

Dar could feel just how wet she was as he slowly thrust back and forth, dragging himself along her rough inner walls.

He dipped his head down and kissed her slowly with the rhythm of his thrusts. They tangled their tongues, and Neko drew her nails slowly down his back as she moaned softly into his mouth.

Neko made him pause and slow down, savor every inch of her sex as he continued to thrust deep into her and drag himself back out to delicious pleasure.

He wasn't sure how long they made love like that; the whole experience was a drawn out, timeless pleasure.

"I'm cumming," he whispered and Neko pulled him in deep, shuddering as he released into her womb.

"Kittens," Neko said with a sigh.

"Kittens?" Dar asked, surprised.

"Again, fill me with Kittens." She kissed his lips slowly and ground herself up into him. His enchantments didn't let him down as he felt himself once again come to attention to try and give Neko kittens.

He knew that demons and spirits rarely had children, but there was a chance. And something about the chance excited him, spurring him on as he entered her once more.

Chapter 23

Somehow, after Neko and Dar's first two times together, it was like someone had given the green light to the rest of his women. They'd immediately dashed in, wanting touches of their own after his return.

Sasha was especially eager, wanting to reaffirm her connection to Dar. The maids were more than happy to entertain Mika and Neko while Sasha got hers.

Dar woke up from a pleasant dream with Mika and Sasha pressed up along his sides and Neko laying on top of him. He tried to figure out how he was going to disentangle himself from them.

He carefully picked himself out of the three women as his stomach rumbled. Neko had pulled him aside before dinner, and he had skipped the meal in favor of enjoying his women. But now that the fun was over, his stomach was seriously protesting.

"Morning, milord," Marcie said, stirring a pot on the stove. "Would you happen to need food?"

"Good girl." Dar ran his fingers through her hair before kissing the side of her head.

The mousy maid melted into him. He hadn't realized how much his women all were needing touch, and they were alone.

Reaching up under her dress, he pinched her ass.

"Thank you, milord." She pressed herself further into him.

Wanting to reward her, he pulled back her top, exposing her collar. He leaned forward, biting down hard enough to make a mark that would last through the day. He could feel her whimper and shiver.

His little submissive maid loved it.

"Something to tide you over."

She carefully righted her dress. "I look forward to next time."

"You and Amber could have joined us," he told her.

Marcie only shook her head. "It wouldn't be right. We are satisfied with what you've given us and wouldn't dare press for more."

Once again, Dar was forced to accept that their society had different norms. Still, he enjoyed having Marcie in a rare moment without her little mistress.

"How is everything else, Marcie? Does Amber need any particular retraining with you?" He kept it playful since that seemed to help the shy maid open up and express her needs better.

"No, master." She blushed. "My mistress takes wonderful care of me, though it is all for you. It took her many attempts to tie me up as she had before, but I don't mind the mistakes, knowing she's making it perfect for you."

He kissed the side of her head and pulled her into a crushing hug. Marcie might not talk much, but that told him volumes.

"It is my job not only to punish you when you deserve it, but to reward you and keep you safe. Is there anything you need from me?" he asked.

She hesitated before asking, "Maybe next time, could you bring things for piercings?" "I can." He wasn't sure what he'd bring. "Have you played with hot wax before?"

There was a thoughtful look in her eyes before she shook her head. "No, but I can see how that would be interesting. I will procure some candles. You are busy. Now, sit. Your stomach is too loud."

His stomach had been gurgling off and on during their conversation, but Dar had ignored it in favor of discussing Marcie's needs. At her encouragement though, his hunger won out, and he sat at the kitchen table. It didn't take long before Marcie came up behind him with a steaming bowl full of the porridge with shaved bison meat in it.

Dar took one bite before realizing it was far creamier than before. "Goat milk?"

"Yes. I fear everything we eat will have a little goat's milk in it for the near future." She shook her head.

"That's probably for the best. Milk helps keep your bones and teeth healthy, along with providing a whole host of good nutrients. It'll probably bring a noticeable improvement to the village's health to have milk with breakfast."

Marcie nodded along with what he was saying, but he didn't really think she understood. "Will the others be up soon?"

Dar looked back at the door. It was slightly ajar, and he could hear the soft snoring from the pile of women. "I don't think so. But, if you could go get some warm milk and waft it near Neko's nose, I'm sure she'll wake up. She missed dinner as well."

"Yes, milord." Marcie bowed, moving the pot off the burner before she left the mansion to retrieve milk.

For a moment, Dar was alone in the silence.

It had been a while since he had been alone. Granterra had been filled with adventures and new people at every turn. For him to sit idle in the dim light with no one around was odd, yet a relief.

His mind began to spin with thoughts and reflections on what had happened recently as he ate his porridge.

Bellhaven was under siege by an enemy it couldn't handle. And it was possibly his fault. He had certainly riled up the hive and taken away their food source, but Bellhaven had also pushed out some of their best defenses by mistreating the demons and spirits.

And the mantises had already been scavenging for food in the woods. It had only been a matter of time before they would have attacked, regardless of him taking out the Mo. He'd just sped the process up a bit, and at least he'd limited their ability to reproduce quite so quickly. He worked to rationalize all of it.

The larger problem was what to do going forward. Tormac and Kindrake were going to go to war after winter thawed and the mountain passes opened back up. The Deep One was likely to come and claim Bellhaven once The White officially pulled back her protection.

Dar paused, starting to piece the various problems together. There was a chance The Deep One would solve the insect devils in an attempt to protect the city. It would certainly be a way to win the loyalty of Bellhaven.

But it was also possible Bellhaven would fall in that time, or The Deep One would lose interest. Dar couldn't take that chance. He needed to deal with the threat and remove it before it became too much to handle.

Things were going to become complex come spring, and Dar knew the only way to ensure Hearthway would survive the turbid waters was to have power.

He sighed, smacking his spoon on the bottom of the bowl as he took his next bite. His problems had grown from lesser devils and some angry villagers to kingdoms and celestial demons. And beyond that, he'd eventually have to go after the other Mo that would be breaking out across the world.

Sasha had told him to stop pushing himself, but the more he thought about everything, the more he realized that was exactly what he needed to do. Understanding a greater dao was just the next step he needed. Dar needed to go far beyond that, and quickly, before he had larger problems to contend with.

He saw the next steps clearly. He needed to form the new greater dao he had in mind, and if he could use that to make a grand dao, then he wouldn't wait for someone else to intervene. He'd go after the insect devils himself. And he'd feed all their corpses to the little dao tree.

There were so many of the mantis and beetle devils that he could fill his tree with powerful fruits. And, with those fruits, he could empower his family and the village.

He chuckled at the thought of the hundred villagers all having the grasp of at least one greater dao. If he could give everyone three lesser dao and push them in that direction, then come spring, it would be a disaster to Kindrake or whoever challenged them. They'd have a solid force.

The idea solidified in Dar's mind, and he knew what he had to do.

Downing the bowl of porridge that had grown cold, he stepped away into one of the side rooms and sat down to meditate.

Cherry and Blair were in deep meditation within his inner world, working on their own dao. He could feel Blair glowing bright with mana; she was well on her way to forming her grand dao. He wondered if he couldn't race her.

Sitting down next to her by the tree, he took the dao book and the three lesser dao he had picked before. Conductive, malleable and tough.

Focusing on each in turn, they all radiated from the power of earth, and he could feel the little dao tree's support as he started to internalize them.

Dar wasn't sure how long he had been meditating, but when he opened his eyes again, he had his new greater dao. A smile crossed his lips, but he wasn't done yet. He now had the dao of iron. It was a common enough metal to make it extremely useful, and he had no doubt having control of iron would come in handy.

Though most of the tools in the village were a soft bronze, iron was expensive mostly because it was so hard to refine. Maybe with this, Dar could help improve the village as a whole.

But now that he had another greater dao, it was time to make another pass at a grand dao. Some instinct inside of him said that it would work this time. The little dao tree pulsed with excitement as he took the three greater dao and sought to find their combination.

But Dar was startled at what happened next. All it took was one pulse from the little dao tree, and two of the three greater dao locked into position. Like two tumblers of a safe hitting their pins, they clicked together. Granite and iron locked together, with just flame still spinning.

Excitement filled Dar. This... this was incredible.

His mind was a flurry of activity as the flame dao circled and spun around the two that were fixed in place by the little dao tree's power. He searched, trying to find where flame fit to make the most complex character Dar had ever seen in his life.

Mana surged around Dar, but it wasn't for him.

He could feel Blair next to him, becoming a vacuum of power as she changed. She was reaching a new level of dao comprehension, and as a result, the air filled with the complete dao. That sparked an idea in Dar.

He drew just a little of the complete dao that surrounded Blair into himself, pushing it towards his current cultivation.

It had an immediate effect. The dao of flame moved faster into a particular position, although it still wasn't connected. But that was all Dar needed. He immediately stopped rotating the dao around the other two and fixed it in place, spinning it in the same spot.

Dar felt Blair's ascension to a grand spirit complete, the mana in the air returning to normal. He hadn't quite found the right orientation, but he was able to hold its position, spinning until it finally clicked.

Elation ran through him—his own grand dao was completed. He took the completed dao and spun it through his body. Instantly, power bloomed in him.

Raging power swelled from deep inside of him, coursing and filling his body until it began to spill out, threatening to tear him apart. Molten dao came to life inside of him, his new grand dao.

Mana surged into him from the surrounding world. And with it, motes of the complete dao covered him. Dar knew that each time he grew to a new rank, it was an opportunity like no other.

Ignoring his new grand dao for the moment, he drew upon the complete dao and pushed it inside himself.

Once again, he had the opportunity to change himself, evolve. Previously, he had made channels to carry mana through his body, and had also expanded his inner world to store more mana within himself.

But this time, he focused elsewhere. He wanted to help shape his mind, open it up, and expand his consciousness. The grand dao brought with it an opportunity to control the world around him, and he knew he needed more awareness and better ability to multitask to make the most of such a power.

He thought about Cherry, who was able to independently control eight different branches while fighting. That was what he wanted. It was what he needed for what was to come.

So, along with flooding his body with mana, he focused on making it grow stronger, particularly focusing on all the enchantments on his body.

They had saved his life time and time again—Lilith's enchantments had been his foundation for his strength. It was time to elevate his foundation and continue his growth.

Even with his eyes closed, a soft glow penetrated his eyelids. He was changing, growing with each second exposed to the complete dao.

He pushed, not wasting a moment of its power for as long as he could, but then it was gone.

The completed dao faded like a scent on the breeze. One moment it was there, completely surrounding him, part of his awareness, and the next second it was gone.

"I can't believe you almost beat me." Blair's voice was the first thing he heard as he cracked his eyes open.

"Sorry?" He wasn't quite sure if he should really be sorry.

"Oh, don't be sorry. I'm just jealous. I've been working on this forever." Blair sat next to him, her wide amethyst eyes staring into his. "Sasha said you weren't even a lesser immortal a few months ago. I'm over a hundred years old, and I was born a greater spirit. Yet only now am I reaching grand."

Dar sighed. He knew that he was progressing at unparalleled speed thanks to Lilith, but it still didn't seem fast enough for the growing dangers. "At least you'll grow at a remarkable rate now." He patted the tree.

"There are better ways to increase each other's dao." She licked her lips suggestively.

Dar laughed, nudging her and wiggling his eyebrows. Her eyes grew larger, and Dar realized he hadn't shut her down like so many times before.

But he realized he didn't really want to. She'd come on strong at first when he'd barely known her, but he couldn't say that was true anymore. He'd even trusted her enough to let her into his inner world to cultivate. She was quickly becoming a part of his life and a part of their family.

Growing more serious, Dar spoke softly, "Blair, you don't have to hold back anymore. I want you to be all of yourself, suggestive comments included."

She started shifting forward, and he laughed, holding her shoulders.

"I'm not saying we are going to take a tumble right here in the dirt, but I don't feel like resisting this anymore. You're amazing, and I can't deny there's something here between us worth exploring."

She was nearly bouncing where she sat. "Really?"

"Yeah. But before we do anything else, I'd like to try to exercise my new dao, and I'm sure you want to use your own."

"Careful what you ask for. In the past, I've barely been able to find it. I came upon it in a fluke. But now I can create it at will. Maybe I'll cover your inner world in it and make it sparkle." She stood up and stepped away from the tree towards the black stone keep's outer wall, preparing to spar.

"I should be telling you to be careful." Dar rolled to his feet. "It is about time I show you that I just might be more than you can handle."

"Oh, I can handle more than you know. Just wait. You've made me wait long enough; I can't wait to make you beg."

Blair's dao activated, and Dar could feel mana drain from the world around him and cover her. Rapidly, the magical energy converted itself into physical form. A clear crystal began wrapping itself around her in a thin crystal armor.

At first he assumed it was salt, but after a second he realized with absolute shock what one of her greater dao was.

"Holy shit. Is that diamond?" Dar's jaw nearly dropped to the floor.

"What's diamond?" she asked. "All I know is I bought a bag of salt once and found these two little pebbles that weren't salt. They were the toughest little things I had ever experienced."

Dar shook his head. He realized they probably didn't even know how to cut diamonds in Granterra. They might not even have the tools. "Where I come from, it is considered the hardest material in the world."

"Oh. Oh!" She took a moment to realize what he was saying. "So this armor should be pretty tough?"

"Extremely. And we also used to tip certain cutting tools with it so that they wouldn't lose their points. You could make amazing weapons. And given their rarity, it makes it even more powerful in trade." Dar almost didn't want to fight her now that she was covered in diamonds.

Blair had no idea just how versatile and powerful her new dao would be.

"Well then, this should be more fun than I thought." Several small spears of diamond grew in the air around her, pointing at Dar.

Dar shook his head, taking in the beauty of Blair while she stood confidently swirling diamond spears around her. It was mesmerizing.

She laughed, enjoying the attention, and Dar realized he'd been staring. He shook his head and activated his grand dao.

Molten lava burst out of the ground before him and splattered onto him. He wrapped it tightly around him, shifting it into metal and rock armor that glowed bright orange.

He was amazed at the power of a grand dao. With a lesser dao, he could only affect his body and something he touched, and greater dao allowed him to mold it into an object but still required touch. Now with a grand dao, he could create using nothing but mana.

There had been no lava in the ground, but he'd been able to call it forward.

And it wasn't just molten granite or molten iron that he had control over. It was all types of lava and molten metals that came to mind. Although he had to admit, he had a certain affinity for iron and granite. The armor he wore now was made up of those two.

"Impressive. It's like the burning rivers I've heard Mika speak of in Mahaklan." Blair stared back, looking more than eager to fight. But Dar did notice beads of sweat were already forming on her brow.

"Then let's start." Dar punched his molten fists together, letting some of it splash down to the ground, burning patches of grass and leaving behind drips of black rock.

Blair's diamond lances shot forward and punched into his molten armor with incredible force, but they didn't penetrate. Instead, the semiliquid of magma absorbed the impact, and they began to burn rapidly.

"I wasn't sure if diamond would burn. But it makes sense—it is pure carbon." Dar brushed the remains of the lances off of himself. Diamond had caused him some concern, but he shouldn't have been worried. Lava was incredibly powerful, and he couldn't wait to test it out.

"On second thought, I'm not going to attack." He realized just how much heat he was putting off. Even an accidental touch would likely burn Blair.

Blair's brow pinched down in frustration. "I thought you wanted to test yourself." She leapt into the air, forming a large crystalline sword and swinging it down at him.

Dar blocked, feeling his enchantments flair to life as he caught her blade. Then he twisted it, throwing Blair down against the ground.

"Going to have to do better than that," he chastised her.

"You really aren't going to hit back?"

"I think I'm a little too hot for you to handle at the moment." He shrugged, leaning against the black stone keep's outer wall before his eyes popped open and he realized two things in rapid succession.

First, he had failed to remember to open the Blackstone Keep when he had had access to the complete dao.

Second, the black stone of the keep was made of lava rock.

He froze. Could it just be a coincidence? Dar couldn't help but feel a small shiver at the way it felt like fate was guiding him on his path.

"What's wrong?" Blair could tell something was amiss.

"I need to try something." He dismissed his molten armor, letting the physical lava he had made transition back into mana.

Blair did the same, her diamond armor disappearing. "Okay, I'm all ears. What are we doing?"

Chapter 24

Dar pushed forward into the Blackstone Keep's training yard and to the door that had blocked his path. He'd meant to break it down when he formed his grand dao, as he had with the gate before, but he'd forgotten.

But, if it was formed of lava rock, he might just be able to control it now.

"Are you going to tell me what's going on?" Blair followed him.

"This keep was already here inside of me when I first became an immortal."

"You didn't make it?" she asked.

"No. I think Lilith, the first witch, put it here. Like she did with the dao tree."

Blair froze on the spot. "Maybe we shouldn't mess with it."

"Calm down. She put it inside of me, and that means she gave it to me. I don't think we have anything to worry about."

Blair hesitated a moment before catching up. "So what's the problem?"

"There used to be a gate blocking me from entering this portion. I knocked it down when I formed my greater dao. I forgot to knock down this door with my grand dao." He pointed at the entrance to the keep. "But as things would happen, the stone is made of once molten rock, and I think I can clear a path myself now."

"That's a coincidence..." She realized it as she said it. "Oh. Yeah, that's kind of creepy."

Dar nodded. It was more than a little unsettling. Had Lilith been able to predict the future? Nothing Cherry had told him pointed to such an ability. But he couldn't help but feel it was all lining up. Had Lilith somehow planned out all of it, and he was just following a path she'd laid out for him?

He looked up at the keep, wondering if it would have the answers. Lilith was dead, but she might have left clues inside.

Pressing his hand to the frame around the door, he melted the area where the lock would be and pulled.

The door came free; the lock still sticking out.

"Why didn't you just bust down the door before?" Blair asked.

"I couldn't—it was too strong."

Her eyes roved over the otherwise normal looking door. Dar knew better; it was covered in enchantments much like himself.

"So what's inside?" She tried to look around him as he paused in the doorway.

He looked as well. It was... plain. It looked like any normal home. Dirty dishes even sat on the counter, long forgotten.

Dar took a step inside, letting Blair join him. The other girls weren't in his inner world. He would have to bring them later.

"Think someone lives here?" she asked.

"No, I don't think anyone has lived here for some time." There wasn't any dust, but there also wasn't the warmth that often accompanied an occupied home.

He walked through the area, feeling a strange nostalgia for a life he didn't remember. Nothing on the first floor caught his eye, so he wandered up the stairs. As he hit the hallway, he saw a master bedroom, and it drew him.

The sheets were ruffled, messed up from someone's sleep long ago.

But what caught his attention was a book. Although, it was more like a tome considering the sheer size of it. Dar picked it up and flipped it open.

Inside were dao characters. There were hundreds, maybe even thousands, of them littering the pages. All of them lesser dao, but the possibilities with all of them were practically endless. And each was labeled. Dar just stood there, too shocked to move.

"What's that?"

"I think it is Lilith's dao book." He turned to hand it to Blair, but it fell right through her fingers when she tried to grab it. "Huh. She must have enchanted it."

"But you can pick it up," Blair gasped. "Lilith's fucking dao book. Do you realize how many demons would kill for that? The White would probably leave her little frosty bitch mountain and come take it if she knew it was here."

Dar nodded, realizing he held one of the most precious treasures in the world. "You'll tell no one?" he asked for confirmation.

"Of course not. That would be a great way to end up dead. Some secrets are worth keeping a secret." Blair shook her head in disbelief. "Damn."

"Damn is right." Dar put the book down, feeling like it was a little too hot to handle at the moment. "I don't even know where to start with it."

"Yeah, that's a brick full of knowledge there. Best keep it here. It's too risky to even take it out of your inner world."

He couldn't agree more, turning and leaving the room. After finding the book, he was curious if Lilith had left anything else.

But, after searching the entire keep, he couldn't find anything more from her. He realized that, beyond power, he'd hoped for something... personal. Maybe even a note with guidance. He was starting to feel out of his depth.

Blair hesitated by his side. "Let's get out of here. We should go celebrate with everyone else that we both reached our grand dao." She injected as much excitement as she could into her voice.

"Yeah. Let's get out of here. This place feels like it is haunted with old memories." He left the dao book upstairs for the moment.

Blair shivered in agreement and grabbed his arm, pulling him out of the keep. When they got close to the dao tree, he brought them both out of his inner world.

They appeared in one of the unused bedrooms.

Blair cast a look at the bed behind him and raised an eyebrow. "Wanna knock one out?"

"Maybe another time. That place got me in a weird mood."

"It was kind of creepy, like being in someone else's home when they aren't home."

Dar stood and offered her a hand up. "Exactly. So strange."

Walking out of the spare room with Blair, he wondered what time it was.

"There you are." Sasha put her hands on her hips until she saw Blair, a knowing smile crossing her lips. "Ah. That's what you've been up to today."

He almost argued, but then smirked, pulling Blair against him. “Caught me red-handed.”

He was ready to push forward with Blair, and he didn’t really want to tell Sasha he’d gone after the same approach as before to create a grand dao. “She helped me with my latest dao.” Technically, it was the truth.

Blair was startled for just a moment before she shifted and hung off of him. “Such a delight.” She traced his jaw with a finger and whispered in his ear. “You owe me, and you know exactly what I want.”

Sasha’s eyes narrowed; she could tell something was slightly off, but she let it go. “Great. Glad you took the easier route offered. Welcome to the family, Blair.”

The salt spirit did a little bow. But then Dar realized that salt spirit didn’t fit her anymore. She was the spirit of crystals in their many forms. Diamond. He shook his head at that little secret she’d hidden from them.

But she’d always be a salt spirit to him.

“Blair, show her your new grand dao.” Dar nudged her forward.

“Dar was pretty impressed.” Blair shone with pride as she raised her palm. A diamond sphere grew in her hand.

Sasha stepped forward and plucked it from Blair, holding up the sparkling orb. “What is it?” She banged it on the table. “Not glass or salt.”

“It’s a gemstone. One that is considered the hardest material,” Dar explained.

“Oh.” Sasha made an appreciative noise as she hefted the sphere. “So you both have a grand dao now?” she asked with a smile. “That’s amazing! There are so many things you can do with it.”

There was a small touch of bitterness in her voice, and Dar wondered if he had run too far ahead of Sasha.

“Now we need to work on getting you your grand dao.” He left Blair’s side and wrapped Sasha in a hug. “Or not, it is entirely up to you.”

"I know what you are doing," she huffed.

He kissed the top of her head. "And I can see that you are pouting."

"I'm so happy for you! Really. It's just... you are hurtling forward in your dao path. I don't want to be left behind." Sasha leaned into him.

Blair quietly stepped away, seeing that Sasha needed some time.

"I won't leave you behind."

Sasha shook her head into his chest. "But what happens when next week you are learning your first celestial dao, and I am nothing but a little greater demon. When some problem arises, you will have to shove me in the back of the cave or stand in front of me the whole time. I refuse to be useless."

Dar wanted to argue, but with her current strength, it was pretty close to what he likely would do. Even with the oncoming insect devil problem, he wanted to stuff Sasha in a safe place.

"Then what do you want?"

"To stand by your side." She put her foot down firmly.

Dar set his jaw and nodded. "Then you need to grow stronger. In my inner world, we found Lilith's dao booklet today. It's in the Blackstone Keep. Take it and grow stronger, but we don't have long, Sasha." He had a feeling that it would work for the women that had joined with him recently.

Her nose flared, and her eyes filled with determination. "If that's what I have to do, then so be it. Bring me into your inner world."

Dar gave her one last kiss and transported her into the Blackstone Keep.

Walking out of his home for the first time since getting his grand dao, he felt great. The world was in a sharper clarity than it had been before, and he felt substantially stronger.

Dar felt like he could defend Hearthway so much better, but now it wasn't just him. With Blair growing in strength as well, that put their village at three grand demons. They were now stronger than Bellhaven had ever been. And only with Tami's family would Kindrake be any stronger.

Dar ached to put his power to use as he looked around, wanting an excuse. When he saw the partially finished wall, a smirk grew on his face.

He walked over and pushed lava up from the ground, pouring it up the sides of the granite foundation. Using his dao, he held it in place while it cooled. He kept going in sections, making each about ten feet tall by ten feet wide and a few feet thick. That was about his limit to the amount of molten material he could control at one time, but that was still amazing.

He used his dao of heat and drained the excess heat to speed it along. He couldn't make something cold, but he could disperse some heat from the several thousand-degree rock.

The end result was a shiny black stone with heavy silver striations. Dar looked it over, pleased.

"What is this?" Bart and Glump came up behind Dar.

"Grand dao," Glump answered before Dar. "An extremely potent one."

Bart watched with awe-filled eyes. "You're making this with your dao?"

"Yup." Dar let himself feel a little smug. Having a grand dao was a massive step. "But these sections are about all I can create at once."

Bart didn't touch the wall. Instead, he pulled a hammer from his belt and swung at it. Rather than chip or break, the wall only dented a barely noticeable amount. "Is this metal?"

"About seventy percent of it is." Dar could feel just how much was there. He had an instinctual feeling of what would have worked, and he realized any percentage of stone to metal would have made a wall, but if he had made it anymore stone, then it would have been brittle and chipped more easily. If he had made it any more metal, then it would have been far softer.

"Can you make molten metal?" Bart asked, his eyes wide with excitement, clearly already running through the possibilities.

"That I can. I can also make iron now."

"Fruit you could share?" Bart asked hopefully.

Dar only laughed. "I'm afraid it won't be that easy, friend. But I can give you the lesser dao and the technique to train towards being able to do it yourself."

"Without the grand dao, you need the material," Glump croaked in reminder.

"I'm a damn blacksmith," Bart chuckled. "I'll get all the iron I need if I can mold it with my hands and mind."

He focused back on what Dar was doing. "If you can make me molten iron, we can work it on the forge. This stuff doesn't seem very pure."

"I'm afraid you are correct. What I'm creating is more like raw iron ore. Maybe I could work on something to help refine it." Dar scratched at his chin as more molten material crept out of the ground, making the next section.

"We know how to refine the ore if you can make us something that can withstand the heat." Bart smiled back at Dar, clearly eager to get working on the new project. "My boys would love to get the forges. You get us up and running and we'll pump out anything the village needs."

"Okay. After the wall, we'll work on making a small foundry." Making a foundry had not been on his village plan, but they would figure it out. It was a natural extension of his new skill. And Bart was just the man to run it. "If you are impressed by my dao, wait until you see Blair's."

Glump looked horror stricken. "She's also a grand spirit now? Your family… has exceeded all expectations."

"I know, and now we hope to start sharing with the village." With his new strength, Dar was ready to start sharing information more broadly, and he trusted Glump. "We have fruits that can help anybody learn a dao, even the humans."

Glump's eyes shifted to Bart. "I had wondered why I could feel mana from you. But we've all been respectful. It's the same with your maids. And since you've returned, they've felt like greater demons."

"I knew I wouldn't be able to hide it for long. Glump, it is about time I used it to help not only my family but the other demons and spirits in the village. Let me finish this and start on Bart's foundry. When dinner comes, I'll lay everything on the table."

"A grand day indeed. Two new grand dao in the village!" Glump shook his head in disbelief. "I look forward to tonight."

The old demon looked like a little kid before Christmas and hurried away, most likely to share the news with his dao companions.

Bart hung back, watching Dar put up another section. "What did you have in mind for the foundry?"

"We just need something simple, right?" Dar asked for clarification. "A vessel for me to pour molten metal into so that you and your guys can work it? I'm thinking a wide, shallow bowl, and then we need to make sure that you can pour out of it."

"Just have it make bars," Bart agreed. "We can work the bars into something else. And yeah, just a large bowl with a pouring lip should work. And we'll need it on a stand next to a grid we can pour into. Beyond that, we just need some sort of heat source so that the bowl stays hot."

"How big do you want it?" Dar asked, thinking through the plans in his head.

Bart held his arms out like he was wrapping them around something. "Maybe an opening this large and a foot or two deep. It'll only make a dozen bars at a time, but it'll be work to keep it heated and scrape off the crud and flux."

"I think we can manage that. Blair's new dao is pretty heat resistant, but it'll burn on direct contact. So we'll need to line it with a solid layer of clay. But I think it'll hold well." Dar chuckled to himself, thinking about making diamond equipment. It was very heat resistant and made entirely of carbon; it was perfect fuel for fire. But it would be near blasphemy to use a diamond bowl for trade work back on Earth.

Bart nodded along eagerly. "Perfect, I'll let you two think about the construction."

The wheels in Dar's head were already spinning as he pushed another section of the wall up. Without having to build something by hauling all the stone out of the cave, he was making extremely fast progress. He'd have the wall done by dinnertime.

Bart stayed to watch a little longer before disappearing, replaced at some point by Cherry.

"Dar. This is incredibly powerful for a grand dao," she whispered.

"I know. I wanted something with power and building capabilities as well."

Cherry watched and the orange glow from the molten wall reflected in her eyes. "You'd stomp Karn with this. His ice would barely even stall you if you threw this at him. But don't get complacent. The White would put this out with a glance."

"What's her dao?" Dar asked. It was the first time Cherry was giving him information on stronger opponents. Before, she'd always thought it was too far above him. He was happy that she considered him so much more powerful.

"Celestial dao are a little different, Dar. They are absolute in some aspect, within a range. She is practically a Drasil."

Dar recognized the word that the townspeople used for the no longer existent gods that once held the Mo back. "So what does it do?"

"She's capable of freezing anything and everything so absolutely that it can be like time stops for the ones that are frozen."

"Absolute Zero," Dar said with a shiver.

Cherry looked at him with a question on her face. "What's that?"

"A theoretical minimum of temperature," Dar explained. "One that supposedly can't be reached. But to be fair, I'm pulling lava out of thin air. I suppose a lot is possible with dao."

"You're still making it come out of the ground," Cherry pointed out.

He raised a brow at her. "You seem to do the same thing with plants."

She shrugged. "It's easier than making a free-floating root."

Dar understood her dao much more now. So much of how his dao worked had to do with his intention, how he visualized it. It was much harder to imagine lava forming in midair than it was to have it come out of the ground.

"I get it now. But the question is, what's next?"

Cherry shook her head in disbelief. "I can't believe I'm saying this, but we work towards two more grand dao, with a celestial dao in mind. Dar, you just entered the real fight. Grand dao is the kind of power that creates or destroys kingdoms. And it's also the level of power that gets attention."

Dar nodded. The difference between a greater dao and a grand dao was massive. He could feel it in his newfound power. He was left wondering what a celestial dao would feel like.

Chapter 25

Dar slapped the rest of the clay over the diamond cauldron for the foundry, using his own dao of heat to bake the clay into a ceramic liner. It wouldn't last forever, but it would do its job of insulating the diamond.

Ceramics were surprisingly heat resistant.

The sun was setting, so he made his way over to the central hearth while the cauldron cooled down. He'd fill it for Bart in the morning.

"Everything go okay?" Bart asked as Dar approached the leader's circle.

Everyone was there, even Samantha. Dar did a double take when he saw her; she looked twenty years younger.

"Went well. We'll pick a spot for it tomorrow, and I'll fill it for your boys." Dar took his seat, turning his attention to Samantha. "Looks like Amber was able to help you?"

"Yes." She blushed. "I'm getting a lot of questions today, and so is Jerry. How do I answer them?"

Dar nodded. That was a great segue into what he wanted to discuss tonight with the group. "We answer them honestly from here on out. I have fruits that will allow humans to step onto the dao path. We'll be providing them out to our townspeople. But, Samantha, we need someone to guide them on the transition."

"I can do that," she agreed. "Do we let the kids eat these? Is it safe?"

That was a great question. Dar thought about it for a moment. "Yes. Let's make sure they stick to something safe though, like the dao of quiet. The last thing we need is for some kid to run around with the dao of combustion and start blowing holes in homes."

The group gave a nervous chuckle; with these sorts of powers, kids would be dangerous.

"You are right. Kids get something relatively safe, and we help them learn. Can we do them last? That way, the rest of us are able to keep up with them." Rex said it in a half teasing, half serious voice. "The last thing the guards need is a few dozen kids bolting through the town with parents chasing after them."

"Another good point," Dar agreed as Amber handed him a bowl of food. "Russ, you look worried." He couldn't help but notice that the gnoll's bestial face was pressed into a frown.

Russ had his own bowl of food and had stared into it long enough that Dar was worried he hadn't heard anything they'd said. "We found some dead bison at the edge of the fields."

"Something got them?" Rex asked.

"I uh... don't want to worry anyone, but we are debating if it was the insect devils that everyone is worried about."

Dar paused with his food halfway to his mouth. "We'll check it out tomorrow. I don't think they should be this far north already... but we can't be too careful."

"Thanks. I didn't want to worry everyone."

Glump patted the younger demon on the back. "It's good. And shows you're progressing. You would have gone and tried to fight them on your own a few weeks ago."

Russ huffed. The young demon had a history of being reckless, but it would seem life in Hearthway had managed to temper him some. "I know."

"Good." Dar went back to eating, speaking around his food. "Blair and I will go with you tomorrow and check it out."

"Won't that leave the village weak?" Rex asked. "Cherry goes where you go."

Dar thought about it, trying to assess the threat. These devils seemed to work and strategize in groups, like an ant colony. "If there's a problem this far north, it's a scout. Only once it goes back to the hive will more come. We are far enough away from the issue that there's little risk to the village. Besides, we have several greater demons here that could help if a scout comes this way."

More than a few of the leaders seemed unsure, but Dar was confident in his assessment.

But the discussion brought up the other topic Dar wanted to share. "I'd like to get to a place where our town doesn't rely on only a few grand demons. I told you about the fruit, but I have another surprise as well. I have a way to speed up everyone's dao path."

The younger members seem surprised, but the old demons like Rex and some of Glump's wives didn't even flinch, but they did lean forward, interested. It seemed that the speed of his and his family's progression hadn't gone unnoticed.

"More importantly, I want to share this with all of you. Glump, what I have right now specializes in helping earth-related dao. Would you like to see if you can push forward?"

The old frog demon looked back at his wives who quickly nodded. "I would be interested. What do I have to do?"

"You'd need to leave for a short while. I can't move it, and you'd need dao characters to practice. I can provide those to you as well, but you have to tell me what you want."

"Dar. You make it sound like there's no limit to what you can provide." The old demon gave him an appraising look that held both warning and fear.

"I'd say that's close enough to the truth."

"What about the rest of us?" Russ nearly shouted.

Dar knew that after a few of them made great strides in their dao path, it would be hard to keep up with demand. "Right now, I can help those with earth-related dao best. If you have companions with those skill sets, they are welcome to join Glump."

Russ jerked his head at one of his wives. Mindy, the Ram demon, stepped into their circle. "I would like to go with Glump."

Rex rubbed his chin. "Would you take someone who would want an earth dao for their second or third greater dao?"

"Of course," Dar was quick to answer. "Pushing more of our village to grand dao is a priority. Blair used this advantage to form her grand dao." He looked over at his family unit and waved Blair over.

She did a double take and pointed to herself in question.

Dar chuckled and nodded, urging her to come over again.

Blair nearly dropped her food as she hurried over. "What can I do for you all?"

"I was just offering to the group to let some of them cultivate under the little dao tree like you did. They seem a little skeptical."

"Oh." Her eyes went wide, and she looked at the group. "Don't be. I wasn't his dao companion, and I used the tree, forming my grand dao in just three days."

There were hisses as several of the demons in the group took sharp breaths.

"How did it work?" Glump asked, anticipation in his eyes.

"Well, I just sat against this tree that Dar has." Those words brought confusion to a few faces. "The tree radiates dao, particularly that of earth and darkness. I just sort of soaked it up, and it helped me align my three greater dao. It is hard to explain without experiencing it."

Rex turned away from the circle, and one of his wives spoke to him briefly before hurrying off into the night. He turned back to the group. "I think there's little harm in trying this. We should all have one person from our families give it a try. If this works, it would be huge."

Bart raised his hand. "Did your dao of iron come from this?"

"Partially." Dar realized that the blacksmith would be eager to try it.

"Then, I'd like to see what it can do myself."

"Each of you should talk with your families. After dinner, I'll take those that want to join to the little dao tree," Dar agreed.

Samantha frowned. "Why are you so secretive about where it is?"

But it was Rex who answered her. "Samantha, I don't think you understand the gravity of what he is offering. Kingdoms would be crushed for such a thing. Frost's Fang itself would move if they knew where it was. For Dar to even let us use it is showing us a great deal of trust."

The woman nodded, not quite satisfied, but apparently dissuaded from pushing further.

"Thank you, everyone. Enjoy dinner, Russ. I'll see you in the morning to come with you to see the bison herd." Dar decided to leave the circle and head back to his girls, pulling Blair back with him.

The white-haired spirit blushed as she held his hand. "We still haven't had our date."

"I know," Dar sighed. "I promise we'll have it soon."

"Is it bad that I'm just happy that everyone thinks I'm your dao companion?" she whispered.

"No, I'd never fault you for being happy." Dar squeezed her hand and pulled her to his side as he sat down among the girls that made up his family.

All of them gave Blair a welcoming smile. Mika bumped hips with her and gave her a pat on the back. "See, I told you it would happen if you were patient."

"Guess you were right." Blair blushed. "Just have to be patient." She said the last bit with a meaningful look at Dar.

He had accepted her into the family, even if they hadn't been physical yet. To him, she was his dao companion now. "So, I wanted to make sure you all knew. We'll have some guests at the little dao tree for the foreseeable future."

Cherry pouted. "Does that mean we can't…" Her tongue pressed against her cheek in a lewd gesture.

Dar looked at her as he continued, "The other piece of news is that the Blackstone Keep in my inner world has opened up. I suggest we try to stay there when we need privacy." He tried to be discreet, but they all knew what he meant.

"Great." Cherry perked up. "I'd hate to miss time with my tree."

There were those crazy eyes again.

"Maybe we should have someone looking after the tree while they are there?" Amber suggested.

"Not a bad idea. But I don't want any of you to think that this stops any of you from using the tree. We all need to keep growing stronger." With that information out, he had to get to the bad news. "Also, I'm going to go with Blair tomorrow and check out the bison herd. Russ says that there were signs of what he believes might have been insect devils killing a few bison."

"That's not right. How could they have ranged this far already?" Tami argued.

Dar nodded along with her. "I feel the same, but it needs to be checked out."

"I wish to come then." Tami set her jaw.

"Mika, can we spare that much room in the boat?" Dar asked the wave spirit.

She tilted her head, making her blue hair splash about. "It's going to get tight. We might have to do one less bison for the three of you."

Dar had slightly hoped she'd say no. One bison wasn't a big deal; they had a surplus at the moment. But it seemed Tami would be able to join.

"Tami, we probably need to talk about what to do with you." Dar put it out there, not hiding anything.

"Do with me?" She leaned back, looking at the group.

Sasha nodded. "She's been in our home long enough to have learned some of our secrets. Can we afford to have them shared with her father?"

"We could just kill her as food for the tree," Cherry suggested, though Dar wasn't sure if she was being serious or just trying to scare the girl.

Tami's head was whipping back and forth as the woman spoke. "Whoa. Why would you kill me?"

"You've noticed the humans following a dao path in the village." Neko nodded to herself. "I've seen you watching a few of them. And you know about Dar's secrets, that he's progressing far too fast and that he learned your dao in just a day."

Neko was right. He'd been casual about his secrets lately.

"I think you're right, Neko. We need to do something with Tami." Dar turned to the deer demon. "So, what's it going to be?"

"What do you mean?" She was struggling like she was about to bolt.

"You said you were under oaths to your father. That means you are going to have to tell him what you saw here, I bet." Dar let out a sigh. She was starting to grow on him.

Tami stayed silent for a moment, working through what to say. "I... I could just not head back to Kindrake. If something prevented me from going back, then my oaths wouldn't come into play."

Dar stared at her for a moment before nodding. "Then you are officially my prisoner. Swear an oath that you won't try to escape, and you'll have some level of freedom in the village."

"I swear on my dao that I won't try to flee Hearthway, or your operations. My movements will be limited to where you go and tell me to go," Tami said quickly.

Dar froze. She'd just said an incredibly restrictive oath. Dar winced, realizing just how much of her freedom she had just willingly given up and knowing they had likely been said similarly to what she'd had to give to her father.

"Would you like to put a little more leniency in that oath?" Dar asked.

"No, it needs to be this way," Tami stated firmly.

That meant that her father had her under tight oaths. What an evil man to have put his own daughter under such restrictions.

"Fine. You can come with us. But I won't be giving you the same benefits for training your dao as the village," Dar told her.

"I agree. You shouldn't help me progress to the grand dao—not while I'm under oaths to someone who would work against you. However, I would be willing to offer my dao to your family." Tami bowed slightly as she finished.

"Why?" Dar didn't understand why she'd offer to help them so much.

"Because I want to," Tami said, sticking her chin out. "This place is... peaceful. That you lead it as you do has earned my respect."

Mika chuckled. "He really is one of a kind. Compared to all the male demons and spirits I've met, Dar is a powerful and merciful leader."

"Glump, Rex, and Russ seem benign enough," Dar argued.

Blair put a hand on his arm to get his attention. "That is because they follow your lead. Glump might normally be pretty placid, but that's mostly because he's a lazy frog who would rather lie in the mud all day. Rex or Russ would be far more aggressive in a leadership position."

"Think about Stupid Bear," Neko pushed. "Imagine what a village would look like under his leadership."

Dar thought about Karn, and the stories he'd heard from Mika, and the islands to the south. Even what he'd heard of Tami's father was brutal.

Was he really that much of an exception? By the looks on all the girls' faces, it would seem he was.

"Well, I'm just going to keep being me. If I start to become too soft or too hard, that's on you girls to slap me upside the head."

"There he goes again," Sasha sighed. "No demon would ask his women to help course correct him."

"Bah," Dar spat. "I'm no demon. I'm an immortal. Besides, I have other needs."

"Yes, you do." Cherry licked her lips.

"Kittens," Neko agreed.

"Kittens?" Sasha turned, surprised by her statement.

Neko nodded, making those ears of hers bounce. "I want Dar to give me kittens."

The group all looked at Dar expectantly.

He shifted, not loving the spotlight at that moment, but he knew he had to address the questions in their eyes. "I know the chances are low for pregnancies among demons and spirits, but I don't see any reason to prevent them. It's not like we are using condoms."

"But do you want... kittens?" Sasha asked.

"I wouldn't mind kids," Dar agreed. "I think the timing is dangerous, but then again, in nine months, I could be a powerhouse beyond what this world has ever seen. So why wait?"

The girls collectively sighed, and Sasha spoke up, "Yes, very different from demons. Most don't want kids. They are a time sink that would take away from their power and prowess."

"Stupid," Dar muttered. But he understood that immortality brought with it different challenges. He wondered if humans would push off kids longer if they were immortal.

He thought about it for a few minutes and realized they probably would. It changed the focus from species survival to personal survival.

Coming out of that thought, he found the girls still staring at him. "Let's round up those that want to cultivate by the little dao tree, and then we'll see if we can't get Neko kittens."

"Yes. Let's hurry." Neko got up and pulled Dar off his stump. "Get people to the dao tree. Hurry. Hurry." She shoved him even as he laughed at her eagerness.

Dar went around and gathered up a small crew to cultivate under the little dao tree. Mindy, Bart, Glump, Darande, and Shelia joined. He walked them into the cave before they stopped.

"Alright, I need all five of you to close your eyes and relax." Dar told the group as Blair joined them.

"I'll get them situated. Otherwise, I think Neko will claw your eyes out." The white-haired spirit laughed with a little nervousness.

He knew she wasn't fully comfortable with their current situation. And their little misunderstanding with Sasha wasn't helping. She was anxious to truly become his dao companion.

Drawing the group of six into his inner world, Dar turned back to the rest of his family. He eagerly pulled them into their bedroom.

"Hold up. Before we go any further, I have a confession." He stopped the girls.

They looked confused, but gave him space.

"I have not consummated dao companionship with Blair. It was a misunderstanding that I've let go too far." He looked at Sasha apologetically.

"Do you accept her as your companion?" Sasha asked, confused.

"Yes, I do."

"Then it'll happen. I'm not happy that you let the lie grow, but I think I understand. Don't do it again?" She pressed her finger into his chest at the last statement.

"I won't. It was silly," he agreed.

"Good. Then, girls, he has far too many clothes on, don't you think?" Sasha ran a finger down Dar's shirt, causing the silk to ripple and peel back. It was like her finger was unzipping the fabric.

Neko was there in an instant, pulling the shirt off while Cherry closed the doors to his room. Mika moved quickly, tugging down on his pants. All of them moved with eagerness, and he enjoyed their touch.

He loved his girls.

CHAPTER 26

"Dar, it's time to get up." Mika shook him gently at first, then harder when he didn't wake up immediately.

"Uh. Time?" Dar asked groggily.

"Time to go." She pushed and pulled, but he was stuck between Neko and Sasha.

The cat girl responded to his movement by holding his arm tighter and nuzzling into his shoulder.

Dar pinched his eyes open and saw his predicament. Scooting the cat girl off his arm as gently as he could, he lifted himself out of the bed. Then he reached forward, grabbing the bed pole and using the dao of granite to help pull him out of bed.

Mika gave him a raised brow. "That's what you use your dao for?"

"It gets harder and harder to escape the bed every morning." He shrugged, grabbing a set of clothes that Sasha had laid out for him. She'd needed to mend them after unmaking them the night before.

Ducking out of the bedroom and closing the doors, Dar realized Tami had been waiting just outside, and he was still naked.

"Hold on." Dar covered himself and got dressed behind the kitchen table.

"Don't mind me." Tami turned away as her face warmed.

"Blair is still in your inner world?" Mika asked.

Without her reminder, Dar might have forgotten. He pushed and Blair popped out, rubbing the sleep from her eyes. "Always a little startling to have that happen. But I'm starting to learn how to feel it coming."

"How is everyone settling in to cultivate?"

Blair covered her mouth as she yawned before answering, "Not a lot of questions. Most of them could feel it when they settled down next to the tree. After that, it's been quiet as they all are taking advantage of the opportunity."

"Progress?" Dar asked.

She gave him an unamused look. "It has only been a single night. We aren't all freaks."

"If you two are done, Russ is probably pacing back and forth by now, waiting. We are usually well on our way by now." Mika swung her trident over her shoulder. "Coming?"

Tami was on her feet and behind Mika in a flash. "Right behind you."

Blair rolled her eyes and sauntered after Mika, swinging her hips exaggeratedly for Dar's pleasure. He took the moment to check her out. Blair had curves where Mika was toned, and Tami was just thin.

"Stop staring and come along, Dar." Mika waved her hand over her shoulder.

He wasn't going to deny it. "Sorry, distracted by the beautiful view." But he sped up, following Mika out to the village proper where, exactly as she predicted, Russ was pacing.

There was a moment's thought that he'd have to fill the crucible full of iron, but then again, Bart was still in his inner world. He could do it when he let him out.

"Finally!" Russ shooed his girls ahead of him towards the Bell River. "It is important we get out there early."

Dar shrugged. He thought it was still plenty early. "It can't be too hard to hunt bison around a herd."

Russ didn't respond to that, instead changing the topic. "How's Mindy?"

"Blair was with them, and Cherry is with them now. According to them, everything is going well." Dar didn't have much more than that to say.

"Good," Russ said excitedly. "Mindy is really sharp; she'll pick up dao quickly."

"Surprised you didn't want to go train." Dar honestly thought the gnoll would want to become stronger, faster.

But he shook his big dog-like head. "Not interested in earth or shadow. A hunter needs to be quick, agile, and able to chase down prey. Wind is what I'd like."

Dar was surprised. The logic made sense, but Dar had thought Russ would be interested in earth. "Surprised. Figured earth would interest you."

"You have to play to your weaknesses sometimes," Russ answered.

Ah, that mindset made far more sense why he'd want to go for wind. At the very least, it showed that Russ was maturing. The demon that had showed up at Hearthway in the first few days wouldn't have come up with a plan like that.

"Good for you." Dar patted him on the back as they got to the river. There, he saw Russ' girls hauling thick cords of rope into the boat. "That's a lot of rope."

"Takes a lot to hang a bison and bleed it out," Russ grunted, picking up more of the rope and throwing it onto the boat.

Dar followed suit, taking an armful of rope and jumping onto the deck of the boat, before pulling hand over hand and helping get the rest of the rope loaded.

"Alright, everyone ready?" Mika called out, getting behind the helm of the boat and using a long pole to push the boat off the shoreline.

"Seems we are on our way despite what we say," Blair said dryly.

"Oh, hush." Mika was excited as she started up the enchanted piece of the boat that functioned much like an onboard motor. Water sloshed out behind them as Mika turned the boat into the river.

Tami ran to the back and grabbed the rails, looking into the wake. "What is this?"

"Dar made it," Mika answered her. "He makes lots of interesting things. Watch this." She slammed the lever forward and the boat's front rose out of the water as the boat zoomed across the river.

Mika and Russ' crew hooted into the wind as they rode across the river. It was a short trip, but they still enjoyed themselves.

Tami was looking a little green as she clung to the rail. "This is very fast."

"It'll be over soon." Dar pointed to the other shore. "It isn't as if we have far to go."

On that note, Mika turned the boat hard and powered down the motor, letting the boat coast into the other shore.

Russ and his girls were jumping off and pulling the boat ashore before they'd even touched ground.

"So, where did you see these odd kills?" Dar asked the gnoll.

"South side. We'll show you." Russ gave one more hard tug on the boat before handing off the rope to Mika, who lashed it to a nearby rock as best she could.

Dar didn't think that rock looked particularly big enough. Touching the ground, he felt granite beneath them and made a thick stone pole that connected to the granite beneath them. "There. That'll be more stable."

"Already making things easier." Mika smiled. "I'll be here at the boat doing some fishing while you guys go scout."

Dar nodded, noting that she didn't participate in the hunting.

When Dar looked up, Russ was already tromping through the woods. Dar and the two girls hurried to keep up with the hunters.

The woods by the river didn't last long before they opened up to a wide field of rolling hills that ran to the northeast, like one massive green carpet.

Bison dotted the landscape, many of them clustered a mile from where they stood in one massive herd.

"That's a lot of them. It's one thing to hear about it, another to see it," Dar commented.

Tami kept an eye out on the field. "Is this what your village uses for food?"

"We had crops growing, but yes, the bison are our principal source of meat. Since the southern woods burned down, we don't exactly have many options for meat," Dar explained as Russ followed the tree line, curving south along the edge of the plains.

"Dar, the herd has been staying away since we found this." Russ pointed up ahead, and sure enough, there were two or three bison's worth of mangled bodies and blood.

Tami hurried over and pulled a few of the limbs up, examining them. "Whatever did this has sharp teeth and brute strength. Half of this is physically torn from the bison, the other half is chewed through."

Dar looked at the surrounding woods for some sort of additional sign that would point to what had killed the bison, but he didn't spot any. So he went off of the limited information they had. They needed to consider what was strong enough.

"Do you think it was one of the beetles?" he asked Tami.

"Could be. I don't think a mantis could fly with one of the bison."

"Fly with it?"

Tami was still sorting through the gunk. "Yeah, I think the bison was dropped. Its legs look broken, and not in a way that some force hitting them from the side would do."

"If we are talking about something that could fly with a bison, it is most definitely the beetles. If it is the insects at all." Dar reasoned. "There really isn't much here for me to put together a full picture. Russ, can we check along the forest line to see if there are any more killings like this?"

"Sure." The demon led them forward, keeping an eye on the herd.

Dar thought about the size of the beetle devils and what they were seeing. The bison that were killed might just be enough food for one or two beetles. More of the herd would be killed if there were more than that. He was relieved the herd was still there; it meant the hive hadn't come yet.

But if it did, they would lose their primary source of meat.

"Let's hope it is some random demon or monster." He wanted to believe that, but it felt too coincidental that it had started just after the insect devils had started to roam.

As they followed the curve where the forest met the fields, Tami held up her hand for everyone to stop.

"There." She pointed to a blood stain not far into the forest.

Dar put his hand on her shoulder to stop her from going ahead. "Allow me to stay in front."

Molten lava pooled out of the ground and ran up his legs until it made a ball in his fist. Squeezing the ball tight, he kept pressure on his ball of lava, ready for a surprise.

He walked forward to where the blood began. It trailed away in a path, as if something had been dragged.

Dar followed the trail, with the girls and the hunters lingering behind him. The bloody path led up to a hole just big enough to stuff a bison through.

"That doesn't look ideal." Dar let more of his molten dao creep up from the ground and clad himself in glowing orange armor.

He found it now served two purposes: protection and lighting for the small tunnel. He slowly moved into the dark space, keeping his senses open.

Once inside, he stretched out with his dao of shadow, reaching out to get a sense of the structure. He found that it was connected to a larger network of tunnels. And the structure felt very familiar.

"Shit. It's the insect devils," he confirmed. "It is set up exactly like the one in the hills, only smaller. And I think it goes further south."

"Is it connected to the other one?" Tami asked, concern in her voice.

"I can't tell. That is too far outside of my reach. How did they expand so quickly?" Dar asked.

Blair wrinkled her nose. "What if they were already this expanded before you attacked? What if you just gave them reason to use it?"

Dar didn't like the idea, but it made sense. It was unlikely that the insect devils had made these tunnels in a day. If they had, that would be a terrifying level of growth.

Dar sensed devils approaching. "Ready for a little fun Blair?"

The salt spirit was wrapped in diamond armor in a moment. "Do we have company?"

"Three beetles coming down the pipe. Let's fight them here so they can't fly." Fighting had its own set of risks, but letting the devils fly would have its own troubles. He'd rather take them on in the narrow corridors. "Everyone else, stay up here. It's tight corridors and the fewer people the better."

"Let me go first. Give me some light." Blair excitedly charged forward.

Dar smiled. It was fun to watch her get so excited about using her new dao. He'd always seen her in more of a meditative state as she'd continually tried to progress down her dao path; he enjoyed seeing her in action.

Dar created a globe of magma in his hand and held it high in the air, washing the tunnel with bright orange light.

Blair's diamond armor sparkled in the light as she charged forward, a lance of diamond smashing into one of the beetles and tearing right through the massive devil. Dar noted it was far more effective than his shadow weapons had been.

The three beetles pulled up short in surprise, but Blair and her new dao weren't stopping. Her lance bent ninety degrees and stabbed into a second beetle.

Beetle number three let out a piercing screech down the tunnel as it used one of the injured beetles' bodies to slam Blair into the wall. The injured beetle used the chance to smash its horn into Blair.

Dar prepared to move forward and help her, but the hit did nothing to the diamond armor, not even scratching it.

Lances of diamond filled the air and came down, silencing the third beetle.

Dar just stood there watching, dumbfounded at the display of violence and power. He was once again reminded of the added power grand dao provided. He now understood why Karn hadn't wanted to fight using dao. A grand demon fighting someone without a grand dao was pointless.

But Dar felt bad for Cherry, because despite all the help she had been, he realized just how weak her grand dao was in the scheme of things. That because she was a spirit, her ability to learn new dao was often limited to what kind of spirit she was.

Blair had made it work for her, but Cherry didn't have great options as a dryad. Plants, especially new growth, weren't... well... diamond or magma.

"What did you think?" Blair bounced back towards Dar.

"You were amazing," Dar replied honestly, absorbing the beetles and banishing his globe of lava to let his dao of shadow loose once again down the tunnel.

The globe of lava had limited his shadow abilities, but as soon as it was back, he regretted that he hadn't used it sooner.

"Incoming," he hissed.

"How many?" Blair asked, excitedly spinning a new diamond lance in her hands.

"Not sure. But a lot." Dar couldn't count the number pouring into the tunnel, but they were coming from many of the side tunnels. And they were moving quickly.

"Just how many damn bugs did that queen make?" He prepared himself. "Let me handle this."

Dar stepped forward, careful to keep his molten dao from harming Blair in the small confines of the tunnel.

He drew upon his newly minted grand dao, filling the ground beneath him with molten magma. The floor of the tunnel didn't hold up to it, melting into the pit he was creating, but that was okay.

Mantises were at the front of the pack, and they weren't smart enough to realize just what magma was. They were recently created and not highly intelligent, and that worked to his advantage.

The mantises took flight to avoid the heat on instinct, moving over it.

Curling tendrils of magma erupted as Dar snatched at the mantises. Each time the magma touched one of the devils, the devil burst into flame and was consumed by the magma instantly.

Dar pulled up the pool of magma he'd made and pushed it down the tunnel, following as it went. The deadly lava flow crept deeper into the devils' hive. The molten liquid sloshed at Dar's behest, splashing those that were trying to escape.

Dar smiled, pleased with how well his grand dao was working when put to the test.

He kept moving, destroying beetles, but then he noticed one approaching that looked different from the rest. It was far larger than the other beetles.

The large, black beetle slapped Dar's lava flow, and the earth swallowed up his lava, dumping further underground.

Dar frowned. It was the first he was seeing a devil use dao beyond that of physical amplification. It felt so wrong, and he realized instantly why. Though they were both connected to the dao, however, the devil didn't use mana.

It all occurred in a blink of an eye, and the next moment, the devil was jumping into the surrounding soil, disappearing like a fish into water.

"Blair. Be ready," he said. The spirit had followed him and watched the tunnel with watery eyes.

"Dar. If they have grand devils among them, then suddenly, the length of these tunnels starts to make sense." She spun with her lance, waiting for it to attack.

When it didn't immediately, Dar figured the best way to force it out would be to go back on the offensive. He drew more magma around his feet and set it rolling forward to melt his prior flow of magma and the earthen spikes that the beetle had created.

A massive clod of earth shot from the wall, impacting Dar and slamming him against the far wall just before a pair of black claws grabbed him. Even as the claws clamped down, the black beetle screamed in pain from Dar's molten armor.

Dar smiled. The beetle had it coming.

Dar broke off eight beads of molten material from his armor and punched them into the soil behind him. The screaming intensified as its clawed arms retreated.

The attack had stopped Dar's lava flow once again, allowing the insect devils further down the hive to run and scatter deeper into the hive. Dar had a feeling they were moving to a connection that led to another hive.

In anger, he drew up a ball of molten material and pressurized it into tiny balls until he almost had molten buck shot. Then he opened his hand, spraying the material into the tunnel walls.

They didn't have quite the force of a shotgun, but it had far more penetrating power with the heat of molten lava. They sizzled paths through the dirt, penetrating several feet deep.

"Where is it?" Blair looked around, shifting nervously.

"I think it's gone. It seems like the black beetle was only trying to stall us for the others to escape." He looked further down the tunnel, letting his shadow dao stretch out for almost a mile. All he found was a rapidly emptying hive. "There's almost nothing left here."

"Do you want to chase after it?" Blair asked, seeming fine with whatever he decided.

"No. I think that, if we keep going like this, then we'll end up in an ambush we can't handle. Did you see the way that beetle went through the earth?"

"Yes. It was like it was flying through air rather than dirt," Blair agreed. "At least they didn't have the brains to just bury us in earth until we suffocated."

Dar shot her a dirty look. "Let's not even give them the idea."

"I don't think devils can understand language," Blair shot back, but kept quiet on the subject after that.

"It would be just our luck to find one that did," Dar spat. "Okay, if we aren't chasing after them, then I want to seal this place."

"Seal it?" Blair asked.

Lava started to flow around Dar's feet. "Yeah, it'll take me a little bit. Want to go up and tell Russ that it's clear and we're okay?"

She hesitated before nodding and turning around. "Stay safe down there."

Dar nodded, but he was positive they had all fled. And even if he was trapped, he had all the food in his inner world. He was confident he'd be able to dig himself out with a shell of molten lava long before he'd need more food.

Magma bled out from the walls around Dar as he descended deeper into the hive, sealing the walls with lava and flooding junctions with molten flow that poured down deeper into the hive.

He did manage to find a few more body stores like they'd found in the first hive. Stuffing those into his inner world, he made quick work of sealing the hive. As he left the cave, it was all still liquid and hot. Even if the black beetle came back, it would have a hard time dispersing his magma. The ridiculous heat coming off of the hive would keep anything from getting close.

CHAPTER 27

Dar came back to the surface to find three bison already strung up near the hole, draining onto the ground as one of Russ' women worked to clean them.

"I see you guys are making quick work." Dar nodded at the bison; it wasn't even midday.

"Got a group that had wandered from the herd. Most of the day is waiting for those types of opportunities and taking them. We can't confront the herd directly," the spirit with light green hair answered.

"Makes sense. You are all lesser demons and spirits. An entire herd of bison can do some serious damage." Dar looked at the herd in the distance. With just the sheer volume of them, if they decided to stampede, it would devastate an entire village. "Where's Blair?"

"Helping the hunting party. I don't think she's going to kill, but she's keeping them safe."

Dar looked at the tunnel he'd just finished filling. "Well, the insects should be gone for now." Dar felt into the stone beneath them, and there was no sign of a devil moving about.

Feeling reassured that nothing would prove him wrong, he nodded. "I'm going to go see what Russ and the party are up to." He wanted to speed up the hunting party so he and Blair could return to Bellhaven.

They had found a second hive—it was worse than Dar had thought.

The insect devils hadn't just occupied the hills northeast of Bellhaven; they had underground hives that stretched for hundreds of miles. They'd created secondary clusters, and if Dar was a betting man, he'd guess that each of them had another grand devil to protect them. Fighting them inside the earth was going to be a losing battle.

He had a feeling that the queen's devils would lean towards earth dao given what she had been eating and feeding them, but Dar wondered what the queen's dao would be.

She was structured much more like the mantis, although far more human looking than other devils he'd seen. But it was a mimicry of humanity; there was just something off about its face and form.

They were up against more than he had imagined. He and the village needed to be prepared. He'd seriously underestimated how far their hives reached, but he hoped that the ettercaps had helped hold them off from stretching too close to their village.

For the time being, they were likely safe, but it didn't mean that they would be for long.

Dar didn't see many options in front of them beyond attacking the source. He needed to strike at the queen before he could raid the rest of the hives, if he could even find them all.

This hive had been below the bison's field, where they regularly hunted, yet Russ and his girls had only just now noticed signs.

Dar shivered. There was a lot of open land in Kindrake between Bellhaven and Frost's Fang. He just had to hope that the insect devils didn't have that many hives.

Spotting Russ and the rest of the group hovering over another few dead bison, Dar waved. "Seems you guys are going to wrap up early."

"All thanks to her," Russ grumbled and pointed at Blair.

She shrugged. "No need to take longer than it had to. I could spear one of these from a hundred yards, no problem."

Dar couldn't help but notice three sparkling spears glittering in the sun, each perfectly spearing through a bison's head.

"Then let's get these dressed and ready. We blocked the hive here, but it has created additional concerns," Dar explained his concern while they worked.

Russ nodded solemnly. "We need to hole up in Hearthway."

Dar knew it took a lot out of Russ to say that. The hunting raids were a big part of his identity in the village. He came back every day victorious with meat to share, and he was celebrated in the village for it.

"It won't be long. Blair and I will need to deal with this problem before it becomes too much."

Tami rose from where she'd been cutting into one of the bison, wiping her forehead and smearing blood on it. "I'm coming too."

"This is going to be a dangerous fight. We're going up against a grand devil as strong as Karn. We won't be able to look after you." Dar hoped to scare her away, but her jaw was set in that all too familiar look. She was going to fight him on it.

Dar held up a hand to stop her protest. He could already see her decision, and she had the right to make it for herself, even if he could have ordered her using the oath she'd sworn. "Fine, if you are willing to put yourself in that sort of danger, we could use the help. Prepare yourself to fight when we get back. We'll pass through

Bellhaven on the way so that you can get your things as well."

Tami nodded. "I'll make sure to stop by the prince and let him know I'm your prisoner as well."

Dar frowned. That would send the message back to her father and bring far more problems down on him. But then he locked eyes with her, and he realized she might have been helping him understand she'd have no choice but to make the stop unless he instructed otherwise.

"Nope. That's straying too far. I'd consider that an attempt to escape." Dar could see the moment she relaxed, her oath to him wiggling a tighter hold on her.

"Understood." She went back to working to field dress the bison. Once they were done, Dar, Russ and Blair all picked up a bison and brought it back over to the spirit working on cleaning up the kills and draining them.

"Already? It isn't even midday." She shook her head. "Hang 'em up. It'll be an hour before they are drained enough to put them on the boat."

Blair wandered over to the edge of the hole that led down to the hive, and Dar followed her. She chipped at the obsidian from where some of his lava had cooled.

"Dar, there are thousands of them. How do we fight this many without collapsing from exhaustion first?"

Dar nodded. They'd both fought with reckless abandon. They could have done likely just as much damage with far less exertion. It was something they'd have to work on as they learned to use their grand dao.

"I don't know, Blair. This has all grown exponentially from what I thought we were up against. When I first went after the Mo, I was expecting a cluster of trolls and gremlins like the ettercaps. We'd just take out the Mo and disperse the others. This... I'm not sure what to do with this. But it won't go away."

She clicked her tongue. "Should have known it wouldn't be so easy. Devils haven't been the blight of this land for so long for nothing. They might not be intelligent, but they have an uncanny knack for survival, even at the worst odds."

"That's one of the things I'm most worried about." Dar took a deep breath, thinking about what little he knew of insects. "I think that, for most insects, there is only one queen at a time, but when one queen dies, another is born."

That was the worst-case scenario in his mind. They'd go through all the work of killing the main hive, only to have every other hive birth its own queen and multiply their problem. It would be worse than cutting the head off a hydra.

"So, what's the plan?" she asked.

"I think we are going to have a very busy winter," Dar sighed. "And I'm even more sure now that we need to prioritize the village's growth along the dao path. Another two grand demons would make a world of difference."

"Agreed. After we deal with the main hive, I think we need groups led by someone strong to go forth and cleanse the rest of the area. Otherwise, come spring, we are going to have a problem too big to deal with."

Dar looked out into the wilderness, wondering just how many hives it would take to stretch from here to the hills by Bellhaven. He estimated at least four, with some good distance between each. And the hive likely had grown out in multiple directions; there were probably at least a dozen secondary hives out there.

What a mess. But he'd start with the main hive.

Even if it created more queens, he knew they'd be far weaker. After all, they hadn't been feeding from a Mo for so long. This queen needed to die before she became any more powerful. Its power felt similar to Karn, so Dar estimated that she had two grand dao, and Dar was just starting to fully understand just how powerful that made her.

He cringed as he thought about Bellhaven. It didn't have the resources to take on that level of threat. He almost dreaded seeing what had become of the city since his last visit.

Blair stood quietly by his side while he thought. She was a comfort as he leaned on her presence.

"We're ready," Russ shouted, breaking Dar's thoughts.

Blair turned angrily towards Russ.

"It's fine." Dar put a hand on her shoulder. "I don't have any more time to dwell on what could be. It's time to take action. We'll head back home first, and then we'll talk with the leaders and the family. I expect we'll be back on our way to Bellhaven tonight."

Blair nodded. "Understood."

Dar could tell that she was rapidly trying to find where she fit into the family. Despite her flippant attitude back at home, out away from everyone, she'd become a force to be reckoned with. And now she had the power to back it up.

Diamond. It still baffled his mind.

***

"... and that's about it. But you can see my concern," Dar finished telling his tale to the leaders. It was lunchtime at Hearthway, but he'd managed to wrangle the leadership and his family to sit down and talk through his concern.

Even a few of the people had emerged from his inner world, a lesser dao or two gained and reporting back to their families.

"You're right. This sounds like a problem that we can't ignore." Rex scratched his chin. "But we only have three grand demons and about two dozen greater demons. If you and your family go take on this threat, we're down to about eighteen greater demons to protect the village."

It was plain to everyone that Rex worried that that might not be enough, and his job was to protect the village.

Dar couldn't blame him. The thought of one or even multiple of those grand beetle devils coming into the village was terrifying. They could very easily tear through it.

"What do you propose, then? Cherry and I are a package deal. And we need Blair for a successful offense against the insects." Dar didn't see a great option, either.

Out of the corner of his eye, he could see Sasha fidgeting. He noted it for later. He knew she was already insecure about her dao path and where she fit when it came to battling enemies.

"We'll have to manage," Bart spoke up. "I'm sure we could fend off a few of those beetles or mantis. If it's like any old infestation, you often only see a few at a time, anyway." He was feeling more confident after learning another lesser dao.

Samantha disagreed. "We should have a plan to hide in the caves. Have an escape plan. And have some bison ready to leave out, potentially satisfy them until our stronger members are back."

"Or a trap," Russ interjected. "If we see some nearby, we leave out some bison and ambush them."

"I was trying to avoid fighting," Samantha said dryly.

As amusing as their suggestions were, Dar wanted to keep them organized. "Rex is in charge of the guard. Let's leave it up to him to do his job keeping the village safe. But if we need to plan out a sheltering option, then I'm expecting everybody to pitch in."

The avian demon smiled and nodded. Dar could tell he already had plans churning in his head.

"Great. Then it's settled. I'm going to round up my girls and we are heading out. Once we deal with this queen, I need the entire village stepping onto their dao paths." Dar looked pointedly at Samantha.

"I already have a plan in place and am working with a few of the older women. Leave some fruits with me and I'll have another dozen done before you get back." She held her chin up defiantly.

Dar pulled a pile of the fruits from his inner world. They were all the dao of quiet. He figured it was a safe dao for everyone to get used to, and it could help protect them if the devils came.

"Get it done. Then we have a plan to discuss. We'll try to get in and get out quickly. You just need to stay safe until then." Dar stood, but Russ had one more thing to say.

"What of those who are still cultivating with you?" Russ worried for his dao companion.

"They are still cultivating. To interrupt them now would harm them." Dar sighed. "I'll have them returned to you as soon as I can."

"Don't worry. It is perfectly safe there," Bart comforted the demon.

It didn't completely solve Russ' worries, but it was the best Dar could do.

If he were to die, he wasn't sure what would become of them. But in the end, if he died, there wasn't anybody to stand up to the queen if she came for the village. Kindrake, even if it tried to help, wouldn't make it in time, and they had their own battles they were preparing for.

Dar could already imagine what would start pouring out of the nests soon; they were multiplying too quickly.

Sasha was already heading towards their home, pulling the maids and the rest of his girls along with her. He knew that they needed to talk, so he broke from the leadership circle, letting them work out the village's defense strategies without him.

Catching up to the girls as they entered the cave mansion, he closed the front door behind him. As he walked in, they were already sitting down. Sasha had a stern look on her face as she commanded the group. Everyone was there, Tami and the maids included, minus Cherry.

Dar pushed and ejected Cherry from his inner world.

The dryad looked around excitedly before reading the mood and jumping into a seat, holding her hands in her lap. “Seems like it’s time to fight?” she asked.

“Yes, dear.” Sasha reached over and patted her on the leg. “It's time for Dar to fight. Again.” Sasha let out a long sigh, before turning a pointed look to Dar. “And we are all going with him.” She gave him a smug smile.

“Sasha—” Dar tried to ease into it.

“Shut it,” she snapped. “I’m going, but I won’t be part of the combat.” Sasha sighed and held her head in her hands. “You aren’t going to leave me behind on this.”

He could see the emotions surging in her eyes. Denying her would only increase the insecurities she already had. If she agreed to stay out of battle, that would have to be good enough.

“Okay, Sasha.” Dar nodded. It hurt to see her like this.

Sasha looked up, surprised by his sudden acceptance. “The maids and I will go as a support team. If you need us to patch someone up, give others here a rest from combat, we’ll be in your inner world to function as such. And, when we get back, all of us will start cultivating under the dao tree.” She scanned the room for any argument, but found none.

Neko’s ears bobbed as she nodded. “We are too weak. I was so excited to make my first greater dao, only to find that Dar is going up against something with two grand dao. I won’t be left behind again.”

"Precisely, Neko." Sasha smiled at the cat girl and reached over Cherry to put a hand on her shoulder. "We have a strong mate, but that just means we have to become stronger, or risk being left behind."

"I'd never," Dar scolded Sasha. "Don't even put that out into the world that I'd leave any of you behind over your combat strength. Not everything is solved by fighting."

His head wife looked properly chastised. "That's not—"

"No. It is what you meant. I'll hear none of it, or you'll get shoved in my inner world, and I won't let you out to prove that I'll never leave you behind." Dar glared at Sasha, daring her to argue.

It had angered him that she felt like she was being left behind—that he'd even consider leaving her behind for not being a fighter. He hated that she didn't see her own worth. She ran their household, and she was a big part of the functioning of the village. She had her own fierceness.

He watched her, but she didn't say a word. "Good." He moved on. "I love you all."

His eyes awkwardly and apologetically landed on Tami. He clearly hadn't meant her in that statement, but he did appreciate her willingness to follow and fight for him.

"I'd never leave any of you behind. Even if I went on a mission that you didn't take part in, I'll always come back." He let his voice drop low. "Understand?"

Neko leapt off her seat and jumped into Dar's lap, butting her head against his chest and rubbing her cheek against him.

"We all share Neko's sentiment." Sasha gave a soft laugh as she calmed down. "Please don't take offense. I just... feel like I've been a burden lately."

Dar shook his head. "You've been leading the village in my absence. Your skill as a merchant was helpful in negotiating trade with Dane. Do not sell yourself short."

Dar set Neko aside and strode over, picking Sasha up and pressing her into his chest. "I'd be lost without you," he whispered in her ear.

She pushed off his chest, looking like she was on the verge of crying, but her face was filled with relief. She nuzzled into him for a quiet moment before pushing out of his arms and clapping her hands. "Everyone. Get your things. We are going on a long trip. Food, water, daily necessities. There's a new home inside Dar's inner world, and we ought to make it our own."

Everyone jumped to their feet, getting ready.

Blair hung back and stepped up to Dar. "I'm glad this is where I ended up." She kissed him on the cheek, but Dar pulled her back for more. He savored her lips for a moment before patting her on the ass.

"Go, get ready. I need you for this."

She gave him a brilliant smile before turning on her heels and wiggling her rear for him yet again.

Tami lingered, clearly not sure what to do. "Will I be going to this inner world?"

"Yes." Dar realized it would be the easiest way for them to travel. Plus, they could rest during the travel as well. He knew Tami would see even more of his secret, but she seemed happy to be under oath to him to keep it safe.

"Understood. I appreciate the comfort and hospitality you've shown me." She bowed, her antlers getting close to smacking Dar in the face. She looked up with a smirk, and Dar realized she knew just where they ended.

He laughed, pushing them to the side. It turned out the deer demon could play, after all.

CHAPTER 28

All the girls except Mika piled into his inner world as Dar got ready to leave. But, as he walked through the village, Bart came running up, clearly wanting to chat.

"I'll go make sure the boat is ready." Mika stepped away tactfully.

For a moment, Dar thought he was going to remind him to fill the crucible so that they could make iron. But the old blacksmith looked tired.

"Is my girl going to be okay?" Bart asked.

"They will be supporting. I'll make sure they stay out of the main conflict," Dar reassured him. Though they were growing in strength, and they might participate in some of the weaker conflicts, Dar didn't think they had the experience to fight alongside him when it came to the queen.

Bart seemed relieved as he patted Dar on the shoulder. "Don't forget, sometimes retreating can be a sound tactical decision. The village leans on all of you and would be worse off for any loss."

"Got it, dad," Dar joked, giving the man a hug. "I'll do everything I can to bring everyone home."

"Atta' boy." He slugged Dar on the shoulder.

Parting on a more positive note, Dar had to push away his own doubts. They were going up against a powerful enemy with a small army. He knew it wouldn't be easy.

Mika waited for him not far outside of the village. "Everything okay?"

"He's just worried about Amber," Dar explained. "And the rest of us."

Mika sighed. "You left me out in all the battle preparations."

Dar knew he had. "You and Neko are both capable fighters, but you have only gotten to a greater dao. It's up to you two on what you want to do. I'll push you both aside if need be for the battle with the queen, though."

"Understood." Mika nodded. "I would like to join you in the fight into the hive. Allow those of us who can't participate in the final battle to fight early on and help you reserve your strength."

Dar knew when to let her get her way, nodding as they reached the boat and climbed in. "Sure. And we'll be on standby for when a grand devil shows up."

Mika got behind the wheel and pushed off the bank, angling downriver and slamming the boat into full speed. "Where are we going?"

"Bellhaven. I know the way from there, and we should see what's happened to the city."

Mika winced. "It isn't going to be pretty, is it?"

"No, I don't think it is." Dar dreaded what the city would look like after just a few days of the insect devils' attacks. "But we need to confirm what the situation is."

"I know. Don't have to like it though."

Dar stepped up behind her while she piloted the boat, wrapping his arms around her. "We don't have to think about it just yet."

"I'm driving," she whined, but she pressed her rear further against Dar's hips.

"You like this," he said as he let his hands wander to her hips, distracting her as she drove. "It's a thrill for you to go fast, but this adds some danger to it, doesn't it?" He nibbled at her ear and the sensitive skin just behind it.

Mika groaned and nodded.

He knew she was a thrill seeker, and they both needed something to distract them on the way to Bellhaven. As his fingers wandered down to her thighs, he could already feel that it was going to be a pleasant trip, considering the circumstances.

***

Mika pulled the boat up into the docks at Bellhaven, breathing hard and grabbing Dar's face before smashing her lips to his. "Fuck. If you ever edge me that long again, I'm going to crash the boat."

"Noted." Dar held up his hands in his defense.

They both lingered on the boat for a moment before realizing they couldn't avoid checking Bellhaven for long. The sun was hanging low in the sky and sunset was only an hour or so away.

The docks were eerily quiet. Not a soul was out and about. Compared to the busy hub it had been before, it was truly chilling. Their boat was only one of two. And the other had its mast down in need of repairs. Every other boat had left. To Dar, that spoke of desperation.

"Well, this isn't creepy," Mika said, lashing the boat between two docks and removing a piece of the enchantment that ran the boat.

"Not at all," Dar said sarcastically.

He had expected a large amount of damage to the city from the devil attacks, but this was a ghost town.

The water sloshed, and the docks creaked loudly in the late afternoon as Dar made his way into the city proper. A few windows cracked to get a look at him, and while it made him feel unwelcome, it was also a sign that people were still alive.

They were just afraid to be outside. The bloodstains in the street spoke of the reason. Every few paces, there was another splash of blood, as if the hive had descended on the city in a massacre.

"These people are terrified." Mika kept her head up, glancing at the sky, expecting something to come at them.

"Yeah. We should keep an eye out," Dar reminded Mika, even though she didn't need it. "If they are staying in their homes, that means they think there is an active danger."

He balled up more of the molten buckshot in his hand, ready for a surprise. Mika had her spear and net at the ready, drawing on her mana. She was ready to use her dao as needed.

The wind cut as something flew at them.

Dar raised a hand and opened his fist, spraying tiny molten balls at the devil that had been dumb enough to attack him.

The mantis devil hit his attack, and small sparks of flame came to life in its chest. The flames burned right through the devil as it screeched in pain, but there wasn't enough force behind Dar's attack to stop it in its tracks.

Dar sidestepped the devil as it continued towards him. It was far too distracted by its own pain to try and catch him.

Mika wasn't about to leave things up to chance, her trident stabbing into its head as it twitched.

"Pretty sure it was already dead," Dar chuckled, absorbing devil into his inner world.

Every devil was more fruit, and he wanted to power up his women and village as quickly as he could. He knew that the eyes lurking in the window slits were watching, but he had accepted that secrecy was over. Enough people knew his secrets that they were bound to spread.

Mika spun, throwing her net into the air as another devil leapt off a building toward them.

Tangled and confused, the devil fell short and skid to a halt in front of Dar. His boot crushed the head like it was nothing.

"Way to get my net filthy," Mika grumbled, pulling it off as Dar absorbed another devil.

"It normally is filled with fish. How is it not already filthy?" he asked back.

"Okay, it's just a new kind of dirty." She stuck her tongue out, pretending to be distracted, even as her eyes scanned the rooftops behind Dar.

The two of them continued up the street. Dar was headed towards the east gates, and then out towards the hills. They walked two more cross streets up, but before they even hit the next street, Dar knew there was a problem.

Blood ran down the cobblestones in large rivulets, and he could smell more of it up ahead. At the next cross section, the street was covered in blood, but no flesh remained.

"I think this is where someone put up a fight." Mika did her best to step around the blood to get to their destination.

"Guards, or maybe the citizens, put together a group to attack," Dar agreed. It was enough blood that dozens of people had died.

Further uphill towards the noble district, Dar could see the fronts of most of the houses smashed in. He shook his head. The leadership of Bellhaven was likely dead given the state of those homes. There were survivors in the city, but that seemed to be after the rest of the city had been picked clean by a swarm of devils.

Fuck. Bellhaven was done for.

Several devils tried to ambush them, intending to use their distraction. But unfortunately for it, Dar had some anger to burn off. Lava shot up from the ground and blasted waves of magma at them, killing the five mantis devils instantly.

"That was a waste of mana," Mika said as she paused. "And I can't cross that."

Dar scooped her up and carried her over the cooling molten material. "Don't worry, I got you."

"My hero," she bantered, blinking her eyelashes at him.

Both of them laughed, but it was more a distraction from their surroundings than finding it funny. It helped lighten the horror of all the blood.

Dar put her down once they were well and clear of the lava and headed for the eastern gates, which were torn from their hinges.

"That was either something huge, or a large number of devils," Dar said. He saw signs that it wasn't just humans that died there.

Splatter of bug guts was mixed in with the blood on the walls. He was glad the humans had put up a fight, but it hadn't been enough. Dar could see where the blood had poured down from the top of the wall and didn't want to see what they looked like on top.

"Bellhaven fought and lost," Mika commented. She'd given up on avoiding the blood and guts at this point. The field outside the city gates was impossible to avoid.

"Do you blame me for this?" Dar gave voice to his doubts.

"Hell no." Mika stopped and planted her trident in the ground. "You might have sped this up, but it was going to happen without you. And think about how much worse it might have been if the devils had another few months to amass with the Mo as food for them. Hell, even Tami has said you likely saved Kindrake City."

Dar raised an eyebrow at that. He hadn't realized Tami had spoken out like that.

"Don't be surprised. She might hide it, but she's smitten with you. She'll find a way to stay your prisoner." Mika picked her trident back up, feeling that her point had been sufficiently made.

"Stay my prisoner?" Dar asked, though he had already suspected it as well. She had alerted him that she'd have to try to notify her father in Bellhaven.

"Yeah, she doesn't want to go back home. At least, I think that's part of it. The other part is that, when you aren't there, she marvels at how kind you are, how much you care for your family. She's jealous of us, yet keeping it contained with a little hope." Mika laid it out for him, raising an eyebrow in question.

Dar sighed. "Another? What do the rest of the girls think?"

Mika was honest to a fault. If any of his girls were going to lay out the dynamics, it was her.

"Neko couldn't care less. She sort of wants to pounce on Tami though. I think it's a predator and prey sort of thing. Blair just wants a piece of you. Now that she's 'in', she has calmed down quite a bit. Cherry... is Cherry, I'm not convinced she realizes there are other people in the room when you're there most of the time."

Mika hesitated before continuing, "Sasha is her biggest hurdle. Her feelings of being inadequate lately are making her not want to include more women that are stronger than her."

Dar clicked his tongue. "I'll handle Sasha. What about you?"

"I do my own thing. I love being part of the family, but what someone else gets doesn't take from me. Something people in Mahaklan used to say. 'The ocean is a big place. Why care if someone else is in it? Focus on the water just before you.'"

"I'm the ocean?" Dar chuckled. "Didn't think I was that big."

She rolled her eyes. "It's just a saying the old men would say. There's a lot of world out there." She looked out to the horizon even as the sun was dipping dangerously low, slowly dying the clouds purple and orange. "Why concern ourselves so much with others when there is so much before you?"

"You almost sound like you disagree with me doing this?"

"No. Not at all. Devils are a scourge that needs to be purged. In this case, it is a matter of perspective. You aren't looking out worrying about what neighboring countries are doing. You are just concerned with what affects our village." Mika smiled up at him.

"Thanks." Dar meant it. She had helped him clear the air on a few things.

"You're welcome, but I think I'm going to have to stop here. In the dark, I'm not going to be much help." She sighed. "Maybe I should work on that dao of shadows, like the maids."

Dar nodded, happy to have Mika be in a safer spot. "Head on in and give them an update. I'll pull the maids out for the rest of the trip once the sun sets."

Mika gave him a wink and a thumbs up before he drew her into his inner world.

Dar continued walking alone until the sun was nearly below the horizon. Then he drew on the maids. They resisted for just a moment before allowing it.

"Milord." Amber bowed while Marcie curtsied. Marcie had a steaming bowl of food in her hands. "What would you have of us?"

"I hadn't thought about eating as we went, but that suddenly smells amazing." It was a pleasant change from the stench of blood. Dar took the bowl from Marcie as he walked.

"Our pleasure. Marcie, take the right. I'll take the left." Amber took up her spot next to him, and he could feel her stretch out her dao of shadows, scouting ahead and around them.

Dar let himself relax for a moment while they kept watch, letting himself recover. He focused just on the food for a moment, enjoying it and its warmth.

But they didn't go far before he felt shadows sharpen and flicker about twenty feet ahead of them. He turned to Marcie with a raised eyebrow.

"Two drones," she said simply.

The dao of shadow was incredibly powerful at night, especially against weaker opponents, but it quickly lost much of its advantage against stronger opponents.

Like an assassin, it worked well against unguarded and unarmored opponents.

"You did well, but be careful. Your shadows will not pierce a beetle and may only be able to kill a single mantis if you catch it unaware," Dar reminded the two of them.

"We understand, milord," the maids both said in unison.

They were really becoming a pair.

"How has training the villagers to become immortals gone?" he asked the two as he finished eating and drew the bowl back into his inner world. He was curious if he could target exactly where it went, intending for it to go back inside the Blackstone Keep.

"Good," Amber kept it short as she kept her dao of shadow active and scanned for more devils in the woods.

Dar decided to help and expanded his dao. His capacity to use mana was far larger than either of the girls, allowing him to wrap his dao around both of theirs and stretch it out further.

"Milord. We were given express orders to make sure you used as little of your strength as possible prior to reaching the hive," Marcie admonished him. "Please withdraw your dao and relax. We have this."

It was hard for him to let the girls take the lead, but their logic made sense. Retracting his dao of shadow, he felt nearly blind.

"Your master is uncomfortable not being in control," Amber explained to Marcie. "Just as you feel comfort in submission, he feels comfortable in control."

Marcie looked up at him in question. "Milord, why don't you order us to do this?"

Dar thought it sounded silly, but he went along with it. "I order you two to keep an eye on our surroundings, kill weak devils, and alert me to stronger ones."

Oddly enough, he felt better.

"See." Amber smiled up at him. "It isn't just the master's job as a dominant to make us feel good, but it is up to us as well to make you feel in control."

Dar hadn't thought of it that way before. Dominance and submission had always felt like a one-sided act. He always assumed it was just the dominant caring for and controlling the submissive, but Amber had opened his eyes to something else.

"Kiss me," he told Amber as he pulled her close.

She pressed her lips to his; the corners turning up in a smile as her tongue licked at his teeth. But then she pulled away. "I am happy to do what you command, but I will lose focus on my other task."

Dar let himself kiss her once more before putting her back down and letting her proceed forward while he did the same with Marcie, who melted as he pinched her rear.

"Thank you both for the relief." Not only had they made him feel more in control, but they had helped wash away the recent memory of walking through Bellhaven.

"Our pleasure, milord. Now relax, we'll see you to the hills." Amber's shadow flickered, and Dar didn't even check to see what she'd killed.

Together, the trio walked through the night. Amber and Marcie killed several lesser devils, only stopping once to ask for his help as a patrol of four mantis came into range. Together, they had each killed one before using their shadows in coordination to kill the last one.

It had been an oddly peaceful walk to the hills before Amber and Marcie disappeared back into his inner world.

Dar had been up for most of the day. As he settled down just before the hills, he brought Neko and Cherry out.

"Cherry, can you bury us in roots like you've done before? Neko, can you keep watch while I get a little rest?"

Without even responding, roots appeared and pulled Dar and Neko down under a tree on the tree line.

"Neko will keep watch. Sleep, Dar." Her tail flicked in his face as Cherry rejoined those in his inner world.

Dar took a moment to ruffle her ears. "Thank you, Neko." He kissed her before laying down for rest.

He could have gone into his inner world, but Dar felt like he would just disturb the girls' training. Instead, he just slept.

CHAPTER 29

Cocooned in vines and with Neko's warmth pressed alongside him, Dar slept soundly despite the fact that he was going into a massive battle. When a little fuzzy tail flicked at his nose to wake him, dawn was already creeping into the sky.

"Dar slept like a rock," Neko chuckled. "Without me to keep the dao of quiet, your snoring would have brought the devils."

"Thank you for that." He ruffled her ears. "Alright, get some rest yourself. I'll keep moving. Tell Cherry and Blair to be ready."

Neko gave him a half-serious salute before letting herself get dragged back into his inner world.

Dar grabbed hold of the roots and tore them apart, releasing himself from the shelter that Cherry had made for him and creeping out slowly.

In the bright light of day, Dar could already see he was going to have a problem. Past the tree line, there were insect devils buzzing through the air, and there were far more than he'd seen the last time. The hills were swarming with them.

He was going to have his work cut out for him, and he was going to need Blair and Cherry sooner than he had hoped.

Pulling on both of them, they appeared before him. Blair was in a sheer nightgown that showed everything off.

"What?" The salt spirit rubbed at her tired eyes.

Cherry was already looking out past the forest and saw why Dar had called them in. "That's a lot more than you and Tami described earlier. By the way, she wants out as well. They all do."

Dar grunted and pushed out Sasha, the maids, Mika, and Tami. "Looks like the hive is far larger than last time we were here."

Tami followed his line of sight, swearing as she saw it too. "How? How are there so many?"

"Two options," Dar started. "Either that queen can make that many in just a few days, or when we attacked the second hive, this is where they ran to escape."

"For my own sanity, I'm going to pretend it's the latter." Sasha shook her head, looking out into the hills. "Those are all lesser devils at least?"

"Afraid so."

Dar watched the swarm to see if it was doing anything in particular. It seemed like it bled off into the distance just as quickly as new ones were coming back. Dar could only guess that they were dropping off food.

"I'd guess there's two to three times what we can see from here, with the rest off gathering some sort of food source," he said.

"That might just be the other population of devils," Tami offered. "Though, with so many insect devils, it is no surprise that they overwhelmed them and hit Bellhaven so quickly."

Dar started getting antsy. It wasn't going to get any better; he was ready to take action. "Let's go. There's just going to be more of them if we wait. I'll lead. Blair, you're on the lookout for anything too big for everyone else to handle. Cherry, you have our rear. Mika, Sasha, Tami, take them out of the sky. Neko, Amber, and Marcie kill them when they are on the ground."

Everyone nodded and Dar started forward, breaking free of the tree line and immediately attracting the attention of some devils flying from the hills. But Dar had anticipated that and kept moving. He raised his hand and fired off a handful of molten beads into the mantises that flew towards their group.

They screamed as several dropped out of the sky, twitching, but the rest kept coming.

Silk ribbons shot into the air, tangling up the still flying insects. Then Mika drew the moisture from the air and threw a wave of water at the devils.

Between the two of them, their attacks grounded almost all the mantises, who were swiftly taken care of by the rest of the girls. Shadows and blades flashed over the mantises, eliminating them without issue.

Drawing the corpses into his inner world, Dar continued on as another group broke from the hive.

Their teamwork was impeccable, taking out the lesser devils they encountered as they moved. Dar didn't even have to break his stride as they continued forward through the attacks.

He knew it would get tougher, though, as soon as drones poured over the hill. Their attack had become noticed.

That only meant that it was Dar's turn to shine.

Dar summoned lava before him and spread it out into a thin, arcing line, flowing it forward with their group.

The drones were mindless attackers, so the second they hit the lava, they screeched, burnt up, and fell into it. They were smart enough to start to notice, and the drones at the front turned to avoid it, but the mass of drones behind them pushed them forward, anyway.

Dar rolled right through the mass of drones, burning them to a crisp until the last of them realized there was a problem and tried to flee.

Amber darted out to his side, but Dar caught her. "Don't chase. Staying together is more important than catching a few drones."

"Sorry, milord."

"It's understandable to want to press the advantage, just know it could turn any second." His eyes lifted to the sky. He could already see several larger forms in a group flying their way.

The beetle devils would be the first real challenge for this group.

"Get ready, Blair. Beetles incoming."

Diamond spears appeared, floating just over Blair's shoulders. "Ready."

Dar fired into the flying group like all the others, but the devils were learning.

They caught wind for a moment and lifted higher into the sky, out of his range, before plummeting back down into their group.

Dar cursed under his breath. He didn't dare fire so close to the girls. While his dao might be powerful, it was too dangerous to risk friendly fire.

Sasha and Mika continued their attack, using ribbons and waves to knock the devils out of the air, but while it had been effective on the mantises, they weren't as good against the beetle devils.

When Sasha's ribbons snagged on one, its powerful wings beat and it lifted off the ground, dragging Sasha up into the sky.

"Let go of it," Dar shouted, worried for her.

But Neko was there first. She leapt high into the air, grabbing Sasha and throwing herself up again onto the beetle. Her dao of claws flashed in the daylight as she tore right through the beetle devil's hard exoskeleton. After several more swipes, the beetle was falling back out of the sky. Sasha's ribbons found other targets to tangle and bring to the ground.

Blair's diamond spears sparkled as they shot into other beetles, cracking through their bodies and exploding in a shower of bug guts.

"Dar. Keep moving. We've got this," Sasha barked, an annoyed look on her face.

He knew she didn't like him feeling like he had to back her up, but he would not apologize for being concerned when she got swept into the air by a devil. He gave her a firm look before drawing in the devil corpses and turning forward to once again push towards the hive.

The ground exploded behind them, but Dar didn't even flinch. He felt Cherry's dao flare to life and heard more screams of insect devils as she tore them apart with roots.

More drones came pouring in, and fighting was becoming instinctive to Dar by that point. He rolled a wave of magma before him, catching and killing the grounded devils easily, sparing moments to pepper incoming waves of flying devils.

Their trek across the ground continued for almost an hour before the hive retracted in on itself. The mass of flying devils in the air pulled back to the hills and grounded themselves. They had killed so many devils, but the hive was still brimming with activity.

"Get ready for a big one." Dar could feel the tension in their party.

There was no response, but he heard the creak of everyone clutching their weapons tighter.

A small rumble of earth was the only warning that Dar had before a black beetle, a grand devil, erupted from the ground before him.

Pent up from only dealing with weak devils so far, Dar exploded into action. His fist wrapped itself in a gauntlet of molten lava as he punched forward.

The devil blocked Dar's blow, only for him to splash the gauntlet past the beetle's guard and into its face. It screamed, reeling back and trying to dive into the ground to recover.

But Dar knew the tactic and wasn't about to let it escape. A large, pitch-black axe appeared in his hands as he swung for the fences, catching the beetle in the side hard enough to lift it off its feet.

Neko pounced over his shoulder, her claws tearing into the beetle as she swiped furiously, taking advantage of it being disoriented. Each pass took away a chunk of its chest until Neko was elbow deep into the bug. It slumped to the ground.

The cat girl spit on the devil and swiped its head off for good measure.

Dar absorbed the corpse; it would be valuable for the little dao tree.

"It's getting dangerous for all of you," he said over his shoulder.

"Not yet," Mika declared. "We'll fight with you until the queen arrives."

Dar wanted to tuck them all away and keep them safe in his inner world, but he'd take the help for the moment.

"We aren't some delicate flowers, Dar. Most of us have been fighting for longer than you've been alive," Tami argued.

Dar could almost feel the approving looks they shot her.

If they were all together in this, then there was little Dar could do to convince them. "Do not hesitate when I try to pull you in. The queen is incredibly fast. Resisting for even a moment could make a world of difference in my ability to counter her attack."

The girls nodded, and Dar continued forward. He wasn't sure what he'd do if he lost one of them. Dar imagined that the monstrosity of the devils would pale in comparison to his anger.

As they moved, the devils felt like they were getting desperate. The drones and mantises threw themselves relentlessly at them, trying to stop them or slow them down.

It wasn't until Dar crested the hill that he saw why.

The queen was pumping out dozens of insect devils each second. The birthing section had regrown and was a squirming monstrosity, spewing out larvae that drones would take and bury in the hillside.

The powerful devil looked up at Dar and company with what resembled a smirk, even as larvae continued to spew out.

But what was more disturbing was watching the larva mature practically before their eyes.

They were buried in the hills and came bursting back out less than a minute later. And what came out was an emaciated version of some insect devil that immediately ran or flew off to a nearby pile of food.

"That's disgusting," Blair spat. "And holy shit, how is it making so many?"

Dar would have thought that removing the Mo would have slowed down the queen. But that clearly wasn't the case.

He realized that he could sense a massive amount of dao coming from the birthing section. "It has something to do with its dao. I can feel it coming from that birthing section."

"You're right." Cherry made a face, even as roots sprouted around them. He smiled. Cherry was ready for a fight.

The lesser and greater devils might as well have been entirely expendable to the queen as they stood in shock as dozens more were birthed. But their moment of surprise was interrupted as more of the emaciated devils burst forth from the hillside and noticed Dar's group.

"Get ready." He peppered the air with beads of molten lava, raining it down among the devils. He might have been able to do more, but with the limited amount of lava he could control at once, the sporadic drops were the most efficient way he could think of harming the large quantity of devils below him.

Devils screamed and curled up on themselves as the beads of magma burned right through them. The hive flooded out to defend itself, so many of them dying to his constant stream of raining magma.

He almost felt sorry for the creatures, but it was working. He was taking them out faster than the queen could produce them. It was even a two for one when he took out a drone carrying a larva, because laying there helpless on the ground, the larva would die too.

One such larva managed to wiggle itself into a drone, feeding on its fallen ally and bursting forth moments later an emaciated mantis. Dar tried not to gag as he watched it unfold.

But the queen had no such issue. She seemed completely unaffected. Beads of magma hit her and congealed into cold black stone as she stood there, glaring up at Dar.

His magma didn't seem to be enough to hurt the grand devil. Even one of the black beetles managed to shrug off his molten rain.

The girls had their hands full as lesser devils welled up the side of the hill and dove in from above. The area rapidly descended into a war of attrition. Thousands of devils fell to their group, yet their own group was exhausting themselves.

Neko and the maids darted in and out of the group with lethal strikes, taking out devils. Sasha, Mika, and

Tami held a front line using their dao to tangle, push, and block the oncoming devils.

Cherry's roots smashed into the nearby devils, crushing them in droves while Blair remained steadfast, waiting for the stronger devils and attacking them as they came.

Meanwhile, Dar stood among it all, continuing to rain down molten droplets that tore through the ranks of weak devils.

He'd expected the queen to attack, but she remained where she was, continuing to birth dozens of new devils every second. Even though devils had stopped coming out of the hive, they were still birthing out of the hills at an alarming rate.

He realized their current plan wasn't sustainable. He could see the girls tiring out, starting to slip up. He needed space to make a much larger attack.

Just then, the queen screamed, and the surrounding hills exploded as a black beetle erupted out of each of them.

"Girls, inside. Now." Dar's tone brooked no argument as he drew them all inside his inner world. He finished just in time as eight black beetles slammed into where their group had just been.

Dar flung himself off the hill towards the queen, wrapping himself in a foot-thick shell of molten lava.

It might have been a fantastic way to protect himself, but it also made him blind. Luckily, it didn't matter for the singular goal he had in mind.

When he felt resistance against his molten shell, he exploded out the top, making the shell splash in every direction.

The queen blocked as much of it as she could, burning one arm to a crisp even as Dar took out one of the black beetles, but he also got his most important target.

The birthing section of the queen was liberally splashed with lava. It caught fire and collapsed on itself from the magma. The queen let out a wail of anger.

Spikes of earth erupted everywhere around Dar, like falling into the maw of some massive beast.

As the danger closed in around him, Dar tried a tactic he'd been thinking about as he'd come to the battle. With his increased dao, he could channel far more mana than before, so he pushed every ounce into his enchantments after he'd improved them with his ascension into a grand immortal. He trusted that Lilith had known what she was doing when she had given them to him, so supercharging them felt like a good use of his mana.

Dar's skin grew bright as dao characters glowed from just underneath his skin. He redoubled his efforts as the earthen spikes crushed against him.

Sure enough, his body held out. The glowing enchantments strained as Dar pushed back, breaking the spikes of earth and launching himself out of the mess.

He nearly flew, surprising even himself with his newfound strength.

The queen whipped around at him, surprised to see him come out alive from her death trap. Her claws flashed and tore off the ruined birthing section. Her burnt arm fell off, but a new one grew in its place.

Dar wasn't sure what its dao was, but between the rapid birthing, the larvae growing uncontrollably quickly, and its own regeneration, Dar assumed there was some sort of insect dao that combined them.

He shivered, not loving that an enemy had that dao.

Pushing, he released Blair and Cherry from his inner world. "The queen seems to be able to heal any damage I do," he grunted. "But I think the hive is empty. Her birthing section is gone. Now it's just her and those eight black beetles."

Blair looked him up and down. "You're glowing."

"I'll explain later. This is taking up most of my capacity for mana."

"I'll tangle with the black beetles." Cherry glared at them. "Do you want the queen, Dar?"

"No. Blair, keep yourself wrapped in armor and distract the queen. Cherry and I will take care of these beetles and join you in a minute." He wanted to ask after the others, but that was a distraction at the moment. He needed to focus on the fight before him. The queen and those black beetles were enough for him to worry about.

"Let's go." Dar sprinted forward, the enchantments glowing all over his body.

Chapter 30

Blair burst forward, wrapped in diamond armor.

The queen separated herself from the burning birthing section, and a pair of buzzing wings flared out of her back as she met Blair's charge head on. As they collided, the queen sent Blair backwards, bouncing along the ground.

Dar paused for a moment to make sure she was okay, but Blair kicked to her feet. Only her armor nicked.

Knowing that she would be fine, Dar started his own fight, jumping into the air as the ground beneath him cracked. He was filled with so much power, so much mana, that his body defied the limits of his mind.

Gripping the black axe handle in his hand, he swiped at the first surprised beetle.

All that could be seen was a black arc in the air as the beetle exploded. Dar twisted himself to the side to recalibrate when he had been able to use more force than he'd expected.

Two more black beetles took the opportunity and slammed into his back, rocketing him back down to the ground, where the earth itself opened up and tried to swallow him.

Dar struggled, but the two beetles pushed him through the earth like it was water before darting off and flying back up through the soil, leaving him behind. Dar screamed, buried over a dozen feet deep in the ground and barely able to move. He fought against the weight above him as he tried to move just his arms.

But being that deep in the ground was no joke. He had thousands of pounds of resistance from the earth above him.

If it weren't for the enchantments on his body, he would have already been crushed. And releasing them to use a dao would put him in danger. But no enchantment made him able to breathe through the ground. Time was running out as the air in his lungs became a valuable commodity.

Dar decided to take a chance. He pushed on his molten dao and formed a shell of lava around him even as his enchantments cut out when he diverted his mana. There was a crushing pain for just a moment, but that was worth extracting himself from the ground.

He hurled himself and the molten shell out of the ground, taking a deep breath of air.

The beetles had forgotten about him. He watched as Cherry stood amid eight massive roots, riding one and using the other seven to keep the beetles at bay.

Blair was still getting pushed back, but she was bouncing to her feet with each exchange, her armor growing back to recover any damages. Though she was looking a little dizzy.

Dar channeled his anger and slammed a column of lava up from the ground, catching one of the beetles that was fighting Cherry. Then he lifted the column into the air and slammed it back down on the queen.

Before he could see the result of his attack, three of the remaining beetles broke off from Cherry and dove at him.

Not wanting a repeat of the prior attack, Dar stuck with his dao, exploding columns of lava up at the three oncoming beetles. Unfortunately, they were fast. They darted out of the way even as earthen spikes threatened Dar.

He had to jump and dodge, as it seemed like the earth itself had become his enemy. One spike caught him in the side, tearing a nasty gash before he could switch his mana to power his enchantments.

With his enchantments active, he shot off the ground, tackling one beetle midair.

It flailed and tried to bite him, but Dar snapped his fist into its face, dazing it, and switched his mana back to his dao, wrapping them both in a molten shell. He managed to cook the beetle before they hit the ground.

Dar's enchantments flared back to life as he hit the ground and rolled to his feet. He got his footing just as the other two beetles pounded into where he'd landed.

Dar clutched at his ribs and came away with a blood-stained hand. The spike had done some damage. As tough as he was, he needed more protection. No one was around to see and Dar wrapped himself in the black armor as he stared down the two beetles.

The two remaining beetles faced off against him, their wings fluttering in preparation for flight, but they hadn't lifted off the ground.

But their standoff was broken as the queen screamed, startling both Dar and the beetles.

Dar recovered first, his axe swinging for one of the distracted beetles.

But it sank into the ground as a pillar pushed Dar up, throwing his swing wide over its head and putting Dar on a pedestal. It was the perfect position for the other beetle to attack him, so Dar tumbled off the pillar, drawing the axe back into his inner world as both of them came at Dar once again.

Something crashed into Dar's side, and he found himself face to face with the queen as she plowed him into the dirt. Her claws raked over him, yet the black armor held, frustrating the devil.

The queen screamed in frustration and flung herself off of Dar.

Dar realized with satisfaction that she was looking extra crispy from his prior attack. He could hurt her. They might just stand a chance. He just had to hit her.

The queen dodged several pillars of magma as he drew them up out of the ground around the devil as she danced back away from him.

"Dar. She's giving up on me," Blair shouted.

With horror, he knew where she'd be going next given her attack on him hadn't worked either.

"Cherry. Run," Dar screamed.

His dryad only had a moment to turn before the queen was on her.

Dirt exploded in the air as the queen attacked. He only had a moment of terror before Cherry's hair fluttered out from behind another tree, clear of the dust cloud.

The queen shot out of the dust cloud, attacking that tree only for Cherry to appear from another. Cherry flitted from tree to tree, moving towards the forest.

The devil screamed in rage and went on a rampage, destroying every tree in sight as Cherry escaped back into the forest where she'd be far stronger.

After he'd gotten over his initial shock, Dar got his head back in the fight. His enchantments flared to life as he jumped onto the nearest beetle, throwing all of his momentary fear into a fist that popped the beetle like an old grape.

The other beetle came swinging, but a diamond spear burst through its chest before it could finish its punch. The diamond tip of the spear swelled, and spikes of diamond ripped the devil apart from the inside.

Dar looked over to see how Cherry was faring. The three devils she'd been fighting earlier were making their way towards the forest, chasing after her and the queen. And Dar's favorite dryad was playing hide-and-go-seek among the trees.

With her ability to pass between the trees, she would be nearly impossible for the devil queen to catch. But the queen and the beetles had a solution for that—they were smashing all the trees.

"We need to stop the queen. Think you can hold her still for a moment?" Dar asked Blair as he grabbed her hips and launched both of them towards the forest.

"When she realized she couldn't hurt me, the queen just stopped fighting me and went for you guys. I think that, unless I can harm her, it's going to be hard to hold her attention. But she's just too fast," Blair growled in frustration.

"Then we'll just have to get her attention. Hold on." Dar landed and lifted Blair up, one hand steadying her stomach and the other cupping behind her rear as he pulled her back.

Blair's eyes went wide. "What are you doing?"

"Go!" Dar threw Blair like a rocket.

Diamond wrapped around her as she embodied a diamond spear before hurtling into the forest and crashing into the queen. She was a lethal missile as she crashed into the queen and ripped her off her feet, hurling the two of them through another half a dozen trees.

That should solve Blair's inability to catch the speedy devil.

Dar could see diamond spikes fly, erupting from where they crashed as he hurried to catch up.

Blair flew backwards through the air a moment later as a mangled devil queen crawled out of the divot in the ground. Spikes of diamonds still stuck in her broken wings.

"Got her good." Blair gave him a thumbs up as he caught up.

"Now we just need to finish this." Dar grabbed her arm and hauled her to her feet.

Cherry appeared next to them. "I can't believe you threw Blair."

"It worked." Blair smiled. "I was able to get my hands on her long enough to drive those spikes through her wings."

But, as she said it, she stumbled just a little, her eyes losing focus. Dar realized that throwing her probably hadn't been great for her equilibrium.

At that point, the three beetles reached them. They flew down and tried to block for the queen, but Dar was having none of that. Dar drew on his dao and made a wall of magma in the air, dropping it down on the devils.

Dust and steam filled the air as Dar watched, waited, and listened for what happened to his opponents. He didn't have to wait long. The three beetles shot into the sky, carrying the queen as she started puking.

No, not puking, Dar realized. She was wrapping herself in gunk.

"After them." Dar was already grabbing both of the girls and using his enchantments to their max as he kicked off the ground and cleared a hundred feet in a single bound. Then he jumped again, trying to keep pace with the three flying devils even as they were burdened from the queen who was rapidly wrapping herself in a cocoon.

"What is it doing?" Cherry said, disgust in her voice.

Dar dreaded what might come of it. "It's a cocoon. Either to heal... or change." He said the last with hope that he was wrong.

"Doesn't matter. We will kill it all the same." Blair narrowed her eyes. "Throw me again. I've got this."

"You sure? It looked like the last one scrambled you a little."

"Just dizzy. I'm fine now. Throw me before they get too far ahead."

Blair was right. Even with Dar's enchantments, the devils were out pacing Dar and the girls, rapidly getting ahead.

Dar landed with a thud and let go of Cherry as he wound up and threw Blair for all he was worth. The air ripped as she flew through it. This time, she was already forming a spearhead of diamond in front of her to help with the air resistance.

Cherry caught Dar as he sagged after the throw. "You're using a lot of strength."

He pulled himself up from his moment of exhaustion. "Keeping this enchantment at this level is exhausting. But we need to finish this."

He drew upon all the surrounding mana he could and tried to fill himself up, despite already feeling like he was bursting at the seams. He couldn't afford to be tired.

He watched as the Blair spear impacted the cluster of flying devils and spikes of diamond bloomed in the air. Dar grabbed Cherry and returned to his massive leaping strides. He tried to catch up as the three beetles and the queen's cocoon fell out of the sky.

This was their chance.

"Put me down," Cherry shouted over the wind.

Dar didn't have time to do it gently, dropping her as he landed again and pushed off, chasing the devil queen.

Cherry flickered in the corner of his eye as she passed between trees, rapidly overtaking him and shooting forward to the next battle.

He could already hear the screams of beetles and explosions of earth as Blair fought three devils on her own.

Cherry's battle cry joined the mix as thuds of wood joined the fray and Dar finally reached the battle.

The beetles were desperately trying to keep the two women off of the cocoon, throwing their bodies and blocking hits instead of really fighting.

Dar drew the black axe from his inner world and took his moment of surprise to attack the cocoon. One swift swing was all he needed to end this.

His axe bit into the cocoon, piercing only a foot deep before it stopped.

A beetle tackled him to the ground just as the cocoon exploded, and a monstrous devil came out, holding the business end of Dar's axe. He barely recognized the devil that had emerged.

The queen unfurled herself. She no longer had any resemblance to a human. She had two rear legs that were more befitting a grasshopper, with a long back now covered by fully healed wings.

Her head had elongated, and sharp mandibles had covered her previously human face. And two pairs of arms, one pair of mantis-like scythes, the other closer to human arms, came out of her torso.

It was a grotesque amalgamation of an insect trying to take the best of anything it could think of and slap it together. But she was thin, almost malformed. Dar had a feeling the transformation hadn't completely finished.

Dar pushed the beetle that had tackled him off and rolled to his feet as the queen snatched up that same beetle and opened her mouth. Staring into her mouth, it was as if it was a black hole, devouring it in a blink of the eye.

The other two beetles flew to her, and she devoured them both, too. As she did, her body filled out, suddenly looking far healthier.

The queen took his axe and tried to break it, but thankfully, the mystical weapon held up under her strength. So instead, she tossed it behind her and far away from the battle.

"Dar, how did she change so quickly?" Blair asked.

"Hell if I know." He thought back to how quickly the larvae had been maturing by the hive and wasn't surprised this was in line with the same dao. "It'll die all the same. Cherry, hang back and try to tie it down with roots. Blair, you are in front with me."

Blair didn't waste a moment jumping in with a spiked club of diamond. She threw her weight into the swing, trying to end it quickly.

Dar was right behind her. The queen might have tossed his axe aside, but he pulled out a heavy sword from his inner world. When he'd tried to use the sword before, it had been too heavy. He'd been baffled then at how he had once been able to wield it.

But now he knew.

With all the mana he was pumping into his enchantments, he was a juggernaut. The swords that had previously given him trouble were like toothpicks as he swung for the queen.

Her mantis arms snapped out and blocked both of their attacks while her human-like arms tried to grab Dar.

He pushed off with his sword to get clear before she could get a hold of him. Thinking back to how the queen had devoured the beetles, Dar couldn't help but feel a cold sweat creep down his back at the idea of those arms getting a hold of him and bringing him to that black hole of a mouth. He did not want to become insect food.

Cherry's vines sprang up around the queen's massive, coiled legs, but the queen sprang forward with such speed that the wind of her passing nearly blew Dar away.

Cherry barely managed to escape into the tree line before the queen nearly reached her.

Blair screamed and threw everything she had at the queen. Weapons of diamond rained down on the queen for just a moment before one of her coiled legs shot out, catching Blair in the chest and launching her into a high arc.

Dar wasn't worried about Blair. She'd land relatively unharmed, but it would take her a minute to get back to the fight.

The queen's head was already tossing back and forth, looking for Cherry.

Dar was somewhat offended that the damn bitch wasn't focused on him. So Dar summoned a black spear from his inner world and hurled it at the devil. That got her attention alright.

She blurred from that spot to one on his right. The next thing Dar knew, he was flying backwards.

Dar crashed into the ground, skidding along it and digging a ditch as he went before finally stopping. He noticed the light from his enchantments was flickering. He was dangerously low on mana.

The queen was back to focusing on Cherry, running through the cluster of trees as Cherry led her on a merry chase.

So Dar took the moment to let go of all the mana he was pumping into his enchantments. Instead, he just breathed, trying to draw in as much mana as he could to restore himself and rally for one more shot. He could see Blair sparkling in the distance as she hustled to get back to the fight.

He also made a mental note that Tami needed to share her dao of speed if they made it through the battle. The devil queen was just too damn fast for them.

Blowing out another breath, Dar prepared himself. He didn't have any more break to take. The queen was about done with the cluster of trees, and Cherry needed a distraction.

Dar didn't activate his enchantments this time; instead, he drew on his dao. It was a risk, but trying the same thing was insanity. His molten dao had a better chance at harming the queen, the only trick was finding a way to hit the devil and hold it still long enough to roast her.

Cherry must have felt him ready himself again because she darted through the trees towards him, leading the devil queen his way.

Dar blasted globes of molten lava at the devil queen, who dismissively tried to bat them away. But, as they splattered over her arms, little tongues of fire flicked out and she screamed, flinging it off.

She tried to remove it before it did any more damage, but Dar wasn't about to give her the chance. Two hands of magma burst out of the ground before him as they tried to grab at the devil queen.

He cursed as she darted away, once again just too fast.

But he'd been watching her movements by that point. As powerful as those two back legs were, they worked in amazingly fast, yet only straight lines.

Just before she did her second dash to him, Dar threw up a wall of magma and dropped to the ground.

The queen exploded through his wall, missing him as her scythe-like arms swished above his head and flung magma everywhere. Finally he covered her in magma.

Dar let the wall of molten material fall on top of him and mute the queen's screams as lava coated her, burning her.

From his hiding place, he summoned a pillar of lava up from the ground, grabbing and trying to hold the queen in place. The thick, viscous material wrapped around her legs, and Dar put all of his effort in pushing her up off the ground. It gave her no purchase to move and use those powerful legs as it cooked her alive.

Despite all the power and fortitude the grand devil had shown in the fight, very few things could withstand being submerged in lava.

Dar held onto his dao, filling it with all the available mana he had as he controlled it, working to keep her powerful legs from touching anything solid. Squeezing himself dry of every drop of mana he had, Dar's focus narrowed down to the singular goal of keeping it trapped. It took his full attention, all sound and even his vision falling away.

It wasn't until a diamond lance poked into his molten lava shelter that he startled and removed himself from the lava, trusting Blair.

"She's dead, you can stop now," Blair said. She was panting, but smiling.

Dar looked over to confirm it and took a few steps to get a better view. The queen devil was well and truly cooking through. He let the lava go, dismissing it as he lay down on the ground, letting his body collapse into the grass. His mind was comfortably blank as exhaustion took him.

CHAPTER 31

The queen was dead, and they were far enough away from the hive that they were in the clear. Though, he wasn't sure if there were any devils left in the hive after their battle.

He was too exhausted for the moment to even move, but he also realized he had a family that was no doubt worried for him in his inner world. That, and right now, he wasn't sure he could lift a finger if a wild animal decided he looked tasty.

Pushing, Dar released all of his women from his inner world as he lay on the ground, catching his breath.

"Well. Something happened here. Wait, where are we?" Sasha did a slow turn, pausing at the smoldering devil queen's corpse. "Oh. Looks like that finished up nicely."

"We're further northeast from the hills," Dar replied to her earlier question.

"Oh, up towards where Toldove used to be." Sasha shaded her eyes and continued to look northeast.

Frost's Fang was that direction, but Dar guessed that it would still be several weeks' walk to get there. It was hard to tell distances with something so large.

Sasha nudged him with her foot. “At least you don’t look beaten up to hell this time.”

“Of course. I’d hate to let you down.”

“But why is your hair so long?” She asked, bending down to pick it up as if to show him. His hair hung down his back and seemed to still be growing.

“Something with my enchantments. I pushed them further than ever before. Maybe the restoration rune is making it grow much faster?” he offered a plausible explanation, but honestly had no clue why his hair grew when he pushed so much mana into his runes.

“Want me to cut it?” Sasha offered.

“Yes, please.”

While Sasha did that, Neko wandered over to the devil queen and poked the smoldering corpse before jumping back, claws out.

When it didn’t move, she grew braver and dragged it back towards Dar. “For the little dao tree.”

Dar gave the corpse one last look, making sure it was truly dead, before absorbing it. “Cherry, that thing had insane regeneration, mind doing me a favor and burying it to put my mind at ease?”

“Nonsense. Let us do it.” Amber stepped forward. “All of you are so tired. Rest.”

Cherry shrugged, so Dar brought the maids, accepting their offer.

Tami awkwardly scratched at her arm. “So, it’s done? The hive near Bellhaven is gone, and the city is saved?”

Mika and Dar shared a look before the wave spirit spoke, “The hive is gone, but Bellhaven… it didn’t look so good when we passed through it.”

Tami’s expression fell. “What do you mean?”

“Blood flowing in the streets, ambushes by devils as we walked through it. There were people, but they were all holed up. Up in the noble district, we saw houses smashed in. I’m not sure what you are going to find,” Dar explained. He didn't voice his assumptions about the nobles of Bellhaven. The way the noble district was smashed made it seem unlikely that many survived.

Tami just sat down in shock. "Those poor people."

He was somewhat relieved she was worried about the general populace and not the prince. "We can try to help them. But that won't be today."

"Why not?" she asked.

"Because I'm not getting up for a few hours," Dar chuckled.

His comment made Sasha straighten. "Bring me into your inner world and pull me out in a few minutes."

"Sure." What was he? A ferry service?

He needed to find a better way for everyone to come and go from his inner world, but he drew Sasha inside again.

Blair fell down next to him and propped her head up on his chest. "I think laying down for a while sounds perfect."

Cherry took his other side. "Agreed, my old bones need to rest."

That made Dar roll his eyes. She looked like she would get carded at a bar, even though she was over a thousand years old.

Neko was the only one still standing as she walked over to some of the shattered trees, picking up a few choice pieces of splintered wood before holding it out to Dar. "Dry this, please."

He paused, but that didn't take much effort. So lifting one hand, he washed the cord of wood in her hands with hot, but not too hot, air.

"If you stack it up, I'll just put a little lava in the center," he said, realizing he could light it far easier.

The cat girl stacked the wood while the rest of the group watched, and Dar put a cup's worth of lava in the center of the stack. The wood caught fire immediately, and they had the start of a fire.

"Maids and Sasha should be ready," Neko reminded him.

He pushed the three women out, and each of them came laden with goods.

Sasha took the lead immediately as she glanced at them all collapsed on the ground. "Mika, go find something we can sit on. Neko, thank you for the fire. Tami, go help Mika."

The maids didn't seem to need any orders as they got to work setting up a pot over the stove and making a meal.

Sasha was pulling goods out of her pouch and laying down some medicine supplies. "Now, who needs to get patched up first."

"Cherry," Dar and Blair said in unison. While they had both managed to come out with just abrasions and bruises, Cherry had a few nasty looking cuts.

She might have avoided most of the queen's attack, but that didn't stop the spray of rocks and wood from clipping her.

"Fine." Cherry crossed her arms in a pout. "Do my right shoulder. That one is starting to hurt."

Sasha spoke to no one in particular as she worked. "I've decided that my dao path is going to lead towards that of mending. While I don't enjoy fighting, I recognize that there will be much of it around all of you. So if I'm not going to fight, then I need to be there for all of you afterwards."

"You don't have to—" Dar started.

"No. I do," she interrupted. "I need my part in this family, and I think I found it. This feels right."

"Good for you," Blair said. "Apparently, my part is to get smacked around by a big devil."

Cherry laughed before Sasha pushed her harder against Dar, trying to get her to hold still. "You did it really well. And don't forget, you also make a great spear."

"Talk about being dizzy. Do you have anything there for that, Sasha?"

"No, but I'll consider it in the future. You were a spear?" Dar's head wife asked.

Dar gave a tired smile and started to tell the entire tale to Sasha and the maids, knowing they'd want all the details. They worked as he spoke, taking in his story from when they'd gone into his inner world to when he'd managed to wrap the queen in magma and kill her.

By the time he finished, the three of them were properly taken care of by Sasha and sitting on split logs while the maids were about done with dinner.

"The question becomes, what will we do after all of this?" Cherry proposed the question that had been on everyone's mind since Dar had started his story.

Marcie came over and served Dar a thick, hearty bison stew first, and he ate a spoonful before replying, "This is great girls." And it was. There was more flavor in it than anything he'd had at Hearthway.

"Thank you, milord. We were able to prepare better with the trip to Bellhaven."

Dar had underestimated just how much the flavor had perked him up. "Cherry, we'll start a herb garden in my inner world."

"One bite and you have him declaring that. Let me try this. And my question still stands, Dar. What next?" Cherry held out her hands for the next bowl the maids ladled.

"We need to go back and check the main hive. It felt like they threw everything at us, but we need to make sure it is clear. In terms of timing, that'll be tomorrow after a night of rest. After that, I'm thinking we check on Bellhaven as we go back to our boat. From there, on to

Hearthway to join everyone for the winter and start training everyone up." Dar took another sip of his stew, feeling confident about what came next.

"Should we leave anyone in Bellhaven?" Tami asked. "They won't be able to defend themselves should more devils come."

"You stay with me," Dar made that clear. "Maybe we could send someone down from Hearthway after a little while, but they'd need to be prepared to empty out their coffers for our help."

"Pretty sure we could just go loot one of the smashed-in noble houses if you want money, Dar," Mika commented.

"It isn't about the money, it is about making a statement," Dar grumbled. "They did this to themselves; if they want our help, they need to pinch their wallets."

The group quieted down after his statement.

"Kittens?" Neko asked hopefully.

That broke the group's mood and had everyone laughing.

"Neko, now isn't the time," Sasha admonished the cat girl. "We have a guest, and Dar is exhausted."

"Let's focus on other things for now," Dar tried to divert the group away from laughing at Neko. "Forget the near present. What is everyone hoping for in the future? We all know Neko wants kittens, but what about everyone else?"

Sasha calmed down and sighed. "I dreamed of making clothing for kings and queens. But, at the rate you are going, I should just keep making your clothes and I'll meet that goal."

Dar nearly choked at the idea of being king. A village leader, sure, but a king?

The idea was wild. Although, she was right; if he kept how he was going, that might just happen.

"What about you, Mika?"

"Live life and enjoy it. I have no need to push a specific way, as long as the current I'm on is pleasant." She smiled, leaning back lazily.

Dar loved the relaxed way she approached life. Mika reminded him to enjoy the moment and live in the present.

"I want my tree to be the biggest in the world." Cherry gave him an exaggerated stare. While it might have seemed like she was joking, her tree was everything to her. That meant Dar was too.

Dar leaned around Sasha to see the maids taking their seats. "You two?"

"We have everything we could want already," Amber answered for both of them.

"Nothing at all?" Dar pushed, hoping to get more out of them.

The two maids looked at each other, a silent conversation passing between them. "We wish to be your shadows. Always there, often unnoticed, but when you need us, we'll be ready." There was a slightly predatory glint in both of their eyes.

He was baffled at how his two soft maids had turned into wanting to be deadly assassins. But he also understood that they had already been in the shadows for so long. Now they could do something about it. And, with all the enemies they seemed to have, he didn't mind having them watch his back.

"I guess I'm running out of time to come up with something witty," Blair said. "I just want to find a place where spirits are treated fairly. Hearthway is what I want, but I also selfishly want to expand our culture outside that community."

"That's not selfish at all. I'd say that's a fantastic goal, and I think Hearthway is going to expand. Technically, we are our own sovereign nation and the closest city to us was just sacked." He paused, realizing what he was suggesting.

Though, with the prince dead, he wondered how much weight the document he had would hold.

"You wouldn't," Tami gasped.

But he could. Dar could roll into Bellhaven and take over, force them to acknowledge Hearthway's treatment of demons and spirits.

"Now, your turn," Dar avoided the question.

"I..." Tami hesitated, looking around the circle. "A family full of love sounds nice. Nothing too grand, just a place filled with love." She tensed up, as if waiting for a rebuke.

Dar knew that he'd opened her eyes to just how harsh her own family had been, but he didn't realize to what extent she'd idolized what they had in his family and Hearthway.

"That's a great goal." Neko rubbed Tami's back.

The tension melted out of the girl, and she ducked her head to hide a blush.

Dar raised his bowl to the group. "Then to a great future. May we all strive towards our goals together."

"Here here!" everyone shouted, but Sasha smirked. "Dar, you didn't think you'd get out of it, did you?"

He smiled. Part of him had. "What I want? To make all of you happy." He enjoyed the scowls he got in response.

"Boo. Give us something real. Come on," Blair heckled him.

Dar didn't have to think. "I want to be able to protect my family and my community. Shelter each and every one of you so you can achieve your own goals. And the prerequisite for that is power. So in short, I want power."

Lilith had pushed him to defeat the devils, but in his mind, that was a secondary mission to keeping his family safe. And he had a feeling the world was going to push that upon him either way.

Everyone around the circle nodded. Power meant everything for survival as the devils became bolder. For his goal and all of theirs, they'd need that power.

"I'd like to add the rest of my dao to your family's dao book." Tami hesitated. "If that's okay?"

She'd asked once before, but Dar hadn't had time to let her actually do it.

Dar knew when Blair had put hers in the family dao book it had been a sign of something. Of accepting her into the family. So instead of answering, Dar let his girls speak.

All of them focused on Sasha.

"That's fine. You can do it tomorrow. Tonight is for resting," Sasha said between bites, as if it was the most casual thing in the world.

But Tami was practically vibrating on her log at the answer. It definitely meant something to her. Her putting her dao in his book tomorrow would be an acceptance that she was part of the family.

"Of course." Tami realized she hadn't said anything back after a moment. "I look forward to it."

"Would anyone like more?" Amber asked, finishing her bowl and standing up.

Everyone sitting around the fire held up their bowls. Amber smiled as she took them and filled them up. The sun started to sink in the night sky, and the group chatted idly about Hearthway and the kingdom.

Dar relaxed. It wasn't about what was said, but the feeling of comfort of having his family around him. Dar sank into the moment, taking it in.

Chapter 32

Dar and his women walked cautiously to the hive, needing to make sure that the threat was resolved. Much to their relief, all that remained was a handful of mantises and drones wandering the site aimlessly—stragglers that had returned to the hive after the battle or those that had been deep in the hive finally surfacing.

It would seem that it was much like an actual insect colony. These devils weren't independent without the queen.

He filled the hive like the other by the bison field. He noted which directions any off shoots went so they could catch any other openings or hives.

Tami was helpful in creating a map, charting down where they'd need to search to weed out the rest of the insect devils. Luckily, all signs pointed to those hives being smaller and on the level of the one they had found up near the bison fields.

For the moment, Dar was okay solving that later, so they headed back towards their boat. He'd focus on helping train up Hearthway to be able to take on the problem. A few small teams could go out and defeat them, and it would be a great training exercise.

Dar strategized as they walked, but was pulled back to the present as they approached Bellhaven, which looked like it was in the process of being looted.

People had come out of their homes, wary but driven by hunger to seek food. It looked like they'd decided to go to the noble district and take what they could carry from the nobles' homes that were destroyed.

From the shape the buildings were in, the noble houses looked like they'd become bigger targets for the devils. Dar wasn't sure if it was just that they'd had more people or some draw to the wealth. The shacks by the docks were relatively untouched.

"We have to check on the prince," Tami said, pulling at Dar's sleeves.

Dar didn't want to, but he knew he had to see if there was leadership left in the city. "Fine."

As they went deeper into the noble district, Dar quickly spotted the prince's manor. It was smashed in like many of the others. Picking through the rubble for food were a number of citizens.

Dar called to them, "Is anyone in that home? Or any of the nobles?"

Most of the looters scattered, but one young boy walked up to Dar. "I'll tell you for a silver."

Dar remembered the kid. It was the same one he'd sent running to warn of Karn's arrival.

Sasha fished a coin out of her dress and handed it to the boy. "Tell us."

He bit the coin and smiled. "I like her. You did good with that one," the boy tried to butter Sasha up.

"Enough, tell us what you know."

"We've all been hiding from the devils. They were snatching anybody that moved in the streets. I got hungry, but that was better than being insect food." The boy shivered a bit. "But then last night, people say they saw a large group heading out from the noble district.

And nothing attacked them! So folks started creeping out of their homes today."

Tami got down on the kid's level. "Did anyone see who was in that group?"

"Nope, people say it was the wizards, but people say lots of things." The kid shook his head. "But we've been digging through the noble homes for food all day and no one has come out to stop us."

Dar sighed. When he had seen the unrestrained looting, he had a feeling that would be the answer. "Thanks kid."

He pulled out an orange from his inner world behind his back and handed it to the kid, who was more excited about the sweet food than the piece of silver. He held it close to his chest as he ran off.

"There you have it, Tami. The city is without leadership. Would it be so bad if I took it over?"

Tami shook her head in disbelief. "I can't believe they ran away. It doesn't make any sense. Why not rebuild?"

She stood for a moment processing the news, so Dar asked her the question again. That seemed to wake her up.

"No, don't take the city over. Let the people run wild for a bit. News will get to Kindrake, and they'll have to do something. That's when you make your move. If you do it now, you'll be blamed for everything."

Dar paused. He hadn't thought about it that way, but she was right. "Going to become my political adviser now?" Dar chuckled.

"I know how the game is played. I've been standing to the side listening to it for over a hundred years," Tami said, and it was clear wheels were starting to turn in her head.

"Won't The Deep One come to Bellhaven if we leave it so empty?" Dar asked. Although, he wasn't sure he wanted to hold the city against such a powerful demon.

"Don't worry about that now; there's little we can do either way. We should get moving. Our village is at risk the longer we leave it without powerful demons and spirits. Dar, is there anything you'd like before we leave?" Sasha asked.

He rubbed his chin in thought. "I'd like to go through the prince's manor. He had quite the collection of maps and books. I doubt the looters have been looking for that, but it will help us understand more of what surrounds us. And, if there's a guard station with any weapons, that wouldn't hurt either."

Dar's mind was on the longer term than just food. He wanted knowledge and tools for the future.

Sasha snapped her fingers and pointed the maids to adjacent homes. They instantly moved to follow her instructions. "We'll spread out and regroup. No use in letting those things or even all their delicate silk go to waste."

"You're going to take their clothes?" Dar asked.

"No, I'm taking their cloth for my own use. Very different." Sasha smiled. "Besides, they aren't here to say we stole anything. Nor to call us robbers."

It reminded Dar of some old sayings. "The robbers are always those that lose, the kings are those that won. At least, according to history."

"I like it." Sasha smiled victoriously. "Since of course we just won."

Dar grunted. "Just don't take any food. The people here need it more. Assuming they manage to regroup, they should have plenty now that their numbers are more depleted in their winter stores."

"Dar, that's dark." Mika wrinkled her nose.

He shrugged. It was the truth.

After that, they worked quietly for the next few hours alongside the looters. They wrapped up and headed back to their boat.

Dar was happy to see the boat in the same condition that they'd left it. Though someone had undone two of the ropes only to find there were no sails, oars, or other means to drive the boat. Mika had disabled the enchantment when they had docked it.

Hopping aboard, Mika instantly got them moving. Dar looked up at the sky, roughly guessing the time based on the sun. If they hurried, they'd be back for dinner at Hearthway.

***

Dar dreaded the walk from the boat back to the village. They'd left the village more unprotected than ever before when the devils far outnumbered them. He was worried he'd made the wrong choice.

But, as he walked through the opening in the obsidian wall, the village was lively as ever. Goats bleated and people moved through the village. The villagers looked like they'd become one with the goats, who had taken the village over.

A few people looked up from their tasks to see Dar and company walking back into the village. Most just waved and continued on with their tasks. He was glad that nothing was so urgent that they needed to stop the group.

Dar couldn't help the sigh of relief that escaped him.

"Dar. Dinner is almost ready. Why don't you tell us about what happened?" Rex waved him down as they were passing through the central hearth.

"Sure." Dar settled comfortably back into the routine of the village, the girls walking off to work on settling in as well.

The other leaders gave their updates, but nothing needed his immediate attention, so Dar let his mind wander a bit.

He was thankful that Hearthway had remained peaceful despite all the surrounding trouble. Simple was good as far as he was concerned. He just wanted to keep his family safe, and if he could create a safe space for others as well, he would be more than happy to do it.

So he settled into the moment of calm. He'd seen enough to know it wasn't going to last forever. Kindrake's war, the devils, there would be more to come. And he fully planned to use the winter to organize. He wasn't going to be able to take it all on just himself. He needed his villagers to grow in power, and he had the tools to do it.

Dar pondered on the queen's dao and the other insects that were probably being buried in his little dao tree as he sat there. He'd likely have several new fruits to offer to the villagers, and he couldn't wait to find out what they were.

***

Winter picked up in the coming weeks, but Hearthway remained as active as ever. Dar could sense mana and dao radiating from the villagers as they continued to work through the cold, shrugging it off with far more fortitude than an average person.

Then again, they were all immortals. Not only that, but they were growing by leaps and bounds. The first group had left with Blair yesterday to go seek out one of the secondary hives with eight villagers that had reached their first greater dao.

"And pour," Bart called.

Dar pushed the crucible of purified iron and it tipped over into the wells that he'd made based on their specifications. It wasn't anything fancy, just ingots, but the blacksmiths were all gathered around. Steam filled the air as they all tried to wave it out of their faces.

It had taken more than a few trials and errors to figure out what Dar could make and how they could remove the impurities. But this time, he knew it was right.

The red-hot liquid rapidly cooled in the casting molds, losing its red-hot glow and turning a metallic silver.

Bart held his hands over the ingots and smiled. "My dao of iron is reacting. They're good, boys!"

The group of blacksmiths cheered and hugged each other, because this wasn't just iron, it was their futures as well. Each of the blacksmiths would have killed to have a supply of quality iron to work with.

Now they had it, and Dar figured more than one of them was going to stay up late at the forges.

"Just don't get so excited that you try to pick one of these up before it cools." Dar gave them all a chagrined smile.

The village was picking up steam in a big way. He had over twenty people in his inner world most days working hard on their own cultivation. Most of the village had opted for an earth-related dao, the potential for them to build things with their dao was far more tempting than the lethality of shadow for most of them.

"Glad it all worked out this time." Sasha leaned against his shoulder.

Dar snaked an arm around her waist and pulled her closer. "Just took a few tries."

"A few." She rolled her eyes.

Sasha had been in a much better mood as of late. With the help of Cherry's knowledge and Lilith's dao book, she had been working hard on her own dao path.

Dar suspected she'd be a grand demon by spring at this rate as she worked towards a dao that Dar thought of as flesh, in hopes of being able to heal the rest of the family when needed.

"The village is really coming together," Sasha sighed. "Enough that it won't need you and Blaire here to protect it in the spring."

"What's that supposed to mean?" Dar looked over his shoulder into her deep blue eyes.

"It means that, come spring, I expect our family to get very busy." Sasha leaned on him, pressing her chest into his back.

Neko happened to see them and came hurrying over. "Kittens?" She tugged at Dar's arm.

He knew exactly where she wanted to take him.

"At this rate, you are actually going to have kittens by the end of winter." Sasha tagged along.

"Nothing wrong with that." Neko only tugged harder at Sasha's encouragement.

"I'm afraid I can't Neko. I have an overdue date with Blair." Dar kissed the overeager cat girl on the top of her head.

Neko pouted until he rubbed her head and she melted. "Tonight." She declared before hurrying off.

"I'm glad she wasn't able to distract you." Blair came around from behind Dar. "We've put this off long enough."

"Oh you know. We only had an emissary from the White, a horde of hungry insect devils and the fall of Bellhaven. Just a few things popping up here and there." Dar dismissively waved his hand.

"Hush, Mika already spilled the secret. Let's go on this magical picnic you have planned." She clung to his arm.

"Have fun." Sasha waved Dar and Blair off.

It would be a pleasantly busy winter for Dar. But spring had a few surprises in store for him.

Afterword

Thanks for joining me in Dao Disciples. Dar is powering up and I wonder just how OP I can make him by the end of the series on book 5. I'm going to do my best to pull the story back to one about Hearthway for book 4. This book stepped off that path, but it was where the story took me.

Other books in the works, Mana 5 is almost done, then it'll go through its editing cycles and be ready 2/9. I'm wrapping up mana this week and then starting in on Dragon 3. I'm excited to have Zach chase down Morgana, and the resulting romantic conflict.

Then what's next... I'm not quite sure. I'm ready to finish Mana and start a new series, but how exactly I'm going to weave that into the sequence, I'm not clear on yet.

Lots of ideas for the two new series, I'm likely going to plan them as trilogies. I have too many ideas I want to write.

Outside of writing, life is good. Like most of the world, I'm realizing mid winter that I need to do some work to fit into suits for weddings in the spring and am dieting.

As always, if you can, drop me a review. It keeps my books alive and greases the gears in Amazon's system.

Leave a Review

Also By

Legendary Rule:

Ajax Demos finds himself lost in society. Graduating shortly after artificial intelligence is allowed to enter the workforce; he can't get his career off the ground. But when one opportunity closes, another opens. Ajax gets a chance to play a brand new Immersive Reality game. Things aren't as they seem. Mega Corps hover over what appears to be a simple game. However, what he does in the game seems to effect his body outside.

But that isn't going to make Ajax pause when he finally might just get that shot at becoming a professional gamer. Join Ajax and Company as they enter the world of Legendary Rule.

Series Page

A Mage's Cultivation:

In a world where mages and monster grow from cultivating mana. Isaac joins the class of humans known as mages who absorb mana to grow more powerful. To become a mage he must bind a mana beast to himself to access and control mana. But when his mana beast is far more human than he expected; Isaac struggles with the budding relationship between the two of them as he prepares to enter his first dungeon.

Unfortunately for Isaac, he doesn't have time to ponder the questions of his relationship with Aurora. Because his sleepy town of Locksprings is in for a rude awakening, and he has to decide which side of the war he is going to stand on.

Series Page

Dao Divinity: The First Immortal

Darius Yigg was a wanderer, someone who's never quite found his place in the world, but maybe he's not supposed to be here...Ripped from our world, Dar finds himself in his past life's world, where his destiny was cut short. Reignited, the wick of Dar's destiny burns again with the hope of him saving Grandterra.

To do that, he'll have to do something no other human of Grandterra has done before, walk the dao path. That path requires mastering and controlling attributes of the world and merging them to greater and greater entities. In theory, if he progressed far enough, he could control all of reality and rival a god.

He won't be in this alone. As a beacon of hope for the world, those from the ancient races will rally around Dar to stave off the growing Devil horde.

Series Page

There are of course a number of communities where you can find similar books.

https://www.facebook.com/groups/haremlit

https://www.facebook.com/groups/HaremGamelit

And other non-harem specific communities for Cultivation and LitRPG.

https://www.facebook.com/groups/WesternWuxia

https://www.facebook.com/groups/LitRPGsociety

https://www.facebook.com/groups/cultivationnovels

Made in the USA
Monee, IL
12 January 2024

51639083R00213